When Staying is the Choice

THE PEOPLE OF CEDAR RIDGE, BOOK 2

Written by Diane Kann

Brought to you by Volans Galaxy Press

Published by Kannceptual Creations LLC

An imprint of Volans Galaxy Press

ISBN: 978-1-971356-41-9

Printed in the United States of America

First Edition, January 2026

Contents

Author's Biography

Diane Kann writes sweet romance stories that celebrate love, second chances, and the quiet moments that change everything. Her stories focus on emotional connection, gentle healing, and relationships built on trust, hope, and heart.

When she's not writing, Diane enjoys spending time in nature with her family and dogs, finding inspiration in peaceful landscapes and everyday moments, and dreaming up tender stories rooted in compassion.

Dedication

For those who know that love isn't always about chasing what's next, but about standing still long enough to truly see one another.

This book is for the hearts that have faced the quiet question—
Should I stay?
And discovered that sometimes, staying is not weakness,
but courage in its most tender form.

For those who choose love not because it is perfect,
but because it is real.
For those who understand that roots can be as powerful as wings,
and that devotion is built in the small, everyday moments
where two lives decide to keep choosing each other.

May this story remind you that staying—
when done with love, honesty, and intention—
can be the bravest romance of all.

— Diane Kann

CHAPTER ONE

The Arrival

The tires of Evan Morales's obsidian-black sedan crunched audibly on the gravel shoulder of the road, a sound that seemed to echo with an almost offensive loudness against the hushed symphony of Cedar Ridge. Towering pines, their needles dense and fragrant, formed a verdant tunnel, dappled sunlight filtering through in shifting patterns onto the dusty, unpaved street. His car, a sculpted piece of urban engineering, gleamed with a sterile precision that felt utterly out of place, a stark anomaly against the weathered charm of clapboard houses and picket fences. Evan, accustomed to the relentless hum of city life, found the silence unnerving, punctuated only by the distant chirping of unseen birds and the gentle rustle of leaves.

He steered the vehicle with practiced ease, his gaze sweeping across the town as if cataloging its components. His mind, sharp and efficient, was already dissecting the scene, assessing its operational flow, its inherent inefficiencies. This was his domain, his expertise: identifying the rot beneath the polished veneer, the hidden cracks in the foundation, and then, swiftly and decisively, implementing the necessary repairs.

Cedar Ridge presented itself as a quaint, almost idyllic postcard, but Evan knew that beneath the picturesque surface, there were invariably systemic flaws demanding his attention. The air itself was different here, thick with the scent of pine and damp earth, a primal perfume that hinted at a slower, more deliberate pace of life. He registered it, acknowledged it, but it hadn't yet penetrated the carefully constructed fortress of his professional detachment. His focus remained on the objective, on the task that had brought him to this remote corner of the world: the Cedar Ridge Collective.

He parked the car in a designated spot outside a building that, from a distance, seemed to embody the town's unassuming character. The sign above the entrance, hand-painted and slightly faded, read "Cedar Ridge Collective – Connecting Community, Cultivating Growth." The words themselves spoke of aspiration, of a purpose that went beyond mere commerce. Evan, however, saw only the operational challenges that awaited him. His mission was clear, etched into the very fabric of his professional identity: assess, rectify, optimize, and depart. He was a consultant, a temporary catalyst, a problem-solver dispatched to mend what was broken. He had no illusions about becoming a part of Cedar Ridge's narrative; he was merely a transient force, a brief, albeit necessary, disruption.

Stepping out of the car, he felt the subtle shift in gravity, the almost imperceptible pull of a place less hurried. He smoothed the lapels of his tailored charcoal suit, the crisp fabric a stark contrast to the worn, natural textures of his surroundings. He carried with him an aura of detached efficiency, a quiet competence that set him apart. His briefcase, a sleek testament to modern design, felt like an extension of his will, a tool designed for action, not contemplation. The scent of pine, once merely an atmospheric detail, now seemed to permeate his very being, a persistent reminder of his departure from the familiar urban landscape. He took a deep, measured breath, preparing himself for the initial assessment, already formulating the strategies that would soon bring order to this seemingly placid, yet undoubtedly flawed, community hub.

The Cedar Ridge Collective stood as the undeniable heart of the town, a place where the pulse of the community was felt most strongly. Evan pushed open the heavy wooden door, a small bell above him tinkling a gentle, almost apologetic welcome. The interior was a revelation, a world away from the sterile efficiency he typically encountered. Worn, polished wooden floors creaked softly under his expensive loafers, bearing the imprint of countless footsteps, of generations who had passed through these doors. The walls were adorned with a vibrant, eclectic collection of local art – colorful landscape paintings, intricate pottery, handcrafted textiles – each piece a testament to the town's creative spirit and its deep connection to the surrounding natural beauty.

His gaze, sharp and discerning, began its systematic sweep. He noted the layout: a central reception area, branching off into various rooms that likely served as offices, meeting spaces, and perhaps even a small retail section showcasing local goods. The air was alive with a low hum of activity, punctuated by the murmur of conversation and the occasional burst of laughter. Well-meaning individuals, their faces etched with the warmth of genuine community, moved about their tasks. He observed their interactions, their cooperative spirit, and while he admired their dedication, he also detected the subtle signs of inefficiency, the unoptimized workflows, the systems that had perhaps outlived their usefulness.

He saw a sign-up sheet for local produce deliveries, a bulletin board overflowing with community notices, and a small counter where transactions were being processed with a charming, if somewhat antiquated, manual system. It was a system built on trust and familiarity, on personal relationships rather than streamlined technology. He understood its appeal, the human element it fostered, but as a consultant, his job was to look beyond sentimentality and identify the tangible areas for improvement. He began to compile a mental list, a preliminary diagnostic of the Collective's operational shortcomings. Outdated inventory management, inefficient communication channels, a lack of standardized procedures – the familiar litany of challenges began to form in his mind, each point a potential target for his intervention.

He approached the main desk, where a woman with kind eyes and a gentle smile was assisting a customer. Her movements were unhurried, deliberate, a stark contrast to the brisk efficiency Evan was accustomed to. He waited patiently, his presence a quiet, observant force in the bustling room. He could already envision the transformation, the streamlined processes, the enhanced productivity he would bring. The building itself, with its history etched into its very structure, spoke of continuity and shared purpose.

These were concepts he understood in theory, but his professional life had been a testament to the pursuit of progress through change, through the constant reinvention of systems. He viewed such concepts as secondary to measurable results, to the quantifiable impact of his interventions. Yet, as he stood there, taking in the eclectic art and the warm chatter, a flicker of something akin to appreciation, however fleeting, touched the edges of his professional armor. It was a charming environment, he conceded internally, but it was also a breeding ground for operational inefficiencies, and that was his sole focus.

Evan located an unoccupied office, a small, utilitarian room tucked away from the main thoroughfare of the Collective. It was functional, devoid of any personal touches, its stark white walls and minimalist furniture reflecting his own professional detachment. He set up his laptop, its sleek design a familiar anchor in this unfamiliar environment. This would be his temporary command center, his sterile bubble amidst the warm, organic fabric of Cedar Ridge. He was keenly aware of his transient status, a temporary necessity, a cog inserted into the machinery of the town's operations to ensure its continued functioning. He anticipated a smooth, albeit brief, engagement, his mind already focused on the technical aspects of his work, on the data he would gather, the analyses he would conduct, the solutions he would implement.

He knew, intellectually, that his presence would be noted by the townsfolk. He could already sense their polite but distant curiosity, their collective reserve. They were individuals, each with their own stories, their own roles within the community, but as a unified entity, they maintained a certain guardedness towards an outsider. He hadn't yet engaged with them on a personal level, nor did he intend to. His interactions would be strictly professional, confined to the parameters of his contract, his objective clearly defined.

The goal was to effect change and move on, leaving behind a more efficient, more robust operation. Any personal connection would only serve to complicate his departure, to blur the lines of his professional detachment. He was here to fix a problem, not to build relationships. The quiet hum of his laptop was a more familiar sound than the gentle rustling of leaves outside, a sound that grounded him in his purpose and reminded him of the life he would return to once his work here was done. He was a stranger in Cedar Ridge, a role he embraced with practiced ease, his mind already several steps ahead, strategizing the most effective path to achieve his objectives.

As he delved into the preliminary data, the hum of the Collective's operations a low thrumming backdrop, his attention was momentarily diverted by the sight of a woman standing just outside the entrance, engaged in conversation with an elderly gentleman. She possessed a quiet strength, an air of rootedness that was palpable even from a distance.

Her posture was open, her engagement with the elder sincere, her hands gesturing subtly as she spoke. There was a natural grace about her, a sense of belonging that seemed to emanate from her very being, as if she were as integral to Cedar Ridge as the ancient pines that surrounded the town.

Evan registered her presence as another facet of the town's established order, a woman deeply intertwined with its rhythm. He noted the ease with which she navigated the conversation, the warmth in her expression. Her focus was entirely on the gentleman before her, her attention unwavering. It was a fleeting observation, a mere snapshot in the larger panorama of his initial reconnaissance, yet it managed to snag a corner of his awareness. He felt a flicker of unacknowledged curiosity, a fleeting question about her role, her connection to this place.

He cataloged her as another piece of the Cedar Ridge puzzle, a component of the community he was tasked with analyzing. But there was something about her stillness, her grounded presence, that momentarily caught his professional eye, a subtle deviation from the expected narrative of a sleepy, rural town. He filed the observation away, a small, insignificant detail in the grand scheme of his mission, and returned his focus to the spreadsheets and operational reports that awaited his meticulous scrutiny. The scent of pine seemed to sharpen for a moment, and the silence of his temporary office felt a shade more pronounced, as if the outside world had briefly intruded upon his carefully constructed equilibrium.

Evan's professional life was a meticulously choreographed ballet of arrival and departure. He was the embodiment of the hired gun, the expert parachute dropped into the heart of a struggling operation to diagnose its ailments, administer swift and decisive treatment, and then, just as quickly, extract himself, leaving behind a healthier, more robust entity. Cedar Ridge and its Collective were simply the latest stage for this well-rehearsed performance. His mandate was etched in the contract, a document he'd scanned and internalized with his usual alacrity: identify the inefficiencies, implement immediate fixes, and, crucially, train the local staff to sustain the improvements.

This wasn't a suggestion; it was the bedrock of his methodology, a pattern of intervention and departure honed over years of navigating the treacherous currents of corporate and community organizations. He saw himself not as a builder of relationships, but as a surgeon of systems. The scalpel of his analysis would expose the rot, the precise application of his solutions would excise it, and the follow-up training would ensure the wound wouldn't fester again. His purpose was to catalyze progress, to be a brief, albeit potent, disruptor, and then to fade back into the anonymity from which he came.

The concept of putting down roots, of becoming a permanent fixture in any of these transient landscapes, was antithetical to his professional identity. His six-month timeline was a firm boundary, a meticulously calculated duration designed to achieve maximum impact with minimum personal entanglement. He was a meteor, streaking across the sky to illuminate, and then vanishing, leaving behind only the memory of its passage and a subtly altered celestial map.

He opened his laptop, the familiar glow of the screen a comforting presence in the sparsely furnished office. The digital interface was his true native tongue, a realm where logic and data reigned supreme, unburdened by the messy nuances of human emotion or the sticky webs of small-town allegiances. The preliminary reports, already uploaded to his secure cloud, were a dense tapestry of numbers, operational metrics, and anecdotal feedback gathered by his pre-arrival research team. His task now was to weave these disparate threads into a coherent diagnosis, to pinpoint the precise points of friction that were hindering the Cedar Ridge Collective's potential.

He began by cross-referencing the financial statements with the reported volunteer hours, looking for discrepancies that suggested either a lack of oversight or an over-reliance on goodwill that wasn't being adequately channeled. The inventory logs, a notoriously difficult area for community-based organizations, were next under his scrutiny. He suspected, with a certainty born of experience, that a significant portion of their resources – be it donated goods or purchased supplies – were likely slipping through the cracks, lost to disorganization or a lack of standardized tracking. He envisioned a streamlined inventory system, perhaps a digital one that could be accessed and updated in real-time, accessible to authorized personnel, ensuring accountability and preventing waste. This was the tangible, measurable impact he strived for, the kind of improvement that would appear on a balance sheet and in the reduced frustration of the staff.

He initiated a series of diagnostic queries, algorithms designed to sift through the operational data and flag anomalies. His mind worked with a speed and precision that few could match, dissecting the information, identifying patterns, and forming hypotheses at a pace that left the ambient sounds of the Collective – the distant chatter, the occasional thud of something being moved, the murmur of voices – as a mere indistinct hum in the background. He wasn't interested in the "why" behind the inefficiencies, not yet.

His focus was on the "what" and the "how much." Was it a lack of proper storage that led to spoilage? Was it a convoluted ordering process that resulted in duplicate purchases? Was it insufficient training that led to errors in reporting? These were the questions he sought to answer with hard data, stripping away any subjective interpretations of intent or effort. The human element, while a factor in any operational environment, was for him a variable to be managed, not a primary focus. His job was to optimize the system, and if that meant highlighting areas where human error or lack of training was the root cause, so be it. The goal was efficiency, and efficiency was an objective, quantifiable outcome.

The initial data analysis painted a picture that was both familiar and, in its own way, uniquely Cedar Ridge. The Collective, it seemed, was a victim of its own success, or rather, of the very goodwill that sustained it. The sheer volume of community engagement, while commendable, was overwhelming its existing infrastructure. The bulletin board, so artfully cluttered with notices of bake sales, lost pets, and volunteer opportunities, was also a testament to a communication system that had long since been outgrown. Information was disseminated organically, through word-of-mouth and scattered paper postings, a system that was charming in its informality but disastrous for ensuring that everyone received the same, accurate message.

This lack of centralized, reliable communication was likely contributing to a cascade of minor issues: missed deadlines for donations, volunteer shifts being forgotten, confusion over event details. He made a mental note to explore the implementation of a unified communication platform, perhaps a simple online portal or a dedicated app, that could serve as a central hub for all official announcements and updates. This would require training, of course, but it was a crucial step towards mitigating the chaos inherent in an unmanaged information flow.

He then turned his attention to the physical layout and workflow within the Collective. His research had indicated that the organization managed a diverse range of activities, from food pantry distribution and local artisan support to community event coordination and educational workshops. The current configuration of spaces, however, seemed to be a patchwork quilt of ad-hoc solutions, with different functions spilling into each other, creating bottlenecks and compromising efficiency. He pictured the food pantry, likely operating out of a small, potentially cramped space, struggling to manage both storage and distribution, leading to potential health code violations and a less-than-ideal experience for recipients.

The artisan showcase, while a wonderful initiative, was probably competing for space with administrative tasks, hindering both the display of goods and the efficiency of daily operations. He began sketching out potential reconfigurations on a digital notepad, imagining a more logical flow, perhaps designating specific zones for each core function, optimizing pathways for both staff and visitors, and ensuring adequate storage and processing areas for each. This would necessitate a review of the building's current footprint and potentially some minor structural adjustments, but the long-term gains in terms of efficiency and safety would far outweigh the initial investment.

His mind was already cataloging the types of training sessions that would be required. For the inventory management, he envisioned a hands-on workshop demonstrating the use of the new digital system, emphasizing data entry protocols and the importance of regular audits. For communication, the training would focus on navigating the new platform, posting updates, responding to queries, and understanding the importance of clear, concise messaging. For workflow optimization, it would involve practical exercises in spatial management and the application of lean principles to their daily tasks.

He understood that resistance to change was inevitable, especially in a community that likely valued tradition and familiarity. His approach would be to emphasize the benefits, not just to the organization as a whole, but to the individuals themselves. Streamlined processes meant less frustration, more time for meaningful engagement, and a greater sense of accomplishment. He had a knack for framing these changes in a way that resonated with people, highlighting how efficiency could actually enhance the very community spirit they so deeply cherished.

He paused, stretching his fingers, the soft glow of the laptop screen reflecting in his eyes. The initial assessment was taking shape, a complex mosaic of interconnected issues. It was a challenging puzzle, but one he was uniquely equipped to solve. He wasn't here to make friends or to become a part of the Cedar Ridge tapestry. His role was far more precise, far more defined. He was the catalyst, the external force introduced to accelerate growth and improve function. The notion of him staying beyond his six-month term was as alien to him as the idea of trading his tailored suits for flannel shirts and hiking boots. He would bring order, instill new practices, empower the local team to carry the torch, and then he would depart, leaving Cedar Ridge stronger, more efficient, and better prepared for whatever the future held. His reputation was built on these successful, albeit temporary, interventions.

He was the specialist, the problem-solver, and his value lay in his ability to effect profound change without becoming entangled in the process. The scent of pine, still a faint, lingering presence in the air, served as a constant reminder of his transient status, a subtle demarcation between his life's work and the world he was merely passing through. He glanced at his watch, a discreet, high-tech device that was as much a tool as his laptop. The first day was progressing as planned. He had initiated the diagnostic phase, and soon, he would be ready to present his findings and begin the implementation phase. The clock was ticking, and Evan Morales was determined to make every second count. He was a man on a mission, and that mission was to optimize, to streamline, and to leave Cedar Ridge better than he found it, before seamlessly rejoining the quiet anonymity of his own life.

The scent of pine, crisp and clean, was the first thing that registered, a pervasive aroma that clung to the very air within the Cedar Ridge Collective. Evan inhaled deeply, a practiced maneuver to clear his mind, though he suspected the scent would soon become an olfactory cliché of this particular assignment. His footsteps echoed on the worn, wide-planked wooden floorboards as he stepped through the main entrance, a solid oak door that creaked a welcoming, if somewhat antiquated, greeting. This was it – the nerve center, the nucleus of the operation he was here to dissect and, hopefully, revitalize.

His initial scan of the space was swift, a practiced sweep that cataloged details with the precision of a seasoned analyst. The main hall of the Collective was a testament to a community's heart, a vibrant, if slightly chaotic, tapestry woven from decades of shared purpose. Sunlight, filtered through large, multi-paned windows, illuminated dust motes dancing in lazy patterns, casting a warm, golden hue across the room.

The walls were adorned with a kaleidoscope of local art – watercolors depicting rolling hills and stoic farmhouses, vibrant textile pieces that spoke of intricate craftsmanship, and even a few rather charming, albeit slightly lopsided, pottery creations. Each piece seemed to whisper a story, a narrative of the people who lived and worked here, their passions and their talents proudly displayed. Evan's gaze, however, didn't linger on the aesthetic. While he acknowledged the inherent charm, his mind was already translating these visual cues into operational data. The art represented a significant commitment of community resources, both in terms of artistic creation and display space. He mentally noted the sheer volume of it, the potential for it to contribute to a sense of clutter if not managed effectively within a defined aesthetic or functional framework.

To his left, a large, bulletin board, a behemoth of cork and wood, commanded attention. It was a visual symphony of community life, a vibrant, almost overwhelming, collage of faded flyers, handwritten notices, and official-looking printouts. Bake sale announcements vied for space with lost pet posters, upcoming workshop schedules were layered over pleas for donations, and community event reminders were tacked precariously over handwritten requests for volunteers. It was, in Evan's professional opinion, a digital desert in an analog age. The sheer density of information, the overlapping layers, and the evident reliance on manual updates spoke volumes about the Collective's communication infrastructure – or lack thereof.

He imagined the frustration of trying to find a specific piece of information, the endless rifling through papers, the missed opportunities due to a buried announcement. It was a microcosm of the systemic inefficiencies he was here to address. His mind immediately began sketching out a more streamlined alternative: a digital platform, easily accessible, where all official communications could be housed, categorized, and updated in real-time. He could almost see the clean interface, the search function, the ability to push notifications directly to registered members. It was a vision of order emerging from this charmingly disheveled chaos.

Across the hall, a counter, seemingly crafted from repurposed barn wood, served as the central point of interaction. Behind it, a small group of individuals were engaged in what appeared to be a variety of tasks. Their energy was palpable, a gentle hum of activity that spoke of genuine enthusiasm, yet their movements seemed, to Evan's trained eye, a little uncertain, a touch uncoordinated. He observed a woman with kind eyes and a smudge of what looked like flour on her cheek meticulously sorting through a stack of what he assumed were donation forms, her brow furrowed in concentration.

Nearby, a younger man, with an earnest expression, was attempting to navigate a labyrinth of boxes and crates, his efforts to find a specific item hampered by the sheer disorganization. There was a warmth radiating from them, a sense of shared purpose and inherent good will, but also, Evan noted with clinical detachment, a distinct lack of standardized procedure. They were, he surmised, the heart of the Collective, the embodiment of its spirit, but perhaps lacking the honed operational expertise required to translate that spirit into maximum impact. He saw their well-intentioned efforts, their dedication, but also the potential for burnout, for frustration stemming from inefficient systems, and for valuable resources to be wasted due to a lack of clear processes.

He continued his silent circuit, his gaze absorbing every detail. The space itself was a patchwork of functionality and history. A section near the back seemed to be designated as a makeshift pantry, shelves lined with an assortment of canned goods and dry staples, some neatly arranged, others in precarious piles. He pictured the logistical challenges of managing such an inventory, the potential for spoilage, the difficulty in tracking stock levels, and the implications for health and safety. Adjacent to this, a small area was dedicated to showcasing local crafts, a few tables displaying pottery, knitted items, and handmade soaps. While the initiative was commendable, the integration with other functions felt...fluid, to say the least.

It was clear that different operational needs were competing for the same limited physical space, leading to a constant negotiation of territory. He began mentally reconfiguring the layout, envisioning distinct zones for each core function – a dedicated intake and sorting area for donations, a well-organized pantry with clear labeling and inventory tracking, and a more prominent, thoughtfully arranged space for the artisan showcase, perhaps with improved lighting and display fixtures. He saw the potential for a clearer workflow, for reduced cross-contamination risks in the pantry, and for a more professional presentation of the artisans' work.

Even the furniture spoke of the Collective's journey. A sturdy, albeit slightly chipped, oak table served as a communal workspace, surrounded by a motley collection of chairs that suggested a gradual accumulation rather than a deliberate design. A faded floral couch in a corner offered a cozy, if somewhat dated, seating area. These were not the sterile, functional pieces of a corporate office; they were items that had likely been donated, cherished, and integrated into the fabric of the Collective over time. Evan, whose own workspace was a paragon of minimalist efficiency, recognized their utilitarian value but also their inherent limitations. They served a purpose, but they didn't necessarily optimize for workflow or ergonomic comfort. He filed away the observation, a minor detail in the grander scheme of operational overhaul, but a contributing factor to the overall atmosphere of gentle, unmanaged charm.

He paused by a window overlooking a small, sun-drenched courtyard. A few wilting potted plants sat on a windowsill, testament to either an absent green thumb or simply a lack of dedicated attention. Even here, the sense of community was evident – a small, hand-painted sign designated the space as a "Quiet Zone," inviting a moment of respite. It was this inherent human element, this ingrained desire to create welcoming spaces, that often posed the greatest challenge, and paradoxically, the greatest opportunity. These were the elements that couldn't be quantified, the intangible qualities that fueled the Collective's existence. His task, however, was to build upon this foundation, to infuse it with the structure and efficiency that would allow its spirit to flourish without being bogged down by operational friction.

His mind, a highly efficient processing unit, was already compiling a preliminary list of immediate, tangible improvements. The bulletin board was at the top, a clear and present need for a centralized communication system. The pantry's disorganization was another priority, requiring a complete overhaul of shelving, labeling, and inventory protocols. The workflow between the different functional areas – donations, pantry, artisan showcase, administrative tasks – needed a more logical flow, a streamlining that would minimize wasted movement and confusion. He envisioned a scenario where volunteers could seamlessly transition between tasks, where inventory was tracked with minimal effort, and where community members could access services and information with ease.

He could see the potential for training sessions already. Workshops on using a new digital communication platform, hands-on guidance in implementing a streamlined inventory management system, and practical demonstrations of efficient workflow techniques. He understood that these changes would require a shift in mindset, a move away from established habits towards new, more efficient practices. It wouldn't be about imposing his will, but about demonstrating the clear benefits, about empowering the individuals who were already so deeply invested in the Collective's success. He pictured himself explaining the new inventory system, not as a rigid set of rules, but as a tool that would free them from tedious manual counts and reduce the likelihood of valuable donations going to waste. He saw himself presenting the digital communication platform not as a replacement for personal interaction, but as a way to ensure that important messages reached everyone, thereby reducing confusion and enhancing participation.

As he continued his walk-through, he noted the presence of a few individuals who seemed to be in administrative roles, hunched over desks laden with paper. Their expressions were often tired, their movements deliberate, suggesting long hours and a constant juggling of competing demands. He understood the inherent strain on such roles within a community organization, where resources are often stretched thin. He made a mental note to investigate their specific pain points, to understand the administrative bottlenecks that were contributing to their workload. Perhaps a digital database for member information, a more efficient system for processing donations, or even just better organizational tools could make a significant difference.

The air, though carrying the persistent scent of pine, also held hints of other aromas – the faint, sweet smell of baked goods from a nearby kitchen, the earthy scent of wood polish from someone tending to the furniture, and the subtle fragrance of lavender from a display of handmade soaps. These were the sensory markers of the Collective's diverse activities, a testament to the many hands that contributed to its operation. Evan, however, was already translating these sensory inputs into a more pragmatic framework. The baking implied a need for adherence to food safety standards, the woodworking for proper storage and handling of materials, and the soap making for ingredient sourcing and quality control. Each aroma was a potential area for operational consideration, a facet of the larger system he was here to optimize.

He found himself pausing in front of a large, framed photograph on the wall, depicting a group of people, young and old, laughing and working together at what looked like a community festival. Their faces were alight with a shared joy, a palpable sense of camaraderie. It was a powerful image, capturing the very essence of what the Collective represented. Evan's gaze, however, was drawn to the logistical elements – the implied coordination, the volunteer management, the resource allocation that must have been required to orchestrate such an event. He could see the potential for improvement even in that snapshot of success, envisioning more efficient pre-event planning, better communication channels during the event itself, and more robust post-event evaluation to inform future endeavors.

His tour concluded back at the entrance, near the creaking oak door. He hadn't spoken to anyone yet, his initial interaction a silent observation, a data-gathering mission conducted through immersion. He had seen the charm, the dedication, the inherent value of the Cedar Ridge Collective. But he had also seen the inefficiencies, the outdated systems, and the potential for significant improvement. He took one last breath of the pine-scented air, a mental catalog of observations already cataloged and cross-referenced.

The building itself, with its worn floors and lovingly displayed art, was more than just a structure; it was a living testament to the community's history and its enduring spirit. His task was not to erase that history or diminish that spirit, but to build upon it, to provide the framework that would allow it to thrive in the modern age. He turned, a quiet determination settling in his gaze. The initial impressions had been formed, and now, the real work of diagnosis and prescription could begin. The challenge was significant, but the potential for positive transformation was even greater. And for Evan Morales, that was a challenge he was more than ready to meet.

The temporary office Evan had been assigned was a stark contrast to the characterful main hall. Tucked away in a small annex adjacent to what seemed to be a storage room overflowing with donated textiles, it was a space that had clearly been cleared out in a hurry, likely for his arrival. A functional, if uninspiring, metal desk stood against one wall, topped with a bare, beige surface that seemed to absorb any hint of warmth. Beside it, a slightly wobbly filing cabinet, its drawers perpetually sticky, stood sentinel. The single window, small and grimy, offered a view of a patch of overgrown weeds and a leaning fence post. It was, Evan reflected with a wry internal smile, exactly the kind of utilitarian, impersonal space he usually preferred.

His work was about systems, about efficiency, about removing the emotional clutter that could impede progress. This room, stripped of any extraneous charm, was an ideal canvas for his analytical mind. He unpacked his laptop, its sleek, professional lines a further incongruity against the room's tired décor. He plugged in his charger, the faint hum of the power adapter a familiar, comforting sound. He'd brought his own ergonomic mouse and keyboard, small comforts that made long hours at a desk more bearable, and these were placed with practiced efficiency on the desk.

He then arranged a small stack of meticulously organized files, each clearly labeled, a testament to his systematic approach. He even placed a small, unobtrusive desk lamp, its cool LED light a sharp counterpoint to the natural, golden hues of the main hall. This was his command center, a zone of focused activity designed to isolate him from the gentle chaos he was here to address. He knew his presence was a necessary intrusion, a temporary measure to inject a dose of modern operational thinking into a community that, while rich in spirit, was perhaps a little behind the curve in terms of infrastructure. He was the external consultant, the problem-solver, the one brought in to optimize, to streamline, to ensure the Cedar Ridge Collective could continue to serve its purpose effectively. His role was defined, his boundaries clear, and he intended to maintain them.

He knew, from his initial briefing and his brief observation, that the townsfolk were likely to be polite, perhaps even curious, but fundamentally cautious. Small towns, he'd found, tended to be insular, their residents bound by shared histories and unspoken understandings. He was an outsider, an unknown quantity, and he expected a certain degree of reserve. He wasn't here to make friends; he was here to make a difference, a distinction he felt was crucial for maintaining objectivity. His focus would be on the data, on the workflows, on the tangible metrics that would demonstrate the impact of his interventions.

Personal relationships, while not actively discouraged, were not part of his agenda. He would interact, of course, answer questions, and explain his findings, but he would do so with a professional detachment, steering clear of the personal entanglements that could cloud his judgment. He anticipated a predictable pattern of engagement: polite greetings, brief conversations about the weather or the Collective's immediate needs, and a general deference to his expertise. He would be the quiet observer, the meticulous analyst, and then, the agent of change.

He'd encountered this dynamic many times before in various communities and organizations. The initial politeness often masked a deeper reticence, a quiet assessment of his capabilities and intentions. He would need to earn their trust, not through charm or personal connection, but through demonstrable competence and tangible results. His reputation preceded him, of course, built on a track record of successful overhauls in similar community-based organizations. But even the most impressive resume could only go so far in a place like Cedar Ridge. Here, actions would speak louder than words, and the effectiveness of his proposed solutions would be the ultimate arbiter of his success.

He settled into his chair, the faux leather squeaking slightly under his weight. He opened his laptop, the familiar glow of the screen illuminating his focused expression. His initial task was to familiarize himself with the Collective's current operational data, to dig into the reports, the financial statements, the volunteer logs that had been provided. This would be the foundation upon which he would build his recommendations. He already had a framework in mind, a series of key performance indicators he would be tracking, from donation processing times to volunteer engagement levels, from resource allocation efficiency to community outreach effectiveness.

He planned to spend the first few days observing, interviewing key personnel – the director, the lead volunteers, the administrative staff – and gathering further qualitative data. He would then cross-reference this with the quantitative data, looking for discrepancies, for areas where perception and reality diverged. It was a meticulous process, one that required patience and a keen eye for detail. He knew that sometimes the most significant inefficiencies were hidden in plain sight, masked by long-standing habits or a general acceptance of the status quo. His job was to shine a light into those dark corners, to challenge assumptions, and to propose solutions that, while potentially disruptive in the short term, would ultimately lead to a more sustainable and effective operation for the Cedar Ridge Collective. He leaned back for a moment, closing his eyes and taking a slow, deliberate breath.

The scent of pine, which had been so pervasive in the main hall, was fainter here, mingled with the musty odor of old fabric and something vaguely chemical, likely from cleaning supplies. It was the smell of a space that was functional but not cherished, a space that served a purpose but didn't evoke an emotional response. And that, he thought, was precisely how he wanted it. This was a workspace, not a sanctuary, and in that distinction lay the key to his professional detachment. He was here to analyze, to strategize, and to implement. The emotional resonance of Cedar Ridge was for the people who lived and worked here; his focus was on the mechanics of its operation. He opened his eyes, his gaze fixed on the glowing screen, and began to type, the rhythmic tap of his fingers a quiet counterpoint to the distant murmur of activity from the main hall.

The waiting game had begun, but for Evan, it was a game he was well-equipped to play. He was confident that his structured approach, his experience, and his unwavering focus on objective outcomes would allow him to navigate the complexities of Cedar Ridge and deliver the improvements the Collective needed. He wouldn't be drawn into the small-town charm, nor would he be deterred by the initial distance. He was here for a purpose, and he intended to fulfill it with precision and efficiency. The temporary office was his staging ground, the data his ammunition, and the future of the Cedar Ridge Collective his objective. He was ready.

Evan found his temporary office, a utilitarian box tucked away from the main thoroughfare of the Cedar Ridge Collective, to be precisely the kind of environment that facilitated his work. It was a space devoid of personal touches, where the scent of old textiles and cleaning supplies offered a muted contrast to the prevailing pine. He unpacked his laptop, the sleek device a stark yet welcome addition to the functional desk. His meticulous arrangement of files, his ergonomic peripherals, and the sharp glow of his LED lamp were all deliberate attempts to create a zone of pure operational focus.

He was here to dissect, to analyze, to optimize – a detached surgeon entering a community organism. He anticipated the town's predictable reserve, the polite caution of a close-knit populace towards an outsider. His objective was clear: to implement improvements, not to forge connections. He understood that his competence, not charisma, would be the currency of his success. The initial data would be his roadmap, his interviews with key personnel the dissection tools. He wouldn't be swayed by the town's perceived charm; his focus remained resolutely on the tangible metrics that would define the Collective's future.

As he settled in, the low hum of his laptop a familiar comfort, Evan allowed himself a brief moment to observe the activity filtering in from the main hall. The sounds of muffled conversations and the gentle clinking of what might be ceramic mugs suggested a community still very much alive and functioning. He was an intruder, yes, but a necessary one, tasked with bringing a fresh perspective, a modern approach to systems that, while perhaps steeped in tradition, might be hindering growth. He was prepared for the subtle resistance, the ingrained habits that would need to be gently, yet firmly, challenged.

His expertise had been sought, and he intended to deliver results, to prove his worth through quantifiable achievements. He leaned back, his gaze drifting towards the small, grimy window. The view was unremarkable – overgrown weeds, a leaning fence post – a visual echo of the very inefficiencies he was here to address. He took another breath, the scent of the temporary office grounding him. This was his arena, and he was ready to begin the analysis.

He began by opening the digital files, a cascade of spreadsheets and reports that represented the Collective's current state. He navigated through the financial statements, the volunteer logs, and the donation processing records, his mind already mapping out potential areas for improvement. He looked for patterns, for anomalies, for anything that deviated from an optimized workflow. It was a process that demanded patience, a willingness to sift through mountains of information to find the critical few insights. He had a framework in mind, a set of key performance indicators that would serve as his measuring stick: efficiency of resource allocation, volunteer engagement rates, community outreach impact. These were the objective markers he would use to guide his strategy. He would need to supplement this quantitative data with qualitative observations, to understand the human element that underpinned the numbers.

A gentle murmur of voices, clearer now, drew his attention back to the window. He shifted his gaze, his professional detachment momentarily giving way to a flicker of passive observation. Just outside the main entrance to the Collective, bathed in the soft afternoon light, a woman was engaged in conversation with an older gentleman. Evan didn't recognize either of them, but the scene held a certain quiet resonance. The woman stood with an air of unpretentious grace. Her posture was straight, her movements deliberate, conveying a sense of an individual who was both comfortable in her own skin and deeply connected to her surroundings. She wasn't making grand gestures or raising her voice; her presence was one of a gentle, yet undeniable, rootedness. He noted the way she inclined her head slightly as she listened, a gesture of genuine attention that spoke volumes about her character. There was a subtle strength in her bearing, an aura of quiet resilience that Evan, accustomed to dissecting motivations and identifying strengths, instinctively registered.

He recognized, with a detached, analytical part of his mind, that she was likely a familiar face in Cedar Ridge, someone woven into the fabric of the town. Her interaction with the elder, a man whose weathered face suggested a lifetime of experience and, Evan surmised, a position of respect within the community, seemed to embody the very essence of Cedar Ridge's established order. It was a brief tableau, a fleeting moment observed through a grimy pane of glass, yet it lodged itself in his periphery. He didn't consciously seek to identify her, didn't feel an immediate urge to engage. She was simply another data point, another element of the complex ecosystem he was here to understand. Her conversation, though inaudible to him, appeared to be one of mutual respect and shared understanding, a dialogue that likely touched upon the rhythms of the town, its concerns, its enduring spirit.

He registered the subtle way her hand moved as she spoke, a natural, unstudied gesture that added emphasis to her words. There was an authenticity to her demeanor that was, even from a distance, palpable. It wasn't a performance; it was simply who she was. He found himself cataloging these observations, not out of personal interest, but as part of his broader assessment of the town's social dynamics. Such interactions, he knew, often revealed more about a community's character than any official report. The way people treated their elders, the ease with which they conversed, the unspoken cues that passed between them – these were the subtle indicators of social cohesion, of shared values, of a collective identity. He filed away the image of the woman, her quiet strength, her evident connection to the man beside her and, by extension, to Cedar Ridge itself. She was, he acknowledged internally, an embodiment of the town's character, a woman deeply intertwined with its rhythm.

His gaze lingered for a fraction of a second longer than strictly necessary. It was a purely observational pause, an involuntary pause in his analytical process. He registered her presence as a significant aspect of the town's established order, a personification of Cedar Ridge's deep roots. There was no judgment, no particular admiration, just a quiet acknowledgment of her significance. He then turned his attention back to the glowing screen of his laptop, the data before him demanding his focus. The brief glimpse of Lena Whitaker, as he would later learn her name, was already being processed, categorized, and filed away within the broader framework of his assessment.

She was another thread in the intricate tapestry of Cedar Ridge, a thread he would undoubtedly encounter again, but for now, his mission lay within the digital confines of his temporary office. The hum of his laptop resumed its steady rhythm, a reminder of the task at hand, of the intricate systems he was here to untangle and refine. The conversation outside had concluded, and the woman had turned, her figure disappearing from view, leaving Evan to immerse himself once more in the world of numbers and operational efficiency. The momentary distraction, however, had served its purpose, adding another layer of subtle observation to his initial reconnaissance of this unfamiliar town. He was here to understand Cedar Ridge, and that understanding extended beyond mere logistical analysis; it encompassed the very essence of the people who comprised it.

CHAPTER TWO

The Heart of the Town

Lena Whitaker was, in many ways, the living embodiment of Cedar Ridge. Her roots here weren't merely planted; they were deeply intertwined with the very soil, the weathered timber of the town's historic buildings, and the rhythms of its seasons. She was a walking testament to a lineage that had contributed to this place for generations, a lineage that understood the profound interconnectedness of every soul within its unassuming borders. This wasn't just a town; it was an ecosystem, and Lena understood its delicate balance with an instinct honed by a lifetime of observation and participation. Her commitment wasn't a choice made in a moment of inspiration; it was an ingrained part of her being, as essential as the air she breathed.

She moved through Cedar Ridge with an unassuming grace, her presence a quiet constant in the ebb and flow of daily life. Whether she was stocking shelves at the general store, tending to a neighbor's ailing garden, or simply sharing a cup of coffee and a moment of quiet camaraderie at the diner, Lena was a pillar of understated strength. Her hands, often dusted with flour from baking or roughened by hours spent mending fences, were capable and kind. They had a way of offering comfort, of fixing what was broken, and of nurturing what was growing. She understood that true community wasn't built on grand pronouncements or sweeping initiatives, but on the quiet, consistent acts of support that formed the bedrock of everyday existence.

Lena's perspective on life was fundamentally shaped by the wisdom of her ancestors, who had navigated the challenges of this region with resilience and a deep respect for the land. They had taught her the value of self-sufficiency, yes, but more importantly, they had instilled in her the understanding that true strength lay not in isolation, but in interdependence. She had witnessed firsthand how the success of one family often rippled outward, bolstering the spirits and the livelihoods of others. Conversely, she had also seen the devastating impact when that delicate web of support frayed, leaving individuals isolated and vulnerable. This was a lesson that resonated deeply within her, shaping her unwavering belief in the power of collective action and mutual aid.

Her family's history in Cedar Ridge was etched into the very landscape. The old Whitaker farm, a sprawling parcel of land on the outskirts of town, had been in their family for over a century. Lena had grown up amidst its rolling fields, learning the language of the soil, the subtle signs of changing weather, and the enduring patience required to coax life from the earth. These experiences had fostered in her a profound respect for the natural world and a deep appreciation for the cycles of growth, decay, and renewal. This intimate connection to the land translated into a broader understanding of community – that like any living organism, it required nurturing, care, and a willingness to adapt to its inherent rhythms.

Lena's unwavering steadfastness wasn't born of a blind adherence to tradition, but from a profound understanding of what made Cedar Ridge endure. She saw the town not as a static entity, but as a living, breathing organism, one that required constant attention and care. Her dedication was not a passive acceptance of her role, but an active, conscious choice to invest her energy and her spirit into its continued vitality. She believed that every individual had a responsibility to contribute to the collective well-being, and she approached this responsibility with a quiet but fierce determination.

Her days were a testament to this commitment. While many saw Cedar Ridge as a sleepy, unassuming town, Lena saw it as a vibrant tapestry of interconnected lives, each thread crucial to the overall design. She was the kind of person who remembered everyone's birthday, who knew who needed a casserole after a loss, and who was always the first to volunteer when a community project arose. Her presence at the weekly farmers' market was more than just a vendor selling her jams and preserves; it was an anchor, a familiar face offering a smile and a word of encouragement. She listened to the concerns of her neighbors, offering practical advice gleaned from her own experiences or simply a sympathetic ear.

The notion of interdependence was not an abstract concept for Lena; it was a lived reality. She understood that the success of the general store depended on the farmers who supplied it, that the local school relied on the dedicated teachers and the engaged parents, and that the overall charm of Cedar Ridge was a collective effort, a shared responsibility. This understanding fueled her own contributions, whether it was organizing the annual town picnic, coordinating volunteers for the library's renovation, or simply lending a hand to a neighbor struggling with a difficult task. She believed that by strengthening one part of the community, you inevitably strengthened the whole.

Her family's legacy was a source of both pride and responsibility. The Whitaker name carried with it a certain weight in Cedar Ridge, a reputation for hard work, honesty, and a deep-seated commitment to the town. Lena felt this legacy keenly, not as a burden, but as an inheritance to be honored and nurtured. She saw herself as a custodian of the values her ancestors had championed, and she strove to live her life in a way that reflected their enduring spirit. This meant always putting the needs of the community before her own, even when it required personal sacrifice.

Lena's steadfastness also manifested in her quiet resilience. She had faced her share of hardships, both personal and communal. She had seen businesses falter, friends move away, and the inevitable challenges that come with living in a place that wasn't always at the forefront of progress. But through it all, she had never wavered in her belief in Cedar Ridge. She had a remarkable capacity to find the silver lining, to identify the lessons in adversity, and to encourage others to keep moving forward. Her optimism wasn't naive; it was a hard-won conviction, forged in the crucible of experience.

She was a natural connector, able to bridge divides and foster understanding. While others might see disagreements or petty squabbles, Lena possessed an uncanny ability to find common ground, to remind people of their shared humanity and their mutual stake in the town's success. She wouldn't shy away from difficult conversations, but she approached them with empathy and a genuine desire for resolution, always prioritizing the health of the community above personal pride. Her mediation style was less about imposing solutions and more about guiding individuals towards their own understanding and compromise.

Evan, the new consultant, represented a new variable in this intricate equation. Lena observed him with a cautious curiosity, her inherent protectiveness of Cedar Ridge piqued by his detached demeanor. She saw his analytical mind, his focus on data and efficiency, but she also recognized what he might be missing: the intangible threads that held their community together, the unspoken bonds, the shared history that informed every decision. She understood that efficiency was important, but she also knew that Cedar Ridge thrived on something far more profound – a sense of belonging, a shared identity that couldn't be measured in spreadsheets.

Her steadfastness, therefore, wasn't just about preserving the status quo; it was about ensuring that progress didn't come at the cost of what made Cedar Ridge unique. She was prepared to engage with Evan, to listen to his proposals, but she would also be a quiet advocate for the heart of the town, for the values that had guided them for so long. She believed that true growth came from within, from strengthening the existing bonds, not from imposing external solutions that might alienate or disrupt the delicate ecosystem she so fiercely protected.

Her commitment was to the soul of Cedar Ridge, a soul she believed was far more valuable than any quantifiable metric. She would be a steady presence, a reminder that behind the numbers and the strategies, there were people, lives, and a deeply cherished way of life that deserved to be understood and respected. Her loyalty was to Cedar Ridge, and that loyalty was as unyielding as the ancient oaks that dotted its landscape.

The hum of the town, a familiar melody Lena had known since childhood, seemed to subtly shift with Evan Morales's arrival. He was a splash of vibrant, almost jarring color against the muted, earthy tones of Cedar Ridge. His tailored suit, a sharp contrast to the worn denim and practical flannels that constituted the town's usual uniform, spoke of a different world, a world of polished boardrooms and fleeting deadlines. Lena watched him from her usual vantage point behind the counter of the general store, the scent of dried herbs and aged wood a comforting buffer. He moved with a restless energy, his gaze sharp and analytical, sweeping over the worn facades of Main Street as if cataloging their imperfections. There was no mistaking his purpose; he was the outsider, the hired hand, the one brought in to dissect and, if possible, to fix whatever perceived ailments plagued their quiet corner of the world.

She saw him at the diner, hunched over a laptop, his brow furrowed in concentration. The chipped Formica tabletop and the clatter of ceramic mugs seemed out of place for such a sophisticated instrument. He asked questions, Lena had heard, not of the usual kind. He wasn't inquiring about Mrs. Gable's prize-winning roses or the best spot for fishing on the river. His inquiries were pointed, data-driven, focused on metrics and outcomes. He wanted to know about foot traffic, revenue streams, efficiency ratings. Lena understood the necessity, of course. The town council, in their earnestness to secure the future of Cedar Ridge, had recognized a need for a fresh perspective, a pragmatic approach to challenges that had perhaps grown too familiar for their seasoned eyes. Evan Morales, with his credentials and his air of confident capability, was that perspective.

Yet, even as she acknowledged the practical value he might bring, a quiet skepticism began to take root within her. It wasn't a judgment of his character, but a deep-seated understanding of Cedar Ridge's unique ecosystem. He saw problems, tangible issues that could be addressed with charts and graphs. He saw inefficiencies that could be streamlined. But could he see the soul of the town? Could he feel the pulse that beat beneath the surface, the invisible threads of connection that bound its residents together? Lena doubted it. His approach, while undeniably efficient, felt... detached. He was a surgeon, precise and skilled, but one who operated without fully appreciating the patient's history, their deeply ingrained habits, their cherished idiosyncrasies.

She remembered seeing him earlier that week, walking down Elm Street, his head tilted back as if trying to decipher the architectural blueprints of the historic homes. He had a way of observing that felt more like surveying, a methodical assessment rather than an appreciation. He'd stopped in front of the old library, a building that held so many of Lena's own memories – summer reading programs, hushed whispers among the stacks, the comforting scent of aging paper. He'd pulled out a small notebook, scribbled a few notes, and then moved on, his expression unreadable. Lena wondered if he'd noticed the slightly crooked sign, the peeling paint on the window frames, or if he'd simply seen an underutilized public space, a prime candidate for renovation or perhaps even consolidation.

The nuances, the intangible elements that defined Cedar Ridge, were likely lost on him. He couldn't measure the warmth of Mrs. Gable's smile when she offered a stranger a tour of her garden, nor could he quantify the quiet satisfaction of a shared meal at the community potluck, where recipes passed down through generations were as much a part of the conversation as the town's current affairs. He focused on the quantifiable, the measurable, the things that could be translated into numbers on a report. He was, Lena surmised, a man of outcomes, and Cedar Ridge was a town built on process, on the journey, on the slow, deliberate unfolding of community life.

There was a particular incident that solidified her initial assessment. A small fire had broken out at the bakery, a beloved institution that had been serving up its flaky pastries and crusty breads for as long as anyone could remember. The fire had been contained quickly, thanks to the swift action of the local fire department and a few quick-thinking neighbors who had rushed over with buckets of water and towels. The damage was minimal, mostly smoke and a scorched patch on the back wall. While the town rallied around, offering support and assistance, Lena had observed Evan Morales's reaction. He'd arrived on the scene, his suit immaculate despite the lingering scent of smoke, and had immediately begun asking about the cost of repairs, the insurance implications, and the potential downtime for the business. He'd been efficient, certainly, but his questions felt clinical, devoid of the shared sigh of relief that had rippled through the onlookers, the genuine concern for Martha, the baker, and the collective gratitude that no one had been hurt.

Lena, who had known Martha since she was a child, had felt a pang of something akin to disappointment. She'd offered Martha a comforting hand on her arm, a silent gesture of solidarity, and had instead seen Evan discreetly taking photographs of the damage with his phone, his focus entirely on the material aspect of the incident. It was a stark reminder of their differing perspectives. For Lena, the fire was a scare, a testament to the community's resilience, and a reminder of the fragility of cherished local businesses. For Evan, it was likely a data point, an operational disruption to be factored into his analysis.

She understood that his role was to identify and address weaknesses, to bring a pragmatic and objective viewpoint. Cedar Ridge, for all its charm and strong community bonds, wasn't immune to the economic pressures that faced many small towns. There were indeed challenges, and his expertise might prove invaluable in navigating them. But Lena couldn't shake the feeling that he was missing the most crucial element: the heart of the matter. He saw the cogs and gears of the town's machinery, but he didn't seem to grasp the invisible current of affection, loyalty, and shared history that powered it.

He was a temporary fixture, a highly skilled technician brought in to tune an instrument he didn't quite understand. Lena envisioned him leaving as abruptly as he had arrived, his reports filed, his recommendations implemented, and the town returning to its familiar rhythm, perhaps a little more efficient, a little more streamlined, but potentially a little less... itself. Her own connection to Cedar Ridge was so deep, so intrinsic, that she couldn't imagine approaching it as a problem to be solved. It was a living entity, a complex tapestry woven with countless individual stories, a place where sentiment and practicality were inextricably intertwined.

Evan Morales, with his sharp suits and his spreadsheets, represented a force that could, perhaps, improve the town's functionality, but Lena worried it might come at the cost of its unique character, its intangible spirit. She would observe, of course, as was her nature, and she would participate as needed, but her role remained that of a quiet guardian, a keeper of the flame, ensuring that in the pursuit of progress, the true heart of Cedar Ridge didn't get lost in the shuffle. His presence was a question mark in the town's ongoing narrative, and Lena found herself waiting, with a mixture of curiosity and apprehension, to see how the chapter would unfold.

The Cedar Ridge Collective. Even the name resonated with a sense of shared endeavor, a deliberate gathering of resources and talents for the betterment of all. For Lena, it wasn't merely a place of commerce; it was the beating heart of their small community, a vital circulatory system that nourished the lives of those who called Cedar Ridge home. She moved through its aisles with an ingrained familiarity, her hands instinctively reaching for the smooth, cool surface of the heirloom tomato crates, the rough texture of hand-knitted woolens, the delicate fragility of hand-blown glass. Each item on display held a story, a silent testament to the dedication and passion of the individuals who had brought it into being.

Lena understood the Collective's multifaceted role. It was a marketplace, yes, but it was so much more. It was a lifeline for the local farmers, providing them with a consistent and fair outlet for their produce, shielded from the caprices of distant distributors and fluctuating market prices. She knew their faces, their families, the generations of soil-tilling knowledge etched into their hands. When she saw Mr. Abernathy's robust pumpkins, their skins a deep, autumnal orange, she didn't just see inventory; she saw the early mornings, the back-breaking work, the hopeful gaze cast towards the sky for rain. When she priced the honey from the Miller family's hives, she remembered Mrs. Miller's gentle explanations about the distinct floral notes of each season, the subtle sweetness of clover in the spring, the richer, darker tones of late summer wildflowers.

Beyond the agricultural bounty, the Collective was a sanctuary for the town's artisans. Here, the intricate beadwork of Sarah Jenkins, whose delicate jewelry captured the iridescence of dragonfly wings, found appreciative eyes. The sturdy, practical pottery of David Chen, his glazes reflecting the earthy hues of the surrounding landscape, was sought after by residents and visitors alike. Lena took pride in curating these displays, arranging the pieces with an artist's eye, ensuring that each creation received the respect and attention it deserved. She believed that these were not just goods for sale; they were tangible expressions of Cedar Ridge's creative spirit, fragments of its soul made manifest.

Her involvement extended beyond mere display and sales. Lena was an active participant in the Collective's operational rhythm. She meticulously tracked inventory, not with the sterile detachment of a corporate accountant, but with a deep understanding of each item's significance. A dwindling supply of Mrs. Henderson's famous blueberry jam wasn't a stock-out; it was a signal to gently inquire if Martha had had a chance to make another batch, a quiet acknowledgment of her efforts and a subtle encouragement. She managed the finances with diligence, ensuring that the profits flowed back into the community, supporting the very people who contributed to the Collective's richness. She saw every transaction not as a simple exchange of currency, but as a reinforcement of the bonds that held them together.

Lena was acutely aware of the Collective's imperfections. The slightly crooked shelving unit in the back, a relic from the town's founding days, still held its share of canned goods. The worn linoleum floor, polished smooth by countless footsteps, bore the faint scuff marks of children's playful dashes. The sign above the entrance, though charmingly hand-painted, had a small chip on its corner, a souvenir from a particularly blustery winter storm years ago. To Lena, these were not flaws to be eradicated, but rather the endearing scars of a life well-lived. They were markers of history, testaments to the enduring resilience of the Collective and the community it served. Each imperfection was a whispered story, a reminder of shared efforts, of challenges overcome, of the collective endeavor that had built and sustained this place.

She recalled a summer when a sudden hailstorm had threatened to decimate the early apple crop. The farmers, their faces etched with worry, had brought their bruised but still edible fruit to the Collective. Instead of discarding it, Lena had organized a "Hailstorm Special," selling the apples at a reduced price for pies and cider. The response had been overwhelming. Residents flocked to the Collective, not just to buy apples, but to offer their own assistance, to share recipes, to simply offer words of encouragement. It was in moments like these that the true strength of the Collective shone through – its capacity to adapt, to support, and to transform potential disaster into a shared experience of resilience and resourcefulness.

The Collective was a place where connections were forged and nurtured. It was where young families discovered locally sourced baby food, learning about the farms that grew their children's nourishment. It was where newcomers, seeking to understand the rhythm of Cedar Ridge, could find not only goods but also conversations, advice, and a welcoming smile. Lena often found herself playing informal matchmaker, introducing a baker in need of specific flours to a farmer who grew heritage grains, or connecting a retiree with a passion for gardening to a young family looking for advice on starting their first vegetable patch. These interactions, seemingly small and insignificant, were the mortar that held the town's foundation together.

She remembered when Evan Morales had first visited. He had walked through the Collective with that same analytical gaze Lena had observed on Main Street, his eyes scanning the shelves, his brow furrowed. He had asked about sales figures, profit margins, inventory turnover rates. Lena had answered his questions with a quiet professionalism, but her heart had felt a slight disconnect. He saw the numbers, the data, the potential for optimization. He didn't see the interwoven threads of dependency and support, the quiet understanding between a farmer and a customer, the shared pride in a locally crafted product. He saw a business; Lena saw a community's heart, beating with a life of its own.

Her role at the Collective was more than a job; it was a stewardship. She was a guardian of its spirit, ensuring that its operations remained rooted in the values that made Cedar Ridge special. She understood that growth and progress were necessary, but not at the expense of the town's intrinsic character. She believed that the Collective's success was measured not just in its balance sheets, but in the strength of the relationships it fostered, the sense of belonging it provided, and the quiet testament it offered to the enduring power of community. It was a place where every purchase was an investment, every interaction a contribution, and every product a reflection of the collective soul of Cedar Ridge.

She felt a deep sense of purpose in her work, a quiet satisfaction in knowing that she was playing a part in maintaining the vibrant, complex, and deeply human pulse of her beloved town. The gentle murmur of conversation, the rustle of paper bags, the scent of fresh produce and handcrafted goods – these were the sounds and smells that formed the symphony of the Collective, a symphony Lena knew by heart, and one she was committed to preserving.

The Collective wasn't just a hub of activity; it was a living, breathing entity, its health directly tied to the well-being of its residents. Lena saw this intrinsically. She understood that when Mrs. Gable, a widow living on a modest pension, needed a few extra pounds of potatoes to get her through the week, the Collective offered that grace without fanfare. It was the unspoken agreement, the shared understanding that everyone looked out for each other. This wasn't charity in the traditional sense; it was community, woven into the fabric of daily transactions. Lena ensured that this ethos was upheld, that the Collective remained a place of generosity and understanding, a safe harbor in an often-uncertain world.

She often found herself explaining this delicate balance to those who, like Evan, approached the Collective with a purely business-minded perspective. "It's not just about the bottom line," she'd say, her voice calm and steady, as she pointed out the hand-painted sign advertising the community's upcoming bake sale, a crucial fundraiser for the local school's art program. "It's about supporting Martha's bakery, which in turn supports our farmers by using their local flour. It's about giving young Sarah Jenkins a place to sell her beautiful jewelry, giving her a pathway to independence. It's about ensuring that when the harvest is bountiful, our farmers don't have to throw away perfectly good produce because they can't find a buyer."

Lena saw her role as a translator, bridging the gap between the quantifiable and the qualitative. She could readily provide Evan with the sales data for the jams, the pottery, the honey. She could articulate the profit margins and the inventory flow. But she could also speak to the immeasurable value of these items. She could describe the joy on a child's face when they received a handmade toy from the Collective, or the comfort a warm, locally sourced blanket provided on a cold evening. These were the elements that spreadsheets couldn't capture, the intangible assets that made Cedar Ridge not just a place to live, but a place to truly belong.

She remembered a particular instance that underscored this. The Collective had hosted a "Meet the Maker" event, featuring a local woodworker who crafted intricate birdhouses. He was a quiet man, a retired carpenter named Thomas, who found solace and purpose in his craft after his wife had passed. The event was a quiet success, drawing a small but appreciative crowd. Evan had attended, observing the interactions with his characteristic observational intensity. Afterward, he'd remarked to Lena, "Interesting model. High engagement, but low sales volume per participant. Perhaps we could explore tiered membership options or offer premium workshops to increase revenue."

Lena had smiled gently. "Thomas isn't just selling birdhouses, Evan," she'd replied, gesturing towards where Thomas was now deep in conversation with a young couple about designing a custom piece for their new garden. "He's sharing his passion, his skill. This young couple is learning about woodworking, about the dedication it takes. They're connecting with him, and through him, with Cedar Ridge. That connection, that shared experience – that's as valuable as any sale." Evan had nodded, his expression unreadable, and Lena knew he'd filed her words away as another data point, perhaps one that didn't quite fit his existing algorithms.

The imperfections Lena cherished were not signs of neglect, but rather of constant, organic evolution. The worn counter, smoothed by generations of hands, bore the faint ring marks from countless coffee cups. The slightly frayed edges of the burlap sacks used for potatoes spoke of their journey from the earth to the shelves. These were not blemishes; they were the patina of authenticity, the visible history of a place deeply intertwined with the lives of its people. They were a testament to the fact that the Collective was not a static entity, but a dynamic, evolving organism, constantly adapting to the needs and rhythms of its community.

Lena often worked late, the soft glow of the single lamp above her desk illuminating stacks of invoices and order forms. In these quiet hours, the hum of the refrigerator and the gentle creak of the old building were her only companions. She would review the previous day's sales, not just noting the figures, but reflecting on the stories behind them. A large order of apples for Mrs. Gable's famous pies, a special request for a particular type of herb from the local apothecary, a spontaneous purchase of a hand-knitted scarf by a visitor who'd been charmed by its vibrant colors – each transaction was a thread in the intricate tapestry of Cedar Ridge life. She saw these as moments of connection, of shared experience, of mutual reliance.

She understood that Evan's objective, to streamline and optimize, was a necessary function in a changing economic landscape. Small towns like Cedar Ridge faced significant challenges, and a fresh, analytical perspective could indeed be beneficial. But Lena held a deep-seated belief that the soul of the town, the intangible essence that made it unique, lay not in its efficiency, but in its humanity. The Collective, in her eyes, was the embodiment of that humanity. It was a place where people came not just to buy, but to connect, to share, to belong. And Lena was its devoted steward, ensuring that its pulse remained strong, vibrant, and deeply rooted in the hearts of its people.

Lena's vision for Cedar Ridge wasn't a grand, sweeping overhaul, but a slow, steady bloom, nurtured by the very roots of the community. She understood that the town's resilience wasn't a matter of attracting outside investment or implementing trendy business strategies, though she wasn't naive enough to dismiss their potential benefits entirely. Rather, its true strength lay in the quiet, unwavering commitment of its residents, in their willingness to pour their hearts and souls into the soil of their shared home. This was the undercurrent of her daily work at the Collective, the unspoken philosophy guiding her every decision. She saw the town not as a collection of individuals, but as a single, complex organism, its health dependent on the vitality of each of its parts.

She often found herself in quiet conversations with individuals who came to the Collective, not just to purchase goods, but to connect. There was old Mr. Silas, who still came by every Tuesday for his loaf of sourdough, his hands gnarled like ancient oak roots. Lena would always take a moment to ask about his prize-winning roses, and he, in turn, would offer sage advice on the best times to prune the berry bushes in the Collective's small community garden. These weren't mere pleasantries; they were the threads of connection, the reaffirmation that each person, regardless of age or contribution, was a vital part of Cedar Ridge's tapestry. She knew that

Silas's quiet pride in his roses was as important to the town's spirit as the robust sales of Mrs. Gable's jams.

Then there were the younger families, their faces often a mixture of exhaustion and fierce love. Lena made it a point to know their children's names, to ask about their latest milestones. She'd guide them towards the organic baby food, patiently explaining which farmer's produce went into each jar, a small act of transparency that fostered trust and a sense of shared responsibility. She saw the Collective as a place where these families could not only nourish their children but also feel nourished themselves, a place that offered them a sense of belonging in a world that often felt isolating. When a young mother, Sarah, confided her anxieties about returning to work, Lena didn't just offer a sympathetic ear; she discreetly mentioned that Mrs. Henderson, who often helped at the Collective during peak seasons, was looking for occasional babysitting opportunities. It was a small gesture, born from knowing her community intimately, and it had the potential to ease Sarah's burden while providing Mrs. Henderson with some much-needed income.

Lena believed that fostering this sense of belonging was paramount to Cedar Ridge's long-term survival. It wasn't about forcing people to stay, but about creating a place where they *wanted* to stay, a place where they felt valued, heard, and understood. This meant nurturing the town's unique character, its quirks and traditions, rather than trying to smooth them over for the sake of standardization. The slightly dilapidated charm of the town square, the annual pie-eating contest that always ended in a sticky, good-natured mess, the way everyone knew each other's business (for better or worse) – these were the elements that defined Cedar Ridge. Lena saw her role as a protector of this essence, ensuring that any progress or development honored, rather than erased, these defining characteristics.

She recalled a town meeting a few years prior, where a proposal had been put forth to redevelop the old, vacant movie theater into a multiplex. The idea had been met with divided opinions. Some saw the potential for economic growth, for bringing in outside entertainment and revenue. But Lena had spoken passionately against it, not because she opposed development, but because she believed the proposed model was fundamentally at odds with Cedar Ridge's spirit. "That theater," she had said, her voice clear and resonating in the hushed hall, "is where generations of Cedar Ridge families have shared their first dates, celebrated graduations, and found a common escape from the everyday. Tearing it down for a soulless chain is like ripping out a page from our town's history book. We need development, yes, but we need development that honors our past and builds upon our strengths, not one that erases them."

Her words, though initially met with some skepticism, had resonated. The proposal was eventually revised, and the old theater, after significant community fundraising and volunteer effort, was transformed into a vibrant community arts center, hosting local theater productions, art classes, and small concerts. It had become a hub for creativity and connection, a testament to what could be achieved when the community invested its own passion and effort. Lena saw this as a prime example of Cedar Ridge's inherent strength: the power of collective will, fueled by a deep-seated love for their home.

Evan Morales, with his sharp suits and sharper business acumen, represented a different perspective, one that Lena found both intriguing and, at times, frustrating. He saw Cedar Ridge through a lens of spreadsheets and profit margins, a landscape ripe for optimization. He'd spent weeks poring over the Collective's books, his brow furrowed in concentration, identifying inefficiencies and suggesting cost-saving measures. Lena appreciated his analytical mind, his ability to spot trends she might overlook. But she also knew that his definition of success was different from hers.

"Lena," he'd said one afternoon, gesturing to a display of hand-knitted scarves, their vibrant colors a cheerful defiance of the muted tones of early spring, "these are lovely, truly. But the profit margin on these is significantly lower than what we could achieve with mass-produced, branded winter wear. We could offer a much wider selection, meet a broader demand, and significantly increase revenue."

Lena had gently picked up a scarf, running her fingers over the intricate stitches. "Evan," she'd replied, her voice soft but firm, "these scarves are made by Mrs. Gable, who knit them while recovering from surgery. It's not just about the wool and the needles; it's about her strength, her resilience, and her desire to contribute. When someone buys one of these, they're not just buying a warm accessory; they're buying a piece of Mrs. Gable's story, a tangible connection to someone in this town. That's a value that can't be quantified on a balance sheet."

She saw his point, of course. The Collective, like any enterprise, needed to be financially sound. But she refused to let that be its sole measure of success. The intangible benefits, the fostering of community spirit, the provision of a platform for local artisans, the strengthening of neighborly bonds – these were the true dividends. She believed that by prioritizing these elements, the financial stability would follow, a natural consequence of a thriving, connected community. It was a slower, more organic growth, but in Lena's view, a far more sustainable and fulfilling one.

Her own commitment to Cedar Ridge was deeply personal. She had grown up here, her childhood etched with the scent of pine needles and the sound of the creek tumbling over smooth stones. She had left for college, for the allure of the wider world, but the pull of Cedar Ridge had been a constant, undeniable force. It was the comfort of familiarity, the deep-seated sense of belonging, the knowledge that her roots ran as deep as the oldest oaks in the surrounding forest. When she returned, it wasn't as a visitor, but as someone coming home, eager to contribute to the place that had shaped her.

She understood that for Cedar Ridge to truly thrive, it needed more individuals like herself, people who were willing to invest not just their time and resources, but their hearts. It needed people who saw the town not as a temporary stop, but as a permanent home, a place to build a future, raise a family, and contribute to a legacy. This was why she championed the various community initiatives, from the farmers' market expansion to the support programs for local entrepreneurs. She saw each success, however small, as a seed planted for the town's future, a testament to the enduring power of collective effort.

Lena often found herself observing the subtle shifts in the town's atmosphere. A new family moving in, their car laden with boxes, always brought a flutter of hopeful anticipation. A successful harvest festival, filled with laughter and shared stories, left her feeling a renewed sense of optimism. Conversely, a period of economic hardship, where businesses struggled and young people felt compelled to leave, cast a shadow over her. These were the rhythms of small-town life, and Lena felt them deeply, her own emotional landscape intricately tied to the well-being of Cedar Ridge.

She knew that the path forward wouldn't always be smooth. There would be challenges, setbacks, and moments of doubt. But she also knew, with a certainty that settled deep within her bones, that Cedar Ridge possessed an inner strength, a resilience forged by generations of people who had loved this land and each other. Her role, as she saw it, was to fan that flame, to nurture that inherent spirit, and to ensure that the heart of Cedar Ridge continued to beat, strong and true, for years to come. It was a commitment that went beyond her work at the Collective; it was a calling, a deep-seated responsibility to the place and the people who had given her so much. And in that commitment, Lena found her own deepest sense of purpose.

The Saturday morning air in Cedar Ridge hummed with a familiar, comforting energy. The town square, usually a quiet expanse of worn cobblestones and sleepy storefronts, transformed each week into a vibrant tapestry of colors, sounds, and smells. Stalls overflowed with the bounty of local farms: ruby-red strawberries glistening under the early sun, pyramids of crisp, green lettuces, and bouquets of fragrant herbs that perfumed the air. The scent of freshly baked bread mingled with the sweet aroma of apple cider, creating an olfactory symphony that drew residents and the occasional visitor alike. Lena, a familiar presence amidst the cheerful chaos, moved with practiced ease, her wicker basket tucked under her arm. She greeted familiar faces, exchanged brief pleasantries, and carefully selected the freshest produce for the Collective's shelves.

It was during one of these routine Saturday excursions, as she was inspecting a crate of heirloom tomatoes at Silas's stall, that she saw him. Evan Morales. He stood a little apart from the main throng, his posture radiating an almost palpable aura of efficiency, a sharp contrast to the relaxed ebb and flow of the market. He was dressed impeccably, as always, a dark blazer over a crisp, lighter-colored shirt, a stark departure from the practical, often flour-dusted attire of the local farmers and artisans. He seemed to be observing, his gaze sweeping across the stalls with an analytical intensity that Lena recognized from their meetings at the Collective. He hadn't yet approached any vendors, his hands clasped loosely behind his back, his expression thoughtful.

Lena felt a peculiar sensation, a subtle shift in her awareness. She'd grown accustomed to Evan's presence at the Collective, his probing questions and calculated suggestions. He was a force of logic, a master of the bottom line, and while she often found herself gently pushing back against his more utilitarian viewpoints, she couldn't deny his sharp intellect. He saw Cedar Ridge as a business, a system to be optimized, and in that he was undeniably skilled. But here, amidst the earthy realities of the farmer's market, surrounded by the tangible products of hard work and dedication, his presence felt... different. Almost out of place, yet undeniably there.

As if sensing her gaze, Evan turned his head. His eyes, a deep, intelligent brown, met hers across the bustling square. For a fleeting moment, the cheerful clamor of the market seemed to recede, replaced by a focused silence between them. He offered a brief, almost imperceptible nod, a gesture of acknowledgment that felt more formal than the easy nods exchanged between neighbors. Lena responded in kind, a small smile touching her lips. She found herself intrigued by the flicker of surprise, or perhaps recognition, that crossed his face before it settled back into its usual composed expression. He was a man who dealt in projections and forecasts, in market shares and revenue streams, but in that brief exchange, Lena saw a spark of something more. It was in the way his gaze lingered for a fraction of a second longer than necessary, in the subtle softening of his features as he met her eyes.

He began to make his way toward her stall, navigating the crowd with a quiet, almost apologetic grace. Lena turned back to Silas, her heart giving an unexpected little flutter, and continued their conversation about the best way to ripen those stubborn last tomatoes. She kept a peripheral awareness of Evan's approach, her senses tuned to his proximity. He stopped a respectful distance away, his presence a quiet hum beside the cheerful chatter of the market.

"Lena," he said, his voice measured, carrying easily over the din. It was the same tone he used in their business meetings, professional and clear. "I was just finalizing the order for the Collective's fall produce. I wanted to confirm our projected needs for root vegetables and inquire about the availability of those specialty squash varieties you mentioned last week."

Lena nodded, shifting her attention fully to him. The initial surprise of seeing him at the market had given way to a comfortable familiarity, even in this new setting. "Good morning, Evan. The root vegetables are looking excellent. I've been speaking with Farmer McGregor; he anticipates a particularly robust harvest of carrots and parsnips this year. As for the squash," she gestured to a display further down Silas's stall, where a few hardy specimens of acorn and butternut squash were already on display, "we've got a good initial stock, but more will be coming in over the next few weeks. We can definitely accommodate the projected quantities."

Evan pulled out a small, sleek tablet from his inner jacket pocket, his fingers moving with practiced speed across the screen. "Excellent. McGregor's parsnips are always superior. And the squash... are we looking at a consistent supply throughout September and October?"

"Absolutely," Lena confirmed, her gaze sweeping over the vibrant display of vegetables. "The farmers are very good about staggering their planting. We'll have a steady flow, with the larger varieties available later in the season." She paused, then added, with a touch of pride, "Some of those larger pumpkins are already growing beautifully out at the Henderson farm. They're promising some truly impressive specimens for the harvest festival."

Evan looked up from his tablet, a faint smile playing on his lips. "The harvest festival," he mused, his gaze briefly sweeping across the bustling square, taking in the families browsing the stalls, the children with sticky faces from sampled pastries, the general atmosphere of relaxed community. "It's... quite an event."

"It is," Lena agreed, her own smile widening. She found his observation, coming from him, particularly interesting. For Evan, an "event" was usually a carefully planned corporate gala or a meticulously orchestrated product launch. This was something far more organic, a celebration born from the land and the people who worked it. "It's a chance for everyone to come together, celebrate the season, and... well, just enjoy being a community."

He met her gaze then, and for a moment, the professional façade seemed to soften, revealing something a little more personal. Lena noticed the intelligence that sparked in his eyes, the quickness of his mind, but also a certain quiet contemplation that was absent in their usual office interactions. He was listening, truly listening, not just to the data, but to the sentiment behind her words. "I can see that," he said, his voice a little softer. "It's a different kind of energy than I'm accustomed to."

"It is," Lena acknowledged. "But it's a good energy, isn't it?" She held his gaze, a silent question hanging in the air. Was he capable of appreciating it? Could he see beyond the inefficiencies, beyond the lack of polished corporate structure, to the genuine warmth and connection that pulsed through Cedar Ridge?

Evan didn't answer immediately. He looked out at the square again, his gaze lingering on a group of children chasing a runaway balloon. A faint, almost wistful expression flickered across his face before he turned back to Lena. "It has its... unique appeal," he conceded, a hint of a smile in his voice. "And the quality of the produce is undeniably superior. That's what's important for the Collective, of course."

Lena heard the familiar refrain of business acumen, but she also detected a subtle shift. It wasn't just about quality; it was about the experience, the atmosphere. He was, in his own way, acknowledging the intangible value of the market, of Cedar Ridge itself. "The quality is a result of the care and dedication of the people here," she said, her voice gentle. "They invest their hearts into what they grow, and you can taste it."

He inclined his head, a gesture of acknowledgment. "I understand that, Lena. And I appreciate your perspective on it. It's... a valuable component of the Collective's brand." He paused, then added, his eyes meeting hers with an earnestness that surprised her, "Your ability to connect the product to the producer, to the story behind it... it's a significant asset."

Lena felt a warmth spread through her chest, a quiet satisfaction at his observation. He saw it. He truly saw the value in what she championed. It wasn't just about profit margins; it was about the human element, the relationships, the shared history. "Thank you, Evan," she said, her voice genuine. "That means a lot."

He gave a small, almost shy smile. "Just stating the facts." He then consulted his tablet again, though his attention seemed less focused. "So, the root vegetables. McGregor is confirmed for X kilograms of carrots and Y kilograms of parsnips. And the squash – can we finalize the order for acorn and butternut? I'll need quantities for the next four weeks."

Lena began to relay the figures, her mind effortlessly accessing the details of the Collective's inventory and the farmers' commitments. As they spoke, their conversation flowed smoothly, the initial professional transaction now imbued with a subtle undercurrent of personal connection. Lena found herself noticing the way Evan's brow furrowed slightly when he concentrated, the way his lips quirked at the corner when he made a dry observation. She saw a man who was accustomed to navigating the complexities of the business world, a man who possessed a sharp intellect and an impressive drive, but who, in this moment, seemed to be experiencing a moment of quiet reflection, a subtle appreciation for the rhythm of small-town life.

Evan, for his part, was struck by Lena's natural ease, her genuine warmth that seemed to radiate from her like the summer sun. He was used to transactional relationships, to people who either wanted something from him or were wary of his business-driven approach. Lena, however, was different. She was grounded, her confidence not born of arrogance, but of a deep-seated connection to her community and her work. He found himself drawn to her quiet strength, her unwavering commitment to the values she held dear, even when they clashed with his own more pragmatic outlook. He'd spent weeks dissecting the Collective's financials, looking for ways to streamline and maximize profit, and while he still believed in the necessity of that approach, Lena had made him see that there were other forms of capital at play – the capital of community, of shared purpose, of genuine human connection.

"And the apples," Evan added, looking up from his tablet, a question in his tone. "Are we still on track for the Fuji and Gala varieties from the orchard up on Miller's Hill?"

"We are," Lena confirmed. "The harvest there has been excellent this year. Mrs. Gable mentioned they might even have some extra Honeycrisps by the end of the month, if you're interested in adding those to the order."

Evan's eyes widened slightly. "Honeycrisp? That's a good call. They're always popular. Let's add a tentative quantity for those. We can adjust based on actual yield, of course." He tapped his tablet again, his focus returning to the task at hand, but there was a subtle shift in his demeanor. The sharp edges of his usual business persona seemed to have softened, replaced by a more relaxed engagement.

Their conversation continued, a seamless blend of business and quiet observation. They discussed delivery schedules, packaging needs, and anticipated seasonal demand. Yet, woven through the professional exchange were moments of shared glances, of brief smiles exchanged, of a mutual acknowledgment that something more than just a supply chain agreement was unfolding between them.

Lena found herself appreciating Evan's ability to grasp the nuances of their operation, his willingness to engage with the specifics of local produce. And Evan, in turn, found himself increasingly disarmed by Lena's passion, her deep understanding of Cedar Ridge, and the quiet warmth that made him feel, surprisingly, at ease. It was a chance encounter, born of necessity and professional obligation, but it held the subtle promise of something more, a recognition that beneath the surface of their differing perspectives, a connection was beginning to form, as unexpected and welcome as the first blooms of spring.

CHAPTER THREE

Cracks in the Plan

The polished chrome of Evan's tablet gleamed under the fluorescent lights of the Collective's back office, a stark contrast to the worn wooden desk it rested upon. He'd spent the better part of the last two days immersed in spreadsheets and inventory logs, his initial optimism steadily eroding with each new discovery. The cracks in his carefully constructed plan weren't hairline fractures; they were widening fissures, revealing a landscape far more complex and entrenched than he had anticipated. His six-month timeline, once a beacon of achievable progress, now felt like an increasingly distant horizon.

He'd arrived in Cedar Ridge armed with data, with proven strategies for organizational optimization, and a healthy dose of confidence. His firm had a stellar track record of turning around struggling enterprises, of injecting efficiency into complacent systems. The Cedar Ridge Collective, with its charmingly rustic façade and its undeniable community spirit, had seemed like a textbook case – a bit behind the times, perhaps, but fundamentally sound. He'd envisioned a swift, decisive overhaul, a series of targeted interventions that would yield measurable results within weeks, not months.

But the reality of Cedar Ridge was proving to be far more nuanced. The "outdated software" he'd flagged in his preliminary report was indeed a symptom, but not the root cause. It was a symptom of a deeper reluctance to invest, a hesitation born from generations of economic uncertainty that had taught the townspeople to be wary of anything that smacked of extravagance or unnecessary risk. The farmers, the backbone of the Collective, were a proud and independent lot. They understood the soil, the weather, the cycles of nature, but the intricacies of modern inventory management or the allure of sophisticated digital platforms felt alien, and frankly, unnecessary, to many. Why bother with newfangled systems when the old ways, however imperfect, had always managed to bring the harvest in?

Evan found himself spending less time strategizing and more time explaining, more time bridging the gap between his world of analytics and their world of tangible, earth-bound realities. He'd expected to encounter some resistance, of course. Change was rarely welcomed with open arms. But the depth of it, the sheer inertia of ingrained habits and deeply held beliefs, was something his models hadn't fully accounted for. He'd projected a smooth transition, a logical progression from problem identification to solution implementation. Instead, he was navigating a minefield of subtle hesitations, polite disagreements, and the occasional outright skepticism.

Take, for example, the issue of online sales. Evan had proposed a robust e-commerce platform, envisioning the Collective's artisanal products reaching a wider audience, tapping into the burgeoning market for locally sourced, high-quality goods. He'd presented projections, sales forecasts, and case studies of similar ventures that had seen significant growth. Lena, bless her earnest heart, had embraced the idea with her usual enthusiasm, but even she had struggled to convince some of the older farmers.

"Online sales? What for?" Silas, a man whose hands were as gnarled and weathered as the ancient oak that shaded his apple orchard, had grumbled during a recent meeting. "Folks come here to buy, to see what they're getting. They like talking to the person who grew it. That's part of the charm, ain't it?"

Evan had patiently explained the reach, the convenience, the potential for increased revenue that could then be reinvested in the Collective, benefiting everyone. He'd even offered to personally oversee the setup and management of the online store for the first few months. But the seed of doubt had been sown, and it had taken root. The idea of their produce being shipped off in anonymous boxes, disconnected from the personal touch, felt like a betrayal of the very ethos they held dear. It wasn't just about the transaction; it was about the connection, the story, the human element that Lena so eloquently championed.

And then there was the issue of standardized packaging. Evan had identified the current haphazard approach as a significant contributor to product damage and an overall unprofessional image. He'd proposed a line of attractive, branded boxes and bags, designed to protect the produce and enhance its visual appeal. This, too, had met with a quiet, but firm, resistance.

"My grandfather used burlap sacks for his potatoes," one farmer had stated, his voice low but steady. "My father used cardboard crates. I use what works. And what works is what I've always used." The implication was clear: his methods were time-tested, reliable, and any suggestion otherwise was an affront to his experience.

Evan realized his mistake. He had focused on the tangible benefits – reduced spoilage, increased shelf appeal, a more cohesive brand identity.

He hadn't adequately considered the emotional attachment, the sense of tradition, the quiet pride that farmers took in their established routines. He'd been so focused on the "what" and the "why" from a business perspective that he'd overlooked the "how" on a deeply personal level. For these people, the tools and methods of their trade were more than just functional; they were imbued with history, with the legacy of those who had come before them.

His carefully mapped-out implementation schedule was becoming increasingly unrealistic. The time allocated for software upgrades was being consumed by workshops on digital literacy. The days set aside for streamlining supply chain logistics were now dedicated to facilitating conversations between skeptical farmers and potential online customers, trying to build bridges of trust. The six-month deadline loomed, and Evan felt a knot of anxiety tightening in his chest. He was a man who thrived on order, on predictability, on the satisfaction of seeing a plan executed flawlessly. This was... messy. It was unpredictable. And it was demanding a level of patience and adaptability he hadn't fully anticipated needing.

He looked at the faces of the Collective's members during the last town hall meeting. Lena, ever the diplomat, was trying her best to mediate, to find common ground. But he saw the furrowed brows, the hesitant nods, the subtle exchanges of knowing glances that spoke of a shared understanding he was still struggling to grasp. They weren't resisting change out of stubbornness, he was beginning to understand, but out of a deeply ingrained caution, a desire to protect the very essence of what made the Collective – and Cedar Ridge – special. They feared that in their pursuit of efficiency and growth, they might lose the heart of what they were.

This fear, he realized, was the most significant unforeseen complication. It wasn't a quantifiable metric, not something that could be easily addressed with a new algorithm or a revised workflow. It was an emotional landscape, a complex web of pride, tradition, and a fundamental desire for connection. His plan, so logical and data-driven, had failed to account for the intangible, for the human element that, ironically, was the Collective's greatest strength.

He sighed, leaning back in the creaking wooden chair. The afternoon sun, now lower in the sky, cast long shadows across the room, painting the worn linoleum floor in stripes of light and shade. He'd anticipated resistance, but not this profound, systemic hesitancy. He'd prepared for logistical hurdles, for operational inefficiencies, but not for the deep-seated cultural undercurrents that shaped the town's approach to progress.

Evan had to recalibrate. He couldn't simply impose his solutions; he had to earn buy-in, to demonstrate that progress didn't have to mean erasure. He had to find a way to weave his expertise into the existing fabric of Cedar Ridge, rather than trying to reweave the entire tapestry from scratch. This meant more listening, more understanding, more adapting his strategies to fit the unique rhythm of this small town. It meant acknowledging that the "charm" Silas spoke of wasn't just a quaint byproduct, but a vital component of their success, a form of capital that his spreadsheets couldn't easily quantify.

He pulled out his tablet again, but instead of diving back into the financial projections, he opened a new document. He titled it "Cedar Ridge: Cultural Considerations." Underneath, he began to jot down notes, not about revenue streams or operational costs, but about tradition, about community, about the intangible value of personal connection. His six-month plan was no longer a rigid roadmap, but a compass, guiding him toward a destination that was proving to be far more challenging, and perhaps, ultimately, more rewarding, than he had ever imagined. The complexity was daunting, but for the first time, he felt a flicker of something beyond professional obligation – a genuine curiosity, a nascent respect for the deeply rooted resilience of this place and its people. He realized that to truly succeed, he needed to become not just a consultant, but a student of Cedar Ridge.

The polished chrome of Evan's tablet gleamed under the fluorescent lights of the Collective's back office, a stark contrast to the worn wooden desk it rested upon. He'd spent the better part of the last two days immersed in spreadsheets and inventory logs, his initial optimism steadily eroding with each new discovery. The cracks in his carefully constructed plan weren't hairline fractures; they were widening fissures, revealing a landscape far more complex and entrenched than he had anticipated. His six-month timeline, once a beacon of achievable progress, now felt like an increasingly distant horizon.

He'd arrived in Cedar Ridge armed with data, with proven strategies for organizational optimization, and a healthy dose of confidence. His firm had a stellar track record of turning around struggling enterprises, of injecting efficiency into complacent systems. The Cedar Ridge Collective, with its charmingly rustic façade and its undeniable community spirit, had seemed like a textbook case – a bit behind the times, perhaps, but fundamentally sound. He'd envisioned a swift, decisive overhaul, a series of targeted interventions that would yield measurable results within weeks, not months.

But the reality of Cedar Ridge was proving to be far more nuanced. The "outdated software" he'd flagged in his preliminary report was indeed a symptom, but not the root cause. It was a symptom of a deeper reluctance to invest, a hesitation born from generations of economic uncertainty that had taught the townspeople to be wary of anything that smacked of extravagance or unnecessary risk. The farmers, the backbone of the Collective, were a proud and independent lot. They understood the soil, the weather, the cycles of nature, but the intricacies of modern inventory management or the allure of sophisticated digital platforms felt alien, and frankly, unnecessary, to many. Why bother with newfangled systems when the old ways, however imperfect, had always managed to bring the harvest in?

Evan found himself spending less time strategizing and more time explaining, more time bridging the gap between his world of analytics and their world of tangible, earth-bound realities. He'd expected to encounter some resistance, of course. Change was rarely welcomed with open arms. But the depth of it, the sheer inertia of ingrained habits and deeply held beliefs, was something his models hadn't fully accounted for. He'd projected a smooth transition, a logical progression from problem identification to solution implementation. Instead, he was navigating a minefield of subtle hesitations, polite disagreements, and the occasional outright skepticism.

Take, for example, the issue of online sales. Evan had proposed a robust e-commerce platform, envisioning the Collective's artisanal products reaching a wider audience, tapping into the burgeoning market for locally sourced, high-quality goods. He'd presented projections, sales forecasts, and case studies of similar ventures that had seen significant growth. Lena, bless her earnest heart, had embraced the idea with her usual enthusiasm, but even she had struggled to convince some of the older farmers.

"Online sales? What for?" Silas, a man whose hands were as gnarled and weathered as the ancient oak that shaded his apple orchard, had grumbled during a recent meeting. "Folks come here to buy, to see what they're getting. They like talking to the person who grew it. That's part of the charm, ain't it?"

Evan had patiently explained the reach, the convenience, the potential for increased revenue that could then be reinvested in the Collective, benefiting everyone. He'd even offered to personally oversee the setup and management of the online store for the first few months. But the seed of doubt had been sown, and it had taken root. The idea of their produce being shipped off in anonymous boxes, disconnected from the personal touch, felt like a betrayal of the very ethos they held dear. It wasn't just about the transaction; it was about the connection, the story, the human element that Lena so eloquently championed.

And then there was the issue of standardized packaging. Evan had identified the current haphazard approach as a significant contributor to product damage and an overall unprofessional image. He'd proposed a line of attractive, branded boxes and bags, designed to protect the produce and enhance its visual appeal. This, too, had met with a quiet, but firm, resistance.

"My grandfather used burlap sacks for his potatoes," one farmer had stated, his voice low but steady. "My father used cardboard crates. I use what works. And what works is what I've always used." The implication was clear: his methods were time-tested, reliable, and any suggestion otherwise was an affront to his experience.

Evan realized his mistake. He had focused on the tangible benefits – reduced spoilage, increased shelf appeal, a more cohesive brand identity. He hadn't adequately considered the emotional attachment, the sense of tradition, the quiet pride that farmers took in their established routines. He'd been so focused on the "what" and the "why" from a business perspective that he'd overlooked the "how" on a deeply personal level. For these people, the tools and methods of their trade were more than just functional; they were imbued with history, with the legacy of those who had come before them.

His carefully mapped-out implementation schedule was becoming increasingly unrealistic. The time allocated for software upgrades was being consumed by workshops on digital literacy. The days set aside for streamlining supply chain logistics were now dedicated to facilitating conversations between skeptical farmers and potential online customers, trying to build bridges of trust. The six-month deadline loomed, and Evan felt a knot of anxiety tightening in his chest. He was a man who thrived on order, on predictability, on the satisfaction of seeing a plan executed flawlessly. This was... messy. It was unpredictable. And it was demanding a level of patience and adaptability he hadn't fully anticipated needing.

He looked at the faces of the Collective's members during the last town hall meeting. Lena, ever the diplomat, was trying her best to mediate, to find common ground. But he saw the furrowed brows, the hesitant nods, the subtle exchanges of knowing glances that spoke of a shared understanding he was still struggling to grasp. They weren't resisting change out of stubbornness, he was beginning to understand, but out of a deeply ingrained caution, a desire to protect the very essence of what made the Collective – and Cedar Ridge – special. They feared that in their pursuit of efficiency and growth, they might lose the heart of what they were.

This fear, he realized, was the most significant unforeseen complication. It wasn't a quantifiable metric, not something that could be easily addressed with a new algorithm or a revised workflow. It was an emotional landscape, a complex web of pride, tradition, and a fundamental desire for connection. His plan, so logical and data-driven, had failed to account for the intangible, for the human element that, ironically, was the Collective's greatest strength.

He sighed, leaning back in the creaking wooden chair. The afternoon sun, now lower in the sky, cast long shadows across the room, painting the worn linoleum floor in stripes of light and shade. He'd anticipated resistance, but not this profound, systemic hesitancy. He'd prepared for logistical hurdles, for operational inefficiencies, but not for the deep-seated cultural undercurrents that shaped the town's approach to progress.

Evan had to recalibrate. He couldn't simply impose his solutions; he had to earn buy-in, to demonstrate that progress didn't have to mean erasure. He had to find a way to weave his expertise into the existing fabric of Cedar Ridge, rather than trying to reweave the entire tapestry from scratch. This meant more listening, more understanding, more adapting his strategies to fit the unique rhythm of this small town. It meant acknowledging that the "charm" Silas spoke of wasn't just a quaint byproduct, but a vital component of their success, a form of capital that his spreadsheets couldn't easily quantify.

He pulled out his tablet again, but instead of diving back into the financial projections, he opened a new document. He titled it "Cedar Ridge: Cultural Considerations." Underneath, he began to jot down notes, not about revenue streams or operational costs, but about tradition, about community, about the intangible value of personal connection. His six-month plan was no longer a rigid roadmap, but a compass, guiding him toward a destination that was proving to be far more challenging, and perhaps, ultimately, more rewarding, than he had ever imagined. The complexity was daunting, but for the first time, he felt a flicker of something beyond professional obligation – a genuine curiosity, a nascent respect for the deeply rooted resilience of this place and its people. He realized that to truly succeed, he needed to become not just a consultant, but a student of Cedar Ridge.

The subtle friction wasn't confined to the farmers; it was present in smaller, quieter ways throughout the Collective's operations. Martha, who had managed the front counter for over twenty years, greeted his suggestion for a new point-of-sale system with a polite but firm smile that didn't quite reach her eyes. "Oh, I don't know, dear," she'd said, her voice soft as worn velvet. "These old machines, they've always worked just fine. I know where every button is, and the customers are used to how I do things." Evan had presented data on improved transaction speed, reduced errors, and better sales tracking.

He'd even offered to set up a training session specifically for her, demonstrating how intuitive the new system was. Yet, she remained unconvinced, her comfort firmly rooted in the familiarity of her current routine. It wasn't a rejection of improvement, he sensed, but a deep-seated apprehension about learning something new, about potentially fumbling in front of customers, about losing the quiet competence she had cultivated over decades. For Martha, the current system wasn't just a tool; it was a symbol of her long-standing dedication and her place within the Collective.

Similarly, young Ben, who handled the unloading and stocking of produce, expressed his reservations about the proposed automated inventory system. He was a practical young man, quick on his feet and adept at judging the weight and quantity of a delivery by sight. "With all due respect, Mr. Hayes," he'd begun, his brow furrowed, "I can usually tell you what we've got in the back just by looking. This... this computer thing, it seems like more hassle than it's worth. What if it makes a mistake? What if it says we have ten bushels of apples when we only have five? Then what?"

Evan tried to explain the accuracy of barcode scanning and the real-time data it provided, the ability to forecast demand and minimize waste. But Ben's concern was less about the technology itself and more about the potential for error and the loss of his own practiced skill. He saw his ability to quickly assess stock as a valuable contribution, and the introduction of a system that might make that skill redundant felt like a personal diminishment. He wasn't afraid of hard work; he was hesitant to embrace a change that, in his eyes, seemed to devalue his experience and innate understanding of the physical goods.

These were not people actively trying to sabotage his efforts. They were individuals who had built their lives and their livelihoods around the existing structure. Their routines were more than just habits; they were the anchors that provided stability in a world that often felt unpredictable. They appreciated the intention behind Evan's proposals – the promise of increased revenue, of greater efficiency, of a more secure future for the Collective. But the perceived cost of that progress felt too high, not in dollars and cents, but in the disruption of comfort, the challenge to ingrained knowledge, and the potential erosion of their sense of self within the community.

Evan found himself spending hours in conversations that didn't directly involve data analysis or strategic planning. He'd sit with Martha over her lunch break, listening to stories about the town's history, about the families who had been part of the Collective for generations. He'd join Ben in the loading dock, helping him sort crates, observing his methods, and gently asking questions about why he did things a certain way. He realized that his initial approach, while efficient and results-oriented, had been too clinical, too detached. He had treated the Collective as a business entity to be optimized, failing to fully appreciate that it was also a community, a network of relationships built on trust, shared history, and a deep understanding of each other's strengths and limitations.

His plan needed more than just revised timelines; it needed a more human touch. He couldn't simply present solutions; he had to facilitate a process of discovery, allowing the members of the Collective to see the value of change through their own experiences and perspectives. This meant demonstrating, not just telling. It meant patience, empathy, and a willingness to sometimes take a step back to allow the community to move forward at its own pace.

The fissures in his plan were not just about the system; they were about the people, and winning their hearts and minds was proving to be a far more complex, and perhaps more crucial, undertaking than he had ever imagined. He understood now that true progress wasn't just about implementing new processes; it was about fostering a shared vision for the future, one that honored the past while embracing the possibilities of what could be. He had to convince them that change wasn't an ending, but a new beginning, one that could strengthen the very foundations they held so dear.

The polished chrome of Evan's tablet gleamed under the fluorescent lights of the Collective's back office, a stark contrast to the worn wooden desk it rested upon. He'd spent the better part of the last two days immersed in spreadsheets and inventory logs, his initial optimism steadily eroding with each new discovery. The cracks in his carefully constructed plan weren't hairline fractures; they were widening fissures, revealing a landscape far more complex and entrenched than he had anticipated. His six-month timeline, once a beacon of achievable progress, now felt like an increasingly distant horizon.

He'd arrived in Cedar Ridge armed with data, with proven strategies for organizational optimization, and a healthy dose of confidence. His firm had a stellar track record of turning around struggling enterprises, of injecting efficiency into complacent systems. The Cedar Ridge Collective, with its charmingly rustic façade and its undeniable community spirit, had seemed like a textbook case – a bit behind the times, perhaps, but fundamentally sound. He'd envisioned a swift, decisive overhaul, a series of targeted interventions that would yield measurable results within weeks, not months.

But the reality of Cedar Ridge was proving to be far more nuanced. The "outdated software" he'd flagged in his preliminary report was indeed a symptom, but not the root cause. It was a symptom of a deeper reluctance to invest, a hesitation born from generations of economic uncertainty that had taught the townspeople to be wary of anything that smacked of extravagance or unnecessary risk. The farmers, the backbone of the Collective, were a proud and independent lot. They understood the soil, the weather, the cycles of nature, but the intricacies of modern inventory management or the allure of sophisticated digital platforms felt alien, and frankly, unnecessary, to many. Why bother with newfangled systems when the old ways, however imperfect, had always managed to bring the harvest in?

Evan found himself spending less time strategizing and more time explaining, more time bridging the gap between his world of analytics and their world of tangible, earth-bound realities. He'd expected to encounter some resistance, of course. Change was rarely welcomed with open arms. But the depth of it, the sheer inertia of ingrained habits and deeply held beliefs, was something his models hadn't fully accounted for. He'd projected a smooth transition, a logical progression from problem identification to solution implementation. Instead, he was navigating a minefield of subtle hesitations, polite disagreements, and the occasional outright skepticism.

Take, for example, the issue of online sales. Evan had proposed a robust e-commerce platform, envisioning the Collective's artisanal products reaching a wider audience, tapping into the burgeoning market for locally sourced, high-quality goods. He'd presented projections, sales forecasts, and case studies of similar ventures that had seen significant growth. Lena, bless her earnest heart, had embraced the idea with her usual enthusiasm, but even she had struggled to convince some of the older farmers.

"Online sales? What for?" Silas, a man whose hands were as gnarled and weathered as the ancient oak that shaded his apple orchard, had grumbled during a recent meeting. "Folks come here to buy, to see what they're getting. They like talking to the person who grew it. That's part of the charm, ain't it?"

Evan had patiently explained the reach, the convenience, the potential for increased revenue that could then be reinvested in the Collective, benefiting everyone. He'd even offered to personally oversee the setup and management of the online store for the first few months. But the seed of doubt had been sown, and it had taken root. The idea of their produce being shipped off in anonymous boxes, disconnected from the personal touch, felt like a betrayal of the very ethos they held dear. It wasn't just about the transaction; it was about the connection, the story, the human element that Lena so eloquently championed.

And then there was the issue of standardized packaging. Evan had identified the current haphazard approach as a significant contributor to product damage and an overall unprofessional image. He'd proposed a line of attractive, branded boxes and bags, designed to protect the produce and enhance its visual appeal. This, too, had met with a quiet, but firm, resistance.

"My grandfather used burlap sacks for his potatoes," one farmer had stated, his voice low but steady. "My father used cardboard crates. I use what works. And what works is what I've always used." The implication was clear: his methods were time-tested, reliable, and any suggestion otherwise was an affront to his experience.

Evan realized his mistake. He had focused on the tangible benefits – reduced spoilage, increased shelf appeal, a more cohesive brand identity. He hadn't adequately considered the emotional attachment, the sense of tradition, the quiet pride that farmers took in their established routines. He'd been so focused on the "what" and the "why" from a business perspective that he'd overlooked the "how" on a deeply personal level. For these people, the tools and methods of their trade were more than just functional; they were imbued with history, with the legacy of those who had come before them.

His carefully mapped-out implementation schedule was becoming increasingly unrealistic. The time allocated for software upgrades was being consumed by workshops on digital literacy. The days set aside for streamlining supply chain logistics were now dedicated to facilitating conversations between skeptical farmers and potential online customers, trying to build bridges of trust. The six-month deadline loomed, and Evan felt a knot of anxiety tightening in his chest. He was a man who thrived on order, on predictability, on the satisfaction of seeing a plan executed flawlessly. This was... messy. It was unpredictable. And it was demanding a level of patience and adaptability he hadn't fully anticipated needing.

He looked at the faces of the Collective's members during the last town hall meeting. Lena, ever the diplomat, was trying her best to mediate, to find common ground. But he saw the furrowed brows, the hesitant nods, the subtle exchanges of knowing glances that spoke of a shared understanding he was still struggling to grasp. They weren't resisting change out of stubbornness, he was beginning to understand, but out of a deeply ingrained caution, a desire to protect the very essence of what made the Collective – and Cedar Ridge – special. They feared that in their pursuit of efficiency and growth, they might lose the heart of what they were.

This fear, he realized, was the most significant unforeseen complication. It wasn't a quantifiable metric, not something that could be easily addressed with a new algorithm or a revised workflow. It was an emotional landscape, a complex web of pride, tradition, and a fundamental desire for connection. His plan, so logical and data-driven, had failed to account for the intangible, for the human element that, ironically, was the Collective's greatest strength.

He sighed, leaning back in the creaking wooden chair. The afternoon sun, now lower in the sky, cast long shadows across the room, painting the worn linoleum floor in stripes of light and shade. He'd anticipated resistance, but not this profound, systemic hesitancy. He'd prepared for logistical hurdles, for operational inefficiencies, but not for the deep-seated cultural undercurrents that shaped the town's approach to progress.

Evan had to recalibrate. He couldn't simply impose his solutions; he had to earn buy-in, to demonstrate that progress didn't have to mean erasure. He had to find a way to weave his expertise into the existing fabric of Cedar Ridge, rather than trying to reweave the entire tapestry from scratch. This meant more listening, more understanding, more adapting his strategies to fit the unique rhythm of this small town. It meant acknowledging that the "charm" Silas spoke of wasn't just a quaint byproduct, but a vital component of their success, a form of capital that his spreadsheets couldn't easily quantify.

He pulled out his tablet again, but instead of diving back into the financial projections, he opened a new document. He titled it "Cedar Ridge: Cultural Considerations." Underneath, he began to jot down notes, not about revenue streams or operational costs, but about tradition, about community, about the intangible value of personal connection. His six-month plan was no longer a rigid roadmap, but a compass, guiding him toward a destination that was proving to be far more challenging, and perhaps, ultimately, more rewarding, than he had ever imagined. The complexity was daunting, but for the first time, he felt a flicker of something beyond professional obligation – a genuine curiosity, a nascent respect for the deeply rooted resilience of this place and its people. He realized that to truly succeed, he needed to become not just a consultant, but a student of Cedar Ridge.

The subtle friction wasn't confined to the farmers; it was present in smaller, quieter ways throughout the Collective's operations. Martha, who had managed the front counter for over twenty years, greeted his suggestion for a new point-of-sale system with a polite but firm smile that didn't quite reach her eyes. "Oh, I don't know, dear," she'd said, her voice soft as worn velvet. "These old machines, they've always worked just fine. I know where every button is, and the customers are used to how I do things." Evan had presented data on improved transaction speed, reduced errors, and better sales tracking. He'd even offered to set up a training session specifically for her, demonstrating how intuitive the new system was.

Yet, she remained unconvinced, her comfort firmly rooted in the familiarity of her current routine. It wasn't a rejection of improvement, he sensed, but a deep-seated apprehension about learning something new, about potentially fumbling in front of customers, about losing the quiet competence she had cultivated over decades. For Martha, the current system wasn't just a tool; it was a symbol of her long-standing dedication and her place within the Collective.

Similarly, young Ben, who handled the unloading and stocking of produce, expressed his reservations about the proposed automated inventory system. He was a practical young man, quick on his feet and adept at judging the weight and quantity of a delivery by sight. "With all due respect, Mr. Hayes," he'd begun, his brow furrowed, "I can usually tell you what we've got in the back just by looking.

This... this computer thing, it seems like more hassle than it's worth. What if it makes a mistake? What if it says we have ten bushels of apples when we only have five? Then what?" Evan tried to explain the accuracy of barcode scanning and the real-time data it provided, the ability to forecast demand and minimize waste. But Ben's concern was less about the technology itself and more about the potential for error and the loss of his own practiced skill. He saw his ability to quickly assess stock as a valuable contribution, and the introduction of a system that might make that skill redundant felt like a personal diminishment. He wasn't afraid of hard work; he was hesitant to embrace a change that, in his eyes, seemed to devalue his experience and innate understanding of the physical goods.

These were not people actively trying to sabotage his efforts. They were individuals who had built their lives and their livelihoods around the existing structure. Their routines were more than just habits; they were the anchors that provided stability in a world that often felt unpredictable. They appreciated the intention behind Evan's proposals – the promise of increased revenue, of greater efficiency, of a more secure future for the Collective. But the perceived cost of that progress felt too high, not in dollars and cents, but in the disruption of comfort, the challenge to ingrained knowledge, and the potential erosion of their sense of self within the community.

Evan found himself spending hours in conversations that didn't directly involve data analysis or strategic planning. He'd sit with Martha over her lunch break, listening to stories about the town's history, about the families who had been part of the Collective for generations. He'd join Ben in the loading dock, helping him sort crates, observing his methods, and gently asking questions about why he did things a certain way. He realized that his initial approach, while efficient and results-oriented, had been too clinical, too detached. He had treated the Collective as a business entity to be optimized, failing to fully appreciate that it was also a community, a network of relationships built on trust, shared history, and a deep understanding of each other's strengths and limitations.

His plan needed more than just revised timelines; it needed a more human touch. He couldn't simply present solutions; he had to facilitate a process of discovery, allowing the members of the Collective to see the value of change through their own experiences and perspectives. This meant demonstrating, not just telling. It meant patience, empathy, and a willingness to sometimes take a step back to allow the community to move forward at its own pace.

The fissures in his plan were not just about the system; they were about the people, and winning their hearts and minds was proving to be a far more complex, and perhaps more crucial, undertaking than he had ever imagined. He understood now that true progress wasn't just about implementing new processes; it was about fostering a shared vision for the future, one that honored the past while embracing the possibilities of what could be. He had to convince them that change wasn't an ending, but a new beginning, one that could strengthen the very foundations they held so dear.

It was a subtle shift, almost imperceptible at first, but Evan began to notice it in himself. His ingrained belief in the necessity of constant movement, of reinvention, of chasing the next challenge, was beginning to waver. He'd always defined success by his ability to conquer, to optimize, to move on to the next project with a fresh set of problems to solve. That perpetual motion was his default, his comfort zone. But Cedar Ridge, with its unhurried rhythms and its deep roots, was beginning to offer a different perspective.

He found himself lingering at the edge of the town square after meetings, watching the way the sunlight filtered through the leaves of the ancient oak trees, the way the locals greeted each other with an easy familiarity that spoke of years of shared history. There was a quiet satisfaction in the deliberate pace here, a sense of building something solid and lasting, rather than the frantic pursuit of ephemeral gains. He started to question his own definition of success. Was it always about the next big win, the next impressive statistic? Or could it also be about nurturing, about tending, about contributing to something that had value beyond immediate financial returns?

This introspection wasn't a comfortable process. It was tinged with a familiar restlessness, a nagging uncertainty that felt alien to his usual driven nature. He'd built his career on the premise that stagnation was the enemy, that the only way to thrive was to constantly push forward, to adapt, to innovate. Yet, here in Cedar Ridge, he was witnessing a different kind of strength – the strength of resilience, of deep-seated tradition, of a community that understood the value of holding steady. He observed the farmers tending their land with a patient, almost reverent, dedication. They didn't rush the harvest; they understood its cycles, its requirements. They had an inherent respect for the natural order, a wisdom that transcended any business model.

Evan had always been a planner, a strategist. His mind was wired to anticipate, to optimize, to build frameworks for progress. But Cedar Ridge was teaching him the value of something less quantifiable: the art of being present. He started to spend less time staring at his tablet and more time simply observing. He'd walk through the market stalls, not to assess inventory or identify inefficiencies, but to listen to the chatter, to absorb the atmosphere. He'd sit on the benches in the park, watching children play, their laughter echoing in the quiet air. There was a profound beauty in this unhurried existence, a stark contrast to the constant hum of activity that characterized his life back in the city.

He recalled a conversation with Lena about the town's annual summer festival, an event that had been a staple of Cedar Ridge for generations. It wasn't a slick, professionally organized affair with corporate sponsors and elaborate marketing campaigns. It was a community-driven celebration, a testament to their collective spirit. The preparations, he'd learned, unfolded gradually over weeks, with everyone pitching in, not because they had to, but because it was an integral part of their shared identity. There was a sense of organic growth, of traditions being passed down and adapted, rather than imposed. This was a stark departure from his usual approach, where efficiency and scalability were paramount.

He found himself wrestling with his own professional identity. Was he the kind of consultant who parachuted in, implemented a few quick fixes, and then moved on, leaving behind a trail of metrics and reports? Or could he be something more? Could he be someone who helped a community preserve its essence while still embracing necessary evolution? The idea of planting himself, of nurturing something, felt both daunting and strangely appealing. The thought of building something that would last, something that wasn't just a temporary fix but a sustainable addition to the fabric of Cedar Ridge, began to take root within him.

This internal shift was subtle, but significant. He found himself less frustrated by the slower pace, and more intrigued by the depth of connection. The people of Cedar Ridge weren't just a collection of individuals; they were a living, breathing organism, each part interconnected, each contributing to the overall health and vitality of the whole. His initial goal had been to optimize the Collective as a business. Now, he was beginning to see that its true value lay not just in its economic output, but in its role as a cornerstone of the community, a facilitator of connection, a keeper of traditions.

The lure of mobility, the constant urge to be somewhere else, to conquer a new challenge, had always been Evan's driving force. It was the adrenaline rush of the new, the thrill of the unknown. But Cedar Ridge was offering a different kind of allure – the quiet satisfaction of belonging, of contributing to something that mattered on a deeper level. He was starting to understand that success wasn't always measured by how far you traveled, but by how deeply you could settle, how effectively you could contribute to the place you were in. The inherent resistance to change he was encountering wasn't just a logistical hurdle; it was a testament to the value these people placed on stability, on continuity, on the enduring strength of what they already had. And for the first time, Evan found himself contemplating the possibility that perhaps, just perhaps, there was more to life than the relentless pursuit of the next horizon.

Lena watched Evan from across the bustling market floor, the low hum of conversation and the scent of fresh produce a familiar soundtrack to her days. He stood near the Collective's main counter, his shoulders slightly hunched, a tablet clutched in his hand like a shield. The familiar flicker of frustration, a subtle tightening around his jaw, was unmistakable. She recognized it from their early meetings, a shadow that had begun to lengthen as the reality of Cedar Ridge's deeply ingrained ways settled in. It was a look she'd seen mirrored in others who came here with grand plans, eager to streamline and modernize, only to find themselves wrestling with an inertia that was as strong and resilient as the ancient oaks bordering the town.

She finished weighing a bag of heirloom tomatoes for Mrs. Gable, offering a warm smile and a brief chat about the unusually late frost. Then, with a nod to Martha, who was expertly handling the cash register, Lena moved towards Evan. She didn't approach him directly, instead weaving through the stalls, her eyes scanning the vibrant displays, her presence a gentle, reassuring constant. She paused by the flower stall, admiring a vibrant arrangement of sunflowers, before finally reaching his side. He looked up, his eyes immediately finding hers, a silent plea for understanding passing between them.

"They're not seeing it, are they?" he asked, his voice a low murmur, barely audible above the ambient noise. It wasn't a question seeking information, but an expression of weariness, of a plan that felt increasingly out of reach. He gestured vaguely with the tablet, as if the data displayed upon it were a tangible representation of their unmet goals. "The efficiency gains, the market reach, the projected revenue... it's all there, Lena. It's quantifiable. But it feels like I'm speaking a different language."

Lena leaned in, her voice pitched to match his, a conspiratorial softness that invited him to step away from the public eye, even if only for a moment. "It's not about the language of numbers, Evan," she said, her gaze steady. "It's about the language of 'us.' This place, the Collective, it's built on more than just transactions and profit margins. It's built on relationships, on trust, on a shared history that runs deeper than any spreadsheet can capture." She gently placed a hand on his arm, a gesture of comfort and quiet solidarity. "You're showing them the 'what' and the 'how,' but you're not always connecting with the 'why' that resonates with them."

Evan sighed, running a hand through his already disheveled hair. "But the 'why' is obvious, isn't it? It's about survival. It's about ensuring the

Collective thrives, so that Cedar Ridge continues to thrive. That means adapting, evolving. We can't just keep doing things the way they've always been done if we want to secure a future." His voice held a note of exasperation, a feeling that his logic was being deliberately overlooked. "I suggested a new system for tracking produce freshness, a simple digital log that would reduce spoilage by almost fifteen percent. And Silas... Silas told me his nose was a better indicator than any computer. His nose, Lena! How do you argue with that?"

Lena chuckled softly, the sound warm and genuine. "Silas's nose has smelled more perfect harvests and predicted more sudden frosts than you and I combined, Evan. That's his expertise. And it's valuable. But so is the data. The challenge isn't to replace his wisdom with technology, but to find a way for them to coexist, to complement each other." She straightened up, her eyes scanning the faces of the shoppers and vendors around them. "You see the cracks in your plan, Evan. I see the foundations of this town. And those foundations are built on continuity. They need to see that progress isn't about erasing what's here, but about strengthening it, about adding a new layer that doesn't undermine the old."

She walked a few steps towards the artisanal cheese stall, picking up a wedge of aged cheddar. "Think about Martha, with her register. She knows every regular customer by name, knows their usual orders, remembers their kids' birthdays. That's not just customer service; that's community. When you proposed the new POS system, you were focused on speed and data entry. She heard a threat to that personal connection, a fear that she'd become just another anonymous transaction point. We need to show her how the new system can *enhance* her ability to connect, not replace it."

Evan watched her, a grudging respect dawning in his eyes. Lena had a way of distilling complex issues into simple, relatable truths, a skill that belied her often understated presence. He'd come to Cedar Ridge armed with analytics and projections, a confident consultant ready to implement proven strategies. Lena, on the other hand, seemed to possess an innate understanding of the town's heart, an ability to articulate its unspoken needs and desires.

"So, what are you suggesting?" he asked, the edge of frustration softening into a genuine desire for her perspective. "Do I just... accept that Silas will continue to sniff his way through inventory?"

Lena smiled, a knowing glint in her eyes. "For now, perhaps. But you can also work *with* Silas. Ask him to teach you. Show him how the digital log can track the *results* of his excellent nose. You can cross-reference his observations with the data. Imagine: 'Silas says these apples are perfectly ripe, and the data confirms their sugar content is optimal.' It validates his expertise while also gathering objective information. It's about building bridges, Evan, not demolishing walls."

She continued, her voice carrying a quiet conviction that resonated deeply within him. "The strength of Cedar Ridge, and of the Collective, isn't in its speed or its scalability in the way you might measure it in the city. Its strength is in its resilience, its deep roots, its ability to weather storms because it's bound together by something more than just commerce. You're trying to inject a dose of modern efficiency, and that's valuable, but it needs to be done with care, like grafting a new branch onto an old, established tree. You can't just hack it on; it needs to be integrated, nurtured, so it becomes part of the whole."

Evan leaned against a nearby display of homemade jams, the sweet aroma a stark contrast to the sterile efficiency he was used to. He'd been so focused on the metrics, on the quantifiable improvements, that he'd overlooked the intangible assets – the accumulated wisdom, the ingrained trust, the sheer emotional capital that held this community together. He had seen resistance as a hurdle to overcome, a problem to be solved. Lena, however, saw it as a symptom, a sign that his approach needed to shift from imposition to integration.

"I've been so busy trying to *fix* things," he admitted, the words tasting like a confession. "I've been looking for the inefficiencies, the outdated processes, and I've been trying to impose my solutions. I haven't spent enough time truly understanding *why* things are the way they are, or what the members of the Collective truly value." He looked at Lena, his gaze earnest. "You've been here longer. You understand this rhythm. How do I... how do I shift my approach without compromising the goals?"

"You listen more," Lena replied, her voice gentle but firm. "You ask more questions, and you're prepared for answers that aren't always in a language you're accustomed to. You don't dismiss Silas's nose or Martha's comfort with her register. You acknowledge their value, their history, and then you find ways to weave in the new. It's about persuasion, not prescription. It's about showing them that the future you envision includes them, respects their past, and enhances what they already cherish."

She paused, her gaze meeting his directly. "Your six-month timeline is ambitious, Evan, and that's a good thing. It provides a framework. But sometimes, the most important progress isn't measured in weeks or months, but in the gradual building of trust. Your frustration is understandable, but it's also a signal. A signal that you need to adapt your strategy, not just your timeline. Cedar Ridge won't be streamlined overnight. It needs to be persuaded, gently and consistently, that the changes you propose will serve its heart, not just its balance sheet."

Lena then turned her attention back to the market, her presence once again becoming that of a friendly, familiar face. "Keep showing them the possibilities, Evan," she said, her voice carrying a note of encouragement. "But remember to show them how those possibilities are extensions of what they already are, not replacements for it. That's the secret to genuine progress here." She gave him a brief, encouraging smile before moving off to greet a customer at the bakery stand, leaving Evan standing amidst the vibrant chaos of the market, his tablet feeling a little heavier, his mind a little clearer, and a new, more nuanced understanding of his task beginning to take root. The cracks in his plan weren't just structural; they were about how to rebuild with a deeper appreciation for the existing architecture.

The initial optimism that had buoyed Evan's spirits in the early days of his Cedar Ridge project had begun to wane, replaced by a creeping sense of urgency that felt increasingly personal. His carefully constructed six-month exit strategy, a roadmap designed to transition his responsibilities smoothly and return him to the city with a sense of accomplishment, now seemed hopelessly optimistic, almost naive. The core of his plan hinged on identifying and nurturing a successor from within the community, someone who could absorb the intricacies of the Collective's operations, understand its unique challenges, and ultimately champion its modernization. But weeks had bled into months, and the search for this elusive individual had yielded only disappointment.

He'd approached the task with the same methodical rigor he applied to any business challenge. He'd observed interactions, held informal interviews, and watched for sparks of aptitude, for that particular blend of insight and dedication that hinted at future leadership. He'd spoken with Martha, whose encyclopedic knowledge of customer habits was legendary, but she was firmly rooted in her front-of-house role, content with the familiar rhythm of the cash register and the warmth of human connection. He'd considered Silas, whose intuitive understanding of produce quality was undeniable, but his expertise was deeply ingrained in a lifetime of sensory experience, not in the systematic oversight required for managing the Collective's broader operations. Even young Amelia, who displayed a sharp mind and a keen interest in the digital aspects of inventory, lacked the years of experience and the deep-seated respect within the community that would be crucial for gaining buy-in from the more traditional members.

Each potential candidate, when examined closely, revealed a vital missing piece. Some possessed the technical savvy but lacked the inherent understanding of Cedar Ridge's fabric; they saw the Collective as a business to be optimized, not a living entity to be nurtured. Others had the community trust and the genuine desire to contribute, but their skills were too specialized, too narrowly focused on individual roles.

They were excellent artisans, dedicated farmers, and skilled craftspeople, but the multifaceted demands of managing the entire enterprise – from financial oversight and marketing strategy to supply chain logistics and member relations – seemed to be a bridge too far. The reality was stark: the skills required weren't easily transferable, nor were they commonly cultivated in a town that had, for generations, prioritized artisanal craft and communal support over corporate-style management.

Evan found himself increasingly isolated in his pursuit. He'd tried to frame the successor role as an opportunity, a chance to shape the future of a beloved institution. He'd offered training, mentorship, even the prospect of a competitive salary and benefits package, hoping to entice someone with ambition. Yet, the response was consistently lukewarm. The idea of leaving the familiar comforts of their established roles, of shouldering the weight of responsibility for the entire Collective, seemed to daunt even the most enthusiastic. It wasn't just a matter of skill; it was a matter of disposition, of a willingness to embrace a different kind of work, a work that often involved navigating delicate interpersonal dynamics and long-term strategic thinking rather than the immediate satisfaction of tangible creation.

The conversations he had, once filled with hopeful brainstorming, now felt like polite rejections. When he spoke to Mr. Henderson, a respected elder known for his meticulous record-keeping of his own farm's yields, he was met with a gentle smile and a reminder that his focus was on his land, not on the broader machinations of the market. When he approached Sarah, who managed the bakery with exceptional efficiency, she expressed her passion for her craft, her joy in the daily baking, and her clear disinterest in the administrative burdens that came with leadership. Each interaction was a small, yet significant, erosion of his carefully laid plans.

The unease that had begun as a subtle tremor now felt like a seismic shift. The initial projection that a suitable candidate would emerge within the first three months, allowing for a further three months of intensive training and handover, was proving to be a fantasy. The problem wasn't a lack of willingness from the community to adapt or improve; it was a fundamental disconnect between the demands of the role he envisioned and the skills and aspirations that currently existed within Cedar Ridge. He had underestimated the depth of specialization and the ingrained nature of the existing roles. The Collective thrived because each member excelled in their domain, contributing to a well-oiled, if somewhat analog, machine. But its very strength, its reliance on individual expertise, was also its vulnerability when it came to centralized leadership.

He replayed his conversations with Lena in his mind. Her insight that the town's strength lay in its deep roots and resilience, rather than its speed or scalability, resonated more powerfully now. He had been so focused on implementing a modern management structure, on installing a linchpin that could operate that structure, that he'd failed to fully appreciate the existing ecosystem. The system, he was beginning to realize with a growing sense of dread, was not designed to be easily handed over to a single, incoming leader who lacked the years of lived experience within its unique context. It was a tapestry woven from the skills and relationships of many, and without his focused guidance, his ability to bridge the gaps and mediate the inevitable tensions, the threads would inevitably fray.

The thought of the Collective faltering, of the progress he'd helped initiate stagnating or even reversing, gnawed at him. He had taken on this project with a genuine desire to help, to lend his expertise to a community he was beginning to admire. The idea of leaving it in a state of disarray, of returning to his city life knowing he had failed to secure its future, was unacceptable. His six-month departure date, once a beacon of freedom, now loomed as a potential deadline for failure.

He sat in his sparsely furnished rented cottage, the scent of pine needles and damp earth filtering through the open window. The tablet lay on the table, its screen displaying a complex organizational chart that now felt like a cruel joke. He'd drawn it with bold lines and clear designations, a testament to his structured thinking. But the names he'd tentatively placed in key leadership positions were either blank or filled with question marks. His meticulously crafted timelines, his projected milestones, all felt like sandcastles against an incoming tide.

The initial plan, the elegant six-month exit, was no longer a viable option. The realization settled heavily in his chest, a physical weight that made it difficult to breathe. He hadn't just encountered resistance; he had encountered a fundamental mismatch. The community was rich in talent, in dedication, in a deep-seated commitment to its way of life. But the specific, multifaceted skillset required to manage and evolve the Collective, coupled with the personal inclination to embrace such a demanding role, simply wasn't present in a readily identifiable form.

He had come to Cedar Ridge to implement a change, to set in motion a process of modernization that would ensure the Collective's long-term viability. Now, he was faced with the stark reality that the most crucial element of that process – the transition of leadership – was proving to be the most formidable obstacle of all. His role, it seemed, was far from over.

The smooth handover he'd envisioned was not just delayed; it was fundamentally impossible within the original timeframe. This meant a reevaluation, a serious and perhaps unwelcome, recalibration of his entire commitment. The project was no longer about a six-month sprint; it was shaping up to be a marathon, and he was the only one with the stamina to keep running, at least for now. The prospect was daunting, but the alternative – watching this vibrant community falter – was unthinkable.

He had to stay. The question was, for how long, and what would that extended stay entail?

CHAPTER FOUR

Seeds of Connection

The weight of Evan's realization pressed down on him, a tangible force that settled in his gut. His meticulously planned six-month departure had dissolved into a nebulous, open-ended commitment, a stark departure from the controlled environment he usually thrived in. He had come to Cedar Ridge with a clear objective: to streamline operations, implement modern efficiencies, and ultimately pave the way for a smooth transition of leadership, ensuring the Collective's future prosperity.

He'd envisioned a swift, surgical intervention, a temporary assignment that would leave him with a sense of accomplishment and a clear path back to his city life. Now, that path was obscured, replaced by the daunting prospect of an extended stay, a commitment he hadn't anticipated and certainly hadn't planned for.

The irony was not lost on him. He'd analyzed market trends, optimized supply chains, and drafted strategic growth plans with the precision of a seasoned architect. Yet, the most critical component of his strategy—the human element, the identification and cultivation of a successor—had proven to be an insurmountable hurdle. Cedar Ridge, for all its charm and its tightly-knit community, lacked the readily available pool of individuals with the precise blend of technical acumen, leadership potential, and deep-seated community trust that the Collective's evolving needs demanded. He'd expected challenges, of course, but not this fundamental disconnect between his structured approach and the organic, deeply ingrained nature of the town's operational fabric.

His initial interactions with Lena had been professional, polite, and somewhat guarded. She was the capable hands-on manager of the Collective's day-to-day operations, a whirlwind of efficiency and quiet competence. Evan, accustomed to a more hierarchical and data-driven management style, had initially viewed her role as essential, but perhaps somewhat limited in its strategic scope.

He'd observed her interactions, the way she navigated the often-complex dynamics of the Collective's diverse membership, with a detached curiosity. Her knowledge of the local producers, their quirks, their strengths, and their limitations, was encyclopedic, a treasure trove of information he'd begun to tap into, albeit in a formal, business-like manner.

But as his extended stay became a concrete reality, so too did the necessity of deepening his working relationship with Lena. The initial awkwardness of his prolonged presence began to dissipate, replaced by a growing recognition of their shared objective: the well-being and continued success of the Cedar Ridge Collective. His six-month plan had relied on a swift identification of a successor, freeing him to return to his city life. That plan had crumbled, leaving him anchored in Cedar Ridge, and Lena, it seemed, was now his most vital link to understanding the intricate workings of the town and its cooperative.

They began to collaborate more closely, their initial professional courtesy gradually evolving into something more akin to genuine teamwork. The need for a shared understanding of the Collective's immediate challenges and future potential became paramount. Evan, no longer focused on the ticking clock of his departure, found himself dedicating more time to understanding the practical realities on the ground, and Lena was his indispensable guide.

One such instance arose from a persistent issue with inventory discrepancies, a recurring headache that had plagued the Collective for years. Evan, armed with his analytical tools, proposed a digital overhaul, a sophisticated inventory management system that promised real-time tracking and reduced errors. Lena, while acknowledging the potential benefits, brought a crucial layer of pragmatism to the table. "Evan," she'd said, her tone patient but firm, during one of their increasingly frequent meetings in the back office, the air thick with the scent of dried herbs and aged wood, "a fancy system is only as good as the people using it. Our folks are used to pen and paper, to a physical count. They trust what they can see and touch."

He'd bristled slightly at first, the familiar defensiveness of a city-dweller encountering what he perceived as rustic resistance to progress. But he remembered her earlier words, her assessment of Cedar Ridge's strength lying in its deep roots and resilience, not in its speed. He took a breath, forcing himself to see beyond the code and the algorithms. "You're right," he conceded, the words feeling surprisingly easy to say. "How do we bridge that gap? How do we make them comfortable with a new system, and more importantly, how do we ensure it actually works for them?"

This was the genesis of their shared project. Evan began to sketch out the technical framework, the logical flow of data, the user interface. Lena, in turn, became his focus group, his sounding board, and his translator. She would take his technical diagrams and translate them into language that resonated with the farmers and artisans. She'd explain the benefits not in terms of efficiency metrics, but in terms of less time spent on tedious counting, fewer mistakes that led to wasted produce, and a clearer understanding of what was available for their customers.

They spent hours together, poring over spreadsheets, walking the aisles of the storeroom, and observing the current manual logging process. Evan, initially focused on the abstract logic of the system, found himself drawn into the tangible reality of the Collective's operations. He learned to identify the different varieties of apples by sight, to understand the subtle differences in the drying process of various herbs, and to appreciate the meticulous care that went into packaging handmade soaps. Lena, for her part, began to see the underlying power of the technology Evan proposed. She recognized how a well-designed system could alleviate some of the burden of her own workload, freeing her up for more strategic tasks, and how it could provide valuable data to inform future purchasing and production decisions.

Their collaboration extended beyond the inventory system. They found themselves working together on the organization of the annual harvest festival, a cornerstone event for the Collective. Evan, with his experience in event planning and marketing, brought a structured approach to logistics, vendor management, and promotional strategies. Lena, with her intimate knowledge of the community, her established relationships with local artisans and performers, and her understanding of what made the festival a beloved tradition, provided the essential local flavor and connection.

They organized meetings with local producers to discuss new product lines, a task that required Evan to shed his corporate armor and engage in the more informal, relationship-driven negotiations that were the norm in Cedar Ridge. Lena was his invaluable ally, smoothing over potential misunderstandings, translating his business-speak into approachable terms, and advocating for the Collective's needs with a quiet authority that commanded respect.

During one such meeting, held in a sun-drenched barn filled with the sweet scent of hay, a veteran apple farmer, a gruff but fair man named Arthur, expressed his reservations about committing to a larger volume of a new heritage apple variety Evan was keen to introduce. Arthur's concern wasn't about the difficulty of growing them, but about the unpredictable demand. "We've always grown what sells, Evan," he'd stated plainly, his hands calloused and stained from years of working the land. "This fancy new one, who's gonna buy it?"

Evan, ready to launch into a detailed market analysis, found himself interrupted by Lena. She didn't dismiss Arthur's concern; instead, she engaged with it. "Arthur," she began, her voice calm and reassuring, "Evan's been doing some research. He believes there's a growing interest in heritage varieties, people looking for something a bit different. And you know how our customers are, they trust our recommendations. If we can offer it, and we make it sound as good as it tastes, I think they'll be eager to try it." She then turned to Evan, a subtle nod encouraging him. "Perhaps we can plan a tasting event for it, make sure people get to sample it before it officially hits the shelves?"

Evan recognized the brilliance of her approach. She validated Arthur's concern, then offered a solution that was both practical and promotional, leveraging the Collective's existing strengths. It was a masterclass in community engagement, a skill he was slowly, painstakingly, beginning to acquire. He found himself admiring her ability to navigate these delicate situations, her intuitive understanding of human dynamics, and her unwavering dedication to the Collective's welfare.

These shared tasks, these moments of collaborative problem-solving, began to weave a new kind of connection between them. The initial reservations Evan had harbored, his subtle skepticism about her organizational capacity, and Lena's initial wariness of the 'city slicker' with his grand plans, began to dissolve. They discovered a shared rhythm, a complementary set of skills, and a mutual respect that transcended their different backgrounds and their initial professional roles.

He started to notice the small things: the way Lena's eyes lit up when she talked about a particularly successful batch of preserves, the quiet pride in her voice when she spoke of the local farmers' hard work, the genuine warmth with which she greeted every customer, whether they were buying a single apple or a week's worth of groceries. These were the details that had been absent from his initial assessment, the human nuances that no amount of data analysis could capture.

Lena, in turn, began to see past Evan's corporate veneer. She noticed his genuine frustration when a plan didn't work, his quiet satisfaction when a problem was solved, and the thoughtful way he listened, even when he disagreed. She saw his commitment, not just to the project, but to the people of Cedar Ridge, a commitment that had deepened considerably since his initial, time-bound arrival. His initial attempts at implementing change had been driven by a sense of duty and a desire to fulfill his contractual obligations. Now, a different motivation was taking root. He was becoming invested.

Their conversations, once strictly business, began to drift into more personal territory. During late evenings spent reviewing sales figures or planning marketing campaigns, they would find themselves discussing their lives outside of the Collective. Evan, usually guarded about his personal life, found himself opening up about the pressures of his city career, the constant demand for results, and a growing sense of professional ennui. Lena, with her calm demeanor and attentive listening, created a safe space for him to express these thoughts, a space he hadn't realized he desperately needed.

Lena, too, shared glimpses into her world. She spoke of her family, her deep roots in Cedar Ridge, and the personal satisfaction she derived from her work at the Collective. She shared stories of past challenges the community had faced and overcome, tales that underscored the resilience and interconnectedness of the town. Evan learned that her role as manager was not just a job, but a continuation of a legacy, a commitment passed down through generations.

The mutual respect that had begun to bloom in the fertile ground of shared responsibilities blossomed further. They learned to anticipate each other's needs, to offer support without being asked, and to celebrate small victories together. The initial friction of their differing approaches had been replaced by a synergistic partnership, where each brought their unique strengths to the table, creating something stronger and more effective than either could achieve alone. The seeds of connection, sown in the soil of necessity, were beginning to sprout, nurtured by shared purpose and genuine collaboration. The Collective, once a project for Evan, was slowly becoming something more personal, and his relationship with Lena was at the heart of that transformation.

Evan found himself increasingly drawn to Lena's perspective, a viewpoint that seemed to bloom from a fundamentally different soil than his own. He'd arrived in Cedar Ridge with spreadsheets and projections, with a mind honed by the relentless pursuit of optimized outcomes. Efficiency was his creed, the measurable increase in output his ultimate metric of success. But observing Lena, witnessing the way she navigated the labyrinthine relationships of the Collective, he began to see that efficiency, as he understood it, was only one facet of a much larger, more intricate gem.

He saw it in the way she handled old Mr. Henderson's insistence on selling his slightly bruised apples at full price, not because they were perfect, but because they were *his* apples, the culmination of decades of his labor. Evan, initially, would have politely explained the grading system, the market value, the necessity of consistency. Lena, however, would listen with an empathetic nod, her gaze steady and understanding. She'd then find a compromise, perhaps a special offer for loyal customers, or suggest a recipe where those apples would be perfect for baking. It wasn't about circumventing the system; it was about honoring the person behind the produce. This, Evan realized, was Lena's value system at play: people first, relationships second, and the tangible product a testament to both.

He observed her interactions at the morning coffee hour, held religiously at the Collective's small café. It wasn't just a social gathering; it was a pulse check, a communication hub disguised as casual conversation. Lena would move from table to table, not just making small talk, but actively listening to concerns about weather patterns, pest infestations, or even the impending school play. She'd offer a word of encouragement, a practical suggestion, or simply a moment of shared understanding.

Evan, standing at a distance with his reusable coffee cup, would meticulously analyze the social dynamics, trying to decipher the unwritten rules of community engagement. He saw a depth of commitment in Lena, a rootedness that transcended a mere job description. Her connection to Cedar Ridge wasn't just professional; it was intrinsic, woven into the fabric of her identity. He recognized that for Lena, belonging wasn't a passive state, but an active participation, a constant nurturing of the bonds that held the community together.

This realization was a slow burn, a gradual dawning that chipped away at his preconceived notions. He'd initially categorized Lena's dedication as a sign of her being perhaps too entrenched, too resistant to change, bound by sentiment rather than logic. Now, he saw it as her greatest strength. Her deep understanding of the community's needs and aspirations allowed her to steer the Collective with a wisdom that his purely data-driven approach could never replicate. She understood that a farmer's pride in their harvest, a baker's dedication to their craft, were not just emotional quirks, but vital components of the Collective's sustainability. Her value was not in maximizing profit margins, but in cultivating a resilient, interconnected ecosystem where everyone felt valued and supported.

He recalled a conversation about the upcoming marketing campaign for the Collective's artisanal cheeses. Evan had presented a sleek, modern design, focusing on the aesthetic appeal and highlighting the artisanal process with sophisticated typography. Lena, while appreciating the design, had gently pushed back. "Evan," she'd said, her voice soft but carrying the weight of experience, "our customers don't just buy cheese. They buy a piece of Cedar Ridge. They buy the story of the cow, the farmer, the cheesemaker who poured their heart into it. We need to show that connection."

She'd then sketched out an alternative, incorporating small portraits of the farmers, handwritten anecdotes about their herds, and a more rustic, hand-drawn feel. It was less about polished perfection and more about authentic storytelling. He saw then that Lena's values were deeply intertwined with the narrative of Cedar Ridge, valuing history, tradition, and the human element above all else.

Conversely, Lena began to see a different facet of Evan. Initially, she'd viewed him as the quintessential city man, all sharp angles and quick decisions, someone who saw Cedar Ridge as a problem to be solved rather than a place to be understood. His structured approach, his insistence on data and processes, had seemed impersonal, even cold. She'd noticed his frustration when things didn't go according to his meticulously laid plans, the slight tightening of his jaw when a delivery was late or a producer missed a deadline. She'd interpreted it, at first, as impatience, a lack of understanding for the organic rhythms of rural life.

But as they worked together, as she saw him wrestling with the inventory system, or meticulously reviewing the nutritional content of new produce for the Collective's health food section, she began to perceive a deeper sincerity beneath his professional veneer. His frustration wasn't born of a lack of empathy, but of a genuine desire to improve things, to bring order to what he perceived as chaos. He wasn't lazy or dismissive; he simply approached problem-solving from a different angle, one rooted in logic and quantifiable results.

She remembered a particularly challenging discussion about expanding the Collective's online presence. Evan had proposed a sophisticated e-commerce platform, complete with real-time stock updates and personalized recommendations. Lena had expressed concerns about the digital literacy of some of their older members, the potential for technical glitches to alienate customers, and the sheer volume of work required to maintain such a system. Evan had listened intently, his brow furrowed in concentration. He hadn't argued or dismissed her points. Instead, he'd asked clarifying questions, seeking to understand the practical implications of her concerns. He'd then spent the next few days researching simpler, more accessible online solutions, even exploring the possibility of a managed service that would handle the technical backend.

"Lena," he'd said, presenting his revised proposal, "I've looked into a platform that's more user-friendly, and we can set up a dedicated support line to help people navigate it. It might not be as cutting-edge as my first idea, but it seems to address your concerns about accessibility and workload." The fact that he'd been willing to scale back his initial vision, to compromise his own pursuit of ultimate efficiency for the sake of the community's comfort and his colleague's perspective, spoke volumes. It showed her that his primary objective wasn't simply to impose his own ideas, but to genuinely help the Collective thrive.

She also saw his vulnerability, a crack in the polished facade. During one of their late-night work sessions, while reviewing a particularly complex financial report, he'd sighed, a sound that carried a weight of weariness. He confessed, without prompting, about the relentless pressure he faced in his city job, the constant expectation to perform, the gnawing feeling that he was always on the verge of burnout.

He spoke of his ambition, but also of a growing disillusionment with a career that felt increasingly hollow, devoid of the tangible impact he craved. Lena listened, offering not solutions, but quiet empathy. She recognized that Evan, despite his outward confidence, was grappling with his own search for purpose and belonging, a search that resonated deeply with her own values.

He wasn't just a city man trying to fix a small-town problem. He was a person trying to find his place, and in his own way, trying to contribute something meaningful. Lena began to see his drive not as an aggressive imposition, but as a testament to his dedication, his belief in the potential of the Cedar Ridge Collective. His frustration wasn't a sign of his being out of touch, but of his earnest desire to find the best path forward, even if that path sometimes diverged from her own well-trodden routes.

She understood that his methodical approach, his analytical mind, were valuable assets, even if they sometimes needed to be tempered with the wisdom of human connection. The tension between their different values was still present, a subtle hum beneath the surface of their collaboration, but it was no longer a source of friction. Instead, it was becoming a point of mutual learning, a dynamic force that was shaping both of them, and in doing so, strengthening the very heart of the Cedar Ridge Collective.

The late afternoon sun, a painter with a palette of molten gold and soft rose, cast long shadows that stretched across the meandering path towards the creek. It was a ritual, unwritten but deeply felt, that as the day's direct demands softened, their paths would often converge by the water's edge. Ostensibly, these meetings were for the casual continuation of their work-related discussions – updates on the marketing campaign, brainstorming for the winter harvest festival, or troubleshooting the latest inventory anomaly. But as the water whispered its age-old secrets over smooth stones and the air grew heavy with the scent of damp earth and wild mint, the conversations inevitably softened, shifting from the practical to the personal.

Evan found himself anticipating these twilight exchanges. He'd arrive, sometimes with a binder of figures still warm from his hands, and Lena would already be there, her silhouette a familiar fixture against the shimmering water. She'd often be tracing patterns in the sand with a fallen branch, or simply watching the gentle flow, a peacefulness emanating from her that Evan had come to recognize as a rare and precious commodity.

"The numbers for the farmers' market outreach are looking good," Evan would start, his voice a little more relaxed here, less the sharp edge of the office. "We've seen a 15% increase in foot traffic since we implemented the new signage, and the social media engagement is... well, it's exceeding projections." He'd offer her a small, almost shy smile, as if pleased with a shared success, a feeling he hadn't experienced in a long time.

Lena would nod, her eyes reflecting the dappled light. "That's wonderful, Evan. Mrs. Gable mentioned she's seen more new faces asking about her jams than ever before. She's particularly pleased with the new display unit. Said it makes her jars look like jewels."

These were the practical anchors, the necessary tether to their shared responsibilities. But the current of their conversations was deeper, pulling them towards unexplored depths. One evening, as they watched dragonflies dart and hover like iridescent jewels over the water's surface, Evan found himself speaking about his life before Cedar Ridge, a life that felt increasingly like a series of temporary stops, each one packed up and left behind with unsettling regularity.

"I never really stayed anywhere for long," he confessed, his gaze fixed on a particularly bold dragonfly. "My father's job in construction... we moved every few years. New town, new school, new friends to make and then leave. By the time I was in college, it felt easier not to put down roots. Less to pack, less to miss." He picked up a smooth, grey stone, turning it over and over in his fingers. "And then, with my career... it was all about the next project, the next promotion. I was always chasing something, but I'm not sure I ever knew what it was."

Lena listened, her presence a quiet anchor. She didn't offer platitudes or easy answers. She simply bore witness to his words, her understanding a palpable comfort. "It sounds... unsettled," she said softly, her voice barely disturbing the stillness of the evening. "Like you were always waiting for the next departure."

Evan finally looked at her, a flicker of surprise in his eyes. "That's exactly it," he said, the simple acknowledgment feeling like a release. "Always waiting for the next departure. I'd become so adept at it, I didn't realize I was missing the arrival. I didn't know how to... be somewhere." He gestured vaguely around them, encompassing the creek, the trees, the quiet hum of the town. "This is the first place I've felt... a pause. A chance to actually see what's in front of me."

Lena smiled, a gentle, knowing smile. "Cedar Ridge has a way of doing that," she said. "It asks you to slow down, to notice. It doesn't demand grand gestures; it thrives on small, consistent acts of presence." She looked down at her own hands, which were calloused from years of working the soil. "My family has been here for generations. My grandparents farmed this land, my parents continued. This creek... it's always been here. I remember learning to skip stones with my grandfather, right here. The feel of the water, the sound of his laughter. It's all woven into me."

She spoke of the deep, intricate tapestry of her family's history in Cedar Ridge. Not in a boastful way, but with a quiet reverence for the lineage of hands that had worked the earth, hands that had nurtured the soil, hands that had built the community. "My grandmother used to say that every seed you plant is a promise," Lena recalled, her gaze distant, as if seeing ghosts of seasons past. "A promise to the future, to the earth, to yourself. She taught me that belonging isn't just about living somewhere; it's about investing in it, tending to it, like you would a precious garden."

Her vision for Cedar Ridge wasn't a grand, sweeping overhaul, but a continuation and deepening of that ancient promise. "I want to see the Collective not just as a marketplace," she explained, her voice gaining a quiet intensity, "but as a living organism. A place where the farmers feel truly supported, where the artisans can pass down their skills, where families can find healthy, local food without breaking the bank. It's about sustainability, yes, but it's also about legacy. About ensuring that the heart of this place keeps beating for generations to come."

Evan found himself captivated by her words, by the depth of her connection to this seemingly ordinary place. He'd always seen land as a commodity, a resource to be managed. Lena saw it as an inheritance, a sacred trust. "So, when you talk about the 'future of Cedar Ridge,'" he ventured, "it's not just about economic growth, is it? It's about continuity, about preserving something vital."

"Exactly," Lena affirmed, meeting his gaze. "It's about honoring the past while building a resilient future. It's about making sure that the children growing up here can still learn to skip stones by this creek, can still taste the richness of soil in their food, can still feel that deep sense of belonging that comes from being rooted."

These quiet moments by the creek became a sanctuary for them both. In the dappled light and the gentle murmur of the water, the walls they'd built around themselves began to crumble. Evan, the man who meticulously guarded his emotions behind a fortress of logic and data, found himself sharing the quiet ache of his rootless existence, the unspoken yearning for a place to call home. Lena, who carried the weight of her family's legacy and the community's expectations, found a listening ear in Evan, someone who, despite his different perspective, genuinely sought to understand.

There was a vulnerability in these shared confessions, a fragile bloom in the fertile ground of their burgeoning connection. Evan spoke of the constant pressure in his previous roles, the hollow victories, the gnawing sense of professional isolation. "I was always the outsider, the one brought in to 'optimize' things," he admitted, his voice low. "And once the optimization was complete, I'd be moved on. It was efficient, I suppose. But it was also… lonely. Like I was just a tool, not a person."

Lena nodded, understanding dawning in her eyes. She'd seen his dedication, his meticulous nature, but had also sensed an underlying weariness. "I think we all crave that sense of being seen, Evan," she said gently. "Not just for what we do, but for who we are. For me, that's tied to this place, to the land, to the people here. It's where I feel most myself."

She spoke of the early days of the Collective, the challenges, the moments of doubt, the sheer hard work it had taken to build it into what it was today. She shared anecdotes about the quirky characters who formed the backbone of Cedar Ridge, the colorful personalities she navigated daily. She recounted the time old Mr. Abernathy, a notoriously cantankerous farmer, had brought her a basket of the first ripe strawberries of the season, a gruff apology for a past disagreement, and a silent offering of reconciliation. "Those moments," she'd explained, her eyes shining, "those are the real currency of a community. More valuable than any profit margin."

Evan absorbed her words, his analytical mind working to process this new data, this understanding of human connection as a tangible, valuable asset. He saw that Lena's strength wasn't just in her knowledge of farming or her business acumen; it was in her profound empathy, her ability to see the inherent worth in every individual and to weave those individual threads into a strong, cohesive whole. He was beginning to understand that efficiency, as he'd once defined it, was a sterile concept without the warmth of human connection, without the rootedness of belonging.

"I used to think that 'belonging' was something you achieved, a status you earned," Evan confessed one evening, kicking a loose pebble into the gently flowing water. "Like a promotion. But here... it feels different. It feels like something you *grow*. Something you participate in."

Lena smiled, a quiet understanding passing between them. "It is," she agreed. "It's a commitment. It's showing up, day after day, not just for the good days, but for the challenging ones too. It's about tending to the relationships, just like you tend to the land."

As the summer deepened, the conversations by the creek became a testament to their evolving understanding. Evan found himself sharing more about his childhood, the quiet yearning he'd always felt for a stable home, a place where he wasn't an ephemeral visitor. He spoke of the disconnect he felt in the fast-paced, transient world of his former career, a world that prioritized constant forward motion over deep connection. Lena, in turn, spoke of the pressures of being a steward of her family's legacy, the quiet burden of expectation that sometimes weighed her down. She confessed her fears of failing to live up to the generations who had come before her, of not being able to maintain the very essence of what made Cedar Ridge special.

"Sometimes I worry," she admitted one twilight, her voice a low murmur against the symphony of crickets, "that I'm too much like my father. Too stubborn, too set in my ways. He loved this land, but he could be... difficult. He saw change as a threat."

Evan, who had initially bristled at any suggestion of change, found himself defending the necessity of adaptation, but with a newfound gentleness. "Change isn't always a threat, Lena," he said softly. "It can be an evolution. Like a plant adapting to new sunlight. It doesn't lose its essence; it just finds a way to grow stronger." He was no longer the relentless optimizer; he was a thoughtful collaborator, his perspective broadened by Lena's deep-rooted wisdom.

In these hushed exchanges, the creek served as their confidante, its ceaseless flow a symbol of both continuity and change. They were learning to speak a new language, one that bridged the gap between Evan's analytical mind and Lena's intuitive understanding, a language of shared vulnerability, mutual respect, and a dawning recognition of their own burgeoning connection.

The seeds of something deeper, something more profound than professional collaboration, were beginning to take root in the fertile soil of their shared experiences by the whispering waters of Cedar Ridge. The nomadic wanderer was finding a semblance of stillness, and the rooted guardian was discovering the courage to embrace gentle growth, all under the watchful gaze of the ancient, flowing creek.

The late afternoon sun, a painter with a palette of molten gold and soft rose, cast long shadows that stretched across the meandering path towards the creek. It was a ritual, unwritten but deeply felt, that as the day's direct demands softened, their paths would often converge by the water's edge. Ostensibly, these meetings were for the casual continuation of their work-related discussions – updates on the marketing campaign, brainstorming for the winter harvest festival, or troubleshooting the latest inventory anomaly. But as the water whispered its age-old secrets over smooth stones and the air grew heavy with the scent of damp earth and wild mint, the conversations inevitably softened, shifting from the practical to the personal.

Evan found himself anticipating these twilight exchanges. He'd arrive, sometimes with a binder of figures still warm from his hands, and Lena would already be there, her silhouette a familiar fixture against the shimmering water. She'd often be tracing patterns in the sand with a fallen branch, or simply watching the gentle flow, a peacefulness emanating from her that Evan had come to recognize as a rare and precious commodity.

"The numbers for the farmers' market outreach are looking good," Evan would start, his voice a little more relaxed here, less the sharp edge of the office. "We've seen a 15% increase in foot traffic since we implemented the new signage, and the social media engagement is... well, it's exceeding projections." He'd offer her a small, almost shy smile, as if pleased with a shared success, a feeling he hadn't experienced in a long time.

Lena would nod, her eyes reflecting the dappled light. "That's wonderful, Evan. Mrs. Gable mentioned she's seen more new faces asking about her jams than ever before. She's particularly pleased with the new display unit. Said it makes her jars look like jewels."

These were the practical anchors, the necessary tether to their shared responsibilities. But the current of their conversations was deeper, pulling them towards unexplored depths. One evening, as they watched dragonflies dart and hover like iridescent jewels over the water's surface, Evan found himself speaking about his life before Cedar Ridge, a life that felt increasingly like a series of temporary stops, each one packed up and left behind with unsettling regularity.

"I never really stayed anywhere for long," he confessed, his gaze fixed on a particularly bold dragonfly. "My father's job in construction... we moved every few years. New town, new school, new friends to make and then leave. By the time I was in college, it felt easier not to put down roots. Less to pack, less to miss." He picked up a smooth, grey stone, turning it over and over in his fingers. "And then, with my career... it was all about the next project, the next promotion. I was always chasing something, but I'm not sure I ever knew what it was."

Lena listened, her presence a quiet anchor. She didn't offer platitudes or easy answers. She simply bore witness to his words, her understanding a palpable comfort. "It sounds... unsettled," she said softly, her voice barely disturbing the stillness of the evening. "Like you were always waiting for the next departure."

Evan finally looked at her, a flicker of surprise in his eyes. "That's exactly it," he said, the simple acknowledgment feeling like a release. "Always waiting for the next departure. I'd become so adept at it, I didn't realize I was missing the arrival. I didn't know how to… be somewhere." He gestured vaguely around them, encompassing the creek, the trees, the quiet hum of the town. "This is the first place I've felt… a pause. A chance to actually see what's in front of me."

Lena smiled, a gentle, knowing smile. "Cedar Ridge has a way of doing that," she said. "It asks you to slow down, to notice. It doesn't demand grand gestures; it thrives on small, consistent acts of presence." She looked down at her own hands, which were calloused from years of working the soil. "My family has been here for generations. My grandparents farmed this land, my parents continued. This creek… it's always been here. I remember learning to skip stones with my grandfather, right here. The feel of the water, the sound of his laughter. It's all woven into me."

She spoke of the deep, intricate tapestry of her family's history in Cedar Ridge. Not in a boastful way, but with a quiet reverence for the lineage of hands that had worked the earth, hands that had nurtured the soil, hands that had built the community. "My grandmother used to say that every seed you plant is a promise," Lena recalled, her gaze distant, as if seeing ghosts of seasons past. "A promise to the future, to the earth, to yourself. She taught me that belonging isn't just about living somewhere; it's about investing in it, tending to it, like you would a precious garden."

Her vision for Cedar Ridge wasn't a grand, sweeping overhaul, but a continuation and deepening of that ancient promise. "I want to see the Collective not just as a marketplace," she explained, her voice gaining a quiet intensity, "but as a living organism. A place where the farmers feel truly supported, where the artisans can pass down their skills, where families can find healthy, local food without breaking the bank. It's about sustainability, yes, but it's also about legacy. About ensuring that the heart of this place keeps beating for generations to come."

Evan found himself captivated by her words, by the depth of her connection to this seemingly ordinary place. He'd always seen land as a commodity, a resource to be managed. Lena saw it as an inheritance, a sacred trust. "So, when you talk about the 'future of Cedar Ridge,'" he ventured, "it's not just about economic growth, is it? It's about continuity, about preserving something vital."

"Exactly," Lena affirmed, meeting his gaze. "It's about honoring the past while building a resilient future. It's about making sure that the children growing up here can still learn to skip stones by this creek, can still taste the richness of soil in their food, can still feel that deep sense of belonging that comes from being rooted."

These quiet moments by the creek became a sanctuary for them both. In the dappled light and the gentle murmur of the water, the walls they'd built around themselves began to crumble. Evan, the man who meticulously guarded his emotions behind a fortress of logic and data, found himself sharing the quiet ache of his rootless existence, the unspoken yearning for a place to call home. Lena, who carried the weight of her family's legacy and the community's expectations, found a listening ear in Evan, someone who, despite his different perspective, genuinely sought to understand.

There was a vulnerability in these shared confessions, a fragile bloom in the fertile ground of their burgeoning connection. Evan spoke of the constant pressure in his previous roles, the hollow victories, the gnawing sense of professional isolation. "I was always the outsider, the one brought in to 'optimize' things," he admitted, his voice low. "And once the optimization was complete, I'd be moved on. It was efficient, I suppose. But it was also... lonely. Like I was just a tool, not a person."

Lena nodded, understanding dawning in her eyes. She'd seen his dedication, his meticulous nature, but had also sensed an underlying weariness. "I think we all crave that sense of being seen, Evan," she said gently. "Not just for what we do, but for who we are. For me, that's tied to this place, to the land, to the people here. It's where I feel most myself."

She spoke of the early days of the Collective, the challenges, the moments of doubt, the sheer hard work it had taken to build it into what it was today. She shared anecdotes about the quirky characters who formed the backbone of Cedar Ridge, the colorful personalities she navigated daily. She recounted the time old Mr. Abernathy, a notoriously cantankerous farmer, had brought her a basket of the first ripe strawberries of the season, a gruff apology for a past disagreement, and a silent offering of reconciliation. "Those moments," she'd explained, her eyes shining, "those are the real currency of a community. More valuable than any profit margin."

Evan absorbed her words, his analytical mind working to process this new data, this understanding of human connection as a tangible, valuable asset. He saw that Lena's strength wasn't just in her knowledge of farming or her business acumen; it was in her profound empathy, her ability to see the inherent worth in every individual and to weave those individual threads into a strong, cohesive whole. He was beginning to understand that efficiency, as he'd once defined it, was a sterile concept without the warmth of human connection, without the rootedness of belonging.

"I used to think that 'belonging' was something you achieved, a status you earned," Evan confessed one evening, kicking a loose pebble into the gently flowing water. "Like a promotion. But here... it feels different. It feels like something you *grow*. Something you participate in."

Lena smiled, a quiet understanding passing between them. "It is," she agreed. "It's a commitment. It's showing up, day after day, not just for the good days, but for the challenging ones too. It's about tending to the relationships, just like you tend to the land."

As the summer deepened, the conversations by the creek became a testament to their evolving understanding. Evan found himself sharing more about his childhood, the quiet yearning he'd always felt for a stable home, a place where he wasn't an ephemeral visitor. He spoke of the disconnect he felt in the fast-paced, transient world of his former career, a world that prioritized constant forward motion over deep connection. Lena, in turn, spoke of the pressures of being a steward of her family's legacy, the quiet burden of expectation that sometimes weighed her down. She confessed her fears of failing to live up to the generations who had come before her, of not being able to maintain the very essence of what made Cedar Ridge special.

"Sometimes I worry," she admitted one twilight, her voice a low murmur against the symphony of crickets, "that I'm too much like my father. Too stubborn, too set in my ways. He loved this land, but he could be... difficult. He saw change as a threat."

Evan, who had initially bristled at any suggestion of change, found himself defending the necessity of adaptation, but with a newfound gentleness. "Change isn't always a threat, Lena," he said softly. "It can be an evolution. Like a plant adapting to new sunlight. It doesn't lose its essence; it just finds a way to grow stronger." He was no longer the relentless optimizer; he was a thoughtful collaborator, his perspective broadened by Lena's deep-rooted wisdom.

In these hushed exchanges, the creek served as their confidante, its ceaseless flow a symbol of both continuity and change. They were learning to speak a new language, one that bridged the gap between Evan's analytical mind and Lena's intuitive understanding, a language of shared vulnerability, mutual respect, and a dawning recognition of their own burgeoning connection. The seeds of something deeper, something more profound than professional collaboration, were beginning to take root in the fertile soil of their shared experiences by the whispering waters of Cedar Ridge. The nomadic wanderer was finding a semblance of stillness, and the rooted guardian was discovering the courage to embrace gentle growth, all under the watchful gaze of the ancient, flowing creek.

The subtle shift in their interactions was as quiet and as natural as the turning of the seasons, yet undeniably present. It manifested not in grand declarations or overt gestures, but in the small, almost imperceptible ways their lives began to intertwine. Lena found herself looking forward to Evan's presence at the Collective, not just for his astute observations on inventory management or his innovative marketing strategies, but for the easy camaraderie that had settled between them. He possessed a quiet competence that was reassuring, and a dry wit that often caught her off guard, eliciting a genuine, unforced laugh that felt as refreshing as a cool breeze on a warm day.

One Tuesday afternoon, during the bustling farmer's market, a minor calamity struck. A stack of freshly printed flyers, detailing the upcoming "Harvest Moon Festival," took an unfortunate tumble from a display table, scattering across the dusty ground like oversized confetti. Before Lena could even sigh in exasperation, Evan was there, his usual precise movements now imbued with a surprising agility. He knelt down, his tie loosened slightly, and began gathering the scattered sheets with a focused intensity. A small smile played on his lips as a gust of wind playfully lifted one of the flyers just out of his reach, sending him scrambling after it with a mock groan. Lena found herself watching him, a warmth spreading through her chest that had nothing to do with the summer heat. His willingness to dive headfirst into such a trivial, yet annoying, mishap, without complaint, spoke volumes.

"Looks like the Harvest Moon is trying to escape us, Evan," she commented, joining him on the ground, her own hands quickly working to collect the errant papers.

He looked up, his eyes crinkling at the corners. "Perhaps it's testing our resolve. Or maybe it's just enjoying the attention," he quipped, his voice carrying a lightheartedness that was becoming increasingly familiar. They worked in comfortable silence for a few moments, the rhythmic rustle of paper and the distant murmur of the market creating a shared soundtrack. It was a simple moment, really, but in its ordinariness, it felt significant. There was no pretense, no expectation, just two people collaborating, sharing a small, silly challenge. When they finally had the flyers restacked, Evan brushed off his hands and offered her a small, triumphant grin. "Crisis averted. The Harvest Moon can now officially begin its reign."

Lena found herself mirroring his smile, a sense of shared accomplishment bubbling up. "Thanks, Evan. I don't know what I would have done without my... crisis manager." The nickname, born of the moment, felt surprisingly apt. He didn't flinch at the implied intimacy of the title; instead, he simply inclined his head with a quiet acknowledgment.

Later that week, while reviewing the budget for the festival, a complex spreadsheet spread before them on Lena's desk, Evan pointed out an oversight he'd made. He'd underestimated the cost of artisanal candle supplies for the evening market. Instead of defensiveness, his reaction was one of open admission and immediate problem-solving.

"My apologies, Lena. I clearly got caught up in the... ambient charm of the festival planning and overlooked the detail on wax procurement. Let me re-run those figures and find us some savings elsewhere. Perhaps we can negotiate a bulk discount with Mrs. Henderson for her famous apple cider donuts and offset the candle cost." His willingness to admit his error, and his quick pivot to finding a solution, further solidified Lena's growing respect for him. It wasn't just his analytical mind; it was his integrity.

"It's fine, Evan," she assured him, though she appreciated his diligence. "These things happen. The important thing is that we caught it. And yes, I think a donut-based financial strategy is exactly what this budget needs." Her response was laced with a humor that felt increasingly natural between them. He met her gaze, and for a fleeting second, the professional veneer dropped away, replaced by a look that was warmer, more personal. It was a look that acknowledged the unspoken current flowing beneath the surface of their working relationship, a current of mutual appreciation and a burgeoning, unacknowledged attraction.

The comfortable silences that had once been a testament to their efficient collaboration now held a different kind of weight. They were no longer just pauses between sentences; they were spaces filled with unspoken understanding, with a shared awareness of each other's presence. Sitting across from each other at the worn oak table in the Collective's office, the scent of dried herbs and woodsmoke mingling in the air, they'd often find themselves simply looking at each other, a gentle smile gracing their lips. It was a quiet acknowledgment of the comfort they found in each other's company, a testament to a connection that was deepening organically, without fanfare or forced effort.

There was an evening, after a particularly long day of inventorying new produce, when they found themselves packing up the last crates. The air was thick with the sweet scent of peaches and the earthy aroma of freshly dug potatoes. Lena, her hands sticky with peach juice, fumbled with a particularly stubborn crate lid. It sprang open unexpectedly, sending a cascade of ripe peaches tumbling onto the floor.

"Oh, for heaven's sake!" she exclaimed, a wave of weariness washing over her.

Evan, who had been meticulously labeling boxes, stopped what he was doing. He didn't sigh or look annoyed. Instead, he simply walked over, his movements unhurried, and began to help her gather the escaped fruit. As they knelt side-by-side, their shoulders brushing, a sense of easy intimacy settled between them.

"Peaches have a mind of their own sometimes," Evan remarked, his voice low and steady. He picked up a particularly bruised peach and turned it over in his hand. "This one's seen better days. But still, nothing beats a Cedar Ridge peach."

Lena looked at him, really looked at him, in the dim light of the emptying storeroom. She saw the quiet determination in his eyes, the genuine care he took in even the smallest tasks. It was more than just efficiency; it was a dedication to the quality of their work, to the integrity of the Collective. "You're right," she said softly, her gaze lingering on his for a moment longer than strictly necessary. "They're the best."

He met her gaze, and the air between them seemed to hum with an unspoken energy. There was a shared understanding, a mutual respect that transcended their professional roles. It was in these unguarded moments, these shared tasks, these quiet acknowledgments, that the subtle shift was most evident. Neither of them was actively seeking romance; they were simply two people, forging a genuine connection through shared purpose and a growing, undeniable regard.

The chemistry was a palpable undercurrent, a silent promise of something more, blooming in the unlikeliest of soils, nurtured by the shared rhythm of their days and the quiet strength of their growing bond. It was a slow burn, this burgeoning attraction, ignited by shared work ethic and mutual respect, fanned by the unexpected sparks of laughter and shared vulnerability, and now, it was beginning to cast a warm, subtle glow on their interactions.

The rhythm of their days at the Collective had developed a certain cadence, a familiar beat that now included the steady presence of Evan. Lena found herself subconsciously adjusting her own movements, anticipating his arrival, even planning tasks that might require his particular skillset or his unique perspective. It wasn't a conscious decision, not an intentional pursuit of romance, but rather an organic unfolding of comfort and companionship. He was no longer just the "consultant" or the "numbers guy"; he was Evan, a steady, reliable presence in the often-turbulent waters of running a community-focused business.

One humid afternoon, a delivery of specialty cheeses arrived, and to Lena's dismay, several of the insulated boxes had not been properly sealed, leading to a concerning temperature rise. The pungent aroma of slightly warmed cheddar filled the air, and Lena's shoulders slumped. "Oh, no. This is not good. Some of these are delicate varieties. I'm afraid we might have to discard them." The thought of the waste, the loss of product and the disappointment for the farmers who had worked so hard to produce it, weighed heavily on her.

Evan, who had been reviewing the latest sales reports, looked up at the concerned frown on her face. He walked over, his eyes quickly assessing the situation. "Let me see," he said, his voice calm and reassuring. He carefully examined the cheeses, sniffing them, feeling the texture of the rind. "Some of these might still be salvageable," he declared, a glint of his analytical mind at work. "If we can get them chilled down immediately, and if the aroma and texture haven't been compromised too severely, we might be able to offer them at a reduced price. We can label them clearly as 'express chilled' and inform customers about the situation. Transparency is key, after all."

Lena watched him, impressed by his pragmatism and his refusal to simply accept the loss. He didn't offer empty reassurances; he offered solutions. Together, they meticulously went through each affected cheese, a delicate process that involved a lot of careful sniffing and probing. Evan's quiet focus, his methodical approach, was a calming influence. He didn't rush her, didn't make her feel inadequate for her initial despair. He simply worked alongside her, a silent partner in problem-solving.

"You know, for someone who deals in abstract numbers," Lena remarked as they carefully placed the carefully selected 'salvageable' cheeses back into the chilling unit, "you have a surprisingly good nose for cheese."

Evan offered a small, almost shy smile. "My grandmother was a formidable cook. Taught me to appreciate the nuances of ingredients. And, if I'm being honest, a good chunk of my previous job involved assessing potential risks and mitigating losses. It's just a different kind of inventory."

The camaraderie that had developed during that impromptu cheese-saving mission was palpable. They had turned a potential disaster into a collaborative success, a testament to their complementary skills and their shared commitment to the Collective. It wasn't a romantic outing, not by any stretch of the imagination, but the shared experience, the successful navigation of a minor crisis, solidified their connection on a deeper level.

Later that week, during a quiet afternoon lull at the Collective, Lena was struggling to assemble a new shelving unit for the artisanal bread display. The instructions were notoriously vague, and the pieces seemed determined to defy logic. Frustrated, she let out a small huff of annoyance. Evan, who had just finished reorganizing the spice rack, noticed her struggle. He walked over, not with an air of superiority, but with a quiet offer of assistance.

"Having trouble with that beast?" he inquired, his eyes twinkling with a hint of amusement.

Lena sighed, leaning back against the offending structure. "It's like it's actively resisting assembly. I think the instructions were written by someone who speaks fluent Swedish and ancient hieroglyphics."

Evan chuckled, a warm, resonant sound. He took the instructions from her, his brow furrowed in concentration as he studied them. "Ah, I see the problem. This piece is supposed to connect here, but it needs to be angled slightly. It's a common design flaw in these cheaper models." He then proceeded to deftly guide the pieces together, his movements sure and efficient, explaining his thought process as he went.

"So, it's not me, it's the shelf?" Lena asked, a sense of relief washing over her.

"Precisely," Evan confirmed, securing the final screw. "The shelf is the villain here. You are the innocent victim. And I, apparently, am the knight in shining... well, practical work boots."

Lena laughed, a genuine, unrestrained sound. The ease with which he'd solved her problem, and the lighthearted way he'd framed it, put her completely at ease. She found herself watching him as he worked, appreciating not just his mechanical aptitude, but the quiet confidence he exuded. There was a subtle shift in how she perceived him now. The initial admiration for his business acumen had deepened, evolving into a genuine liking for his character, for the way he navigated the world, both the world of numbers and the world of practicalities.

These small interactions, these shared moments of problem-solving and gentle humor, were the threads weaving a subtle, undeniable attraction into the fabric of their working relationship. There were no whispered confessions of love, no longing gazes across crowded rooms. It was far more nuanced than that. It was in the way their laughter sometimes overlapped, in the lingering warmth of a shared glance after a successful task, in the comfortable silences that no longer felt like empty spaces but like contented pauses in a shared journey.

They were building something, not just for the Collective, but between themselves, a quiet connection forged in the everyday rhythm of Cedar

Ridge, a testament to the subtle power of shared purpose and genuine regard. The attraction wasn't a sudden inferno, but a slow, steady bloom, as natural and as vital as the crops ripening under the summer sun. It was an acknowledgment, unspoken yet deeply felt, that something had shifted, and the comfortable professional dynamic had begun to blossom into something far more resonant.

Evan had always equated freedom with unburdened movement. For years, his life had been a curated sequence of departures and arrivals, each destination a temporary waypoint on a journey that seemed to have no ultimate destination. He'd packed and unpacked his life with an almost practiced efficiency, believing that shedding possessions and relationships was the key to shedding limitations.

This philosophy, deeply ingrained from a childhood spent chasing his father's next construction project, had become his personal definition of liberty. Freedom was the absence of ties, the ability to pivot on a dime, the liberation from the perceived constraints of permanence. He saw attachment as a cage, a vulnerability that would inevitably lead to pain or stagnation. He'd prided himself on his ability to detach, to observe from a distance, to remain unaffected by the emotional currents that seemed to anchor others.

But Cedar Ridge, and Lena's presence within it, was slowly but surely chipping away at the foundations of that belief system. The quiet rhythm of the town, the deep roots that ran through its inhabitants like ancient trees, the way Lena spoke of her family's history with such reverence – it all presented a stark contrast to his own transient existence. He found himself wrestling with a growing internal dissonance. Was his constant motion truly freedom, or was it simply a sophisticated form of running away? Was his carefully constructed detachment a shield, or a self-imposed exile?

Lena, with her unwavering connection to this patch of earth and its people, embodied a different kind of strength, a resilience born not from evasion, but from deep, unwavering commitment. He'd observed how she navigated challenges within the Collective, how she embraced the messy, complicated reality of community life with a grace he hadn't thought possible. She wasn't bound by obligation; she was connected by choice, by love, by a profound sense of responsibility that seemed to fuel her, rather than diminish her.

One evening, as they walked along the familiar path by the creek, the conversation, as it often did, drifted towards the personal. The air was alive with the hum of cicadas, a sound that Evan was beginning to associate with a sense of grounding, a stark contrast to the sterile hum of office buildings he was accustomed to.

"I've been thinking about what you said the other day, about 'being somewhere,'" Evan began, his voice softer than usual, almost hesitant. He picked up a smooth, grey stone, turning it over in his fingers. "You said Cedar Ridge asks you to slow down, to notice. It's taken me a while to... process that. My entire adult life has been about not noticing, about moving on before anything can really take root. I always thought that was the ultimate freedom." He tossed the stone gently into the water, watching the ripples spread and dissipate. "The freedom to leave, to start over, to avoid any messy entanglements."

Lena walked beside him, her gaze thoughtful. She didn't interrupt, allowing his words to settle in the quiet space between them. The water's murmur seemed to absorb his confession, a gentle undertow to his introspection.

"But lately," he continued, his gaze fixed on the darkening water, "I'm starting to wonder if that's just... a gilded cage. A constant state of 'almost.' Almost building a life, almost forming a lasting connection, almost truly belonging. It's exhausting, you know? Always being ready to pack up. Always keeping one foot out the door." He looked at Lena, a flicker of something akin to vulnerability in his eyes. "Is it really freedom if you're always running from something? Or is it just... perpetual escape?"

Lena stopped, her hand reaching out to gently touch a wild mint plant that grew along the bank, its scent rising in the cooling air. "I've never thought of it that way, Evan," she said, her voice low. "For me, freedom has always been tied to agency. The ability to choose my path, to shape my life. And for me, that path has always been here. It doesn't feel like a cage because it's a choice I've made, and continue to make, every single day."

She turned to face him, her expression earnest. "I understand your perspective, though. The idea of being 'tied down' can feel restrictive, especially if you haven't experienced the joy and strength that can come from deep connection. But for me, these roots... they aren't shackles. They're anchors. They give me stability, a foundation from which to grow. They're also a source of immense strength. Knowing my family's history here, knowing that generations before me have tended this land, built this community... it's a legacy I'm proud to be a part of, not burdened by."

Evan listened intently, the analytical part of his brain processing her words, while a more intuitive part felt a stir of recognition. He'd always seen Lena's connection to Cedar Ridge as a given, a hereditary trait. He hadn't truly considered the active choice involved, the ongoing commitment that sustained it.

"But what if your path leads you away from here?" he ventured, the question born from his own ingrained nomadic impulse. "What if there's an opportunity, a calling, somewhere else? Doesn't that commitment become... a limitation?"

Lena's smile was gentle, understanding. "That's where agency comes in, Evan. If that happened, if a genuine calling pulled me elsewhere, then *choosing* to stay would still be an act of freedom. Or choosing to go would be an act of freedom. It's about making conscious decisions about your life, not being swept along by circumstance or fear. For me, the freedom is in the *choice*, not necessarily in the absence of connection." She paused, her gaze drifting towards the water. "Sometimes, the greatest freedom is found in choosing where to plant yourself, and then tending to that space with all your heart."

She looked back at him, her eyes reflecting the twilight sky. "Your life has been about movement, and that's valid. It's how you've learned, how you've grown, how you've protected yourself. But perhaps freedom isn't just about the ability to move *away* from things, but also the ability to move *towards* them. To move towards connection, towards belonging, towards a place that feels like home. It's a different kind of bravery, I suppose. The bravery to be vulnerable, to invest, to risk."

Evan felt a subtle shift within him. Lena wasn't dismissing his life's philosophy; she was offering an alternative interpretation, a new lens through which to view the concept of freedom. He'd always seen attachment as a surrender of control, a concession to external forces. Lena, however, presented it as an active embrace, a deliberate investment of self. Her perspective didn't invalidate his experiences; it simply broadened his understanding of what it meant to be truly free.

"So, you're saying," he mused, the words forming slowly, deliberately, "that freedom isn't about being unattached, but about choosing where your attachments lie? And that those attachments, when chosen consciously, can actually empower you?"

"Exactly," Lena affirmed, her smile widening. "They can be the very things that allow you to soar, rather than the things that hold you down. When you're anchored, you have a stable point from which to explore, to create, to contribute. You're not constantly looking for a place to land; you're building upon a place that already holds you." She nudged his arm gently. "And sometimes, the greatest adventures are found not in seeking new horizons, but in deepening your understanding of the one you're already on."

He considered her words, the implications rippling through his carefully constructed worldview. He'd always seen Lena as the embodiment of Cedar Ridge, a product of its environment. He hadn't fully appreciated the conscious agency she possessed, the active role she played in shaping her life and the life of the community. He'd assumed her roots were a given, an inherited condition. But Lena was demonstrating that those roots were actively tended, consciously chosen, and fiercely protected.

"It's a different way of thinking about personal agency, isn't it?" Evan said, a new line of thought opening up. "I've always believed that agency meant the freedom to break free, to escape constraints. But you're suggesting that agency can also be about choosing to embrace those constraints, to weave them into the fabric of your life in a way that strengthens you."

"Precisely," Lena agreed, her gaze steady. "It's about owning your choices, whatever they may be. If someone feels compelled to leave Cedar Ridge to pursue a dream, that's their agency. If I feel compelled to stay and nurture this place, that's mine. Neither choice is inherently superior. The key is that it's a conscious, deliberate decision. It's not about being dictated by circumstances, or by fear, or by an ingrained belief system that might not serve you anymore."

Evan nodded slowly, the concept resonating deeply. He thought of his father, always chasing the next job, the next horizon, never truly finding peace. Had that been freedom, or a restless dissatisfaction born from an inability to commit? He'd always admired his father's independence, but now he saw the potential for a profound loneliness in it, a constant searching that never yielded a true sense of arrival.

"It's the 'might not serve you anymore' part that's hitting home," Evan admitted, his voice barely above a whisper. "My whole framework for understanding the world, for understanding myself, was built around that idea of constant movement as freedom. It's served a purpose, I suppose. It kept me safe, emotionally detached, adaptable. But maybe it's time to re-evaluate. Maybe staying put, putting down roots, isn't a sign of weakness or stagnation, but a different kind of strength. A strength that comes from commitment, from vulnerability."

Lena reached out and placed a hand on his arm, her touch light but grounding. "It takes courage, Evan. The courage to be still, to be present, to invest in something beyond yourself. And it's okay to question the beliefs you've lived by. That's growth. That's evolving."

They continued their walk, the conversation now infused with a new layer of understanding. Evan, the meticulous planner, the strategic optimizer, found himself letting go of the need to control every outcome, to rationalize every emotion. He was beginning to appreciate the quiet wisdom in Lena's grounded perspective, the profound strength in her chosen attachments. He saw that her deep connection to Cedar Ridge wasn't a limitation; it was a source of her power, a wellspring from which she drew resilience and purpose.

Lena, in turn, found herself reflecting on Evan's inherent drive, his ability to analyze situations and identify potential pathways, even if those pathways had always led him away from stability. She recognized that his constant movement, while perhaps born from a need to avoid attachment, also represented a powerful sense of personal agency, a refusal to be defined by external expectations or geographical boundaries. She saw that his questioning of his own philosophy wasn't a sign of weakness, but a testament to his capacity for self-awareness and growth. He was challenging his own assumptions, just as she was encouraging him to.

As they reached the edge of the woods, the lights of Cedar Ridge twinkling in the distance, Evan stopped. He turned to Lena, a genuine smile gracing his lips. "Thank you, Lena. For... offering a different perspective. It's a lot to unpack, but I think... I think you might be onto something."

Lena returned his smile, a warmth spreading through her. "We're all just trying to figure it out, Evan. The trick is to be open to the possibility that our own maps might not be the only ones that lead to a good place."

The conversation had been a subtle recalibration, a gentle challenge to deeply held beliefs. Evan was beginning to understand that freedom wasn't just about the absence of ties, but about the power of choosing those ties wisely. Lena was seeing that a grounded perspective could be complemented by an appreciation for the courage it took to forge one's own path, even if that path was one of constant movement.

The seeds of connection between them were not just about shared work or mutual admiration; they were about a deeper, more profound understanding of each other's fundamental beliefs, and a growing respect for the validity of those differing viewpoints. The assumptions they had carried, the frameworks they had built their lives upon, were starting to feel a little less rigid, a little more open to the possibility of redefinition, all thanks to the quiet wisdom shared under the Cedar Ridge stars.

CHAPTER FIVE

The Edge of Departure

The calendar pages, once a blur of anonymous weeks, now seemed to mock Evan with their deliberate, stark progression. Six months. The arbitrary deadline his initial contract had stipulated felt less like a professional benchmark and more like a ticking clock, each day a diminishing step closer to an unforeseen precipice. When he'd first arrived in Cedar Ridge, the six-month mark had been a distant, almost irrelevant detail, a professional courtesy to be fulfilled before he'd seamlessly pivot to the next engagement. It was a clean exit strategy, one that aligned perfectly with his lifelong habit of keeping his feet light, his possessions minimal, and his emotional baggage even lighter. Now, the approaching date felt like a physical weight in his chest, a subtle but persistent ache that amplified with every sunrise.

It wasn't just the abstract concept of a deadline; it was the tangible, growing reality of what his departure would mean. Cedar Ridge, with its unapologetic embrace of community and its quiet insistence on belonging, had slowly, insidiously, begun to weave itself into the fabric of his own existence. The days of detached observation had given way to moments of genuine connection, his carefully constructed walls chipped away by the persistent, gentle warmth of its inhabitants.

He found himself anticipating conversations, not dreading them. He looked forward to the mundane rituals – the morning coffee at the diner, the shared laughter during workdays at the Collective, even the occasional, slightly exasperating, town hall meetings. These weren't just interactions; they were threads of a tapestry he was becoming a part of, a tapestry he'd never intended to weave.

Lena, of course, was the central figure in this unexpected shift. Their conversations, once polite and professional, had evolved into something far more intimate, a shared exploration of vulnerability and truth. She'd challenged his deeply ingrained notions of freedom, offering a perspective that resonated with a part of him he'd long suppressed. He'd arrived in Cedar Ridge a connoisseur of transient experiences, believing that true liberty lay in the ability to shed all ties. But Lena, with her unwavering groundedness, had shown him a different kind of strength, a resilience born from deep, conscious connection. She hadn't just spoken of belonging; she embodied it. And in her quiet way, she had begun to plant seeds of belonging within him, too. He found himself imagining Cedar Ridge without Lena, a landscape rendered flat and colorless, and the thought sent a pang of disquiet through him.

The subtle shifts in his own perspective were mirrored by the changing attitudes of the townsfolk. Initially, he'd been the outsider, the temporary consultant, the man from the city with the sharp suits and the even sharper mind. They'd been polite, respectful, but distant. They'd observed him, much as he had observed them, cataloging his efficiency, his problem-solving skills, his detached professionalism. But as the months wore on, and as Evan began to engage, to listen, to contribute beyond the scope of his contract, something began to shift. He'd rolled up his sleeves, literally and figuratively, tackling the seemingly insurmountable logistical challenges that had plagued the Collective for years. He'd brought an order to their chaos, a clarity to their vision, and in doing so, had earned their respect, and something more akin to trust.

He noticed it first in the small interactions. Mrs. Gable at the bakery, who'd previously offered him a perfunctory nod, now insisted he try her new lavender scones, her eyes twinkling with genuine warmth. Old Man Hemlock, the gruff but kindly owner of the hardware store, started holding back the latest edition of his favorite architectural magazine, a silent acknowledgment of their shared professional interest.

Even the younger members of the Collective, who'd initially viewed him with a mixture of awe and suspicion, began to seek his advice on their own projects, their voices tinged with an eagerness that went beyond mere deference. They saw him not just as a problem-solver, but as a contributor, a potential ally, a member of the extended Cedar Ridge family.

Then came the whispers, the murmured conversations that he'd overhear just as he entered a room, the sudden hush that fell when he approached a group. They were no longer whispers of professional assessment, but of a different, more personal nature. He'd catch snippets, like "He's done wonders for us," or "Such a shame he'll have to leave," or the one that pricked him the most, "What will we do without him?" They weren't just talking about the Collective's operational efficiency anymore; they were talking about *him*. His absence, once a hypothetical scenario, was now a looming, tangible loss.

These conversations, though laced with a genuine appreciation for his work, also carried an undercurrent of apprehension. The townsfolk had grown accustomed to his presence, to the steady hand he provided. He had become a familiar fixture, a part of the town's evolving narrative. His departure would leave a void, not just in the Collective's operations, but in the very fabric of their daily lives.

The ease with which they had accepted his arrival, viewing him as a temporary solution, had given way to a subtle, unspoken desire for his permanence. This was a complication Evan had never factored into his carefully constructed professional life. He dealt in project completion, in measurable outcomes, in clean breaks. He didn't deal in the emotional fallout of his successes.

The anxiety of it all began to manifest in subtle ways. Evan found himself checking the calendar with an almost obsessive regularity, the approaching date a dark cloud on his mental horizon. He'd wake up in the middle of the night, a cold sweat prickling his skin, his mind racing with scenarios of his departure. What would he say to Lena? How would he explain the growing attachment he felt, an attachment he was still struggling to fully comprehend? He'd always prided himself on his ability to compartmentalize, to separate his professional life from his personal one. But Cedar Ridge, and Lena, had blurred those lines into an indistinguishable haze.

One afternoon, while overseeing the final stages of a renovation project on the community hall, he found himself in a hushed conversation with Mayor Thompson, a man whose pragmatic approach to town governance had always impressed Evan. The Mayor, usually all business, seemed unusually contemplative.

"Evan," he began, his voice low, almost conspiratorial, as they stood surveying the newly painted walls, the scent of fresh timber and paint still hanging in the air, "the word is out. Six months. That's the end of the line, isn't it?"

Evan nodded, a familiar knot tightening in his stomach. "That was the original agreement, Mayor."

"And we're all incredibly grateful for what you've accomplished," Thompson continued, his gaze earnest. "You've truly... revitalized things here. The Collective is stronger than it's been in years. People are talking about the future again, a future that feels… hopeful." He paused, running a hand through his thinning grey hair. "But it's also made us… comfortable. Reliant, perhaps. We've gotten used to your steady hand, your foresight. The thought of you leaving… well, it's a bit unnerving, to be honest."

"I understand," Evan said, though the words felt inadequate. Understanding was a professional concept; this was something far more complex.

"Do you?" the Mayor asked, his eyes meeting Evan's directly. "Because I'm not just talking about the operational side, Evan. I'm talking about the… the shift. You've changed things here, not just the buildings. You've changed the atmosphere. People feel… seen. Heard. And that's largely thanks to you. Lena's been instrumental, of course, but you've brought a different kind of expertise, a different perspective that's really… resonated."

Evan felt a flush creep up his neck. He hadn't intended to have such an impact, to become so integral. His objective had been to optimize, to implement, to move on. He hadn't anticipated the personal investment that would naturally follow such deep engagement.

"I'm glad I could be of service," he managed, the standard professional platitude feeling hollow on his tongue.

"Service is one thing," Mayor Thompson said, his voice deepening with a sincerity that caught Evan off guard. "Connection is another. And I've seen you connect, Evan. It's not just your work. It's the way you talk to people, the way you've started to… belong, in your own way." He gave Evan a knowing look. "It's going to be hard for a lot of people here when you go. Harder than they might admit. And I suspect, harder for you too."

The Mayor's words hung in the air, a confirmation of Evan's deepest anxieties. He was no longer an impartial observer. He was a participant, and his departure would be felt. He'd come to Cedar Ridge to escape the complexities of attachment, only to find himself entangled in a web of his own making, a web woven from genuine respect and a nascent sense of belonging.

The professional timeline, once a clear path forward, had morphed into a looming deadline, fraught with unspoken emotional consequences, for himself and for the town that had inadvertently captured a piece of his heart. He was at the edge of departure, but for the first time in his life, the thought of leaving felt less like freedom and more like a profound loss.

The whispers had become a constant hum, a subtle soundtrack to Evan's days in Cedar Ridge. They weren't the sharp, analytical murmurs of the initial weeks, but something softer, laced with a hopeful undertone that both unsettled and intrigued him. It was the sound of a community that had braced itself for his eventual departure, only to find itself wishing he would stay.

He noticed it most acutely at the Collective. The once-formal interactions, punctuated by efficient exchanges of information, had evolved. Now, there was an undercurrent of personal investment, a palpable desire that he remain. He'd be discussing the latest inventory figures with Sarah, the bright-eyed young woman who managed the online sales, and she'd trail off, her gaze drifting towards the window overlooking the town square. "It's just... it's been so much better since you've been here, Evan," she'd say, her voice barely above a murmur.

"Things just... run. And people are happier. I know it sounds silly, but I think everyone feels a bit more optimistic." She'd then offer him a shy smile, as if confessing a secret. He'd offer a polite nod, a carefully neutral response, but inside, the confession echoed. He was becoming more than just a consultant; he was becoming a symbol of something positive, something they hoped would endure.

Then there was Mark, a burly, quiet man who ran the woodworking division. Mark wasn't one for idle chatter. He communicated through the precise angles of a dovetail joint or the smooth finish of a sanded surface. Yet, during a recent site visit to assess the lumber supply, Mark had surprised him. They were standing by a stack of freshly cut oak, the air thick with the scent of sawdust and earth.

"This oak," Mark had said, his voice rough but steady, "it's good quality. Strong. Lasts a long time." He'd paused, then added, his gaze fixed on a point beyond Evan's shoulder, "Like the kind of foundation you're building for us here. Solid." The analogy, so simple and direct, resonated more deeply than any lengthy speech. It was a tacit acknowledgment of his contribution, but more than that, it was a quiet expression of a wish for continuity, for the preservation of that solid foundation.

These small affirmations, these hesitant expressions of hope, were becoming harder to dismiss. They chipped away at his carefully constructed resolve to maintain his professional distance, to keep his exit strategy clean and uncomplicated. He found himself actively listening for these undertones, piecing together the collective sentiment of Cedar Ridge. It was a growing realization that his impact extended far beyond the balance sheets and operational efficiencies. He was becoming a part of the town's narrative, an unexpected character in their ongoing story.

Lena, of course, was the one who saw it most clearly. One evening, as they sat on her porch swing, the crickets chirping their nightly symphony, she'd turned to him, her eyes reflecting the soft glow of the porch light. "You know, Evan," she'd said, her voice gentle, "people are starting to talk. Not about the Collective's profits, but about *you*. They see what you've done, and they... they hope. They hope you'll stay."

He'd felt a familiar tightness in his chest. "It's just my job, Lena. A six-month contract."

She'd smiled, a knowing, tender expression. "And contracts can be renewed. Or... new ones can be made. People here have a way of making space for what they value." She'd reached out and gently touched his hand. "And they value you, Evan. More than you realize."

Her words were a balm and a burden. They validated the growing disquiet within him, the gnawing feeling that his carefully planned departure was no longer a simple professional transition, but a potential rupture. He'd started to anticipate the unspoken questions that lingered in the air after his more significant interventions at the Collective. Questions like, "Who will manage the next phase?" or "Will we be able to maintain this momentum without him?" These weren't just logistical queries; they were tinged with an anxiety that mirrored his own burgeoning apprehension.

He saw it in the way Mrs. Gable, the proprietor of the local bakery, now held back a particularly exquisite blueberry scone for him each morning, her eyes crinkling at the corners. "For the man who's making such a difference," she'd say with a wink, as if he were a king bestowing favor upon her humble establishment. He'd always paid for his pastries, meticulously, but now there was an added element, a gratuity of sorts, that transcended mere currency.

Even Mr. Henderson, the taciturn librarian who usually communicated in hushed whispers and stern glances, had begun to engage him in brief, earnest conversations about community outreach programs. He'd shown Evan a worn photograph of the library's original dedication ceremony, a sepia-toned image of stern-faced founders. "We're trying to build something new, Mr. Davies," Henderson had said, his voice a low rumble, "but we need to remember the strength of what came before. And we need people who understand how to build on that. People like you." The unspoken plea for continuity was clear.

He remembered a recent town hall meeting, a typically boisterous affair where differing opinions often clashed. The topic was the expansion of the local farmers' market, a project he'd helped streamline. Amidst the usual debate, a voice from the back, belonging to a young mother he'd only met a few times, had cut through the noise. "But who's going to see it through?" she'd asked, her voice carrying a note of genuine concern.

"Evan's been so good at making sure everything actually *happens*. It's not just about ideas; it's about making them real." The entire room had fallen silent, a collective breath held, as if awaiting his response. He'd offered a carefully worded assurance about a transition plan, but the question had landed heavily. They weren't just looking for a problem-solver; they were looking for a steady hand, a reliable presence.

The collective hope wasn't overtly declared; it was a tapestry woven from small gestures, from averted gazes that held a plea, from quiet conversations that paused as he approached. It was in the extra effort people made to include him in their informal gatherings, the invitations to barbecues and impromptu coffee breaks that he'd previously politely declined, citing work. Now, the thought of declining felt like a rejection, not just of an invitation, but of a burgeoning connection.

He found himself replaying conversations, dissecting the subtle nuances of tone and expression. He'd see it in the way Martha from the town council, a woman who'd initially viewed him with a healthy dose of skepticism, would now meet his gaze with a hopeful nod when discussing future projects. She'd even started to proactively seek his input on long-term planning, not just immediate crisis management.

"We're thinking about the next five years, Evan," she'd said last week, her tone surprisingly earnest. "And honestly, we're all wondering how we'll navigate that without your... foresight. You've brought a perspective we desperately need to maintain."

This growing awareness was a disquieting revelation. He had arrived in Cedar Ridge with a clear objective: to optimize the Collective and depart.

He had envisioned himself as a surgeon, performing a precise operation, then leaving the patient to recover. But Cedar Ridge, with its deep roots and its unwavering sense of community, had proven to be less a patient and more a vibrant ecosystem, one that absorbed him, nurtured him, and now, seemed reluctant to let him go.

The townsfolk's hope was a quiet force, a testament to the impact he had unexpectedly made. It was a hope for continuity, for the preservation of the positive changes he had helped implement. And it was a hope that he, Evan Davies, the transient consultant, might somehow become a permanent fixture in their lives. This burgeoning sentiment, though flattering, presented him with a conflict he hadn't anticipated, a quiet battle between his ingrained habit of detachment and the undeniable pull of a place that had begun to feel like home.

He was no longer just observing Cedar Ridge; he was becoming a part of its unfolding story, and the thought of his chapter ending, of his departure, now felt like a premature closing of a book that was just beginning to capture his full attention.

The worn leather of the journal felt cool and familiar beneath Lena's fingertips, a silent confidante in the quiet hours of the evening. Moonlight, filtered through the lace curtains of her bedroom, cast dancing shadows across the pages, illuminating the tangled thoughts that had taken up residence in her mind. Evan. The name itself was a soft hum in the chambers of her heart, a melody that had become increasingly difficult to ignore. He was a man of quiet competence, of unwavering dedication, a force of nature that had subtly, irrevocably, altered the rhythm of Cedar Ridge. And Lena, more than most, felt the shift, not just in the town's prosperity, but in the landscape of her own emotions.

She traced the curve of a word, a frustrated sigh escaping her lips. The dilemma wasn't about Evan's potential departure; that was a decision solely his to make. The true crux of her internal struggle lay in the delicate dance between her burgeoning affection for him and her fierce, unwavering belief in the sanctity of genuine belonging. She watched him, saw the genuine pride in his eyes when a project at the Collective succeeded, the quiet satisfaction that settled over him like a well-worn blanket. He'd breathed new life into the town, not through grand pronouncements, but through a meticulous application of his skills, a dedication that was both admirable and, she had to admit, incredibly attractive.

Yet, there was a part of her, a persistent, principled part, that recoiled at the thought of him altering his own trajectory solely for Cedar Ridge. He was a man with a life, with ambitions that undoubtedly stretched beyond these quiet streets. To ask him to stay, to implicitly or explicitly pressure him into a commitment he hadn't fully chosen, felt like a violation of the very essence of what drew her to him – his integrity, his authentic self. She cherished the way he navigated their interactions with a thoughtful consideration, a genuine respect for her opinions, even when they differed. She wouldn't be the one to erode that by imposing her own desires.

The journal entry blurred as a wave of longing washed over her. She wanted him to stay, not out of obligation, but out of a desire that stemmed from his own heart. She wanted him to discover, for himself, that Cedar Ridge held something more for him than a successful consultancy. But how to convey that without sounding like a desperate plea, without adding another layer of pressure to the already considerable weight he seemed to carry? He was so accustomed to being the solution-provider, the strategist, the one who brought order to chaos. Could he, she wondered, ever see himself as someone who *belonged*, rather than simply someone who *served*?

Lena closed her eyes, picturing his face. The subtle lines around his eyes that deepened when he smiled, the way his brow furrowed in concentration, the quiet warmth that occasionally flickered in his gaze when he looked at her. These were the details that had woven themselves into the fabric of her days, the small observations that, collectively, had begun to feel like an anchor. She'd seen the ease with which he'd fallen into conversations with the townsfolk, the genuine curiosity he displayed, the way he listened, truly listened, not just to the words but to the unspoken sentiments beneath them. He was adapting, integrating, finding his footing in a way that transcended his professional role.

But was it enough? Was it enough for him? That was the question that gnawed at her. Her own journey to Cedar Ridge had been born of a need for solace, a desire to reconnect with a heritage that felt like a distant echo. She'd found it here, a grounding presence in a world that had often felt too fast, too transient. She understood the quiet pull of a place that offered a sense of continuity, of history, of community. And she saw that Evan, too, was beginning to feel that pull, that subtle magnetism of a life lived at a different pace, with different priorities.

Her fingers stilled on the journal. The conflict wasn't about whether Evan *could* stay, but whether he *should*, and more importantly, whether he *wanted* to, on his own terms. She didn't want to be the architect of his compromise. She wanted him to choose Cedar Ridge, not because she, or anyone else, willed it, but because it resonated with something deep within him, because it offered him a future he actively desired. This meant she had to be a silent observer, a supportive presence, a gentle nudge in the right direction, rather than a forceful hand.

She thought of their conversations, the easy camaraderie that had blossomed between them. There were moments, silences filled with unspoken understanding, glances that lingered a fraction too long, that hinted at something more profound than friendship. And Lena, for the first time in a long time, allowed herself to entertain the possibility of that 'more'. But even as her heart fluttered at the prospect, her mind cautioned restraint. She had to ensure that any future, any potential 'us,' was built on a foundation of mutual respect and genuine desire, not on the shifting sands of obligation.

The external pressure was already mounting, a subtle but pervasive current flowing through the town. People were openly discussing the possibility of Evan's extended stay, their hopes and wishes woven into casual conversations, whispered at the market, and discussed at the diner. Lena heard it all, and while a part of her thrilled at the acknowledgment of his worth, another part felt a pang of unease. She knew Evan's nature. He was driven by logic, by purpose. The idea of being rooted, of staying somewhere simply because it was nice, or because people wanted him, might not be enough to sway his carefully calibrated decision-making process.

She needed him to feel the same sense of belonging she had found, a sense that was not imposed but discovered. She needed him to see the value in the slow burn of a community, the quiet rewards of contributing to something lasting, something that would outlive any contract. And she needed to believe that if he did choose to stay, it would be a choice that honored his own spirit, his own needs, his own definition of a fulfilling life. This meant she had to resist the urge to guide him, to nudge him, to steer him towards a decision that would satisfy her own evolving desires.

The journal lay open, a testament to her internal turmoil. She wanted to write about the ache in her chest when she thought of him leaving, the quiet panic that would grip her if he simply packed his bags and disappeared, a ghost of a memory in Cedar Ridge. But she also wanted to document her resolve, her commitment to allowing him the space to make his own choices, however painful those choices might be for her. It was a tightrope walk, balancing her burgeoning feelings with her deeply held principles.

She thought of the way he'd approached the challenges at the Collective, not with a heavy hand, but with a collaborative spirit, always seeking input, always valuing the existing knowledge within the community. He had a rare gift for making people feel heard, for empowering them. It was this very quality, this respect for autonomy, that she now had to extend to him. She couldn't expect him to honor the autonomy of others if she herself was unwilling to grant him the same courtesy.

The moonlight shifted, casting a softer glow. Lena closed the journal, her decision solidifying like a well-formed stone. She would be his friend, his confidante, the one who listened without judgment. She would offer her perspective, her love for Cedar Ridge, but she would not offer him ultimatums or veiled expectations. His decision would be his alone. And if, by some beautiful twist of fate, he chose to stay, it would be because he had found his own reason, his own belonging, here. And then, and only then, would she allow herself to fully embrace the promise of what might be.

Until then, she would hold her breath, and she would wait, her heart a fragile bird beating against the bars of its cage, hoping for a future that was truly, and freely, chosen. The quiet hum of his presence in town had become a soundtrack to her life, and the thought of that music fading was a prospect she was only just beginning to comprehend, and a prospect she was determined to face with grace, and with unwavering respect for the man who had so unexpectedly captured her attention, and her heart.

The worn leather of the journal felt cool and familiar beneath Lena's fingertips, a silent confidante in the quiet hours of the evening. Moonlight, filtered through the lace curtains of her bedroom, cast dancing shadows across the pages, illuminating the tangled thoughts that had taken up residence in her mind. Evan. The name itself was a soft hum in the chambers of her heart, a melody that had become increasingly difficult to ignore. He was a man of quiet competence, of unwavering dedication, a force of nature that had subtly, irrevocably, altered the rhythm of Cedar Ridge. And Lena, more than most, felt the shift, not just in the town's prosperity, but in the landscape of her own emotions.

She traced the curve of a word, a frustrated sigh escaping her lips. The dilemma wasn't about Evan's potential departure; that was a decision solely his to make. The true crux of her internal struggle lay in the delicate dance between her burgeoning affection for him and her fierce, unwavering belief in the sanctity of genuine belonging. She watched him, saw the genuine pride in his eyes when a project at the Collective succeeded, the quiet satisfaction that settled over him like a well-worn blanket. He'd breathed new life into the town, not through grand pronouncements, but through a meticulous application of his skills, a dedication that was both admirable and, she had to admit, incredibly attractive.

Yet, there was a part of her, a persistent, principled part, that recoiled at the thought of him altering his own trajectory solely for Cedar Ridge. He was a man with a life, with ambitions that undoubtedly stretched beyond these quiet streets. To ask him to stay, to implicitly or explicitly pressure him into a commitment he hadn't fully chosen, felt like a violation of the very essence of what drew her to him – his integrity, his authentic self. She cherished the way he navigated their interactions with a thoughtful consideration, a genuine respect for her opinions, even when they differed. She wouldn't be the one to erode that by imposing her own desires.

The journal entry blurred as a wave of longing washed over her. She wanted him to stay, not out of obligation, but out of a desire that stemmed from his own heart. She wanted him to discover, for himself, that Cedar Ridge held something more for him than a successful consultancy. But how to convey that without sounding like a desperate plea, without adding another layer of pressure to the already considerable weight he seemed to carry? He was so accustomed to being the solution-provider, the strategist, the one who brought order to chaos. Could he, she wondered, ever see himself as someone who *belonged*, rather than simply someone who *served*?

Lena closed her eyes, picturing his face. The subtle lines around his eyes that deepened when he smiled, the way his brow furrowed in concentration, the quiet warmth that occasionally flickered in his gaze when he looked at her. These were the details that had woven themselves into the fabric of her days, the small observations that, collectively, had begun to feel like an anchor. She'd seen the ease with which he'd fallen into conversations with the townsfolk, the genuine curiosity he displayed, the way he listened, truly listened, not just to the words but to the unspoken sentiments beneath them. He was adapting, integrating, finding his footing in a way that transcended his professional role.

But was it enough? Was it enough for him? That was the question that gnawed at her. Her own journey to Cedar Ridge had been born of a need for solace, a desire to reconnect with a heritage that felt like a distant echo. She'd found it here, a grounding presence in a world that had often felt too fast, too transient. She understood the quiet pull of a place that offered a sense of continuity, of history, of community. And she saw that Evan, too, was beginning to feel that pull, that subtle magnetism of a life lived at a different pace, with different priorities.

Her fingers stilled on the journal. The conflict wasn't about whether Evan *could* stay, but whether he *should*, and more importantly, whether he *wanted* to, on his own terms. She didn't want to be the architect of his compromise. She wanted him to choose Cedar Ridge, not because she, or anyone else, willed it, but because it resonated with something deep within him, because it offered him a future he actively desired. This meant she had to be a silent observer, a supportive presence, a gentle nudge in the right direction, rather than a forceful hand.

She thought of their conversations, the easy camaraderie that had blossomed between them. There were moments, silences filled with unspoken understanding, glances that lingered a fraction too long, that hinted at something more profound than friendship. And Lena, for the first time in a long time, allowed herself to entertain the possibility of that 'more'. But even as her heart fluttered at the prospect, her mind cautioned restraint. She had to ensure that any future, any potential 'us,' was built on a foundation of mutual respect and genuine desire, not on the shifting sands of obligation.

The external pressure was already mounting, a subtle but pervasive current flowing through the town. People were openly discussing the possibility of Evan's extended stay, their hopes and wishes woven into casual conversations, whispered at the market, and discussed at the diner. Lena heard it all, and while a part of her thrilled at the acknowledgment of his worth, another part felt a pang of unease. She knew Evan's nature. He was driven by logic, by purpose. The idea of being rooted, of staying somewhere simply because it was nice, or because people wanted him, might not be enough to sway his carefully calibrated decision-making process.

She needed him to feel the same sense of belonging she had found, a sense that was not imposed but discovered. She needed him to see the value in the slow burn of a community, the quiet rewards of contributing to something lasting, something that would outlive any contract. And she needed to believe that if he did choose to stay, it would be a choice that honored his own spirit, his own needs, his own definition of a fulfilling life. This meant she had to resist the urge to guide him, to nudge him, to steer him towards a decision that would satisfy her own evolving desires.

The journal lay open, a testament to her internal turmoil. She wanted to write about the ache in her chest when she thought of him leaving, the quiet panic that would grip her if he simply packed his bags and disappeared, a ghost of a memory in Cedar Ridge. But she also wanted to document her resolve, her commitment to allowing him the space to make his own choices, however painful those choices might be for her. It was a tightrope walk, balancing her burgeoning feelings with her deeply held principles.

She thought of the way he'd approached the challenges at the Collective, not with a heavy hand, but with a collaborative spirit, always seeking input, always valuing the existing knowledge within the community. He had a rare gift for making people feel heard, for empowering them. It was this very quality, this respect for autonomy, that she now had to extend to him. She couldn't expect him to honor the autonomy of others if she herself was unwilling to grant him the same courtesy.

The moonlight shifted, casting a softer glow. Lena closed the journal, her decision solidifying like a well-formed stone. She would be his friend, his confidante, the one who listened without judgment. She would offer her perspective, her love for Cedar Ridge, but she would not offer him ultimatums or veiled expectations. His decision would be his alone. And if, by some beautiful twist of fate, he chose to stay, it would be because he had found his own reason, his own belonging, here.

And then, and only then, would she allow herself to fully embrace the promise of what might be. Until then, she would hold her breath, and she would wait, her heart a fragile bird beating against the bars of its cage, hoping for a future that was truly, and freely, chosen. The quiet hum of his presence in town had become a soundtrack to her life, and the thought of that music fading was a prospect she was only just beginning to comprehend, and a prospect she was determined to face with grace, and with unwavering respect for the man who had so unexpectedly captured her attention, and her heart.

Evan found himself standing at the window of his temporary lodgings, the faint glow of Cedar Ridge's streetlights a familiar, almost comforting, sight. It was a stark contrast to the sterile gleam of cityscapes he'd grown accustomed to, a visual metaphor for the shift occurring within him. For weeks, the thought of his departure had been a constant companion, a silent countdown ticking away the remaining days of his contract. It was the natural order of his professional life: identify a problem, implement a solution, move on to the next challenge. This was the rhythm he understood, the predictable ebb and flow that had defined his existence for so long. Yet, lately, that certainty had begun to fray at the edges, replaced by a disquieting ambivalence.

The initial thrill of possibility, the anticipation of a clean break and the freedom to chase new horizons, had been steadily eroded by an unexpected weight of... obligation? Responsibility? He wasn't entirely sure of the exact nomenclature, but the feeling was undeniable. Cedar Ridge, and more specifically, the Collective, had become more than just a project. It had become a living, breathing entity that relied on his expertise, a cause that had, to his own surprise, ignited a flicker of genuine passion within him. He'd arrived with a carefully constructed plan, a series of logical steps designed to streamline operations and improve efficiency. But somewhere along the line, the cold, hard data had transformed into something more tangible, something with faces and stories and dreams.

He thought of Mrs. Gable, her initial skepticism melting away as she'd described her grandmother's long-forgotten jam recipes. He pictured young Liam, his eyes wide with excitement as he'd helped Evan troubleshoot the irrigation system for the community garden, the pride that had bloomed on his face when he'd finally coaxed the stubborn valve into submission. These were not mere statistics; they were the threads that were weaving themselves into the fabric of his professional purpose, adding a richness and depth he hadn't anticipated. His usual exit strategy, the polished professional detachment, felt increasingly like a betrayal, not just of the town, but of himself.

The idea of leaving now felt less like liberation and more like abandonment. He'd always viewed himself as a catalyst, a temporary force of change. But what if he was becoming something more? What if his impact had extended beyond the measurable improvements in output and revenue, what if he had inadvertently planted roots, however shallow? The thought sent a peculiar jolt through him. Roots implied permanence, a commitment that ran counter to his deeply ingrained migratory instinct. His life had been a series of meticulously curated departures, each one a testament to his ability to adapt and excel in new environments. The notion of willingly foregoing that for the predictable comfort of familiarity felt... alien.

And then there was Lena. Her name surfaced unbidden, a soft counterpoint to the more pragmatic concerns swirling in his mind. He found himself replaying their conversations, the easy flow of their dialogue, the intelligent spark in her eyes when she challenged his assumptions. She saw Cedar Ridge with a clarity that was both refreshing and a little unnerving. She understood its quiet strengths, its enduring spirit, in a way that he, as an outsider, was only beginning to grasp. He'd initially sought her out for her historical knowledge of the town, her insights into its past. But he'd found himself increasingly drawn to her present, to her steady presence, her unwavering belief in the potential of this place.

He'd noticed the subtle shift in her demeanor too, a growing warmth, a certain guarded optimism whenever they spoke. He wasn't oblivious to the undercurrents, the unspoken possibilities that flickered between them during their shared moments. The thought of leaving Cedar Ridge meant leaving her behind, and that prospect now carried a weight that surprised him. It wasn't just a matter of professional completion; it was about the potential for something more, something he hadn't actively sought but was beginning to crave. The idea of returning to his transient lifestyle, to a series of anonymous hotel rooms and fleeting encounters, suddenly felt hollow, devoid of the purpose and connection he'd discovered here.

He sighed, running a hand through his hair. His analytical mind, usually his most trusted tool, was struggling to process this new data. He was programmed for objective assessment, for dispassionate decision-making. But Cedar Ridge, and Lena, had introduced variables that defied his usual algorithms. He found himself weighing the intangible against the tangible, the abstract concept of 'belonging' against the concrete reality of his contractual obligations and his personal history. He had always prided himself on his independence, his self-sufficiency. The idea of relying on anyone, or anything, for his sense of purpose was a foreign concept. Yet, here he was, questioning the very foundations of his existence, drawn by an invisible force to a place he'd initially viewed as a temporary assignment.

He thought back to the meeting with the town council, the earnest pleas for him to extend his consultancy. He'd offered a polite, professional refusal, citing his existing commitments and the need for continuity. But even as the words left his lips, a part of him had recoiled. The idea of simply walking away, of severing ties with the progress he'd helped initiate, felt... wrong. He'd always been good at leaving things better than he found them, but this felt different. This felt like leaving something unfinished, something that still needed him, not just as a consultant, but as someone who cared.

The days that followed were a blur of internal debate. He found himself lingering at the Collective longer than necessary, engaging in conversations that strayed far from operational efficiency. He'd ask about families, about local traditions, about the unspoken hopes and fears that permeated the town. He was gathering data, he told himself, expanding his understanding of the community's needs. But beneath the veneer of professional curiosity, a deeper motivation was at play. He was searching for reasons to stay, for justifications that would allow him to reconcile his ingrained migratory instinct with this nascent sense of rootedness.

He started noticing the small things, the nuances of Cedar Ridge that had previously escaped his notice. The way the light changed on the rolling hills at different times of day, the distinct scent of pine and damp earth after a rain shower, the friendly nods from strangers he passed on the street. These were the markers of a place that was settling into his consciousness, becoming more than just a geographical location. He'd always been adept at observing, at analyzing. Now, he was beginning to feel, to experience.

He found himself looking forward to his interactions with Lena with a quiet anticipation. Their conversations had become a lifeline, a space where he could voice his unspoken doubts without fear of judgment. She possessed a unique ability to listen, not just to his words, but to the unarticulated anxieties that lay beneath. He valued her perspective, her grounded understanding of community, her unwavering faith in the potential of human connection. She didn't offer solutions; she offered understanding, and in his current state of ambivalence, that was more valuable than any strategic plan.

He realized, with a jolt, that his professional definition of success was no longer sufficient. He had always measured his accomplishments by quantifiable metrics, by the impact he had on an organization's bottom line. But Cedar Ridge had shown him a different kind of success, one measured in the smiles of satisfied residents, the renewed sense of pride in a shared endeavor, the quiet hum of a community finding its voice. He had always been the architect of change, the one who initiated it. Now, he was contemplating the possibility of being a part of something that was evolving organically, a process that required patience, and perhaps, a willingness to be changed himself.

The thought of leaving him to his own devices, to navigate his own professional future, was a constant undercurrent in Lena's days. She saw the internal conflict playing out on Evan's face, the subtle tightening of his jaw when the topic of his departure arose, the way his gaze would drift towards the distant horizon as if searching for answers. She understood his need for autonomy, his deeply ingrained habit of moving on. It was a part of his identity, a defining characteristic that had served him well in his career. Yet, she also recognized the burgeoning connection he had formed with Cedar Ridge, a connection that seemed to be pulling him in a new direction.

She watched him at the Collective, saw the genuine pride he took in the success of their initiatives. He had a rare gift for empowering others, for fostering a sense of shared ownership. He didn't impose his will; he collaborated, he listened, he guided. It was this very quality, this respect for the autonomy of others, that made her own internal debate so profound. She wanted him to stay, desperately, but she refused to be the architect of his compromise. His decision, if it came, had to be his own, a genuine choice born from his own evolving desires.

She recalled a conversation they'd had by the riverbank, the setting sun painting the water in hues of orange and gold. He had spoken, tentatively at first, about the transient nature of his work, the constant pursuit of the next challenge. "It's efficient," he'd said, his voice a low murmur, "but sometimes... I wonder what I'm really building." The question had hung in the air, heavy with unspoken longing. Lena had listened, offering no easy answers, no platitudes. She had simply acknowledged the validity of his question, the profound uncertainty that lay beneath his polished exterior.

She saw the growing ambivalence in him, the subtle shift from his initial professional detachment to a more vested interest. He had arrived with a clear objective: to revitalize the Collective. But Cedar Ridge, in its quiet, persistent way, had begun to offer him something more than a successful consultancy. It was offering him a sense of belonging, a tangible connection to a community that was embracing him, not just for his skills, but for the person he was revealing himself to be. He was no longer just the consultant; he was becoming Evan, a valued member of their unfolding narrative.

Lena found herself walking through town with a newfound sense of awareness, observing the subtle ways Evan had impacted its landscape. It wasn't just the increased efficiency at the Collective, or the improved infrastructure. It was in the conversations she overheard at the general store, the hushed whispers of hope and anticipation about his potential to stay. It was in the way people's faces lit up when they spoke of him, a mixture of gratitude and genuine affection. He had, without even realizing it, become an integral part of Cedar Ridge's tapestry.

Her own feelings for him had deepened in tandem with his integration into the town. The initial intrigue had blossomed into a quiet admiration, and then, into something deeper, something that made her heart ache with a mixture of hope and apprehension. She longed for him to stay, not just for the town's sake, but for her own. But she also understood the magnitude of the decision he faced. To stay would mean redefining his entire professional and personal trajectory, a choice that could not be made lightly, or under duress.

She recalled his frustration during one of their late-night meetings at the Collective. He had been wrestling with a particularly complex issue, his usual calm demeanor frayed by the weight of responsibility. Lena had simply sat with him, offering a quiet presence, a cup of tea. He had eventually confessed, "I'm so used to being the one who fixes things, Lena. Sometimes I forget that maybe, just maybe, I don't have to carry it all alone." That vulnerability, that admission of dependence, had struck a chord within her. It was a crack in the facade, a glimpse of the man beneath the skilled strategist.

And now, she saw him grappling with a different kind of dilemma. The external pressure to stay was undeniable, a gentle but persistent tide of goodwill from the townsfolk. He felt their hopes, their implicit request for his continued presence. But his ingrained habit of moving on, of seeking new challenges, was a powerful internal force. He was caught between the allure of the known, the comfort of his nomadic lifestyle, and the burgeoning pull of Cedar Ridge, a place that was offering him something he hadn't realized he was missing.

Lena found herself strategizing, not for Evan's benefit, but for her own peace of mind. She couldn't force his hand, couldn't orchestrate his decision. Her role, she realized, was to offer him the space to discover what he truly wanted, to create an environment where he could hear his own heart above the din of external expectations. She would be a steady presence, a source of quiet encouragement, but the ultimate choice would be his alone. The thought of him leaving was a bitter pill to swallow, a prospect that sent a shiver of unease down her spine. But the thought of him staying out of obligation, out of a sense of duty rather than genuine desire, was a far more painful one. She wanted him to choose Cedar Ridge, not because of her, or anyone else, but because it resonated with something deep within him, because it offered him a future that he actively, unequivocally, desired. This internal conflict was a mirror of Evan's own, a testament to the profound impact he had had, not just on the town, but on her own heart.

The nights had become a canvas for Evan's shifting emotions. He'd lie awake, staring at the unfamiliar ceiling, his mind a battlefield of conflicting desires. The ingrained restlessness, the familiar hum of anticipation for the next adventure, was now being challenged by an equally powerful, and far more unsettling, sense of inertia. He'd always viewed his ability to adapt, to thrive in new environments, as a strength. It was the hallmark of his professional identity. But now, the prospect of packing his bags, of saying goodbye to Cedar Ridge, felt less like an exciting new beginning and more like a profound loss.

He found himself replaying conversations with Lena, dissecting her words, searching for hidden meanings. She had a way of asking questions that subtly nudged him towards introspection, of making him confront the unspoken aspects of his own motivations. He remembered a recent discussion about the town's historical preservation society. Lena had spoken with such passion about the importance of safeguarding Cedar Ridge's heritage, about the deep-seated sense of continuity that it offered its residents. At the time, he'd listened with professional detachment, cataloging the information. But now, those words echoed in his mind, resonating with a newfound significance. He had always been a builder, a creator of new things, but had he ever truly considered the value of preserving, of nurturing what already existed?

The thought of leaving the Collective, of abandoning the projects he'd initiated, felt like a betrayal of the trust that had been placed in him. It wasn't just about completing a contract; it was about seeing things through, about ensuring the sustainability of the improvements he'd helped implement. He'd spent years cultivating an image of efficiency and detachment, a man who delivered results and moved on. But Cedar Ridge was chipping away at that carefully constructed persona, revealing a man who craved something more than just professional success. He craved connection, purpose, a sense of belonging that transcended the transactional nature of his work.

He found himself observing the townsfolk with a new perspective. He no longer saw them as clients or stakeholders, but as individuals with their own stories, their own dreams, their own unique contributions to the community. He saw the quiet pride in Mr. Henderson's eyes as he discussed the upcoming harvest festival, the infectious enthusiasm of the children who flocked to the revitalized playground, the unwavering dedication of Mrs. Gable, who continued to share her family's recipes with anyone willing to learn. These were the threads that held Cedar Ridge together, the intangible bonds that made it more than just a collection of buildings and streets.

And then there was Lena. Her presence in his life had become a grounding force, a quiet anchor in the swirling sea of his indecision. He found himself seeking her out, not for professional advice, but for the simple comfort of her company. Their conversations had a rhythm all their own, a delicate dance of shared thoughts and unspoken understandings. He admired her deep connection to Cedar Ridge, her unwavering belief in its potential. But more than that, he found himself drawn to her quiet strength, her genuine warmth, the way she made him feel seen, truly seen, for the first time in a long time.

The prospect of returning to his old life, to the endless cycle of transient projects and superficial connections, now seemed... unappealing. He'd always embraced the freedom of his nomadic existence, the liberation from any kind of rootedness. But now, that freedom felt like a gilded cage, a testament to his inability to commit, to invest, to truly belong. He had mastered the art of leaving, but he was beginning to question if he had ever truly learned the art of staying.

He found himself lingering at the Collective, not out of obligation, but out of a genuine desire to connect with the people he was working with. He'd initiated informal get-togethers, not for strategic planning, but for simply sharing a meal, sharing stories. He saw the surprise, and then the pleasure, on their faces. He was stepping outside his professional comfort zone, venturing into uncharted territory, and to his astonishment, he found he rather enjoyed it.

The idea of leaving Cedar Ridge was no longer a simple matter of fulfilling a contract. It was becoming a complex emotional equation, a calculation that involved not just professional obligations, but personal desires, burgeoning connections, and a nascent longing for something he couldn't quite articulate. He was at a crossroads, his carefully constructed life beginning to unravel, and for the first time, Evan wasn't entirely sure which path to take. The clarity he usually possessed was clouded by a growing ambivalence, a quiet but persistent doubt that threatened to upend everything he thought he knew about himself and his future. The allure of the unknown, once his sole driving force, was now tinged with the bittersweet possibility of leaving something truly valuable behind.

The air in Cedar Ridge buzzed with the vibrant energy of the annual Summer Solstice Fair. Bunting, strung between the sturdy oak trees that lined Main Street, fluttered a cheerful welcome, a kaleidoscope of reds, yellows, and blues against the impossibly blue sky. Laughter, a joyous symphony, spilled from the bustling stalls, mingling with the sweet, nostalgic scent of cotton candy and freshly baked pies. Evan, a casual observer on the periphery of the jubilant scene, felt an unfamiliar sense of detachment, a lingering dissonance from his internal debate. He was here, physically present, but a part of him remained locked in the silent wrestling match that had consumed him for weeks.

He watched Lena from across the town square. She was at the historical society's booth, a charmingly rustic display of old photographs and handwritten letters, her hands gracefully arranging a display of intricately embroidered linens. The sunlight caught the auburn highlights in her hair, transforming them into a halo of spun gold. She was speaking with Mrs. Gable, her head tilted slightly, a genuine smile gracing her lips. Even from this distance, Evan could sense the warmth radiating from her, the effortless way she connected with the older woman, her gaze attentive, her voice soft and reassuring. It was a tableau of quiet contentment, a scene steeped in the very essence of belonging that had begun to intrigue him.

He'd seen Lena engage with the town in countless ways since his arrival. She was a constant, a steadfast presence, her contributions woven seamlessly into the fabric of Cedar Ridge. He'd observed her meticulously organizing the town's centennial archives, her dedication to preserving the past a testament to her deep respect for its roots. He'd seen her patiently guiding newcomers through the labyrinthine process of navigating local bureaucracy, her innate kindness a bridge between the unfamiliar and the accepted. And here she was, at the heart of a community celebration, not as an organizer, but as an integral, beloved part of its very soul.

There was a profound difference between him and Lena, a fundamental divergence in their approaches to life and work. He was a strategist, a problem-solver, someone who arrived, implemented, and departed, leaving behind a trail of improved efficiencies and optimized systems. His successes were quantifiable, measurable, etched in balance sheets and progress reports. He had always prided himself on his adaptability, his ability to seamlessly integrate into any environment, to achieve his objectives, and then to move on, unburdened by attachment. It was a life of deliberate transience, a series of meticulously planned departures.

Lena, however, was a cultivator. She planted seeds of connection, nurtured relationships, and patiently waited for them to blossom. Her impact wasn't measured in immediate results or tangible outputs, but in the slow, steady growth of community, in the deepening of shared purpose, in the quiet satisfaction of knowing she was contributing to something enduring. Her happiness, Evan realized with a sudden, sharp clarity, wasn't derived from the thrill of the next challenge, but from the quiet joy of being rooted, of being a part of something that was larger and more significant than herself.

He saw it in the way she interacted with everyone around her – the easy camaraderie she shared with Mr. Henderson, who was manning the pie-tasting stall, her laughter mingling with his booming chuckle; the gentle way she reassured a frazzled young mother whose child had wandered too close to the bouncy castle; the genuine interest she displayed in the children who tugged at her skirt, eager to show her their painted faces and glitter-dusted hands. She wasn't performing; she was simply *being*, her authentic self radiating a warmth that drew people in, that made them feel seen and valued.

Evan found himself comparing Lena's interactions to his own. He could facilitate a productive meeting, he could negotiate a complex deal, he could devise an ingenious solution to a logistical nightmare. But could he elicit that same spontaneous warmth, that same effortless connection?

He had always viewed emotional engagement as a potential distraction, a deviation from the objective pursuit of goals. He had built a career on maintaining a professional distance, on keeping his emotions carefully compartmentalized. But watching Lena, he began to question the true efficacy of his approach. Was a life lived solely in pursuit of transient achievements truly fulfilling?

He thought back to the hours he'd spent at the Collective, meticulously analyzing data, streamlining processes, and implementing new systems. He'd achieved the quantifiable goals he'd set out to accomplish. The Collective was more efficient, more profitable, more effective. But had he truly connected with the heart of the organization, with the people who poured their lives and dreams into its mission? He had provided solutions, but had he fostered a sense of shared purpose? Had he, in his relentless pursuit of improvement, inadvertently overlooked the very thing that made the Collective thrive – the human element, the deep-seated commitment of its members?

The image of Lena, bathed in the golden light of the summer sun, stood in stark contrast to his own internal landscape. He saw her as an embodiment of what he had unconsciously been searching for, a tangible representation of a different kind of success, a success measured not by profit margins, but by the depth of one's roots, the strength of one's connections, the quiet joy of contributing to something enduring. He had always believed that his independence was his greatest asset, his ability to navigate life without the burden of attachment. But now, he was beginning to see that same independence as a form of isolation, a self-imposed barrier to genuine fulfillment.

He watched as a young boy, no older than six, ran up to Lena, a triumphant grin on his face, holding out a clumsily drawn picture of a sun with a smiling face. Lena knelt down, her eyes crinkling at the corners as she looked at the drawing. "Oh, that's beautiful, Leo!" she exclaimed, her voice brimming with genuine delight. "You've captured the sunshine perfectly." She praised his efforts, her words encouraging and sincere, and the boy beamed, his small chest puffing out with pride.

Evan felt a pang of something akin to envy. He had never experienced that kind of unadulterated joy, that simple pleasure derived from fostering another person's happiness. His own achievements, while significant in his professional sphere, often felt hollow in comparison. They were milestones, boxes to be checked, steps on a ladder that seemed to stretch endlessly upwards, with no discernible summit. Lena, on the other hand, found her fulfillment in the smaller moments, in the quiet acts of kindness, in the tangible impact she had on the lives of those around her.

He had always viewed his professional life as a series of well-executed missions, each one a testament to his skill and efficiency. He was a man who delivered results, a man who solved problems. But watching Lena, he realized that true fulfillment wasn't about solving problems; it was about building something that mattered, something that would outlast his own involvement. It was about planting seeds, not just reaping harvests. It was about cultivating relationships, not just managing projects.

The realization settled upon him, not with the suddenness of a thunderclap, but with the quiet inevitability of a rising tide. His life, for all its outward success, had been characterized by a profound lack of genuine belonging. He had been a perpetual outsider, a skilled observer, a temporary participant. He had excelled at blending in, at adapting, at becoming whoever he needed to be to achieve his objectives. But he had never truly *belonged*. He had never found a place where his presence was not merely tolerated, but cherished, where his contributions were not just valued, but deeply appreciated.

He saw the effortless way Lena navigated her interactions, her confidence stemming not from arrogance, but from a deep-seated understanding of her place in the world. She was not seeking external validation; she was deriving her sense of worth from within, from her commitment to her community, from the genuine connections she had forged. She was a living, breathing embodiment of what it meant to be rooted, to be a part of something larger than oneself, and the appeal of that existence, once alien and uninteresting, now felt profoundly seductive.

He thought of his own transient existence, the endless cycle of hotel rooms, airport lounges, and impersonal office spaces. He had always rationalized it as a sign of his freedom, his independence. But now, he saw it for what it truly was: a manifestation of his fear of commitment, his inability to truly invest himself in any one place or any one person. He had been so busy chasing the horizon that he had failed to notice the beauty of the landscape that lay at his feet.

Lena's interaction with a group of children gathered around the historical society's booth provided another poignant illustration. They were fascinated by the old photographs, their young minds struggling to comprehend a world without smartphones and instant communication. Lena patiently explained the context of each image, her voice animated as she described the lives of the people who had inhabited Cedar Ridge generations before. She wasn't just sharing historical facts; she was weaving a narrative, connecting the past to the present, and in doing so, instilling in these young minds a sense of continuity, a profound understanding of their place in a long and rich lineage.

Evan felt a stir of something akin to yearning. He had always been the one to look forward, to innovate, to push boundaries. But Lena's focus on the past, on the enduring legacy of those who came before, offered a different perspective, a crucial counterpoint to his own forward-thinking approach. He realized that true progress wasn't just about forging ahead; it was also about understanding where one came from, about honoring the foundations upon which the present was built.

He observed the ease with which Lena accepted a plate of cookies from Mrs. Gable, her gratitude evident in her smile. It was a simple exchange, a fleeting moment, but it spoke volumes about the nature of their relationship, a relationship built on mutual respect, shared history, and genuine affection. He had always operated on a more transactional basis, his interactions dictated by the demands of his work. The idea of engaging in such casual, unscripted exchanges, of simply enjoying the company of others without an ulterior motive, felt both foreign and strangely appealing.

The fairground was a tapestry of interconnected lives, a vibrant illustration of what he had been missing. He saw the shared laughter between friends, the comforting embraces of family members, the quiet nods of acknowledgment between neighbors. These were the threads that bound Cedar Ridge together, the invisible bonds that created a sense of collective identity. He had always been a solitary figure, an island unto himself, his successes and failures borne in isolation. But here, surrounded by the warmth of human connection, he felt a profound sense of his own solitude, a stark realization of the emptiness that had characterized his carefully constructed life.

As the afternoon wore on, Evan found himself drawn closer to the heart of the fair, his initial detachment slowly giving way to a reluctant curiosity. He saw Lena again, this time at the community garden's information booth, her face flushed with a healthy glow from the sun. She was discussing the benefits of composting with a group of enthusiastic young gardeners, her passion for the earth evident in her every word. She wasn't just sharing knowledge; she was inspiring a generation, instilling in them a love for nature, a respect for the environment.

He realized that Lena's contributions, while often quiet and understated, were deeply impactful. She wasn't seeking recognition or accolades; her reward lay in the knowledge that she was making a tangible difference in the lives of others, in the growth and well-being of her community. It was a profound lesson in the true meaning of purpose, a revelation that resonated deeply within him. He had always equated success with outward achievement, with the attainment of ambitious goals. But Lena's example showed him a different path, a path paved with genuine connection, with selfless contribution, with the quiet satisfaction of knowing that one's life had a purpose beyond the pursuit of personal gain.

He watched as she patiently answered a question from a young girl about the best way to grow tomatoes, her explanation clear and encouraging. The girl's face lit up with understanding, her small hand already sketching out plans in a notebook. It was a microcosm of Lena's influence – fostering growth, inspiring confidence, and nurturing a love for the simple, profound act of cultivation. Evan found himself reflecting on his own professional life. He had always focused on optimizing systems, on increasing efficiency. But had he ever truly considered the human element, the cultivation of individual potential, the nurturing of collective growth?

The summer sun began its slow descent, casting long shadows across the town square. The laughter and chatter softened, replaced by a more contented hum. Evan remained on the periphery, an observer no longer detached, but deeply engrossed. He had come to Cedar Ridge with a clear objective: to implement a solution, to achieve a measurable outcome, and then to move on. But he had inadvertently stumbled upon something far more profound, something that had begun to unravel the very foundations of his carefully constructed identity.

He saw Lena sharing a quiet moment with a group of friends, their conversation punctuated by easy laughter. She was not the focal point, not the center of attention, but an integral part of their shared experience, a thread woven seamlessly into the fabric of their lives. Her belonging was not a performance; it was an inherent quality, a reflection of her deep connection to this place and its people.

In that moment, bathed in the soft, fading light of the summer solstice, Evan understood. He understood the profound difference between transient success and meaningful engagement. He understood the quiet allure of belonging, the deep-seated human need to be a part of something larger than oneself. He had spent years mastering the art of leaving, of moving on, of shedding attachments. But watching Lena, he realized that the true art of living lay not in perpetual motion, but in the courage to put down roots, to invest oneself in a community, to find one's purpose in the quiet, enduring beauty of belonging.

The carefully constructed walls he had built around his heart began to crumble, revealing a landscape he had long ignored, a landscape yearning for the same kind of cultivation, the same kind of connection, the same kind of belonging that Lena so effortlessly embodied. The path ahead remained uncertain, but for the first time, Evan felt a flicker of hope, a nascent desire to explore the possibility of a different kind of life, a life where leaving was not the ultimate goal, but a distant memory, overshadowed by the profound and enduring power of staying.

CHAPTER SIX

The Question of Freedom

Evan's internal monologue, usually a well-ordered ledger of pros and cons, had become a churning vortex since his arrival in Cedar Ridge. He'd spent his entire adult life building a fortress of independence, brick by meticulously placed brick. His philosophy, as solid and unyielding as the skyscrapers he'd navigated, was simple: freedom was found in the absence of anchors. It was the glorious, unburdened ability to pivot, to explore, to simply *go*. Staying put, in his estimation, was a slow surrender, a voluntary abdication of potential. It was the comfortable cage of routine, the velvet-lined trap of familiarity, and for Evan, it was the antithesis of a life well-lived.

He traced the rim of his coffee mug, the ceramic cool against his fingertips. This belief wasn't a recent acquisition; it was the bedrock of his identity, forged in the crucible of constant professional relocation. Each new city, each new project, had been a fresh canvas, an opportunity to redefine himself, to test the limits of his adaptability. He'd seen it as a badge of honor, this perpetual motion.

The ability to detach, to sever ties cleanly and efficiently, was not a weakness but a strength, a testament to his self-sufficiency. He'd prided himself on not being beholden to any one place, any one set of circumstances. Why would anyone choose to limit their horizons when the world was a vast expanse of untapped possibilities? To remain in one place felt like willingly clipping one's own wings, settling for a single melody when a symphony was available. The very notion of 'roots' struck him as an unnecessary entanglement, a self-imposed tether that would inevitably restrict his ability to soar.

His professional life had been a masterclass in this ideology. He'd been the quintessential problem-solver, the consultant who arrived with a polished strategy, executed with ruthless efficiency, and then, with a polite nod and a completed report, vanished. The satisfaction came not from the lingering presence of his solutions, but from the clean break, the knowledge that he had made his mark and then gracefully exited, leaving the established order to carry on. This nomadic existence had instilled in him a deep-seated aversion to obligation.

Obligations were liabilities, points of potential failure, emotional baggage that weighed down the spirit. He viewed the world through the lens of choices, and his primary choice had always been the freedom to choose *again*. The path of least resistance, he believed, was often the path that led to stagnation. He saw himself as a navigator of opportunities, constantly charting new courses, and a fixed point on a map felt like a surrender to the inevitable.

He remembered conversations with colleagues, friends, even fleeting acquaintances, who spoke of the comfort of routine, the security of a familiar environment. They spoke of small-town charm, of knowing your neighbors, of a predictable rhythm. For Evan, these were alien concepts, the whispers of a life he had actively, and with considerable satisfaction, avoided. He saw their contentment as a quiet form of resignation, a settling for less. He'd always felt a subtle impatience with their perceived limitations, a mild bewilderment at their willingness to trade the infinite for the finite. The thrill, for him, was in the unknown, the challenge of adapting to new landscapes, both physical and social.

This ingrained perspective bled into his personal life, or rather, his carefully managed lack thereof. Relationships, he'd learned early on, were complex ecosystems. They required nurturing, compromise, and a willingness to be vulnerable – all things that ran counter to his meticulously constructed independence. The potential for heartbreak, for disappointment, was too great a risk. Why invest so deeply when the inevitable end, in his worldview, was departure? It was far more efficient, far more self-preserving, to maintain a respectful distance, to engage on a surface level, and to always, always have an escape route clearly marked. He saw this not as a failing, but as a shrewd act of self-preservation. His freedom was a precious commodity, and he was its diligent guardian.

He'd often thought of his life as a series of perfectly executed maneuvers, each one a calculated risk that paid off handsomely. He was the architect of his own destiny, and that destiny was one of perpetual motion. The idea of putting down roots, of becoming inextricably linked to a single location, felt like a betrayal of his own agency. It was the surrender of his most valuable asset: his ability to move. He was a bird in flight, not a statue on a pedestal. The world was his to explore, and Cedar Ridge, while possessing a certain rustic allure, was just another temporary stop on a much grander itinerary. He viewed the commitment to a single place as a sacrifice of experiences, a deliberate dimming of the vast spectrum of life's potential. Every town he bypassed, every opportunity he declined by staying put, represented a loss of potential growth, a forfeiture of the lessons learned from navigating the unfamiliar.

His very definition of success was tied to his mobility. Success was the ability to adapt, to thrive in any environment, and then to move on, leaving behind a legacy of improved systems and optimized outcomes. It was a career built on the premise that the best solution was always the next one, the one that lay just over the horizon. He associated staying in one place with a kind of professional complacency, a lack of ambition. It was the opposite of progress, a plateau in the ascent. He felt, in a way, that he owed it to himself to see and experience as much as he possibly could. To confine himself to one town, even one as charming as Cedar Ridge, would be to deliberately limit his understanding of the world, to trade breadth for depth in a way he found unappealing.

He took another sip of his coffee, the slightly bitter taste a familiar comfort. This internal dialogue, this justification of his life's trajectory, was an old friend. He'd had this conversation with himself countless times before, usually in the quiet hours of hotel rooms or the sterile anonymity of airport lounges. But here, in Cedar Ridge, amidst the gentle hum of a community that seemed to value stillness, his arguments felt... less convincing. They were well-rehearsed, certainly, but the conviction behind them was starting to fray at the edges, like a well-worn map.

He believed that true freedom was inextricably linked to the absence of obligation, to the unimpeded ability to choose one's path at any given moment. This wasn't a cynical view, but a practical one, born from years of orchestrating his own existence. He saw himself as a craftsman of his own life, and his primary tool was his mobility. The ability to depart, to shed the skin of a previous identity and adopt a new one, was the ultimate expression of self-determination. He viewed the concept of 'settling down' not as a comfort, but as a surrender, a concession to the perceived limitations of a fixed existence.

He believed that staying in one place was akin to choosing to live in a single room when an entire mansion, filled with unexplored corridors and hidden treasures, awaited. The potential for discovery, for personal evolution, lay in the journey, not in the destination. His entire identity was woven from the threads of his travels, each stamp in his passport a testament to his commitment to the pursuit of new experiences and the expansion of his own capabilities. He equated stagnation with a kind of death, a cessation of growth, and therefore, a diminishment of his very being.

Lena watched Evan, his brow furrowed in thought as he stirred his coffee, a familiar gesture that spoke of a mind perpetually at work. He carried his conviction about freedom like a well-worn coat, something he'd tailored to fit him perfectly, yet it seemed to chafe against the contours of Cedar Ridge. His belief in freedom as the unfettered ability to leave, to detach, to remain unburdened by anchors, was a philosophy he'd articulated with compelling logic, and Lena understood its appeal. She'd seen its manifestation in his life, the clean lines of his career, the carefully curated independence. But as she listened, a counter-melody began to form in her mind, a different kind of freedom, one that resonated with the quiet hum of the town she called home.

"Freedom," Lena began, her voice soft but firm, "isn't just about the ability to leave, Evan. It's also about the courage to stay." She met his gaze, her eyes reflecting the morning light filtering through the cafe window. "It's about choosing to plant yourself, to dig your roots deep into the soil, even when you have the wings to fly anywhere you please." She paused, letting the words settle between them, a stark contrast to his own carefully constructed definitions. "For me, freedom isn't the absence of anchors. It's about consciously choosing the anchors that bind you, the ones that tether you to something meaningful, something you're willing to invest in."

Evan's expression shifted, a subtle widening of his eyes that suggested he was genuinely considering her words, even if a flicker of ingrained skepticism remained. Lena pressed on, elaborating on this alternative perspective. "Think about it. When you're constantly on the move, always ready to pivot, there's a certain thrill, I get that. It's the excitement of the unknown, the vastness of possibility. But what do you gain from that perpetual motion? What do you *build*?" She gestured with her hands, illustrating her point. "True freedom, for me, is found in the deliberate act of building. It's in making a conscious choice to be part of something larger than yourself, to contribute to a community, to nurture relationships, to take responsibility for the impact you have."

She spoke of her own life in Cedar Ridge, not as a limitation, but as a chosen path, a deliberate engagement. "When I decided to open the bakery here, it wasn't an escape from anything, it was an embrace of everything Cedar Ridge offered. It was the promise of connection, the opportunity to become a familiar face, a reliable presence. That, to me, is freedom. The freedom to show up, day after day, and make a difference, however small." She leaned forward slightly, her tone earnest. "It's about recognizing that your actions have ripples, and choosing to create positive ones. It's about the freedom that comes from knowing you're indispensable, not in a way that burdens you, but in a way that fulfills you. It's the freedom of purpose."

Lena elaborated on the idea of intentionality. "It's easy to drift, Evan. To let life happen to you. But the real freedom, the profound kind, comes from steering your own ship. And sometimes, steering your ship means charting a course *into* a harbor, not just sailing away from it. It's about choosing where you want to dock, where you want to build your life, and then dedicating yourself to making that place better.

It's about the agency in saying, 'This is my home, this is my community, and I am committed to its well-being.'" She smiled, a gentle, knowing smile. "It's a different kind of adventure, I'll grant you. It's not about scaling new peaks every week, but about tending the garden you've cultivated. And there's a deep satisfaction in that, a sense of belonging that no amount of travel can replicate."

Her perspective on responsibility was also a stark contrast to Evan's aversion to obligation. "I don't see responsibility as a cage," she explained, "but as the framework for genuine freedom. When you take on responsibility for your family, for your neighbors, for the town's future, you're not limiting yourself, you're expanding your capacity for impact. You're giving yourself a reason to be here, a purpose that transcends your own immediate needs or desires. This creates a different kind of freedom – the freedom from existential loneliness, the freedom from the constant gnawing question of 'what's next?' You already know what's next, and it's something you've actively chosen to build."

Lena also touched upon the emotional depth that came with commitment. "Staying also allows for vulnerability, doesn't it? When you're always leaving, you're always protecting yourself. You keep people at arm's length, because getting too close means more pain when you go. But if you choose to stay, you allow yourself to be truly known. You open yourself up to the possibility of deep connection, to love, to friendship that can withstand the storms. That kind of emotional freedom, the freedom to love and be loved without reservation, is something you can't find on the road. It's built over time, through shared experiences, through weathering difficulties together."

She spoke of the intricate web of relationships that formed the fabric of a community like Cedar Ridge. "Every person here is connected, in ways big and small. When someone is struggling, others step in. When there's a celebration, everyone participates. That interconnectedness, that mutual reliance, isn't a weakness, it's a source of immense strength. It's a different kind of freedom, Evan. The freedom of knowing you're not alone, the freedom of belonging to a tribe. It's a quiet freedom, perhaps, not as flashy as yours, but it's a freedom that sustains you, that nourishes your soul."

Lena then addressed the idea of personal growth through contribution. "You talk about growth through new experiences, and that's valid. But there's also growth that comes from deep engagement. When you commit to a place, you're forced to confront your limitations in new ways. You have to learn to navigate complex relationships, to compromise, to find solutions that work for everyone, not just for yourself. That kind of growth, the growth of character, is profoundly transformative. It shapes you into a better version of yourself, not just a more experienced one."

She considered the quiet satisfaction of contribution. "Imagine the feeling of seeing a project you helped champion come to fruition, or witnessing a neighbor you supported overcome a challenge. That's a tangible reward, a sense of accomplishment that comes from being an active participant, not just a transient observer. It's the freedom of making a lasting impact, of leaving a legacy that's more than just a completed report. It's about weaving your story into the larger narrative of a place."

Lena's words hung in the air, a gentle challenge to Evan's deeply ingrained worldview. She wasn't dismissing his definition of freedom, but offering an expanded one, one that embraced commitment, responsibility, and the profound rewards of belonging. She saw his restlessness, his drive for new horizons, but she also saw the potential for a different kind of fulfillment, one that lay in the deliberate choice to stay and to grow where he was planted.Her perspective was rooted in the quiet strength of community, in the enduring power of connection, and in the deep, abiding freedom that came from choosing to be truly present in the world.

She believed that the richest experiences weren't always found in the act of leaving, but in the courageous, intentional decision to stay, to contribute, and to become an integral part of something that mattered. It was a freedom that asked for more, but in return, offered a depth of experience and a richness of life that she believed was unparalleled. She was offering him a different lens through which to view his own life, a possibility that his meticulously constructed fortress of independence might have inadvertently excluded something vital, something essential to a truly full and meaningful existence. The gentle persuasion in her voice was not about conversion, but about offering an alternative, a resonant counterpoint to his own, a melody that spoke of a different kind of liberation, one found not in escaping, but in embracing.

Evan remained silent for a long moment, his gaze fixed on the swirling patterns in his half-empty coffee cup. The air in the cafe, usually a comfortable hum of morning chatter and the hiss of the espresso machine, felt charged, thick with unspoken thoughts. Lena's words had landed not like a criticism, but like a gentle unveiling, a mirroring of a vague disquiet that had begun to stir within him. He'd always prided himself on his foresight, on his ability to anticipate outcomes, to strategize his way through life. Yet, Lena's articulation of freedom – the freedom *to stay*, the freedom *to build* – had pricked at a fundamental assumption he'd held about his own existence.

"You're right," he finally conceded, the words feeling heavy on his tongue. He looked up, meeting Lena's steady gaze. "I've always seen my ability to leave as the ultimate expression of freedom. The freedom from obligation, from entanglement. The power to simply... opt out. It's a very efficient way to avoid pain, to avoid disappointment. If you never plant anything deeply, you can't be truly devastated when it's uprooted." He traced the rim of his cup, a faint tremor in his fingers. "But I suppose," he continued, his voice dropping to a near whisper, "that efficiency comes at a cost. A cost I hadn't fully accounted for."

He thought about the trail of superficial connections he'd left in his wake. Friendships that had never quite solidified, romantic relationships that had flickered and died as soon as the first hint of permanence loomed. He'd been so focused on not being tied down that he'd inadvertently built himself a gilded cage of solitude. "I've been so adept at avoiding roots," he admitted, a wry smile touching his lips, "that I've perhaps forgotten how to grow. Or rather, how to grow *with* something. With someone."

The thought was unsettling. His life had been a series of deliberate choices, each one designed to maximize his autonomy. He'd excelled in his career, amassed a comfortable fortune, and experienced a vast array of landscapes. By all external measures, he was a success. Yet, a persistent, hollow echo had begun to resonate within him, a feeling that something vital was missing.

"Perhaps my freedom has been less about liberation and more about... avoidance," he mused, the realization dawning slowly. "I've been so focused on not being trapped that I haven't considered what I might be missing by *not* being bound. Not bound by debt, or by a demanding job, or by a difficult relationship, yes. But also, not bound by purpose, by shared history, by the quiet satisfaction of contributing to something that will outlast me." He looked out the window, watching a group of children laughing as they chased a stray dog down the street. Their exuberance felt alien, a world away from his carefully controlled existence. "There's a certain bravery in that choice, Lena. To choose to stay. To choose to be vulnerable. To choose to invest yourself in a place, in people, knowing that it comes with the very real possibility of getting hurt."

He turned back to her, a genuine curiosity in his eyes. "You spoke of this 'freedom of purpose' you find here. Can you... can you elaborate on that? What does that feel like, day to day? Is it truly... fulfilling?" He was grappling with the idea that his pursuit of an absolute, untethered freedom might have inadvertently led him to a less rich, less profound form of existence. He'd always associated growth with movement, with acquiring new skills and experiences. Lena's perspective suggested a different kind of growth, one that happened in place, through deepening engagement.

Lena took a slow sip of her tea, her expression thoughtful. She understood Evan's perspective; she'd seen its allure in her own life before Cedar Ridge. There had been times, especially in her early twenties, when the world had beckoned with a siren song of endless possibilities. The desire to see and experience everything, to remain unburdened by the expectations of a small town, had been a powerful pull. She'd even entertained the idea of moving to a larger city, of pursuing a more ambitious career path. But something had held her back. A quiet voice, perhaps, or a deeper instinct.

"It's not always a grand, earth-shattering feeling, Evan," she began, her voice soft. "It's more like a steady hum. A deep, underlying current of knowing. When I open the bakery every morning, I know why I'm doing it. It's not just to bake bread; it's to provide a service, to be a reliable part of people's routines. Mrs. Gable, who's been coming in for her sourdough every Tuesday for ten years, she's not just a customer; she's part of the fabric of my day. Her smile, her small talk about her garden – that's part of the purpose."

She gestured around the cafe, encompassing the scattered patrons. "It's in the interactions. Mr. Henderson, who always orders the same black coffee and reads his newspaper from front to back. Sarah, the young waitress, who's saving up for nursing school and is so eager to learn. I see their struggles, their triumphs, their everyday lives unfolding, and I'm a small, consistent part of it. I'm not just serving them; I'm participating in their lives, in a quiet, unassuming way."

Lena leaned forward, her gaze earnest. "And it's not just about the people. It's about the place itself. When a new business opens downtown, there's a collective ripple of excitement, and maybe a little anxiety too. When the town council debates a new park project, there's a genuine investment from so many people because they'll be the ones using it, their children will play there. That shared investment, that collective ownership – that's where the purpose lies. It's the feeling that your efforts, your presence, contribute to the well-being of something larger than yourself."

She thought about the time the old oak tree in the town square had been struck by lightning. The community had rallied, not just to clear the debris, but to find ways to preserve what remained, to plant saplings, to ensure its legacy. Lena had been there, donating flour for the bake sale that raised funds for the tree's preservation. "That kind of collective action, that shared commitment to preserving and improving what we have – that's incredibly powerful. It's a tangible manifestation of purpose. It's knowing that you're not just a tenant in the world, but a steward. And there's a deep sense of fulfillment in that, a sense that your life has meaning beyond your own immediate gratification."

Lena acknowledged Evan's point about vulnerability. "You're right about the fear of getting hurt," she conceded. "When you commit to staying, you open yourself up to more potential pain. You become more susceptible to the losses that life inevitably brings. My grandmother passed away last year, and it was devastating. If I had been someone who constantly moved, I might have experienced that loss more distantly, perhaps even felt a sense of relief that it wouldn't tie me down. But because she was *here*, because she was a constant presence in my life, the grief was profound. And yet," she smiled a small, bittersweet smile, "that profound grief was also a testament to the profound love and connection that existed. It was the price of admission for a life deeply lived."

She paused, considering her own fear of the unknown, a subtle counterpoint to Evan's fear of being tied down. "And in turn," Lena continued, her voice thoughtful, "I wonder if my own steadfastness has sometimes made me a little... cautious. A little afraid of stepping too far outside the familiar. When you've built something solid, something you can rely on, the prospect of dismantling it, of venturing into entirely uncharted territory, can feel overwhelming. There's a comfort in routine, a safety in predictability. Perhaps, in my desire for security and belonging, I've sometimes shied away from the exhilarating chaos of pure exploration. The very freedom you champion, Evan – the freedom to embrace the unexpected, to reinvent yourself on a whim – that's a freedom I might have unconsciously suppressed."

She admitted that her perspective, while deeply felt, could also be myopic. "My world is Cedar Ridge. My focus is on what happens here, on the people and the rhythms of this town. And that's a good thing, for the most part. But it can also mean I miss the bigger picture, the wider currents shaping the world beyond our valley. I can get so caught up in the details of the community that I forget there's a whole universe of experiences and ideas out there that I haven't even begun to touch. It's a different kind of limitation, isn't it? Not being tied down, but perhaps being too firmly planted."

Evan listened intently, the nuances of Lena's perspective resonating deeply. He saw the truth in her admission, the subtle acknowledgment of her own potential limitations. It wasn't a matter of one being right and the other wrong, but of two equally valid, yet vastly different, approaches to life. His pursuit of freedom had been about maximizing options, about maintaining the ability to pivot. Lena's had been about deepening engagement, about cultivating meaning within a chosen context.

"So, it's a balance, then?" Evan ventured, the question hanging in the air. "A constant negotiation between the desire for autonomy and the need for connection? Between the pull of the horizon and the anchor of home?"

Lena nodded slowly. "I think so. Perhaps true freedom isn't found in an absolute adherence to one extreme, but in finding a personal equilibrium. In understanding the value of both the open road and the rooted hearth. In recognizing that the courage to stay can be as profound as the courage to leave, and that the growth that comes from deep roots can be just as significant as the growth that comes from new soil." She looked at him, a gentle smile playing on her lips. "You've shown me the beauty of embracing the unknown, Evan. The exhilarating possibilities that lie beyond the familiar. And you've made me question if I've perhaps held onto my own sense of security a little too tightly."

Evan felt a shift within him, a softening of the rigid boundaries he'd erected around his life. Lena's words weren't a judgment, but an invitation to a broader understanding. He saw that his meticulously crafted independence, while offering a certain kind of liberation, had also served as a barrier. A barrier to the messy, unpredictable, and profoundly rewarding nature of genuine human connection.

"And you've shown me," he said, his voice imbued with a newfound sincerity, "that 'anchors' don't always have to be chains. They can be foundations. They can be the very things that give life weight, that give it substance. I've always seen commitment as a constraint, but you've helped me see it as a catalyst. A catalyst for purpose, for belonging, for a kind of fulfillment I haven't allowed myself to experience."

He considered the possibility of weaving his own narrative into the tapestry of Cedar Ridge, not as an outsider passing through, but as a contributor, a participant. The idea was both daunting and strangely exhilarating. It meant relinquishing some of his hard-won autonomy, embracing a degree of vulnerability he'd long avoided. But it also promised a richness, a depth, that his life had, until now, lacked.

"The question of freedom," Evan continued, more to himself than to Lena, "is far more complex than I ever allowed myself to believe. It's not a simple binary choice between leaving and staying. It's about the conscious decision of *how* you choose to be free. And perhaps," he looked at Lena, a flicker of hope in his eyes, "perhaps there are different kinds of freedom, and I've been so focused on one, I've missed the profound beauty of another."

He felt a sense of gratitude for Lena's willingness to share her perspective, to challenge his deeply ingrained beliefs without judgment. Her quiet strength, her unwavering conviction in the value of connection and community, had opened a door in his mind that he hadn't even realized was closed. He realized that his journey of self-discovery wasn't about finding a new destination, but about redefining what it meant to arrive, to belong, and to truly live. The implications of this conversation stretched far beyond the cozy confines of the cafe; they touched the very core of his identity and the future he might choose to build. He was no longer just an observer of life, but a potential participant, and the idea, though terrifying, was also undeniably liberating.

Lena smiled, a genuine warmth radiating from her. "It takes courage to see things differently, Evan. And it takes a willingness to be open to what that difference might mean." She reached across the table, her fingers lightly brushing his. "Perhaps freedom isn't about having all the options, but about choosing the ones that truly nourish your soul. And sometimes," she added, her eyes twinkling, "those are the choices that require the most bravery." The unspoken invitation hung between them – to explore this newfound understanding, to see if the rigid lines of his carefully constructed life could indeed soften, making room for the vibrant, messy, and deeply meaningful connections that Cedar Ridge, and perhaps Lena herself, had to offer. The conversation had moved beyond abstract philosophy and into the realm of personal possibility, a space where the questions of freedom and belonging could intertwine, creating a future that neither of them had previously envisioned.

The weight of responsibility settled upon Evan's shoulders not like a sudden burden, but like a slow, insidious seep, gradually saturating the very fabric of his being. He had arrived in Cedar Ridge with a carefully constructed exit strategy, a mental blueprint that accounted for every variable except one: the undeniable, emergent impact he had on the lives of others. His initial objective had been to fix what was broken, to inject efficiency and vision into the struggling agricultural collective, and then, with a clean break, to return to his predictable, untethered existence. But Lena's quiet observations, the genuine gratitude in the eyes of the collective's members, and the sheer, tangible progress they had made together had begun to chip away at his carefully erected defenses.

He found himself staring at spreadsheets detailing the collective's renewed profitability, the optimistic projections for crop yields, and the meticulous plans for expanding their market reach. These were not just numbers; they were the fruits of sustained effort, of collaborative problem-solving, of a shared vision that had, against his initial cynical predictions, taken root. He'd meticulously mapped out every step, anticipated every potential pitfall, and implemented solutions with a detached pragmatism that had always served him well. Yet, now, the thought of simply walking away, of handing over the reins to an as-yet-unidentified successor, felt like an act of deliberate sabotage.

He pictured the faces of the collective's members: young Maria, whose innovative ideas for organic pest control had significantly reduced their reliance on expensive chemicals; old Mr. Henderson, who, after years of quiet resignation, now spoke with renewed vigor about passing on his generations of farming knowledge; and the newer families, who had invested their meager savings and their hopes in this venture, drawn by the promise of a sustainable livelihood and a community that supported its own. These weren't abstract stakeholders in a business transaction; they were individuals whose lives were now inextricably linked to the success of the collective, and by extension, to his leadership.

The notion of a 'successor' felt hollow, almost dismissive. He had poured not just his expertise, but a significant portion of his time and emotional energy into this project. He had learned to navigate the delicate balance between firm direction and collaborative decision-making, a skill he hadn't realized he possessed until he was forced to employ it. He had fostered an environment where mistakes were seen as learning opportunities, not failures, and where collective input was genuinely valued. To leave now, without a clear, capable hand to guide them, felt like abandoning a ship in the middle of a storm, leaving its passengers to the mercy of the waves.

He remembered a conversation with Maria just last week. She had been animatedly describing her excitement about a new irrigation system she had researched, a system that would further optimize water usage and increase crop resilience. Her eyes had sparkled with a blend of intelligence and earnestness, and she had looked to him, not just for approval, but for guidance on how to present it to the rest of the board. In that moment, he hadn't seen himself as a transient consultant; he had seen himself as a mentor, a vital link in her professional development, and by extension, in the collective's future.

The conflict raged within him. His ingrained instinct for self-preservation, his deeply ingrained belief in the power of detachment as a shield against disappointment, warred with the burgeoning sense of obligation, of a responsibility that transcended mere professional duty. He had always prided himself on his ability to be objective, to make decisions based on logic and data, unclouded by personal sentiment. But the data now included the undeniable human element, the fragile ecosystem of trust and hope he had helped to cultivate.

He sat at his desk in the small, utilitarian office he had set up at the collective, the afternoon sun casting long shadows across the worn wooden floor. The air was thick with the scent of drying herbs and freshly tilled earth, a stark contrast to the sterile environments he was accustomed to. He picked up a well-worn ledger, its pages filled with meticulous records of planting schedules and harvest yields. This was more than just a business; it was a living, breathing entity, sustained by the sweat and dedication of the people who believed in its mission.

He had always viewed his contributions as finite, a series of discrete projects to be completed and then moved beyond. He was a problem-solver, a catalyst for change, but never a permanent fixture. The idea of being indispensable had always struck him as a weakness, a dangerous dependence. Yet, here he was, wrestling with the very real possibility that his departure *would* create a void, a disruption that could undo months of painstaking work and extinguish the newfound hope of many.

He thought about the long-term implications. The collective was on the cusp of securing a significant contract with a regional distributor, a deal that would provide financial stability and open up new avenues for growth. But it required a unified front, strong leadership, and a clear vision for the future – things that were still in development, still reliant on his steady hand. If he were to leave before that contract was solidified, before the leadership structure was firmly established, the entire enterprise could crumble. The thought sent a cold dread through him, a feeling far more potent than any personal inconvenience.

This wasn't just about professional reputation or financial gain. It was about the trust placed in him, the faith that had been invested, however implicitly. He had promised efficiency, and he had delivered. He had promised a turnaround, and he had achieved it. But he had also, unintentionally, fostered a sense of community, a spirit of collaboration that was far more complex and delicate than any business plan could account for. To sever that connection abruptly felt not just professionally irresponsible, but morally questionable.

He realized with a jolt that his carefully constructed worldview, built on the principles of detachment and calculated self-interest, was beginning to fracture. The allure of absolute freedom, the ability to move unburdened by obligation, was starting to feel less like liberation and more like a profound, albeit self-imposed, isolation. He had been so focused on the mechanics of business that he had overlooked the profound human dynamics at play, the intricate web of relationships that sustained any endeavor, particularly one rooted in community and shared purpose.

The question wasn't simply whether he *could* leave, but whether he *should*. And if he stayed, what would that look like? Could he truly commit to this place, to these people, beyond the scope of his initial contract?

The idea was both terrifying and, in a strange way, compelling. It meant re-evaluating his own definition of success, of freedom, and of the meaning of a life well-lived. It meant embracing a responsibility that extended beyond profit margins and efficiency reports, a responsibility to the people whose lives he had, however inadvertently, intertwined with his own. The weight of that realization was immense, a testament to the unexpected depth of the soil he had been asked to cultivate.

Evan stood at the precipice, not of a physical cliff overlooking the rolling farmlands of Cedar Ridge, but of a much more daunting internal landscape. His carefully constructed exit strategy, once as solid and reassuring as a fortified wall, had begun to crumble, revealing a vast, uncharted territory within himself. The pragmatic part of his brain, the part that had always excelled at identifying the next objective, the next problem to solve, the next market to penetrate, screamed at him to move on. Cedar Ridge, the collective, had been a project, a successful one, he could grant himself that much. The numbers were undeniable, the turnaround spectacular. He had delivered precisely what he'd been contracted to do, and then some. The logical conclusion was to collect his fee, offer a gracious handshake, and disappear back into the anonymity from which he'd emerged, a ghost in the machine of commerce.

Yet, something held him captive. It wasn't a chain, not a legal obligation, but something far more insidious and compelling. It was the echo of laughter in the barn during that impromptu harvest festival, the quiet pride in Mr. Henderson's weathered eyes when discussing the irrigation system Evan had championed, the burgeoning confidence of Maria as she presented her latest organic initiative. These were not the results of sterile business transactions; they were the vibrant hues painted onto the canvas of his professional life, colors he hadn't anticipated, colors that refused to fade. He had come to Cedar Ridge as a surgeon, intending to excise the rot and leave a clean wound. Instead, he had found himself becoming a gardener, tending to delicate seedlings, nurturing them with care, and now, witnessing the first tender shoots of growth, he felt an inexplicable reluctance to abandon the garden altogether.

The whispers of his own ambition still beckoned, promising new frontiers, greater challenges, the intoxicating thrill of conquest. He envisioned himself dissecting the complexities of a failing tech startup, revitalizing a struggling manufacturing plant, orchestrating a corporate takeover that would make headlines. These were the games he knew, the arenas where his sharp intellect and detached decisiveness had always triumphed. But the thought of returning to that purely transactional existence now felt... barren. He'd always believed that freedom lay in the absence of ties, in the ability to pivot at a moment's notice, unburdened by any lingering attachments. But the weight he felt now wasn't the weight of responsibility in the conventional sense; it was the weight of potential, the untapped promise of something more profound than mere professional achievement.

Lena's presence was a significant part of this internal turbulence. Her quiet strength, her unwavering belief in the community and its potential, had become a mirror reflecting back to him a version of himself he hadn't dared to acknowledge. She saw past the polished façade of the consultant, past the calculated maneuvers and the strategic brilliance, and glimpsed something genuine, something that resonated with her own deep-seated values.

Their conversations, often stretching late into the evening, had moved beyond the logistics of the collective and delved into the shared vulnerabilities and quiet hopes that underpinned their respective journeys. He found himself confessing fears and aspirations he'd buried deep, truths that had been locked away for so long they'd almost atrophied. Lena listened, not with judgment, but with a gentle understanding that disarmed him completely. Her steady gaze, her thoughtful responses, had created a space where his defenses felt less necessary, where the carefully constructed walls he'd built around his heart began to soften.

The burgeoning feelings for her were a complication he hadn't factored into his initial calculations. He had meticulously analyzed market trends, assessed financial risks, and projected operational efficiencies. He had not, however, allocated any resources to the unpredictable, often irrational, force of human attraction. Her laugh, a clear, melodious sound that often punctuated their discussions, had become a sound he actively sought out. The way her brow furrowed in concentration when discussing crop rotation, the way her eyes lit up when a new idea sparked, the simple, unguarded way she moved through her day – these were details that had, without his conscious consent, etched themselves into his memory. He found himself watching her, not with the analytical gaze of a business strategist, but with the captivated attention of someone discovering something precious.

This was no longer about the collective's bottom line, though that remained a vital concern. This was about the intricate, often messy, tapestry of human connection. He had witnessed firsthand the power of shared purpose, the resilience that bloomed when people felt seen, heard, and valued. He had been a catalyst, yes, but he had also become a participant. The notion of simply walking away, of severing the threads he had helped to weave, felt like a betrayal, not just of the collective, but of a nascent part of himself that had begun to flourish in the fertile ground of Cedar Ridge.

He paced his small office, the scent of drying lavender and aged wood a comforting balm. The ledger lay open on his desk, a testament to the tangible progress made. But his gaze kept drifting to a framed photograph tucked away in a corner – a candid shot Lena had taken of him during a board meeting, a moment of shared laughter with Mr. Henderson. He looked... relaxed. Engaged. Present. It was a side of himself he rarely saw captured, a reflection of a man unburdened by the constant need to prove himself, a man finding a quiet satisfaction in the work itself and the people it served.

The question of freedom was no longer about the absence of constraint, but about the presence of purpose. Was he truly free if he was constantly chasing the next horizon, never allowing himself to deeply invest in the present? Was true freedom found in the ability to detach, or in the courage to commit? His professional life had been a testament to the former, a relentless pursuit of upward mobility and objective achievement. But Cedar Ridge had introduced him to the latter, the quiet, profound freedom that came from belonging, from contributing to something larger than oneself, from nurturing the seeds of possibility.

He stopped by the window, gazing out at the patchwork of fields stretching towards the horizon. The sun was beginning to dip below the hills, painting the sky in hues of orange and purple, a daily masterpiece that never failed to inspire awe. He could leave tomorrow, disappear into the anonymity of the city, and resume his life of calculated independence. He could meticulously document his successes, deliver his final report, and move on, leaving Cedar Ridge to forge its own path. But the thought no longer brought the clean sense of closure it once would have. Instead, it brought a hollow ache, a premonition of emptiness.

He had always viewed himself as an independent entity, a solitary explorer navigating the vast seas of opportunity. He was the captain of his own ship, charting his own course, beholden to no one. But Cedar Ridge had shown him that even the most self-sufficient vessel could be enriched by the currents of community, by the shared labor of a crew, by the lighthouse of a guiding star. Lena was that star, a beacon of warmth and resilience in the often-harsh landscape of his ambition. Her belief in him, in the collective, had given him pause, had forced him to re-examine the very foundations of his existence.

He thought about the upcoming harvest season, the critical period for securing the distributor contract, the ongoing development of the new farmer mentorship program he'd initiated. These were not tasks that could be easily delegated or completed in his absence. They required continuity, a steady hand, and a deep understanding of the nuanced dynamics at play. To walk away now would be to risk undoing all the progress, to extinguish the fragile flame of hope that had been painstakingly kindled.

This wasn't about obligation; it was about choice. A conscious, deliberate choice to invest his energy, his skills, and his heart in a place that had unexpectedly captured them. It was about recognizing that his greatest professional triumphs might not be the ones that garnered the most attention, but the ones that fostered the most profound, lasting impact on the lives of others. It was about understanding that true freedom wasn't about escaping ties, but about choosing which ones were worth forging. The path ahead was unclear, fraught with uncertainties, but for the first time in a long time, Evan felt a stir of something akin to excitement, a quiet anticipation of a future he hadn't dared to imagine, a future that might just be rooted in the simple, profound soil of Cedar Ridge. He had arrived with an exit strategy, but he was beginning to suspect he might be staying for the long haul, not out of duty, but out of a burgeoning, undeniable desire.

CHAPTER SEVEN

Unspoken Feelings

The subtle shift in the air whenever Lena entered a room was becoming as predictable to Evan as the sunrise. It wasn't a dramatic shift, no theatrical spotlight, but a quiet recalibration of his senses, a subtle tuning of his awareness. He found himself unconsciously tracking her movements, his gaze snagging on the way she tucked a stray strand of hair behind her ear, the focused intensity in her eyes as she listened to a farmer's concerns, the easy warmth that radiated from her even in the most mundane of interactions. These were observations he wouldn't have deemed relevant in his previous life, the kind of details that would have been pruned from his mental landscape in favor of profit margins and strategic objectives. But here, in Cedar Ridge, they were becoming the very fabric of his days.

Their conversations, ostensibly about the burgeoning organic produce line or the logistics of the upcoming farmer's market, now carried a subtext, an undercurrent of something more profound. It was in the way their voices softened when discussing personal aspirations, in the hesitant sharing of past disappointments that had shaped their present trajectories. Evan, who had built his career on an impenetrable shield of professional detachment, found himself confessing vulnerabilities he'd long suppressed, not in a grand outpouring, but in quiet admissions, like pebbles dropped into a still pond, sending ripples of introspection across the surface. Lena, with her innate empathy and intuitive understanding, created a safe harbor for these confessions. She didn't offer platitudes or easy solutions; instead, she met his hesitant revelations with a steady gaze and a quiet nod, a silent acknowledgment that said, "I see you."

One afternoon, during a late-night strategy session in the dimly lit back room of the general store, the scent of aged wood and brewing coffee hanging heavy in the air, Lena was sketching out a marketing plan for the artisan cheeses. Her brow was furrowed in concentration, her pen gliding across the paper with practiced ease. Evan, ostensibly reviewing budget spreadsheets, found his attention drifting. He watched the way the faint lamplight caught the curve of her cheekbone, the way her lips parted slightly as she considered a new angle.

Without conscious thought, he reached across the table, his fingers brushing hers as he gestured towards a particular statistic. The contact was fleeting, a mere whisper of skin against skin, yet it sent a jolt through him, an electric current that hummed beneath his professional veneer. Lena's eyes flickered up to meet his, and for a suspended moment, the world outside the small room ceased to exist. Her gaze held a question, an unspoken curiosity that mirrored his own burgeoning unease, and a tentative hope. He saw a flicker of surprise, quickly masked by her usual composed grace, but he felt it – that shared awareness, that subtle recognition of a boundary being tested. He quickly withdrew his hand, a faint flush creeping up his neck, and forced his attention back to the numbers, but the ghost of her touch lingered, a warm ember against his skin.

It was in these small, almost imperceptible moments that the unspoken attraction between them grew, a delicate bloom pushing through the cracks of their carefully constructed defenses. At the town hall meeting, where the future of the community solar project was being debated, the room buzzed with opinions and passionate arguments. Evan, usually a detached observer in such forums, found his focus drawn to Lena, who sat on the panel, her presence a steadying force amidst the passionate discourse. When Mr. Henderson, his voice laced with concern, voiced his doubts about the upfront costs, Lena's response was measured and reassuring. She spoke of long-term savings, of energy independence, of investing in the future of their children. As she spoke, her eyes met Evan's across the room, a silent exchange of understanding, a shared commitment to the vision they were both working to realize.

He saw a spark of appreciation in her gaze, a subtle acknowledgement of his support, and he felt an answering warmth bloom in his chest, a quiet pride in her leadership. Later, as the meeting dispersed and people mingled, he found himself navigating the crowd, drawn to her like a compass needle to true north. When he finally reached her, her smile was genuine, tinged with a shared relief that the contentious issue had been navigated with relative grace. "You looked like you wanted to jump in there a few times," she remarked, her voice low and conspiratorial as they stood near the exit. He chuckled, a genuine sound that surprised even himself. "My job is to consult, not to commandeer," he replied, though he knew, with a certainty that unsettled him, that he was increasingly inclined to commandeer if it meant supporting the vision she championed. Her laughter, a clear, bell-like sound, seemed to echo in the suddenly quiet hallway, and he found himself holding her gaze a moment longer than strictly necessary, the hum of unspoken feelings a palpable presence between them.

Another instance, during a visit to Maria's farm to assess the progress of the new composting initiative, Lena had stumbled slightly on a patch of uneven ground, her hands flying out for balance. Evan was instantly there, his arm steadying her, his touch firm yet gentle. The accidental contact, a brief tightening of his grip as he ensured her footing was secure, felt more significant than any planned handshake. Lena looked up at him, her eyes wide for a fleeting second, a silent acknowledgment of the unexpected intimacy of the moment.

The air between them crackled, charged with an awareness that had nothing to do with compost or crop yields. He saw a subtle blush creep up her neck, and he felt a corresponding heat rise within him. He lingered for a beat longer than necessary, his hand still resting on her arm, before releasing her with a regretful slowness. "Careful," he murmured, his voice a little rougher than usual. Her response was a soft "Thank you," her gaze holding his, and in that shared glance, a whole universe of unspoken emotions seemed to unfold. It was a dance of subtle gestures, of fleeting touches, of conversations that veered into the personal with a disarming ease. They were navigating uncharted territory, each step tentative, each glance freighted with a significance that transcended their professional roles.

The burgeoning feelings were a complication Evan had not factored into his meticulously crafted business plans. He had always prided himself on his ability to remain objective, to keep his personal emotions separate from his professional life. Lena, however, was proving to be an anomaly, a variable that defied his calculations. Her genuine passion for Cedar Ridge, her unwavering belief in the power of community, resonated with a part of him he had long neglected. He found himself wanting to impress her, not with grand pronouncements or displays of financial acumen, but with his earnestness, his commitment to the town's future. He would find himself carefully considering his words during meetings, hoping to earn her nod of approval, her subtle smile of encouragement. It was a far cry from the detached pragmatism that had defined his career.

During a particularly challenging negotiation with a potential distributor who was pushing for unfavorable terms, Evan felt Lena's quiet support from across the table. She offered no interruptions, no overt gestures, but her steady presence, her unwavering belief in the collective's value proposition, bolstered his resolve. When he finally secured a deal that was fair to the farmers, she met his gaze with a look of profound gratitude and admiration. Later, as they walked back to their respective cars under the darkening sky, the air cool and crisp, she spoke, her voice soft. "You handled that beautifully, Evan. You really fought for them." The praise, delivered with such sincerity, felt more valuable than any financial bonus. He found himself wanting to share more of these victories with her, to have her witness his efforts, to feel her quiet acknowledgment.

The unspoken attraction wasn't just a matter of shared glances or lingering touches; it was woven into the very fabric of their interactions. It was in the way they instinctively deferred to each other's expertise, the way they anticipated each other's needs. When Evan was engrossed in spreadsheets late into the evening, Lena would often appear with a fresh cup of coffee, her presence a silent offering of support. And when Lena was wrestling with a particularly complex issue related to agricultural policy, Evan found himself offering insights gleaned from his diverse business experience, not as a consultant, but as a partner. There was a comfort in this shared endeavor, a sense of camaraderie that was slowly, subtly, morphing into something deeper.

He found himself replaying their conversations, dissecting the nuances, searching for hidden meanings. A casual comment about his preference for strong coffee, a shared laugh over a particularly absurd town ordinance, a moment of shared frustration over a bureaucratic hurdle – all these seemingly insignificant details were being stored and analyzed, not with the cold logic of a strategist, but with the hopeful curiosity of someone discovering a new language. Lena's laughter, in particular, had become a sound he actively sought out. It was a genuine, unrestrained sound that could cut through the most serious of discussions, reminding him of the joy and light that existed beyond the realm of business.

One evening, after a long day of meetings, they found themselves the last ones to leave the community center. The silence that settled between them was not awkward, but comfortable, companionable. Lena was tidying up some flyers, her movements efficient and graceful. Evan watched her, a sense of quiet contentment washing over him. "You know," he began, his voice soft, "when I first came here, I thought of this as just another project. A job to be done, and then I'd move on." He paused, searching for the right words. "But it's... become more than that."

Lena turned, her expression open, receptive. "It's the people, isn't it?" she offered, her gaze steady. He nodded, a small smile touching his lips. "It's the people," he confirmed. "And it's... the way things are built here. Slowly, surely, with a lot of heart." He met her eyes, and in that moment, the unspoken feelings between them were as clear as the stars beginning to dot the twilight sky. There was an understanding, a shared recognition of the emotional landscape they were both exploring, a landscape far more complex and beautiful than any financial projection. He knew, with a certainty that resonated deep within him, that his exit strategy was no longer just about leaving Cedar Ridge, but about whether he was ready to leave Lena.

Lena found herself caught in a familiar eddy of conflicting emotions whenever Evan was near. It was a sensation she'd learned to navigate with practiced grace, a subtle tightening in her chest that wasn't unpleasant, but certainly demanded attention. His presence, once a mere professional necessity, had become an anchor in the often-turbulent waters of her days. She admired his sharp intellect, the way he could dissect complex problems with an almost surgical precision. But it was more than just his mind; it was the way that mind was slowly, perceptibly, shifting focus.

The rigid lines of his corporate world seemed to be softening, blurring into the more organic, interconnected landscape of Cedar Ridge. She saw it in the way he listened, truly listened, when the farmers spoke of their struggles, not as problems to be solved with a quick fix, but as deeply human concerns that deserved empathy. She saw it in his growing appreciation for the seemingly small things – the taste of fresh-picked berries, the quiet satisfaction of a well-tended garden, the camaraderie forged over shared labor. These weren't the metrics of success he'd once chased, and witnessing this evolution felt like watching a rare bloom unfurl in slow motion.

Yet, as these feelings deepened, a protective instinct, honed by years of self-reliance, kicked in. Lena understood, with a clarity that sometimes ached, that Evan's time in Cedar Ridge was, by his own admission, a temporary assignment. He had a life, a career, a world outside this valley that awaited his return. To acknowledge the burgeoning connection, to allow her own heart to fully open, felt like placing an invisible chain around his ankle, an expectation he might not be willing or able to fulfill. She valued his autonomy, his freedom to choose his path without undue influence. It was a principle she held dear, both for herself and for those she cared about. She wouldn't be the one to complicate his decisions, to add the weight of her feelings to a choice he already had to make. So, she kept her emotions carefully contained, a well-guarded fortress around her heart. She offered him friendship, unwavering support for the projects they shared, and a listening ear, but she carefully avoided any action or word that might imply a claim, a demand, or even a fervent hope for a future that was entirely his to shape.

Their conversations, which had started with budgets and logistics, now frequently drifted into more personal territories, but Lena always steered them back before they could become too revealing. When Evan spoke of his past, of the pressures he'd faced, the sacrifices he'd made, she would offer a quiet understanding, a shared nod, but she wouldn't pry, wouldn't ask for details that might make him feel exposed or obligated. Similarly, when he, in turn, would inquire about her life, her dreams, her history in Cedar Ridge, she would answer truthfully, but with a deliberate restraint. She spoke of her passion for the land, her commitment to the community, but she carefully omitted the deeper currents of longing that sometimes stirred within her. It was a delicate dance, a constant act of balancing honesty with discretion. She wanted him to see her, to understand her, but not to feel burdened by her.

There were moments, of course, when the façade threatened to crumble. A shared laugh that lingered a beat too long, a casual touch that sent an unexpected jolt through her, a look in his eyes that seemed to hold a question she couldn't bring herself to answer – these were the cracks in her armor. One evening, while reviewing the finalized plans for the community garden expansion, they sat close together at her kitchen table, the scent of rosemary and basil from her window boxes filling the air. Evan pointed to a section of the diagram, his finger brushing against hers.

The contact was accidental, a fleeting graze, but it sent a tremor through Lena. She quickly pulled her hand back, her heart thumping against her ribs. She met his gaze, and for a fleeting instant, she saw a flicker of something in his eyes – curiosity, perhaps, or a mirroring of her own surprise. She quickly looked away, busying herself with rearranging a stack of papers, her cheeks flushing. "That seems to be the most efficient layout," she managed, her voice a little breathier than usual. Evan cleared his throat, his own voice a touch deeper. "Yes, I think it will work well. Plenty of space for everything." The unspoken hung heavy in the air between them, a palpable awareness of the charged moment. Lena's internal dialogue was a frantic scramble:

Don't push, don't lean in, don't let him see how much that small touch affected you. She reminded herself of his impending departure, of the life he had to return to. His presence here was a gift, a temporary intersection of paths, and she would cherish it without trying to alter its course.

She noticed the subtle ways Evan had begun to integrate himself into the fabric of Cedar Ridge. He'd started volunteering at the local food bank, his initial awkwardness quickly giving way to a quiet efficiency. He'd even taken it upon himself to organize a small, informal workshop for local business owners on basic financial planning, a gesture that went far beyond his contractual obligations. Lena observed these actions with a mixture of pride and a quiet, persistent ache. They confirmed her growing admiration for him, his capacity for growth and genuine care. But they also served as a stark reminder of his temporary status. These were the actions of someone investing in a community, yes, but perhaps not necessarily of someone planning to stay. And Lena, fiercely protective of her own emotional landscape, refused to build her hopes on such uncertain foundations. She admired his contributions, she appreciated his growing understanding of what made Cedar Ridge special, but she wouldn't allow herself to become a reason for him to stay, or worse, a reason for him to feel guilty if he left.

Her interactions with him became a careful calibration. She would engage with his enthusiasm, validate his insights, and even share in his small victories, but she would never cross the invisible line into expecting more. When he spoke of potential future projects, she would listen with interest, but she would avoid any language that implied a shared future, a joint endeavor beyond the scope of his current contract. It was a form of self-preservation, a way to ensure that if and when he left, the void he left behind would be filled with gratitude for the time they had shared, not with the crushing weight of unfulfilled expectations. She knew his intelligence was a powerful force, but she also knew that intelligence could lead him back to his old life, to the world where he truly belonged, or so she told herself. She wouldn't let her burgeoning feelings cloud his judgment, or more importantly, her own perception of reality.

One afternoon, while visiting the old apple orchard that was slated for revitalisation, they stood amidst the gnarled trees, the scent of ripe fruit heavy in the air. Evan was tracing the lines on a faded blueprint, his brow furrowed in thought. Lena watched him, a soft smile playing on her lips. He was so different from the man she'd first met, so much more grounded, more... present. "It's a lot of work," he mused, more to himself than to her. "But the potential is undeniable." Lena nodded, her gaze sweeping over the rows of trees. "It's the history, too," she said softly.

"These trees have seen generations of families. They deserve a second chance." Evan looked up, his eyes meeting hers. There was a warmth in his gaze, a shared understanding that transcended the words. "You have a way of seeing the soul in things, Lena," he said, his voice low. Lena's heart gave a familiar flutter. She wanted to return the compliment, to tell him how she saw the growing soul in *him*, but she held back. Instead, she offered a small, almost shy smile. "We all do, in Cedar Ridge," she deflected, turning her attention back to the blueprint. "We believe in second chances." It was a carefully crafted response, one that acknowledged his observation without revealing the depth of her own feelings. She wanted him to see the beauty of the town, the strength of its people, but she didn't want him to feel obligated to stay because of her.

The conflict was internal, a constant tug-of-war between her growing affection for Evan and her unwavering commitment to his freedom. She found herself replaying their conversations, not with the strategic analysis of a business deal, but with the hopeful interpretation of someone looking for signs. Had he meant something more when he'd asked about her favorite books? Was there a hidden depth to his casual comment about enjoying the quiet evenings in Cedar Ridge? These were the mental gymnastics she performed in the solitude of her own thoughts, always followed by a firm self-correction.

He's here for a job, Lena. Don't build castles in the sky. She reminded herself of his responsibilities, his commitments, the life that was waiting for him beyond the valley. To allow herself to fall completely, to invest her heart in a future that was so uncertain, felt reckless.

She saw how he interacted with the children at the community center, his initial reserve melting away as he patiently explained the rules of a board game or listened to their enthusiastic tales of playground adventures. She saw the genuine respect he earned from the town elders, who initially viewed him with a healthy dose of skepticism. These were the signs of a man finding his place, of a man connecting with a community on a deeper level. And while a part of her reveled in these observations, another part recoiled, instinctively raising its defenses. She couldn't be the reason he felt tied down, the reason he stayed when his heart, his career, pulled him elsewhere. Her love, if it could even be called that yet, had to be a gift, not a burden.

One crisp autumn evening, as they were packing up after a community meeting, the air filled with the scent of woodsmoke and fallen leaves, Evan hesitated at the door. "Lena," he began, his voice uncharacteristically hesitant. "I've been thinking... about the proposal for the new farmers' market stalls. I think we could explore some funding options that would make it more accessible for smaller producers." Lena turned, her expression open and encouraging. "That's a great idea, Evan. I'm glad you see the need." He met her gaze, a flicker of something unreadable passing between them. "It's not just about the business side, is it?" he said, his voice barely a whisper. Lena's breath hitched. This was it, the precipice.

She could lean in, acknowledge the unspoken, invite him to explore the territory beyond their professional roles. But the image of his future, his freedom, flashed before her eyes. She couldn't be the one to hold him back. She offered a small, knowing smile, a smile that held warmth but also a gentle restraint. "No, Evan," she said softly. "It's never just about the business side here." She turned and walked out into the cool night air, leaving him standing in the doorway, the unspoken words hanging heavy between them, a testament to her guarded heart and her unwavering respect for his autonomy. She wouldn't make him choose, not yet, perhaps not ever. Her feelings were her own, a quiet garden cultivated within the walls of her heart, a place he was welcome to visit, but where he was never expected to stay.

Evan found himself increasingly adrift in a sea of introspection, and Lena was the constant current pulling him under. It wasn't a drowning he feared, but a profound immersion, a surrender he hadn't anticipated. He'd arrived in Cedar Ridge with a clear objective: to streamline, to optimize, to impart his expertise and then depart, leaving behind a more efficient, albeit temporary, imprint. But Lena had become an unlooked-for variable, a beautifully complex equation that defied his usual methods of calculation. He'd catch himself observing her, cataloging the minute shifts in her expression, the way her eyes crinkled at the corners when she genuinely smiled, the subtle tilt of her head when she was considering something with earnest thought. These weren't observations born of professional curiosity; they were the quiet observations of a man noticing the intricate details of a landscape he was beginning to find himself drawn to, a landscape that included her.

He'd replay their conversations, dissecting not just the business proposals and the logistical challenges, but the nuances, the pauses, the unspoken sentiments that seemed to hum beneath the surface of their words. When she spoke of the land, of its resilience and its demands, there was a deep reverence in her voice that resonated with something primal within him, something he'd long suppressed beneath layers of corporate ambition and restless ambition. He admired her quiet strength, the unshakeable core of her that allowed her to navigate the often-unpredictable rhythm of rural life with grace and determination. It was a stark contrast to the performative resilience he'd witnessed in his previous life, the kind that was often a mask for deeper insecurities. Lena's strength felt authentic, rooted in a connection to something tangible, something real.

The question of 'staying' had begun to morph from a hypothetical scenario into a tangible consideration. Initially, it was about the town, about the potential for sustained growth and community well-being. He saw the tangible benefits of his work, the positive impact on the lives of the people here, and that offered a unique kind of satisfaction, one that transcended the bottom line. But now, the contemplation of permanence was inextricably linked to Lena. What would it mean, truly, to remain? Not just as a consultant, a temporary fixture, but as someone weaving himself into the fabric of Cedar Ridge? The thought, once anathema to his ingrained wanderlust, now held a surprising allure. His life had been a series of destinations, of projects to be completed, of challenges to be conquered. He'd always been moving, always looking ahead to the next horizon. But Lena... Lena felt like a destination in herself, a place of quiet solace and vibrant life that he hadn't known he was searching for.

He'd find himself walking through the town square on evenings after their work was done, the scent of woodsmoke and damp earth a comforting balm. He'd see the lights in the windows of homes, imagine families gathered, and the sterile efficiency of his own apartment felt increasingly stark and temporary. He'd catch himself thinking of Lena, wondering what she was doing, if she was reading a book by the fire, or perhaps still tending to her garden, even as the air grew cooler. These were not the thoughts of a man planning his exit strategy; they were the nascent musings of someone contemplating an arrival, a settling.

The idea of building something with Lena, something beyond the scope of their current professional collaboration, began to take root. It was a fragile seedling, easily overshadowed by the ingrained habits of a lifetime spent on the move, but it was there, persistent and undeniable. He pictured shared mornings, the quiet hum of a shared life, the comfortable rhythm of two people building a future together. It was a vision that was both exhilarating and terrifying. His identity had always been tied to his independence, his ability to forge his own path, to adapt and thrive in any environment. The prospect of anchoring himself, of willingly surrendering a portion of that autonomy, was a profound internal shift.

He remembered a conversation they'd had last week, standing by the old oak tree at the edge of Miller's farm. The sun was setting, casting long shadows across the fields, and the air was alive with the chirping of crickets. Lena had been talking about the history of the farm, how generations of her family had worked this land. "It's more than just soil and crops," she'd said, her voice soft but firm. "It's a legacy. It's about what you leave behind, for the people who come after." At the time, he'd nodded, acknowledging the sentiment with his usual professional courtesy. But now, the words echoed in his mind, imbued with a new significance. What was he leaving behind? What legacy was he building, if any? His career was a series of achievements, of boxes ticked, but in the grander scheme of things, what was the lasting impact? The thought was unsettling.

He found himself scrutinizing his own motivations, the deeply ingrained drive that had propelled him forward for so long. Was it ambition, or was it a fear of stillness? A fear of confronting himself in the quiet moments, away from the demands of deadlines and high-stakes negotiations? Cedar Ridge, and more specifically, Lena, seemed to be holding up a mirror to his soul, reflecting back a man he hadn't fully acknowledged. He saw the wanderlust, the restless spirit that craved new experiences, but he also saw a burgeoning yearning for something deeper, something more enduring.

The complexity of his feelings for Lena was a constant undercurrent in his thoughts. It wasn't just admiration for her competence or appreciation for her warmth. It was something that stirred a deeper ache, a desire to be known, to be understood by her on a level that transcended their professional roles. He found himself unconsciously seeking her approval, not in a way that felt subservient, but in a way that indicated a desire for her to see him, truly see him, beyond the polished veneer of his corporate persona. He wanted her to recognize the man beneath the calculated moves, the man who was slowly, tentatively, discovering a new sense of self in the quiet embrace of this small town.

He recalled a moment from earlier that day, when they'd been reviewing the financial projections for the new community center. A minor discrepancy had surfaced, a decimal point out of place that could have led to significant overspending. Lena had spotted it immediately, her brow furrowed in concentration, and then she'd looked at him, a flicker of a shared understanding in her eyes as if to say, "We'll fix this, together." In that brief exchange, he'd felt a profound connection, a sense of partnership that was more satisfying than any solo triumph. It was in these small moments, these shared challenges and quiet victories, that the possibility of a shared future began to feel less like a fantasy and more like a plausible, even desirable, reality.

The fear of disrupting her life, of introducing his own uncertainty into the steady rhythm of her existence, was also a significant consideration. Lena had a life here, a purpose that was deeply intertwined with the well-being of Cedar Ridge. He was a temporary visitor, a catalyst for change, perhaps, but not a permanent fixture. Or at least, he hadn't been. Now, the lines were blurring. The thought of imposing his presence, of potentially altering the course of her life with his own indecision, was a heavy burden. He respected her independence, her self-sufficiency, and he wouldn't want to be the reason she felt she had to compromise her own needs or desires.

His mind often drifted to the hypothetical scenarios. What if he stayed? What would that look like, not just for him, but for them? Could he find a way to contribute meaningfully, to build a life here that was both fulfilling for him and beneficial to the community, without overshadowing Lena's own contributions? He saw the potential for a symbiotic relationship, where his business acumen could complement her deep understanding of the town's needs, creating something truly impactful. It was a delicate balance, and one he was still grappling with.

He remembered the way she'd looked at him when he'd presented his initial strategy for revitalizing the old mill. There had been a spark of respect in her eyes, but also a subtle question, a silent inquiry about his intentions, his commitment. He hadn't been able to articulate his evolving feelings then, not truly. He'd offered professional reassurance, but inside, a storm of conflicting emotions had been brewing. The desire to impress her, to earn her trust, had become as strong as the desire to achieve his professional goals.

The ingrained pattern of his life was one of constant movement, of seeking out the next challenge, the next opportunity for growth. He thrived on the adrenaline of innovation, the satisfaction of solving complex problems, and the thrill of venturing into the unknown. Cedar Ridge, with its quiet predictability and its deep-rooted traditions, had initially felt like a temporary respite, a place to recharge before plunging back into the fray. But Lena had introduced an element of stillness, a gravitational pull that was slowly, inexorably, reorienting his internal compass.

He found himself noticing the small things that made Lena who she was. Her laugh, a clear, melodic sound that could brighten even the gloomiest day. The way she'd absentmindedly tuck a stray strand of hair behind her ear when she was deep in thought. The quiet determination in her eyes when she faced an obstacle. These were the details that were etching themselves into his memory, becoming the building blocks of a desire he was only just beginning to understand. He wanted to be near her, to share in her world, to understand the quiet strength that emanated from her.

He wrestled with the idea of permanence. His identity had been forged in the crucible of constant change. He was a problem-solver, a strategist, a man who could adapt to any situation. But Cedar Ridge, and Lena, were presenting him with a different kind of challenge: the challenge of belonging. Could he, a man who had always been on the periphery, find a true sense of home here? Could he build something lasting, not just professionally, but personally? The questions gnawed at him, disrupting his sleep, occupying his thoughts during long drives and quiet evenings.

He saw the trust Lena placed in him, the way she readily shared her insights and her concerns. It was a trust he valued, and one he didn't want to betray. If he were to leave, as his former self would have automatically planned, it would feel like a betrayal, not just of her, but of the man he was becoming. The thought of leaving this place, of leaving *her*, was starting to feel like a genuine loss, a departure from a path he was beginning to believe was meant for him.

He acknowledged the conflict within him, the ingrained wanderlust battling with this nascent desire for rootedness. He'd always seen himself as a rolling stone, gathering no moss. But perhaps, he mused, there was a different kind of fulfillment to be found in the quiet accumulation of shared experiences, in the slow, steady growth of a life built not on constant motion, but on connection. Lena was the embodiment of that connection, the anchor that was grounding him in a way he'd never thought possible.

He thought about his past, about the solitary pursuits, the transient relationships, the constant striving for external validation. He'd been so focused on what he could achieve, what he could conquer, that he'd neglected to consider what he truly wanted, what would bring him a lasting sense of peace and fulfillment. Cedar Ridge, with its unpretentious charm and its genuine community spirit, was offering him a glimpse of that possibility. And Lena, with her quiet strength and her unwavering integrity, was the catalyst, the gentle force that was nudging him towards a life he hadn't dared to imagine.

He knew, with a certainty that both thrilled and terrified him, that his time in Cedar Ridge had become something far more profound than a business assignment. It was becoming a crossroads, a point of decision that would define not just his career, but the very essence of who he was and who he was meant to become. And the thought of Lena, of a future with her, was the most compelling reason of all to explore the possibility of staying.

The fluorescent lights of the Cedar Ridge Collective hummed, a steady, monotonous drone that usually faded into the background of Evan's concentration. Tonight, however, the sound seemed amplified, a counterpoint to the accelerated rhythm of his own heart. Lena was across the large oak table, her brow furrowed in a familiar intensity as she pored over spreadsheets that seemed to multiply with each passing hour. An unexpected snag in the solar panel installation timeline had thrown their carefully laid plans into disarray, and the late hour had found them still here, wrestling with the logistics.

He'd already run through the calculations half a dozen times, his mind sharp and analytical, yet lately, his focus was increasingly divided. A significant portion of his attention was dedicated to the woman illuminated by the pool of light cast by her desk lamp. The way her hair, usually pulled back in a practical braid, had loosened, stray tendrils framing her face. The slight impatience that flickered across her features when a complex problem resisted an easy solution. He knew these details intimately now, not as data points, but as part of a living, breathing landscape that had become more captivating than any mountain vista or bustling metropolis he'd ever encountered.

Lena sighed, a soft exhalation that barely stirred the air. She rubbed her temples, and Evan's instinct was to offer a gesture of comfort, a hand on her shoulder, a quiet word of reassurance. But the professional boundary, so clearly defined at the beginning of their collaboration, had become increasingly blurred, a hazy line that he hesitated to cross, lest he misinterpret the signals or, worse, shatter the delicate equilibrium they'd found.

"This is... stubborn," she murmured, her voice tinged with fatigue. "I've run through every scenario, and I still can't see how we can make up this lost time without compromising on the quality of the installation. Mr. Henderson is expecting a fully operational system by the end of next week, and right now, that feels like an impossible target."

Evan pushed his chair back, the scrape against the polished floor unnervingly loud in the quiet room. He moved to stand behind her, leaning over the table to get a closer look at the numbers. The scent of her, a subtle blend of earth and something faintly floral, filled his senses, a familiar and comforting aroma that had become intrinsically linked to Cedar Ridge itself. He could feel the warmth radiating from her as he leaned in, a palpable presence that drew him in.

"Let me see," he said, his voice a low rumble. He pointed to a section of the spreadsheet. "What if we reroute the supply chain through the distribution hub in Oakhaven? It's an extra fifty miles, but their turnaround time is significantly faster, and I've had good dealings with them in the past. It might shave off a day, perhaps two, if we factor in expedited shipping."

Lena turned her head slightly, her eyes meeting his. In the soft glow of the lamp, they seemed deeper, more luminous than usual. There was a flicker of something in their depths – surprise, a touch of hope, and something else, something more vulnerable that made his breath hitch. It was a look that invited, that welcomed his proximity, that acknowledged the unspoken connection that had been building between them, slow and steady, like the growth of the ancient trees outside.

"Oakhaven... that's a good thought, Evan," she said, her voice softer now, less strained. "I hadn't considered them, mainly due to the distance. But if their efficiency is as good as you say..." She paused, her gaze holding his, and the silence stretched, filled with the unspoken. It was a moment poised on the precipice of something more, a fragile bubble of shared vulnerability. He could feel the weight of her gaze, the unspoken question in her eyes:

Could we do this? Could we rely on each other like this?

He found himself wanting to reach out, to brush a stray strand of hair from her cheek, to tell her that he saw her, truly saw her, not just as a client, a colleague, or a formidable businesswoman, but as Lena, a woman whose quiet strength and inherent goodness had slowly, irrevocably, captured his attention. He wanted to confess the growing realization that his departure from Cedar Ridge was no longer a foregone conclusion, that the idea of leaving her behind felt like an amputation.

His mind raced, cataloging the possibilities, the risks, the sheer audacity of what he was contemplating. He could stay. He *wanted* to stay. The thought, once a foreign concept, now felt like a natural extension of himself, like a deep, rooted desire he hadn't known he possessed. He saw a future here, a life interwoven with the rhythm of this town, with the warmth of its people, and most importantly, with Lena. He pictured shared mornings, the quiet camaraderie of building something meaningful, not just a project, but a life.

"We can make it work," he said, his voice a little hoarser than intended. He leaned in a fraction closer, the space between them charged with a silent energy. "I'll call them first thing in the morning, personally expedite the order. We'll push the installation crew to put in extra hours. We'll find a way."

Lena's gaze softened further, a hint of a smile playing on her lips. "You always have a solution, don't you, Evan?" she said, the observation carrying a weight that went beyond his professional capabilities. It was an acknowledgment of his presence, his commitment, his growing indispensability.

The air crackled with anticipation. It felt as though the dam of unspoken feelings was about to break. He saw it in the slight parting of her lips, the subtle widening of her eyes, the way her shoulders relaxed almost imperceptibly. He felt it in the thrumming in his own chest, the urgent need to bridge the remaining distance, to confess the truth that was bubbling up inside him. He was no longer just the consultant, the outsider. He was becoming a part of Cedar Ridge, and Lena was the heart of that becoming.

He opened his mouth, the words of his confession – of his burgeoning affection, of his hope for a future beyond this project – poised on his tongue. He could almost taste the vulnerability, the raw honesty of admitting that she had become more than just a professional acquaintance, that she had become the focal point of his thoughts, the quiet hum beneath the surface of his ambition. He wanted to tell her that Cedar Ridge was no longer just a project site, but a potential home, and that she was the reason why.

But then, as if summoned by the very intensity of the moment, his phone, lying forgotten on the table, let out a sharp, insistent beep. A notification, an email alert from a client in a different time zone, demanding his attention, a stark reminder of the world outside their quiet bubble. The interruption was brutal, jarring.

Lena blinked, the spell broken. Her gaze shifted from his eyes to the buzzing phone, a subtle withdrawal. The vulnerability receded, replaced by a polite, professional distance. She picked up the phone, her fingers hovering over the screen. "Looks like the outside world is still calling," she said, a faint, almost imperceptible tremor in her voice.

Evan felt a pang of disappointment, sharp and unexpected. The moment, so pregnant with possibility, had slipped through his fingers. The unspoken confession, the vulnerability he'd glimpsed, retreated behind a wall of professional courtesy. The charged atmosphere dissipated, replaced by the familiar hum of the lights and the rustle of papers.

He cleared his throat, the sound unnaturally loud. "Right," he said, forcing a lightness he didn't feel. "We should probably wrap this up. Get some rest."

Lena nodded, her movements crisp and efficient once more. She gathered the spreadsheets, her focus now entirely on the task at hand, as if the intimate moment had never occurred. "Yes, of course. Thank you for your help, Evan. Oakhaven... I'll look into that first thing."

He watched her, a sense of frustration and a quiet ache settling in his chest. He had been so close. So incredibly close to saying what needed to be said, to acknowledging the profound shift that had occurred within him. But the timing, the circumstances, had conspired against him. The unspoken feelings, the potent awareness of their shared connection, remained suspended in the air, a silent testament to the moment that had passed, leaving him to wonder if, and when, such an opportunity would present itself again. The night, which had promised a revelation, now held only the lingering echo of what might have been, and the quiet resolve to find another way, a better way, to finally articulate the truth that was now so undeniably a part of him.

The silence that followed was no longer comfortable; it was heavy with the weight of all the words left unsaid. He retreated to his own corner of the table, the spreadsheets now a frustratingly mundane distraction from the far more complex landscape of his heart. He knew, with a certainty that settled deep in his bones, that this was not a problem that could be solved with calculations or strategic rerouting. This was a matter of courage, of vulnerability, and of seizing the fleeting moments when the universe seemed to conspire to bring two people closer, even if only for a breath. He would have to find his courage, and he would have to find it soon.

The hum of the Cedar Ridge Collective, once a comforting backdrop to his work, now felt like a constant, low-grade thrumming in Evan's ears, a persistent echo of the internal disquiet that had taken root. The spreadsheets, the project timelines, the intricate dance of logistics – they had been his sanctuary, a predictable world governed by logic and measurable outcomes. But lately, that world felt increasingly fragile, threatened by a force far more powerful and unpredictable than any logistical snag: his own evolving feelings, and the equally unsettling realization of Lena's.

He found himself watching her, not just with the professional scrutiny he'd initially employed, but with an analyst's keen eye for subtle shifts in expression, for the unconscious gestures that betrayed her inner landscape. The way her shoulders would sometimes slump, a barely perceptible giving-in to weariness, and then, just as quickly, straighten with renewed resolve. He saw the slight tightening of her jaw when a problem proved particularly stubborn, and the almost imperceptible softening around her eyes when a solution finally emerged. These were not the data points of a business transaction; they were the intimate brushstrokes of a portrait he was unwillingly, yet undeniably, painting in his mind.

His fear, a cold knot in his stomach, was the fear of losing it all – not the career he'd meticulously built, nor the professional reputation he'd cultivated, but the quiet, unexpected sense of belonging that had begun to bloom within him. Cedar Ridge, with its weathered charm and its fiercely independent spirit, had slowly, insidiously, worked its way under his skin. And Lena, with her quiet strength, her unwavering integrity, and the surprising vulnerability she occasionally let slip, had become the heart of that burgeoning connection.

The thought of leaving this place, of severing the threads he was weaving into its fabric, felt like tearing himself in two. He pictured his life back in the city, the sterile efficiency, the relentless pace, and a profound sense of emptiness washed over him. Was he truly willing to trade this burgeoning sense of peace, this unexpected joy, for the familiar, yet now hollow, echo of his old life? The freedom he'd once craved, the ability to pack up and move on at a moment's notice, now felt like a cage, a self-imposed limitation that denied him the deeper fulfillment he was beginning to crave. He was terrified of the regret that would gnaw at him if he walked away from this, from her, from the possibility of a life that felt, for the first time, truly his own.

He replayed their late-night conversations, the moments of shared frustration, the brief flashes of laughter, the quiet understanding that had passed between them without words. Each interaction was a carefully guarded secret, a precious jewel he turned over and over in his mind, afraid to expose it to the harsh light of day, lest it shatter. He analyzed Lena's responses, searching for any hint of reciprocation, any sign that the unspoken feelings simmering beneath the surface were not solely his own. He saw it in the way she held his gaze a moment too long, in the soft lilt of her voice when she spoke his name, in the subtle tension that seemed to dissipate whenever he was near. But always, just as he felt on the verge of a breakthrough, a familiar wave of caution would wash over him. He was a man who dealt in certainty, in calculated risks, and this... this was a leap into the unknown, a venture where the stakes were immeasurably higher than any business deal.

The fear of regret was a powerful inhibitor. It whispered insidious doubts in his ear:

What if this is just a fleeting infatuation? What if you're mistaking professional camaraderie for something more profound? What if you're sacrificing a future of limitless possibilities for a transient comfort? He envisioned himself years down the line, a successful consultant perhaps, but a lonely man, haunted by the ghost of Cedar Ridge, of Lena's smile, of the life he'd been too afraid to embrace. This fear of losing the life he *knew* was always an option, the life of freedom and opportunity, wrestled with the nascent desire for the life he was beginning to *want*. It was a paralyzing conflict, leaving him adrift in a sea of 'what ifs.'

Across the table, Lena, too, was wrestling with her own brand of fear. She watched Evan, his profile sharp and defined against the glow of his laptop screen, his brow furrowed in concentration. He was a man of sharp intellect and unwavering focus, a force of nature in the business world. And in the quiet intimacy of these late nights, he had become something more. He had become a steady presence, a welcome distraction, and, terrifyingly, a cornerstone of her increasingly complex emotional landscape.

Her fear was the fear of losing him. Not just as a consultant, or a collaborator, but as a connection that had unexpectedly, profoundly, touched her life. Cedar Ridge was a small town, a place where roots ran deep, and Lena was deeply rooted. Her life here was a carefully constructed edifice of hard work, community involvement, and a quiet satisfaction derived from building something meaningful. Evan, with his city sophistication and his pragmatic approach, was an anomaly, an outsider who had managed to breach the defenses she hadn't even realized she'd erected.

She remembered the initial skepticism, the professional distance she'd maintained. He was a temporary fixture, a problem-solver here to fix a specific issue and then move on. But he hadn't just fixed the issue; he'd somehow become integral to the fabric of her days. His insights, his quiet encouragement, the way he challenged her assumptions without ever undermining her authority – these were gifts she hadn't anticipated. And the burgeoning affection, the flutter of anticipation she felt whenever he was near, was a dangerous, exhilarating complication.

The thought of him leaving, of the familiar presence simply vanishing from her life, sent a chill down her spine. It wasn't just the loss of his professional expertise; it was the void he would leave behind. He had seen her, truly seen her, beyond the role of business owner, beyond the stoic facade she often wore. He had a way of looking at her that made her feel seen, understood, and, in a way that was both terrifying and wonderful, cherished. The idea of that gaze being withdrawn, of that understanding fading into memory, was a prospect that felt akin to a physical ache.

Lena's fear was rooted in the deep-seated desire for connection, for a partnership that transcended the transactional. She had always prided herself on her independence, on her ability to stand on her own two feet. But Evan had, subtly and irrevocably, chipped away at that self-reliance, not by diminishing it, but by offering a complementary strength, a silent affirmation that she didn't have to carry the weight of the world alone. His departure would mean returning to that solitude, a solitude that now felt less like independence and more like a profound loneliness.

She found herself scrutinizing his every word, every gesture, for signs that he might be feeling the same pull, the same quiet yearning for something more. But his professionalism, a finely honed shield, often masked the depths of his emotions. He was courteous, engaged, even warm, but always with that underlying reserve, that professional boundary that seemed to keep him at arm's length. Was it a conscious effort to maintain distance, or a reflection of his own inner conflict? She couldn't be sure, and the uncertainty gnawed at her.

The conflict within her was a delicate balance between the ingrained pragmatism of her small-town upbringing and the burgeoning hope for something unexpected. She knew the risks of investing emotionally in someone who was, by all accounts, a transient figure. Cedar Ridge was a place of stability, of permanence. Evan represented the opposite – mobility, opportunity, a world far removed from the quiet rhythm of her life. To allow herself to fall for him would be to invite heartache, to open herself up to a pain that might be far more devastating than the quiet ache of solitude.

Yet, the connection was undeniable. It was in the shared silences that were more comfortable than any conversation, in the easy camaraderie that had developed, in the way their eyes met across the room, a silent acknowledgment of a shared understanding. She saw the flicker of something in his eyes when he looked at her, a depth that hinted at a world of unspoken emotions. But was it enough to overcome the inertia of his life, the allure of his established career, the freedom of his rootless existence?

This fear of losing what she was beginning to cherish, this fear of the emptiness that his departure would leave, was a quiet melancholy that underscored their interactions. It was a gentle ache, a persistent hum beneath the surface of their shared purpose. It was the unspoken tension that hung in the air between them, a fragile barrier of unspoken feelings, a quiet acknowledgment of the precipice they both stood upon. They were two souls, drawn together by circumstance, now navigating the treacherous waters of unspoken emotions, each holding their breath, afraid to make the first move, afraid of the consequences, afraid of losing it all. The beauty of their nascent romance was tinged with this gentle sorrow, a poignant reminder of the precarious nature of beginnings, and the deep, universal fear of what lies beyond the horizon.

CHAPTER EIGHT

The Town's Breath

The shift in the town's collective consciousness was subtle, yet palpable, like the changing of the seasons that Cedar Ridge observed with such ingrained respect. It wasn't a dramatic upheaval, no sudden surge of gossip or hushed whispers carrying malicious intent. Instead, it was a gentle, organic reorientation, a quiet acknowledgment that Evan, the outsider consultant, had become something more. The initial curiosity, the polite observation of a temporary visitor, had slowly, surely, transformed into a deeper, more invested interest. The townsfolk, accustomed to their predictable patterns and the familiar faces that populated their days, had begun to weave Evan into the tapestry of their own narratives.

Mornings at Millie's Diner, once a predictable symphony of clinking mugs and the sizzle of bacon, now held an undercurrent of speculative murmurs. Over steaming cups of coffee, conversations that had once revolved around the progress of Mrs. Gable's prize-winning dahlias or the upcoming bake sale at the community hall, now frequently veered towards the man who had so unexpectedly settled into their midst.

"He's a good sort, that Evan," Martha, a fixture at the counter with her perpetually flour-dusted apron, would remark, her voice carrying over the din of the morning rush. "Saw him helping young Timmy with that broken fence on Elm Street last week. Didn't have to, but he did. Just rolled up his sleeves."

Across from her, old Silas, a man whose weathered face seemed to hold the history of Cedar Ridge itself, would nod slowly, his gaze fixed on the condensation forming on his iced tea glass. "He's got a good heart, that's for sure. And he's doing good things for the Collective. Lena's looking brighter these days, too. Seems to have a spring in her step again."

The "Lena" mention was usually accompanied by a knowing glance, a shared understanding that passed between the town's elders like an unspoken code. They had watched Lena blossom under the town's protective embrace after her parents' passing, seen her shoulder the weight of the Collective with a quiet strength that had always impressed them. But they had also witnessed the subtle erosion of her spirit in recent years, a weariness that had settled around her like a fine dust. And now, with Evan's presence, there was a palpable shift, a rekindling of an inner light that warmed the hearts of those who cared for her.

The younger generation, too, contributed to this burgeoning collective awareness. At the town's only convenience store, tucked between the racks of fishing lures and brightly colored candy, casual conversations often turned to Evan.

"Did you see him at the Farmer's Market on Saturday?" Chloe, a recent high school graduate saving up for college, would exclaim to her friends. "He was actually talking to Mr. Henderson about his organic tomatoes. Not just polite small talk, like he was genuinely interested. And he bought a whole basket! My dad says he's never seen anyone care so much about vegetables."

The observations weren't limited to casual encounters. The sheer length of Evan's stay had become a topic of gentle, yet persistent, interest. He had arrived with the promise of a temporary fix, a six-month contract to streamline operations at the Cedar Ridge Collective. Six months had stretched into nine, then twelve, and now, as the leaves began to turn a vibrant hue of crimson and gold, he showed no signs of packing his city-tailored suits.

This prolonged presence was a silent testament to his growing investment. He wasn't just fulfilling a contract; he was *living* in Cedar Ridge. He had found a small, charming cottage on the outskirts of town, its porch swing perpetually inviting. He had joined the local book club, surprising everyone with his insightful, if sometimes overly analytical, contributions. He had even, to the amusement and delight of many, started volunteering at the town's annual Fall Festival, his initial awkwardness quickly melting away as he helped set up the pie-eating contest and, much to his own chagrin, found himself adorned with a garland of corn husks.

The townsfolk, pragmatic and observant, saw these actions not as mere acts of social courtesy, but as genuine attempts to integrate. They saw the effort, the willingness to shed his city persona and embrace the rhythm of their slower, more connected way of life. They saw the way his eyes lit up when he spoke about the progress of the Collective, the genuine pride he took in its achievements. And, most importantly, they saw the way his gaze lingered on Lena.

It was in the way he would subtly position himself to catch her eye during town hall meetings, the almost imperceptible softening of his features when she spoke, the way he would instinctively reach for her hand, only to pull back at the last moment, a silent testament to their shared, unspoken tension. They saw the easy laughter they shared, the comfortable silences that stretched between them, filled with an understanding that transcended words.

"He's good for her," Eleanor Vance, the matriarch of the town and a close friend of Lena's late mother, declared one afternoon over tea with her sister. "He listens to her, truly listens. And he doesn't try to fix her, just... supports her. It's a rare thing to see."

Her sister, Beatrice, a more reserved woman, simply offered a contented sigh. "He seems to make her happy, Eleanor. And that's all we've ever wanted for our Lena."

The speculation, therefore, wasn't idle gossip; it was rooted in genuine affection and a vested interest in the well-being of their community, and especially of Lena. Evan's extended stay had become a quiet question mark hanging in the air, a hopeful anticipation that this outsider, this man who had so gracefully navigated their town's subtle currents, might choose to stay.

The conversation at the hardware store often revolved around the practicalities of Evan's continued presence. "Think he'll buy that old Miller place?" Frank, the owner, would ponder, wiping grease from his hands with a rag. "It needs a lot of work, but it's got good bones. And it's close to Lena's place. Good investment, if you ask me."

These weren't just idle musings; they were the town's way of processing a potential change, of mentally preparing for the possibility of Evan becoming a permanent fixture. It was a collective hope that this man, who had brought a fresh perspective and a revitalizing energy to their beloved Collective, would also find a lasting place for himself within the heart of Cedar Ridge.

The town's rhythm was a complex interplay of individual lives, each contributing to the overarching melody. Evan's presence had introduced a new, intriguing note, one that resonated with a particular warmth and promise. The townsfolk, in their own quiet way, were observing, waiting, and, most importantly, hoping. They saw Evan not just as a consultant, but as a potential son-in-law, a new neighbor, a contributing member of their close-knit community. And in their collective awareness, the unspoken question wasn't *if* Evan would stay, but *when* he would finally make it official. The air in Cedar Ridge, once thick with the scent of pine and damp earth, now held a subtle undercurrent of anticipation, a collective breath held in eager expectation.

The unspoken question about Evan's future was not a source of anxiety for the townsfolk, but rather a topic of gentle, hopeful speculation. It was woven into the fabric of their daily interactions, a subtle undercurrent beneath the surface of their usual conversations. They had witnessed Evan's genuine engagement with Cedar Ridge, his deep dives into the Collective's operations, and the undeniable spark that had ignited between him and Lena. These were not the actions of a man merely passing through.

At the weekly farmer's market, the banter among vendors and shoppers often included a nod to Evan. "Did you see him yesterday, helping Mrs. Peterson unload her crates of apples?" remarked Sarah, who ran the local bakery stall, her voice a cheerful lilt. "He didn't have to, but he was right there, making sure none of them got bruised. That's more than some folks who've lived here twenty years would do."

This sentiment was echoed by others. Silas, the retired carpenter whose pronouncements carried a quiet authority, offered his perspective from his usual perch on a hay bale. "He's got that look about him, the look of a man who's found where he belongs. You see it in how he talks about the Collective, the pride in his voice. And you see it when he looks at Lena. It's a look I've seen before, in men who've finally found their true north."

The elders of Cedar Ridge, in particular, seemed to harbor a quiet but firm conviction that Evan was here to stay. They had a deep understanding of the town's pulse, an intuitive sense for when a new heartbeat began to align with their own. Lena, they knew, was the heart of Cedar Ridge for many of them. Her quiet resilience, her dedication to the community, her unwavering spirit – these were qualities they cherished. And to see her find a kindred spirit, someone who saw and appreciated her for all that she was, brought them a profound sense of peace and contentment.

Younger residents, too, were caught up in the collective narrative. At the small diner where many of the town's teenagers worked after school, the topic of Evan and Lena was a frequent, though usually hushed, subject.

"My sister's friend saw them walking by the lake last night," whispered Kevin, a lanky teenager wiping down tables. "Said they looked like they were holding hands, but then they let go real quick when they saw Mr. Henderson's truck. They're totally into each other, I'm telling you."

The 'walking by the lake' anecdote, likely embellished, spoke to a broader observation: the growing comfort and affection between Evan and Lena. It wasn't just about shared work; it was about shared moments, stolen glances, and a burgeoning intimacy that was becoming increasingly apparent to the watchful eyes of Cedar Ridge.

Evan's efforts extended beyond the Collective's immediate needs. He had taken it upon himself to research and propose grants for community projects, initiatives that would benefit not just the Collective but the town as a whole. His meticulous research and eloquent proposals had already secured funding for a much-needed upgrade to the town's aging library and a new playground for the local park. These actions, visible and impactful, solidified his integration into the community fabric.

"He's invested, you see?" commented Eleanor, the owner of the local general store, as she bagged groceries for a regular customer. "He's not just looking at profit margins; he's looking at how to make Cedar Ridge a better place for everyone. That's the kind of spirit we need around here."

The townsfolk also observed Evan's quiet contentment. His city apartment had been put up for rent, a clear signal that his ties to his former life were loosening. He had embraced the slower pace of Cedar Ridge, finding joy in the simple things – tending to his small garden, enjoying the quiet mornings with a cup of coffee on his porch, and engaging in conversations that ran deeper than the superficialities of urban life.

This sense of settledness was infectious. It fostered a quiet hope that Evan's extended stay would evolve into a permanent residency. The conversations in Millie's Diner, the post-office chats, the chance encounters at the grocery store – all of them carried a similar undertone: a hopeful curiosity about the future, and a gentle, collective wish for Evan to find his permanent place in Cedar Ridge, alongside Lena.

The townsfolk had seen outsiders come and go before. Some had arrived with grand plans and departed with bruised egos, unable to comprehend the unique rhythm and interconnectedness of their small town. Others had found the quietude stifling, yearning for the constant stimulation of city life. But Evan was different. He had approached Cedar Ridge with respect, with a genuine desire to understand and contribute, and, most importantly, with an open heart.

His integration had been a gradual process, each step deliberate and thoughtful. He had learned the names of everyone at the Collective, remembered their families' milestones, and offered assistance without being asked. He had attended local events, not as a spectator, but as a participant, his initial reserve melting away with each shared laugh and friendly handshake. His willingness to engage, to be present, had resonated deeply within the community.

The collective awareness of Evan's growing connection to Cedar Ridge was not driven by gossip, but by a genuine, almost familial, sense of care. They saw him as someone who was not just working *in* their town, but working *for* it. They saw his dedication to the Collective as a reflection of his commitment to the town's well-being. And they saw his burgeoning relationship with Lena as a promise of continued happiness and stability for one of their own.

The unspoken question of Evan's departure had transformed into a silent, shared anticipation of his arrival. The townsfolk, in their collective wisdom, seemed to understand that love, and belonging, could be as strong a draw as any career opportunity. They had watched the subtle shifts in Lena, the return of her radiant smile, the newfound lightness in her step, and they attributed much of it to Evan's presence.

The conversations, once filled with a gentle concern for Lena's solitary future, now buzzed with a hopeful undercurrent. "He's a keeper, that one," Frank from the hardware store had remarked to Silas just the other day, his voice filled with a quiet certainty. "He's got the right kind of grit, the kind that sticks. And he's got a good heart. Lena deserves that."

This sentiment was widespread. The collective awareness of Evan's integration was a testament to his character. He hadn't just adapted to Cedar Ridge; he had, in his own quiet way, become a part of it. And as the seasons continued to turn, painting the landscape in hues of amber and gold, the townsfolk of Cedar Ridge held their collective breath, waiting for the moment when Evan's presence would be no longer an extended visit, but a permanent, cherished part of their town's ongoing story. They sensed, with the quiet understanding of a close-knit community, that the question was no longer about if he would stay, but simply when he would finally, unequivocally, call Cedar Ridge home.

The hum of activity at Henderson's General Store was a familiar soundtrack to the rhythm of Cedar Ridge. It was a place where necessities were purchased, but more importantly, where connections were forged and maintained. The scent of aged wood, beeswax polish, and the faint, sweet aroma of fresh-baked bread from Sarah's bakery – a constant, comforting presence – hung in the air. Today, however, beneath the usual pleasantries and exchanges of local news, a subtle undercurrent of hopeful speculation swirled. As Evan, clad in his usual practical attire that had long since replaced his city suits, browsed the aisle for gardening supplies, heads turned, not with suspicion, but with a quiet, shared sentiment.

"He's got a real green thumb, that Evan," remarked Mrs. Gable, her voice carrying a warmth that mirrored the vibrant hues of the dahlias she so meticulously cultivated. She nudged her husband, Arthur, with an elbow. "Remember how those hydrangeas by the town hall looked before he started fussing over them? Almost gave up on them, they did. Now look at 'em. Blooming like they've got something to prove."

Arthur, a man of few words but keen observation, merely grunted in agreement, his gaze lingering on Evan's focused expression as he examined a bag of compost. To Arthur, Evan's dedication to the Collective had been impressive enough, but his quiet investment in the town's aesthetic – the small gestures that made Cedar Ridge more beautiful – spoke volumes. It was this holistic approach, this genuine care for the town in its entirety, that was slowly but surely etching Evan's name into the very bedrock of their community.

Miles away, at the Cedar Ridge Post Office, the air was thick with the scent of paper and ink, and the hushed tones of its patrons. Evelyn, the postmistress, a woman whose memory for faces and their associated parcels was legendary, paused her sorting as Evan entered to mail a package. She watched him with a knowing smile. He was a regular now, his mail a mix of industry-related documents and the occasional book order, hinting at his continued pursuit of knowledge beyond his professional obligations. The casual exchanges at the counter had evolved from polite inquiries about the weather to more personal, hopeful questions.

"Anything exciting coming in the mail today, Evan?" Evelyn would ask, her tone laced with a subtle, encouraging curiosity. Today, as he handed over the securely taped box, she added, "Heard you were talking to Mayor Thompson about those new streetlights for Elm Street. Sounds like a good plan. You're really looking out for this town, aren't you?" Her words, seemingly casual, were a reflection of the town's collective consciousness. They saw Evan's engagement not just as a professional duty, but as a genuine commitment to improving Cedar Ridge. He wasn't just fixing problems; he was proactively seeking ways to enhance their shared space, to make it safer, brighter, and more inviting. This forward-thinking approach, this desire to invest in the town's future, was a quality they deeply admired and quietly celebrated.

Later that afternoon, the comforting aroma of coffee and frying bacon wafted from Millie's Diner, the unofficial heart of Cedar Ridge's social circuit. The clatter of ceramic mugs and the murmur of conversation provided a familiar backdrop. Evan, taking a rare moment of respite from his intensive work at the Collective, sat at a corner booth, a half-eaten sandwich on his plate and a thoughtful expression on his face. He was sketching out some ideas on a napkin, his brow furrowed in concentration. Martha, her apron dusted with the perpetual flour of her baking endeavors, refilled his coffee cup.

"Working hard or hardly working, Evan?" she quipped, her eyes twinkling. She leaned in conspiratorially. "You know, Arthur Gable was saying the other day that if anyone could figure out a way to bring some of those young families back to Cedar Ridge, it'd be someone like you. Someone with fresh ideas, someone who isn't afraid to look at things a bit differently." She straightened, a flicker of genuine hope in her gaze. "We've got so much to offer here, but sometimes... sometimes we get stuck in our ways. It's good to have someone like you, who can see the possibilities we might be overlooking."

Her words, though directed at him, were also a public declaration of the town's evolving perception. Evan was no longer just the consultant brought in to fix a problem. He was seen as a catalyst, a potential force for positive change that could extend far beyond the boundaries of the

Collective. The townsfolk recognized his analytical mind, his ability to see efficiencies, and they began to wonder if those same skills could be applied to broader community initiatives. Could he help revitalize the struggling downtown shops? Could he propose innovative solutions for the town's infrastructure? These were the whispered questions that echoed through the diner, fueled by a growing belief in Evan's potential to contribute to the very soul of Cedar Ridge.

The conversations weren't always explicitly about Evan's professional capabilities. They often veered into the realm of personal connection, a testament to his growing presence in their lives. Silas, the retired carpenter, a man whose opinions were sought and respected, had been overheard at the hardware store discussing Evan's presence with Frank, the owner.

"He's got that quiet way about him, you know," Silas had mused, his voice a low rumble. "Doesn't boast, doesn't make a fuss. Just... does. Saw him last week, helping old Mr. Abernathy fix his leaky porch roof. Didn't even know the man. Just saw him struggling and pitched in. That's the kind of neighborly spirit we value here. It's not just about the Collective for him, is it? It's about being part of the fabric of this town." Frank had nodded, running a hand over a display of screws. "That's right, Silas. And you see it in Lena, too. She's got that spark back in her eyes. He's good for her. And if he's good for Lena, he's good for Cedar Ridge."

This sentiment, the interconnectedness of Evan's well-being with Lena's happiness and, by extension, the town's collective spirit, was a recurring theme. The townsfolk had witnessed Lena's quiet strength, her dedication to Cedar Ridge, and the subtle weight she had carried in recent years. To see her smile more freely, to witness the easy camaraderie and the palpable affection between her and Evan, brought a collective sigh of relief and a burgeoning sense of joy. It was as if Evan's presence had not only revitalized the Collective but had also breathed new life into the heart of their community.

The post office, the general store, the diner – these were the conduits through which these hopes and observations flowed. They were the places where the subtle whispers of "What if?" coalesced into a shared, hopeful murmur. It wasn't a demand, but a gentle, heartfelt wish. The townsfolk, in their innate pragmatism, understood that a contract was a temporary arrangement. But Evan's actions, his deep dives into the town's history and its future, his willingness to engage with every facet of Cedar Ridge life, suggested something more profound. He was laying roots, not just professionally, but personally.

Chloe, who worked part-time at the convenience store while attending community college, often found herself chatting with customers about Evan. "He's always so polite," she'd say, stacking shelves with brightly colored sodas. "And he actually listens when you talk to him. Last week, I was telling him about how much I miss having a proper bookstore, and he actually asked me what kind of books I liked and if I'd ever heard of this author who writes historical fiction set in small towns. It was like he was genuinely interested, not just making conversation. Maybe he could help bring one back? Or at least help us start a book club like he's in." Her youthful optimism, mirroring the town's collective yearning, highlighted the idea that Evan's influence could extend beyond the professional sphere, enriching the cultural landscape of Cedar Ridge.

The unspoken narrative was clear: Evan had brought more than just business acumen to Cedar Ridge. He had brought a fresh perspective, a willingness to invest, and, perhaps most importantly, a genuine affection for the town and its people. The townsfolk saw not just a capable consultant, but a potential neighbor, a friend, a part of their extended family. They saw the way his eyes crinkled when he smiled, the quiet thoughtfulness in his interactions, and the undeniable bond he had forged with Lena. These were the qualities that resonated, the indicators of a man who wasn't just passing through, but was deeply integrating into the very essence of Cedar Ridge.

The hope that Evan would choose to stay was not a fleeting fancy, but a deeply rooted aspiration. It was woven into the fabric of their daily lives, a quiet testament to the positive impact he had already made. They saw his potential to contribute not just to the Collective's bottom line, but to the town's overall well-being, its sense of community, and its future prosperity. In the quiet corners of Cedar Ridge, in the shared glances and the murmured conversations, a collective wish was forming, a silent prayer that the outsider who had so gracefully become one of them would ultimately decide to make Cedar Ridge his permanent home. They had seen his dedication, his character, and the undeniable happiness he brought to Lena. Now, they simply hoped he would recognize what they already knew: that Cedar Ridge was, and always would be, a place where a good heart could truly find its home.

Lena had always been a quiet observer, a part of the Cedar Ridge tapestry, woven with threads of steadfastness and a deep, abiding love for her home. She understood the subtle currents that flowed beneath the surface of everyday life, the unspoken hopes that residents shared like secrets whispered on the wind. Lately, those currents had been focused on Evan. She saw the way heads turned at the General Store, the extra seconds Evelyn lingered at the post office counter, the hopeful glances exchanged at Millie's Diner. It was a collective breath held, a community waiting to exhale with relief and joy if their burgeoning hope for Evan's permanence was realized.

She found herself, perhaps unexpectedly, becoming a subtle ambassador for Cedar Ridge. It wasn't a role she actively sought, nor one she would ever articulate aloud. It was more of an instinct, a quiet channeling of the town's heart into her conversations with Evan. She wouldn't pressure him, wouldn't voice the collective yearning directly, for she understood the sanctity of his personal choices. But she could, she realized, paint a picture of what Cedar Ridge meant to its people, of the unique rhythm that Elias had spoken of, the quiet dignity that Silas admired, the vibrant spirit that Mrs. Gable cultivated in her garden.

During one of their shared quiet evenings, a rare moment of stillness after a particularly demanding week for Evan at the Collective, Lena found herself tracing the rim of her teacup, the steam rising like a gentle exhalation. "You know," she began, her voice soft, almost hesitant, "there's a certain... magic to Cedar Ridge. It's not something you can quantify, not something that shows up on a balance sheet." She paused, looking out the window at the darkening sky, the first stars beginning to prick through the twilight. "It's in the way people here still look out for each other. It's in the shared history that lives on in the old buildings, in the stories we tell. It's in the understanding that even when things get tough, we're not alone."

She turned back to him, her eyes reflecting the lamplight. "When you first arrived, I think a lot of us were just... curious. You were an outsider, coming to tackle something so vital to our town's survival. But you didn't just tackle it, Evan. You embraced it. You've taken the time to understand not just the mechanics of the Collective, but the *people* it serves. You've seen the heart of this place." She chose her words carefully, weaving in the essence of what she knew the townspeople felt. "It's easy to see the potential for growth, for efficiency. But the real value, the enduring legacy, is in the community itself. It's in the feeling that you belong, that you're a part of something bigger than yourself."

She saw a flicker of understanding in his eyes, a softening that went beyond the polite attentiveness he always showed her. "That's... a beautiful way to put it, Lena," he said, his voice a low rumble that resonated with a quiet sincerity. "And I see it. I feel it. It's something I've been trying to articulate myself, in my own way."

"And you have," Lena affirmed, a small smile gracing her lips. "You've shown it in how you've talked to Mrs. Gable about her prize-winning roses, and how you helped Mr. Abernathy with his porch. You've shown it by taking the time to listen to Chloe at the convenience store talk about her dreams of a bookstore. Those aren't just random acts, Evan. Those are the gestures that build a home, that weave you into the fabric of a place." She leaned forward slightly, her gaze earnest. "Cedar Ridge... it has a way of getting under your skin, doesn't it? It's not just a place to work; it's a place to *live*. To be a part of something. To have roots."

She didn't explicitly say,

'We hope you'll stay.' She didn't need to. She was giving him the keys to understanding the profound impact his potential decision would have, not just on the Collective's future, but on the very soul of Cedar Ridge. She was showing him the quiet gratitude that existed for him, the unspoken welcome that had been extended, the burgeoning hope that he would see what they all saw: a place where he could truly belong.

Later, during a leisurely walk through the town square, she pointed out the old gazebo where summer concerts were held, the worn benches where elders shared stories, the vibrant flowerbeds that Mrs. Gable and others tended with such care. "This isn't just landscaping, Evan," she explained, her voice carrying the pride of a native. "This is a collective effort. It's a shared expression of love for our town. People pour their time, their energy, their passion into making this place beautiful, not for individual recognition, but because it's *our* town. It's a testament to what we can achieve when we work together, when we care."

She felt him listening, truly listening, not just to her words, but to the underlying sentiment. He was absorbing the quiet pride, the deep-seated connection that bound the residents to their home. She saw it in the way his gaze lingered on the children playing in the park, in the thoughtful way he greeted Silas, the retired carpenter, who was sketching out a new birdhouse design on a park bench.

"It's the intangible things, isn't it?" Evan mused, his voice thoughtful. "The sense of history, the shared experience, the collective investment in the present and the future. I've been so focused on the quantifiable metrics of the Collective, on the spreadsheets and the operational efficiencies, that sometimes I forget the most important asset a community has is its people, and their connection to each other."

Lena smiled, a genuine, heart-felt smile that reached her eyes. "Exactly. And you've become a part of that connection, Evan. You've shown that you understand that. You've shown that you care about more than just the bottom line. And that means the world to people here." She squeezed his hand, a silent acknowledgment of the unspoken conversation they were having, a conversation that echoed the hopes of the entire town.

She was Lena, the woman who loved Cedar Ridge, and in her quiet way, she was also its advocate, whispering its worth into the ears of the man who might just become its future. She believed that by showing him the depth of what Cedar Ridge offered, not just in terms of opportunity, but in terms of heart and belonging, he would see the profound resonance of a life lived here. And perhaps, just perhaps, he would choose to make it his own.

The subtle shift in Evan's interactions with the residents of Cedar Ridge had not gone unnoticed. What had begun as a professional necessity, a deep dive into the operational intricacies of the Collective, had gradually evolved into something far more profound. He found himself looking forward to the impromptu conversations at Millie's Diner, not just to glean information, but to genuinely connect.

He'd started timing his visits to coincide with the lunch rush, not for the bustling atmosphere, but for the easy camaraderie that permeated the air. Millie, with her flour-dusted apron and an uncanny ability to remember everyone's usual order, had become a reliable source of town gossip, yes, but more importantly, a warm and welcoming presence. He'd learned about the upcoming bake sale for the library, the progress on the community garden's expansion, and the latest antics of the mayor's mischievous golden retriever, all offered with a smile and a genuine interest in his reaction. These weren't interviews; they were simply conversations, woven into the fabric of daily life in Cedar Ridge.

His initial approach to Cedar Ridge had been analytical, a dissection of systems and strategies. He'd arrived with a clipboard and a set of objectives, viewing the town and its people as variables in a complex equation. But Cedar Ridge, in its quiet, persistent way, had begun to rewrite his calculations. He'd started attending the Thursday night bingo at the community hall, not out of any particular fondness for the game, but because he'd overheard Evelyn, the postmistress, lamenting the dwindling number of players. He sat with Silas, the retired carpenter, his weathered hands calloused from years of skilled labor, and listened to his stories of Cedar Ridge's past, of the days when the lumber mill was the heart of the town.

Silas's eyes would light up as he spoke of the collective spirit that had built the very foundations of the town, a spirit that Evan was now beginning to truly understand. He saw how Silas, despite his age, still offered his woodworking skills for community projects, mending fences and building park benches with the same dedication he'd once applied to crafting intricate furniture. It was a quiet, unassuming generosity, a palpable demonstration of belonging.

One crisp autumn evening, as the scent of woodsmoke mingled with the decaying leaves, Evan found himself at the annual Fall Harvest Festival, an event he'd initially marked down as another data-gathering opportunity. But as he navigated the stalls laden with local produce, homemade jams, and artisanal crafts, he realized he was no longer just observing. He was participating. He watched as Lena, her usual quiet grace amplified by the festive atmosphere, effortlessly guided a group of children through a pumpkin-decorating station.

He saw the easy way she interacted with everyone, her genuine warmth a beacon that drew people in. He found himself joining a group of men setting up the string lights for the evening's barn dance, their laughter echoing under the darkening sky. He learned how to tie a proper knot from a farmer named Jed, whose hands were as rough as tree bark but whose smile was as bright as the harvest moon. He even found himself engaged in a surprisingly deep conversation with Mrs. Gable about the optimal soil pH for growing heirloom tomatoes, a topic he'd never imagined himself discussing with such earnestness.

The realization dawned on him slowly, like the creeping dawn over a mountain range: he was becoming a part of it. It wasn't a sudden epiphany, but a gradual integration, like a river slowly carving its path through stone. He saw how Elias, the gruff but fair-minded manager of the local farm supply, would always offer a friendly nod and a genuine inquiry about Evan's well-being, even if their conversations rarely extended beyond the weather or the latest crop yields. He witnessed the quiet support network that existed, the way neighbors would rally around a family in need, whether it was a meal train during an illness or a helping hand with a barn raising. He saw it in the way Chloe, the young woman who worked at the convenience store, would leave little handwritten notes with her recommendations on his coffee order, her small gestures of familiarity chipping away at his professional detachment.

He began to understand that the Collective wasn't just an economic engine; it was a vital organ within the larger body of Cedar Ridge. Its success was intrinsically linked to the well-being of the town, and vice versa. He saw how the Collective's need for specialized equipment had spurred a local mechanic, Frank, to invest in new diagnostic tools, expanding his business and creating new employment opportunities. He observed how the Collective's surplus produce was being channeled to the local food bank, ensuring that no one in Cedar Ridge went hungry. These were not isolated incidents; they were threads in a complex tapestry of mutual reliance, a testament to the town's collective spirit.

During one of their frequent evening walks, a comfortable silence punctuated by the chirping of crickets, Evan found himself looking at Lena, the lamplight casting a soft glow on her face. "You know," he began, his voice softer than usual, "I've been so focused on the numbers, on the projections, on the feasibility studies... I think I was missing something. Something much more important." He gestured vaguely towards the dimly lit houses they passed, each one a repository of stories and lives. "It's the human element, isn't it? The way everyone here seems to know everyone else, to rely on each other."

Lena turned to him, a gentle smile playing on her lips. "That's Cedar Ridge, Evan," she replied, her voice a melodic counterpoint to the night sounds. "It's not just a collection of houses; it's a community. People here invest in each other, not just their time or their resources, but their hearts. They celebrate each other's triumphs and they lift each other up during hard times. It's a... a reciprocal kind of living."

"Reciprocal," Evan echoed, tasting the word. "That's exactly it. I see it everywhere I go. At the diner, at the hardware store, even at the bingo nights. People aren't just interacting; they're supporting. They're woven together." He paused, gathering his thoughts. "I used to think of 'community' as a demographic. A market segment. But here... it's tangible. It's the way Mr. Henderson at the bakery always sets aside a loaf of his rye for Silas, even though Silas hasn't ordered it. It's the way Evelyn organizes the secret Santa for the elderly residents every Christmas, even though it's a lot of work. It's the unspoken understanding, the shared history, the collective ownership of this place."

He looked out at the starlit sky, a vast expanse that seemed to mirror the depth of his burgeoning feelings. "I've spent so much of my life building things, solving problems, moving forward. But I never really stopped to consider what 'home' truly means. I always thought it was about a place, a structure. But it's not, is it? It's about belonging. It's about feeling seen, and valued, and... connected." He turned back to Lena, his gaze earnest. "And I'm starting to feel that here, Lena. More than I ever expected to."

The statement hung in the air, a quiet acknowledgment of a significant internal shift. He was no longer an outsider looking in; he was beginning to feel the pull of the current, the subtle but undeniable force that held Cedar Ridge together. He'd attended a town hall meeting about the proposed expansion of the local park, and while his initial intention was to assess the financial implications, he'd found himself captivated by the passion of the residents.

He'd listened to Elias passionately advocate for the need for more green space for the town's children, and he'd heard Mrs. Gable speak about the importance of preserving the natural beauty that made Cedar Ridge so unique. He'd even seen young Chloe speak up, her voice trembling slightly but her words clear, about how she imagined a small amphitheater for local musicians, a place for art and expression to flourish. These weren't abstract policy discussions; they were heartfelt pleas, rooted in a deep love for their town.

He found himself actively seeking out these moments of connection. He'd volunteered to help organize the Cedar Ridge Days parade, not because it was a strategic move, but because he'd seen the sheer joy it brought to the children. He'd spent an entire Saturday afternoon helping Jed and a few others repair the roof of the old community hall, his hands now stained with grease and sawdust, but his heart feeling lighter than it had in years. He'd even started learning the names of the dogs that roamed the streets, offering a friendly scratch behind the ears to Buster, the perpetually happy beagle, and a gentle word to Daisy, the elderly terrier who seemed to have a permanent place by the bakery door.

The weight of expectation, once a source of pressure, now felt more like a warm embrace. He noticed the subtle smiles, the lingering glances, the genuine warmth in people's greetings. It was as if the town itself was holding its breath, not in anticipation of his departure, but in hope of his return. He'd find himself replaying conversations, not just for the information, but for the underlying sentiment, the shared laughter, the moments of quiet understanding. He'd even started looking at the property listings, not with the detached curiosity of an investor, but with a nascent sense of possibility, of a future that might, just might, include him. The idea of leaving Cedar Ridge, which had once seemed like a logical, even inevitable, conclusion, now felt like a betrayal, not just of the town, but of a part of himself he was only just beginning to discover. The equation he'd arrived with was being fundamentally rewritten, not by external forces, but by the quiet, persistent, and utterly captivating heart of Cedar Ridge.

The air in Cedar Ridge, usually alive with the gentle hum of everyday life, seemed to have acquired a new resonance, a subtle vibration that spoke of held breaths and unspoken questions. It wasn't an anxious hush, but a pregnant pause, a collective holding of breath that seemed to emanate from the very cobblestones of Main Street, to whisper through the rustling leaves of the ancient oak trees, and to settle like a fine dust over the rolling hills. Evan, who had arrived in this town with a meticulously crafted agenda and a mind geared for objective analysis, now found himself the unwitting center of this town-wide anticipation. His personal decision, once a matter confined to the quiet deliberations of his own mind, had somehow become a shared concern, a topic of hushed conversations over coffee at Millie's, of lingering glances at the general store, and of thoughtful nods exchanged between neighbors tending their gardens.

He felt it in the way Millie's eyes would crinkle at the corners when he entered the diner, a hint of an inquiry behind her usual warm greeting. He noticed it in the way Silas, his face etched with the wisdom of years, would lean in a fraction closer when they spoke, as if trying to read the unspoken thoughts behind Evan's carefully chosen words. Even Elias, whose gruff demeanor usually masked a deep well of practicality, had taken to pausing mid-sentence when Evan entered his office at the farm supply, his gaze steady and questioning. It was a subtle shift, a collective turning of attention, that spoke volumes without a single syllable being uttered. His presence, once that of a temporary visitor, a temporary interloper, had somehow solidified into something more significant, something that mattered to the fabric of Cedar Ridge.

This pervasive sense of shared anticipation was both flattering and unnerving. It was a testament, he knew, to the way he had, perhaps unintentionally, begun to weave himself into the town's tapestry. He had come to study the Collective, to analyze its economic impact, and to determine its future viability. But in doing so, he had inadvertently become a part of the narrative he was meant to observe. The town, in its quiet, persistent way, had embraced him, and now, it seemed, they were waiting for him to reciprocate that embrace, to make a choice that would resonate far beyond his own personal life. It was as if Cedar Ridge itself was holding its breath, waiting to see if one of its own, a newly adopted member, would decide to stay.

He saw this anticipation reflected in the eyes of the children he'd helped with the parade preparations. Their boisterous energy, usually focused on the colorful floats and the marching band, would momentarily pause when he passed, replaced by wide-eyed stares and shy smiles. They had come to expect him, to see him as a fixture, a reliable presence in their vibrant community. He remembered a conversation with young Lily, a bright-eyed girl with a penchant for asking very direct questions, who had tugged on his sleeve one afternoon. "Are you staying, Mr. Evan?" she had asked, her voice full of innocent earnestness. "Because if you stay, maybe you can help us build a really, really big treehouse in the park!" Her simple question, devoid of any agenda, had struck a chord deep within him, highlighting the innocent hope that was being placed upon his decision.

The pressure of this collective expectation was a new kind of weight, different from the deadlines and deliverables of his former life. It wasn't the sterile pressure of corporate targets, but a warm, encompassing pressure, imbued with the hopes and dreams of an entire community. It was the feeling of being counted on, not just for his analytical skills, but for his presence, his potential contribution to the ongoing story of Cedar Ridge. He found himself replaying conversations, not just for the information exchanged, but for the subtle nuances, the unspoken hopes that lay beneath the surface. When Elias spoke of the Collective's need for long-term investment, his eyes, usually sharp and business-like, held a flicker of something softer, a hint of a plea for continuity. When Evelyn organized the annual book drive for the school, her tired smile seemed to carry an added layer of anticipation, as if she were hoping he would be there to help sort the donations, just like he had last year.

He understood, with a clarity that was both profound and slightly overwhelming, that his decision was no longer solely his own. It was intertwined with the collective well-being of Cedar Ridge. His departure would leave a void, not just in the professional sphere of the Collective, but in the hearts of the people who had come to know and accept him. It would be like removing a thread from a carefully woven tapestry, leaving a gap that would be noticeable, felt by all. This sense of interconnectedness, this understanding that his actions had ripples that extended far beyond himself, was a powerful force, shaping his thoughts and influencing his feelings in ways he had never anticipated.

He had attended a town meeting regarding the potential expansion of the local farmers' market, a project he had initially approached with a view to assessing its economic viability. But as he sat in the packed community hall, listening to the passionate voices of the residents, he realized his perspective had shifted dramatically. He heard Lena speak about the importance of the market not just as a place to buy fresh produce, but as a vibrant hub for community interaction, a place where friendships were forged and where the spirit of Cedar Ridge truly flourished.

He heard Jed, the farmer he had befriended, talk about how the market provided a crucial outlet for his small farm, allowing him to sustain his livelihood and continue the legacy his family had built. He saw the nods of agreement, the shared smiles, the palpable sense of unity that filled the room. This wasn't just a discussion about commerce; it was a testament to the town's shared values, its commitment to preserving its unique character. And in that moment, surrounded by the collective will of Cedar Ridge, Evan felt a profound sense of belonging, a yearning to contribute to something so much larger than himself.

The anticipation that hung in the air wasn't just about his decision, but about the future it represented. It was the quiet hope that the momentum he had helped to build, the connections he had forged, would continue to grow and flourish. It was the implicit trust that he understood the essence of Cedar Ridge, its quiet strength, its unwavering spirit of community. He remembered a conversation with Mrs. Gable, the matriarch of one of the founding families, as they admired the blooming roses in her garden. "Cedar Ridge has a way of holding onto the good," she had said, her voice soft but firm. "It remembers kindness, it nurtures growth, and it holds its own when the winds of change blow. We're all a part of that, you see. We all contribute to the holding." Her words had resonated deeply, echoing the sentiment he felt pervading the town – a sense of shared responsibility, of collective ownership of their cherished home.

He found himself increasingly drawn to the smaller, more intimate moments of connection. He would linger after his visits to the Collective's office, listening to the quiet conversations of the employees, noticing the easy camaraderie, the shared jokes. He had even started to learn the names of the various plants in the community garden, offering a word of encouragement to Silas as he meticulously staked the tomatoes, and sharing a smile with Lena as she pruned the nascent berry bushes. These weren't part of his original mandate, but they had become integral to his experience, to his understanding of what made Cedar Ridge tick. The anticipation of the town was not a demand, but an invitation, a gentle nudge towards a future where his presence would be a source of continuity, a pillar of support.

He knew, with a certainty that had solidified over weeks of observation and participation, that his professional detachment had long since dissolved. The equations he had once labored over had been replaced by the intricate, yet beautiful, dynamics of human connection. The objective data points had transformed into the warmth of a shared smile, the comfort of a familiar greeting, the quiet strength of a community that had learned to rely on each other. The anticipation of Cedar Ridge was not a pressure to be endured, but a testament to the fact that he had, against all odds, found a place to belong. He was no longer just an observer; he was a participant, a stakeholder in the vibrant, unfolding story of this remarkable town. And as the days turned into weeks, and the leaves began to paint the landscape in hues of amber and gold, the question of whether he would stay or go had become less about his professional obligations and more about answering the silent, hopeful question in the collective breath of Cedar Ridge.

Chapter Nine

The Crossroads Decision

The initial purpose of his arrival in Cedar Ridge, a mission etched into his mind with the precision of a surveyor's tool, had been the stabilization of the Collective. It was a task that had seemed straightforward, quantifiable, a matter of data points and strategic adjustments. He had arrived armed with spreadsheets and projections, his focus solely on the economic architecture of the town's central cooperative. The personal had been a negligible variable, an anomaly to be factored out. But the resonance of the town, its quiet insistence on his participation, had blurred those initial lines, weaving him into the very fabric he had come to analyze. Now, standing at this crossroads, the stark reality of his original objective resurfaced, not as a distant memory, but as a pressing, tangible concern.

He found himself drawn back to the quiet hum of the Collective's main office, the air thick with the scent of old paper and fresh coffee, a familiar aroma that had once signified only work, but now carried a deeper emotional weight. He pulled out his laptop, not to finalize plans for his departure, but to revisit the very foundation of his commitment.

He opened the detailed operational reports, the ones he had painstakingly compiled and updated in the initial months, tracing the intricate pathways of supply chains, the delicate balance of member contributions, and the complex web of distribution networks. He began to map out, with the same meticulousness he applied to his financial analyses, the potential fallout should he suddenly withdraw his oversight.

The system, he acknowledged with a degree of professional pride, was significantly more robust than when he had first set foot in Cedar Ridge. He had implemented new inventory management protocols, streamlined communication channels between different departments, and initiated a training program for younger members eager to take on more responsibility. He had seen the seeds of self-sufficiency he had sown begin to sprout, promising a healthier, more sustainable future for the Collective. Yet, as he delved deeper into the data, a disquieting pattern emerged. The improvements, while substantial, were still heavily reliant on his continued presence, his guiding hand.

He traced the flow of crucial decision-making processes. While many day-to-day operations ran smoothly, the more complex challenges, the ones requiring nuanced negotiation with external suppliers or the strategic reallocation of resources during unexpected market fluctuations, still gravitated towards him. The younger members, though bright and enthusiastic, lacked the years of experience, the deep understanding of the Collective's unique history and its intricate social dynamics, that were often necessary to navigate these situations effectively. They were learning, yes, but they were not yet ready to bear the full weight of leadership.

He created a flowchart, a visual representation of the potential disruptions. If he were to leave now, the immediate consequence would be a void in critical leadership. The existing operational framework, while functional, was like a finely tuned engine that required a skilled mechanic to keep it running at its optimal performance. Without that mechanic, even minor glitches could escalate into significant breakdowns. He foresaw delays in contract negotiations, potential misinterpretations of market trends leading to inefficient resource allocation, and a general hesitation in decision-making as individuals grappled with responsibilities they weren't fully equipped to handle.

He zoomed in on the training program he had established. The participants were diligent, absorbing information with impressive speed. He had identified a few individuals with exceptional potential, Elias's son, for instance, who possessed a sharp analytical mind, and Lena, who had a natural talent for understanding the needs of the producer members. He had envisioned them as his successors, gradually taking over more complex tasks, building their expertise under his mentorship. But the timeline for true mastery, for the development of the deep-seated intuition that came from years of practical application, was longer than his own personal timeline allowed for a clean exit.

He scribbled notes in the margins of his digital document, marking areas of particular vulnerability. The relationship with the regional agricultural board, for example, was one he had personally cultivated. He had earned their trust, demonstrating the Collective's reliability and its commitment to sustainable practices. The board members, accustomed to dealing with him, might view a new, less experienced representative with a degree of skepticism, potentially jeopardizing access to crucial support programs and favorable loan terms. This wasn't about his ego; it was about the tangible resources that flowed into Cedar Ridge, resources that directly impacted the livelihoods of its residents.

He thought about Silas, his weathered hands now steady as he worked on the irrigation systems, but his mind still sharp and focused on the bigger picture. Silas had been instrumental in helping Evan understand the historical context of the Collective, the unspoken traditions and the deep-seated values that underpinned its operations. Silas was a repository of invaluable knowledge, but he was also nearing retirement. His informal mentorship was vital, but it was not a structured succession plan. Evan's departure would mean a loss of that institutional memory, a severance of the generational link that Silas so carefully maintained.

The stark realization began to dawn, not as a personal dilemma, but as a concrete logistical problem. His departure wasn't just a personal choice; it was an operational risk. The systems he had improved, the efficiencies he had introduced, were like newly planted trees. They needed time to grow strong roots, to withstand the inevitable storms. Uprooting him now, before those roots had taken hold, would be like abandoning a fledgling sapling to the harsh elements.

He recalled a conversation with Evelyn from the bakery. She had spoken with such warmth about the Collective's role in supporting her business, allowing her to source her flour locally and to participate in the town's farmers' market without the burden of heavy overheads. She had expressed her hope that the Collective would continue to thrive, ensuring that the unique character of Cedar Ridge, its independent spirit, would endure. Her words, at the time, had been a comforting affirmation of his work. Now, they echoed with a different kind of weight, a reminder of the tangible impact his presence, or absence, would have on the lives of people like Evelyn.

He accessed the financial projections for the coming fiscal year. They were optimistic, but contingent on the continued smooth operation of the Collective. The projected increase in profits from the expanded organic produce line, a venture he had personally championed, relied on efficient harvesting, processing, and distribution. Any disruption in these areas, any hesitation in decision-making, could easily erode those gains, pushing the Collective back into the precarious financial position from which he had worked so hard to rescue it.

This wasn't about personal fulfillment anymore, or the quiet allure of small-town life that had begun to seep into his consciousness. This was about responsibility. It was about the practical, undeniable consequences of his actions, or inactions. He had come to Cedar Ridge to fix a problem, and in doing so, he had become an integral part of the solution. To walk away now, before the solution was truly solidified, would be to betray the very reason he had been sent, and more importantly, to let down the people who had come to depend on him.

He felt a strange, almost detached calm settle over him as he reviewed the data. The emotional turbulence that had characterized his internal debate began to subside, replaced by a focused clarity. The void he had to confront wasn't just an emotional one, a space left by a potential absence. It was a functional void, a gap in operational capacity that his departure would create. And that void, he realized with a growing sense of certainty, was too significant, too disruptive, to be ignored in favor of personal desires. The needs of the Collective, the tangible well-being of Cedar Ridge, demanded a pragmatic, if unromantic, decision. He had to ensure the stability he had fought so hard to achieve.

The familiar cobblestones of Main Street felt like a second skin beneath his worn boots. Each crack, each uneven stone, was a memory etched into the pavement, a silent testament to countless journeys taken. He walked without a destination, his feet guiding him through the heart of Cedar Ridge, a place that had, against all his calculated expectations, begun to feel like a destination in itself. The morning sun, still shy of its zenith, cast long shadows that danced with the rustling leaves of the ancient oaks lining the square.

He passed the familiar awning of the "Daily Grind," the aroma of brewing coffee a comforting, persistent hum that had become as much a part of his Cedar Ridge soundtrack as the distant chirping of crickets or the gentle murmur of the creek. He saw Mrs. Gable, her silver hair pulled back in a neat bun, sweeping the sidewalk in front of her flower shop, a ritual as predictable as the sunrise. A wave, a nod, a brief exchange of pleasantries – these small, unremarkable interactions were the threads that wove the town together, creating a tapestry of interconnected lives.

He found himself lingering near the town square, watching children chase pigeons with gleeful abandon, their laughter a bright, unburdened melody. He observed the weathered faces of the older residents, their expressions etched with the quiet wisdom of years lived fully, of challenges met and overcome. These were faces that had seen seasons change, generations rise and fall, all within the embrace of this seemingly tranquil landscape. There was a profound sense of continuity here, a palpable rhythm that was utterly alien to his own past.

His life had been a series of arrivals and departures, a nomadic existence dictated by project timelines and career advancements. He had always viewed movement as progress, the shedding of old skins for new, more polished ones. Growth, in his lexicon, was synonymous with distance traveled, with the accumulation of diverse experiences in disparate locations.

He leaned against the cool stone of the war memorial, its bronze figures stoic and enduring, a stark contrast to the ephemeral nature of his own transient existence. He thought of his previous postings, the sterile corporate apartments, the transient friendships that dissolved as quickly as they were formed. He had collected data, analyzed markets, and implemented strategies, but he had rarely planted roots. The concept of belonging, of being intrinsically part of a place, had always been an abstract notion, something observed from the outside, like a naturalist studying an unfamiliar ecosystem. Cedar Ridge, however, had invited him in, not as an observer, but as a participant. It had subtly, persistently, woven him into its narrative, its quiet embrace a far more potent force than any spreadsheet could ever quantify.

He walked past the small library, its brick façade softened by climbing ivy, a sanctuary of quiet contemplation. He remembered browsing its shelves in his early days, seeking information about the local economy, and stumbling upon volumes of local history, tales of hardship and resilience that spoke of a deep-seated connection to this land. He had been a surveyor, charting the economic terrain, but he had inadvertently discovered the emotional geography of Cedar Ridge. The town wasn't just a collection of businesses and residences; it was a living entity, imbued with the memories and aspirations of its people.

He continued his perambulation, his thoughts a swirling eddy of introspection. Was it possible, he pondered, to find true growth not in the constant pursuit of the new, but in the deliberate act of staying? Could commitment, the deep, unwavering commitment to a place and its people, be a more profound catalyst for personal evolution than a hundred different zip codes? He had always equated stagnation with immobility, with the risk of becoming jaded, of losing the edge that relentless change had honed. But Cedar Ridge offered a different perspective. It suggested that growth could also be found in nurturing, in the patient cultivation of what already existed, in the deepening of understanding that only time and shared experience could provide.

He paused by the bridge that spanned the creek, the water flowing with a gentle, persistent current, carving its path through the landscape with unwavering resolve. It didn't rush; it simply persisted, its journey a testament to the power of endurance. He watched a kingfisher, a flash of iridescent blue, dive into the water, emerging moments later with a triumphant glint in its eye. It was a simple, natural act, yet it resonated deeply. The kingfisher didn't migrate thousands of miles to find its sustenance; it found it in the familiar waters of its home. It was a creature of its environment, intrinsically connected to the ecosystem that sustained it.

He thought of Elias, his son, young Liam, who was already showing a keen interest in the cooperative's operations, his bright eyes absorbing every detail with an insatiable curiosity. Liam was growing up in Cedar Ridge, his roots sinking deep into the rich soil of this community. Evan knew, with a certainty that surprised him, that Liam's future was inextricably linked to this town, not out of obligation, but out of genuine connection. And if Liam's future was here, how could he, Evan, so readily sever his own ties? His past had been defined by what he left behind; his future, he was beginning to suspect, might be defined by what he chose to build, and to nurture, in a place that had unexpectedly captured his heart.

He rounded a corner and found himself facing the imposing, yet welcoming, structure of the Collective's main building. It was the epicenter of his initial mission, the symbol of his objective, and now, it represented something far more complex. He had come to Cedar Ridge with a purpose, a quantifiable goal, but the town had subtly shifted his perspective. It had introduced variables he hadn't anticipated – loyalty, community, a sense of belonging. These were not elements that could be easily measured or dismissed. They were the intangible forces that gave Cedar Ridge its unique character, its enduring strength.

He found himself tracing the intricate network of pathways that crisscrossed the fields surrounding the Collective, the very fields he had helped to optimize. He saw the farmers, their faces etched with the sun and wind, working in quiet unison, a testament to the power of shared labor. They were not just individuals cultivating crops; they were stewards of the land, bound by a common purpose. Their connection to Cedar Ridge was not merely economic; it was ancestral, spiritual. He had witnessed this deep connection, had been drawn into its orbit, and now the thought of leaving felt like a betrayal of that unspoken pact.

He stopped by the community garden, a riot of color and life, where residents of all ages worked side-by-side, tending to their plots with a shared sense of pride. He saw Martha, her hands stained with earth, showing a young girl how to plant seeds, her voice gentle and encouraging. It was a microcosm of the town itself, a place where knowledge was passed down, where bonds were forged through shared effort and mutual respect. He, who had always sought his growth in the vastness of the world, was beginning to understand that growth could also be found in the quiet, persistent tending of a small patch of soil, in the cultivation of relationships that deepened with each passing season.

He remembered his initial assessment of Cedar Ridge as a town on the cusp of decline, its economic foundations shaky, its future uncertain. He had seen it as a challenge, a problem to be solved. But as he walked these streets, as he observed the enduring spirit of its people, he recognized that Cedar Ridge possessed a resilience, a deep-seated strength, that transcended mere economic indicators. It was a strength born of shared history, of mutual reliance, of an unwavering commitment to each other. He had come to save the Collective, but in a far more profound sense, Cedar Ridge had saved him, offering him a glimpse of a life rich with connection, a life where belonging was not a given, but a cultivated treasure.

The crossroads ahead was no longer just a professional decision; it was a deeply personal one, a choice between the familiar path of transient success and the uncharted territory of rooted commitment. He looked at the sun-drenched landscape, at the sturdy oak trees that had weathered countless storms, and a nascent understanding began to take root within him – that true growth might not be about moving on, but about digging in.

The late afternoon sun cast a warm, golden hue across Lena's porch, illuminating the dust motes dancing in the air and the gentle smile that graced her lips as Evan approached. He'd found himself drawn to her, not in a desperate plea for a solution, but in a quiet search for understanding, for a mirror to the eddy of emotions churning within him. He hadn't come to ask her what he *should* do, but rather, to articulate what he was *feeling*, to see if the chaotic landscape of his inner world could find some semblance of order in the shared space of conversation.

"Hey," he said, his voice softer than usual as he stepped onto the worn wooden planks, the familiar creak a comforting sound that always seemed to welcome him. He'd learned to appreciate the subtle symphony of Cedar Ridge, the small sounds that wove themselves into the fabric of daily life, a stark contrast to the sterile silence of his previous existence.

Lena rose from her rocking chair, her movements fluid and unhurried. "Evan. I was hoping you might stop by." Her eyes, the color of warm honey, held a depth of understanding that always disarmed him. He knew she wouldn't pry, wouldn't push, but would simply offer a safe harbor for his thoughts.

"I... I needed to talk," he admitted, running a hand through his hair, a nervous habit he hadn't quite shaken. He'd spent years projecting an image of unwavering control, of strategic decisiveness, but here, with Lena, the carefully constructed façade felt like a burden he was eager to shed.

She gestured to the swing beside her. "Come, sit. Tell me what's on your mind." The ease with which she invited him into her space, into her quiet rhythm, was something he was still unaccustomed to, yet deeply craved.

He sat down, the gentle sway of the porch swing mimicking the back-and-forth of his own indecision. He began to speak, not of projections or market analyses, but of the internal wrestling match that had become his constant companion. He spoke of the ingrained instinct to move, to seek out new challenges, to constantly redefine himself through distance and acquisition. It was a identity forged in the fires of ambition, a life measured by the miles traveled and the goals achieved.

"I've always been a nomad, Lena," he confessed, his gaze fixed on the distant treeline, the silhouette of the hills against the fading sky. "My entire career has been built on movement. On dissecting systems, optimizing them, and then moving on to the next. It's... it's what I know." He paused, searching for the right words to articulate the unfamiliar pull he felt towards this quiet, unassuming town. "But Cedar Ridge... it's different. It's not just a project anymore. It's become... something more."

He explained the conflict, the cognitive dissonance between his ingrained professional identity and the burgeoning sense of belonging that had taken root in his heart. He spoke of Liam, of the simple joy of watching his son thrive in this environment, of the unspoken promise of a childhood grounded in community, not in transient addresses. He spoke of the farmers, their weathered faces and their deep connection to the land, a connection that resonated with a primal part of himself he hadn't known existed.

"I feel this... this tug," he admitted, his voice raw with the vulnerability of it all. "On one hand, there's the life I've always known, the path of perpetual forward momentum. It's familiar, it's predictable in its own way. And then there's... this. This feeling of being rooted, of being *part* of something. And it scares me, Lena. It scares me because it's uncharted territory. It's not a calculated risk; it's a leap of faith."

He looked at her then, his eyes searching hers for any hint of judgment, any subtle indication of what she expected. But Lena's expression remained one of unwavering empathy. She listened with a quiet intensity, her presence a steady anchor in the storm of his uncertainty.

When he finally fell silent, the only sounds were the gentle creaking of the swing and the distant chirping of crickets, a natural lullaby that seemed to absorb the weight of his confession. Lena reached out, her hand resting lightly on his arm, a gesture of comfort that spoke volumes.

"Evan," she began, her voice a soothing balm, "I hear you. I hear the struggle, the uncertainty. And I want you to know, truly know, that whatever you decide, my feelings for you... they don't change. They are genuine, and they are not dependent on your career path or your next destination."

Her words were a release, a quiet affirmation that settled deep within him. He had braced himself for the possibility of conditional affection, for the fear that his choice might dictate the future of their nascent relationship. But Lena's sincerity was a gift, a testament to the depth of her own heart.

"But," she continued, her gaze steady and unwavering, "you're right. This choice has to be yours. It can't be made out of obligation, or even out of a desire to please me. Because if you stay here for the wrong reasons, if it's just to tick a box or to fulfill a perceived expectation, it won't be fair to you, and it won't be fair to us."

She emphasized the word 'you,' her focus entirely on his agency, on his inherent right to choose his own path. "True belonging, Evan, isn't something you can force. It's something you cultivate. It's a conscious decision to invest yourself, to be present, to be vulnerable. And that kind of commitment, it needs to come from within you. It needs to be a choice you make for yourself, because it's what your heart is truly asking for."

Her words weren't advice in the traditional sense, but rather, a gentle redirection, a reminder of the power he held within his own hands. She wasn't telling him to stay or to go; she was empowering him to make the decision that resonated most deeply with his own truth.

"If you decide to stay," she went on, her voice soft but firm, "I want it to be because you want to build a life here, with Liam, and... and with me, if that's what you want too. Not because you feel you *should*. And if you decide to leave, I will understand that too. My life is here, and I've learned to find my own contentment within it. But I also know that sometimes, the bravest thing we can do is to follow our own path, even if it leads us away from what feels comfortable."

She looked out at the darkening sky, the first stars beginning to prick through the deepening indigo. "Cedar Ridge has a way of weaving itself into you, Evan. It demands a certain kind of attention, a certain kind of stillness. It's not a place for those who are just passing through. It's a place for those who are willing to dig in, to plant their roots, and to weather the seasons together."

He absorbed her words, each one a carefully placed stone in the foundation of his burgeoning understanding. Lena wasn't trying to sway him; she was reflecting his own internal struggle back to him, validating his feelings while simultaneously reminding him of the fundamental importance of his own autonomy. She was offering him a love that was steadfast, a support that was unconditional, but she was also demanding honesty, both with himself and with her.

"I've always thought of growth as... expansion," he mused, the rhythm of the swing slowing to a gentle pause. "As acquiring new experiences, pushing boundaries, seeing more of the world. But maybe... maybe growth can also be about depth. About delving deeper into a single place, into a single connection, and finding there a universe of its own."

Lena smiled, a knowing, gentle smile. "Perhaps. Or perhaps growth is simply about becoming more fully who you are meant to be, wherever that may lead." She turned to him, her gaze soft. "Don't let anyone else define that for you, Evan. Not your past, not your career, and certainly not my feelings, as much as I cherish them. This decision, this crossroads, it's entirely yours to navigate."

He felt a sense of peace settle over him, a quiet calm that had eluded him for weeks. He hadn't come to Lena for answers, but in speaking his truth to her, in witnessing her unwavering support and her gentle insistence on his agency, he had found a clarity he hadn't anticipated. The path ahead was still uncertain, the decision still heavy, but for the first time, he felt capable of facing it, armed not with a strategy, but with a quiet understanding of his own heart.

The choice was his, and in that realization, there was a profound freedom. He had come seeking to understand his feelings, and in Lena's honest gaze, he had found not just understanding, but the courage to begin to define his own future. The scent of honeysuckle, heavy on the evening air, seemed to promise something new, something rooted, something real.

The golden light of late afternoon had long since softened, yielding to the deepening hues of twilight. Evan sat on Lena's porch swing, the gentle creak a familiar rhythm against the quiet hum of Cedar Ridge settling in for the evening. He'd come to Lena seeking solace, not solutions, and in their conversation, he'd found something far more profound: a mirror held up to his own soul. Her words had not dictated a path, but rather illuminated the landscape of his own heart, revealing the power he held in his hands. He had been wrestling with a decision, feeling the weight of obligation, the pressure of perceived expectations, but Lena's perspective had shifted the ground beneath him.

He thought back to her emphasis on agency.

"This choice has to be yours. It can't be made out of obligation, or even out of a desire to please me." Her voice, steady and kind, echoed in his mind. He'd been so consumed by the idea of *what he should do* that he'd lost sight of *what he wanted.* The ingrained patterns of his past, the drive for external validation, the constant pursuit of the next challenge – these had become the lenses through which he viewed his present dilemma. He'd framed the decision as a binary, a forced hand dealt by circumstance. Stay and betray his ambition, or leave and sever the nascent threads of connection he was beginning to cherish.

But Lena had gently, so gently, nudged him to reframe it. It wasn't about being forced to stay, or being destined to leave. It was about *choosing*. He could choose to stay, not because Liam needed stability, or because he felt indebted to Cedar Ridge, or even solely because he cared deeply for Lena. He could choose to stay because he saw genuine value and purpose in this place, a life that resonated with a deeper, quieter part of himself. He could choose to invest himself here, to cultivate belonging, not out of necessity, but out of a sincere desire. This realization was not a lightning strike, but a slow dawn breaking within him. The oppressive weight of a forced decision began to lift, replaced by the liberating power of self-determination.

He looked at Lena, her silhouette a comforting presence against the darkening sky. She had offered him a love that was a safe harbor, but she had also demanded an honesty that was a sharp, clear compass. She hadn't tried to manipulate his decision, hadn't played on his emotions or his burgeoning feelings for her. Instead, she had amplified his own voice, urging him to listen to its true desires.

"True belonging, Evan, isn't something you can force. It's something you cultivate. It's a conscious decision to invest yourself, to be present, to be vulnerable." He had been waiting for an external sign, a definitive reason to stay or go, when the answer had been within him all along, waiting to be acknowledged.

He replayed the conversation in his mind, the subtle shifts in his own internal monologue. He had arrived at Lena's feeling like a ship tossed at sea, rudderless, at the mercy of the tides. He'd spoken of his nomadic past, the thrill of the chase, the constant reinvention of self. He had articulated the fear of stagnation, the dread of losing the sharp edge of his ambition. But beneath those anxieties, Lena had heard the yearning for something more grounded. She had seen the flicker of hope when he spoke of Liam's laughter echoing through the town square, of the quiet satisfaction of a shared meal with neighbors, of the earthy scent of rain on fertile soil. These weren't fleeting observations; they were the whispers of a soul seeking a different kind of fulfillment.

He had always associated growth with expansion, with the relentless acquisition of more – more knowledge, more experiences, more achievements. His life had been a testament to that philosophy, a carefully curated collection of accomplishments designed to propel him ever forward. But Lena's perspective offered an alternative: growth could also be about depth. It could be about delving into the rich soil of a single place, of a single relationship, and discovering an entire universe within its confines. He thought of the farmers he'd met, their lives etched with the rhythm of the seasons, their wisdom rooted in a profound understanding of the land. They weren't defined by what they *had*, but by what they *knew* and what they *tended*. There was a quiet strength in that, a resilience that transcended the transient victories of his corporate world.

The choice, he realized, was not a betrayal of his past, but an evolution. To choose Cedar Ridge would not be to abandon the man he had been, but to become a fuller, more integrated version of himself. It would be to acknowledge that ambition, while a powerful engine, was not the sole determinant of a life well-lived. He could still be driven, still be innovative, still seek challenges – but those pursuits could be grounded in a sense of place, in a commitment to community, in a love that was allowed to flourish without the constant threat of displacement. The concept of building something that wasn't destined to be sold, or optimized, or moved on from, began to feel not like a compromise, but like a profound opportunity.

He had always prided himself on his strategic thinking, his ability to dissect complex problems and arrive at optimal solutions. Yet, in this instance, his usual methods felt inadequate. The 'problem' wasn't a market inefficiency; it was a fundamental question of identity and purpose. And the 'solution' wasn't a calculated risk with predictable returns, but a leap of faith into the unknown, guided by intuition and a dawning sense of inner truth. Lena's quiet faith in his ability to navigate this was a powerful catalyst. She hadn't offered him advice, she had offered him her belief – her belief in him, and her belief in the possibility of a different kind of future.

The fear hadn't vanished entirely, of course. The instinct to flee the unfamiliar, to seek the comfort of the known, was deeply ingrained. The thought of explaining his decision to his colleagues, of facing the raised eyebrows and the whispered questions about his sanity, still sent a ripple of unease through him. But now, those anxieties were secondary to a growing sense of conviction. He was not choosing comfort over ambition; he was choosing authenticity over pretense. He was choosing to honor the quiet longing that had taken root within him, the desire for a life that was not just lived, but deeply felt.

He could picture it now, not as a grand, decisive moment, but as a series of small, deliberate choices. Waking up in his own bed, the light filtering through the same window each morning. Walking Liam to school, waving goodbye to a teacher who knew his name and his son's. Sitting on his own porch, not as a visitor, but as a resident, the creak of the wood a sound of belonging. Attending a town meeting, not as an observer, but as a participant, his voice carrying the weight of invested interest. These were not the milestones of a high-stakes business deal, but they held a richness, a texture, that his previous life had lacked.

Lena's hand found his, her touch warm and grounding. He hadn't spoken aloud for several minutes, lost in the quiet revolution unfolding within him. He looked at her, and saw not just the woman he was falling in love with, but a reflection of the best version of himself. She had shown him that true strength wasn't about outward control, but about inner conviction. It wasn't about always being decisive, but about being honest with oneself.

"I think," he began, his voice husky with emotion, "I think I've been waiting for someone to tell me it was okay to stay. To tell me that staying wasn't a failure, but a choice. A strong choice." He turned his hand to clasp hers, his thumb brushing against her knuckles. "And you... you didn't tell me what to do. You just... showed me that I could."

He felt a profound sense of gratitude, not just for her words, but for her presence. She had created the space for him to hear himself, to untangle the knots of obligation and desire. The journey ahead would still have its challenges, the transition would undoubtedly be complex, but the fundamental decision, the choice to anchor himself here, felt solid, real, and deeply his own. He was no longer adrift. He was choosing his harbor.

"It's not about giving up anything, is it?" he mused, more to himself than to her. "It's about gaining something else. Something... lasting." He looked out at the fireflies beginning to dot the darkening yard, their ephemeral lights a testament to the beauty of fleeting moments, yet also a promise of their recurring cycles. Cedar Ridge felt like that – a place where fleeting moments could accumulate, weaving themselves into a rich tapestry of lived experience.

Lena squeezed his hand. "It's about choosing where you want to invest your energy, Evan. Where you want to plant your roots. And that's a decision only you can make. But know this," she added, her eyes shining in the dim light, "wherever you choose to plant them, I'll be here, tending the soil beside you, if you'll have me."

The offer, so simple and yet so profound, settled over him like a comforting blanket. He didn't have to choose between his past and his future, between ambition and love, between himself and the life he was building. He could, with conscious intent, weave them all together. The crossroads was not an ending, but a beginning, and he was finally ready to step forward, not with the calculated certainty of a strategist, but with the quiet courage of a man who had found his own true north. The decision was his to make, and in that, there was an exhilarating, terrifying, and ultimately liberating freedom. He had found not just a place, but a possibility, and the choice to embrace it was entirely his.

The words settled between them, not a conclusion, but a commencement. Evan's hand, still clasped with Lena's, felt the warmth of her response, a silent affirmation that amplified the quiet revolution within him. He had arrived at Lena's porch seeking clarity, and she had gifted him something far more potent: the permission to define his own path, the courage to listen to its whispers. He had spoken of his internal shift, the burgeoning realization that this wasn't about an obligation, but about an investment, a conscious cultivation of a life that resonated with a deeper, more authentic part of himself. The crossroads wasn't a point of no return, but a fertile ground where multiple possibilities could coexist, nurtured by intention.

"It's not a surrender," Evan said, the words gaining strength as he spoke them, echoing the newfound conviction in his heart. "It's a commitment. Not an endless one, not a vow etched in stone that binds me forever. But a commitment to this place, to the work we've started, to... to the possibility of something real." He squeezed Lena's hand, a tangible connection to the anchor he was choosing to drop. He envisioned the coming months, not as a holding pattern, but as a deliberate exploration. He would dedicate himself to the Collective, not with the desperate urgency of a rescue mission, but with the steady hand of a builder. He wanted to see the seeds of their initial efforts blossom, to witness the tangible impact of sustained effort, to understand the subtle nuances of community-driven growth. This was not about settling for less, but about discovering a different, richer kind of more.

He thought of the tangible improvements still needed at the Collective. The dilapidated greenhouse that held so much promise, the community garden plots that needed more than just tilling, the workshops that could be expanded to encompass more skills, more artisans, more shared knowledge. These were not just tasks; they were opportunities to weave himself into the fabric of Cedar Ridge, to contribute in a way that felt meaningful, not just profitable. He pictured himself in worn denim, hands calloused from working the soil, sharing laughter with neighbors over a shared meal, the satisfaction of tangible progress a quiet hum beneath the surface of his days. This was a different kind of ambition, one that measured success not in quarterly reports, but in the flourishing of a community, the well-being of its people, and the enduring strength of its shared spaces.

Lena's gaze was steady, her eyes reflecting the faint glow of the porch light. "That's the essence of it, isn't it?" she mused softly. "Intentionality. Choosing where to place your energy, where to invest your heart. It doesn't mean you have to abandon the things that shaped you, Evan. It means you get to decide how they inform your present." She released his hand briefly to rest a palm on his forearm, a comforting weight. "You can bring your drive, your innovation, your strategic mind, and anchor them here. You can build something that lasts, something that matters beyond the next transaction."

He nodded, absorbing her words, letting them seep into the core of his decision. He had always associated growth with outward expansion, with the relentless pursuit of the next horizon. But Lena had shown him the power of inward exploration, of delving deep into a single patch of ground and discovering its infinite richness. Cedar Ridge, with its quiet rhythms and its deep-rooted connections, offered that kind of depth. He imagined the seasons turning, each one bringing its own unique challenges and rewards, his understanding of the land, and the people who worked it, deepening with every passing month. This wasn't a retreat from the world; it was a conscious choice to engage with a different, perhaps more profound, facet of it.

"I need to see what happens when I don't have an exit strategy," Evan confessed, a vulnerability in his tone that surprised even himself. "When the only way forward is to dig in, to make it work. To truly belong, not just visit. I want to see what kind of person I become when I'm not constantly looking for the next best thing, or running from the current one." He admitted the ingrained fear that had always propelled him – the fear of stagnation, the dread of becoming irrelevant. But now, that fear was being overshadowed by a potent curiosity, a desire to explore the untapped potential within himself, a potential he suspected could only be unlocked through sustained commitment.

He thought of Liam. He saw his son not as a reason *to* stay, but as a part of the tapestry he was choosing to weave. He imagined Liam growing up here, his laughter echoing not just in their temporary rented home, but in a place they could truly call their own. He saw Liam building friendships that weren't subject to the whims of his father's career, developing a sense of rootedness that had always eluded him. The thought brought a warmth to his chest, a quiet certainty that this choice was not just for him, but for his son as well. Cedar Ridge offered a foundation, a sense of continuity, a chance for Liam to experience the kind of stable childhood that Evan himself had craved.

"It's not about setting a date for leaving," Evan continued, his voice gaining a steady rhythm. "It's about setting a date for starting. For truly investing. I'll give the Collective my full attention, my full effort. I want to implement the changes we've discussed, to mentor the new apprentices, to see the local produce program thrive. And I want to do it without the constant hum of 'what if I had stayed in the city?' or 'when will this project be done so I can move on?' I want to be present, fully present, for at least a year. Maybe longer. Whatever it takes to truly see it through, to see what can be built when you're committed to staying."

He was not defining the end point, but the starting line. He was embracing the uncertainty, not as a threat, but as an opportunity for growth. He knew there would be challenges, moments of doubt, times when the ingrained urge to escape would resurface. But he also knew, with a certainty that resonated deep within him, that he had found something here that was worth fighting for, worth nurturing. This was not a passive decision, a surrender to circumstance, but an active, courageous embrace of a life he was consciously choosing to build. The weight of indecision had lifted, replaced by the exhilarating, albeit slightly daunting, freedom of commitment.

Lena reached out, her fingers gently tracing the line of his jaw. "A year," she murmured, a hint of a smile playing on her lips. "That's a good, solid chunk of time. Enough to put down roots, to see how they hold. Enough to get your hands dirty, really dirty, and find out what you're made of when the soil clings to you." Her eyes met his, filled with a quiet understanding and a shared anticipation. "And if, after that year, or two years, or however long it takes, you find that you've built something here that you want to continue building, then that's a wonderful thing. And if you find that your path leads elsewhere, then you'll have gained invaluable experience, and the knowledge that you gave it your best, your most honest effort."

He felt a profound sense of peace wash over him. Lena's acceptance of his choice, her unwavering support for his exploration, was a gift beyond measure. She wasn't asking for guarantees, but offering a sanctuary, a space where he could discover himself without fear of judgment. He realized that his previous life had been a constant performance, a carefully constructed facade of competence and control. Here, in Cedar Ridge, with Lena by his side, he felt the permission to be simply himself, imperfect and evolving.

"It's about more than just the Collective, though, isn't it?" Evan mused, his gaze drifting to the stars beginning to prick through the twilight sky. "It's about... belonging. It's about finding a place where I'm not just an outsider looking in, but someone who's part of the story. Someone who contributes, who cares, who is cared for." He thought of the genuine warmth he had already experienced from some of the townsfolk, the way Mrs. Gable had insisted he take an extra slice of pie, the easy camaraderie he had felt at the hardware store. These were small gestures, easily dismissed in his previous life, but here, they felt like the building blocks of connection.

He was not, he acknowledged, naive. He understood that building true belonging took time, effort, and vulnerability. It meant attending town meetings, even when he felt unqualified to speak. It meant offering help, even when he felt his skills were insufficient. It meant opening himself up to the possibility of rejection, and the certainty of imperfection. But the prospect no longer filled him with dread. Instead, it sparked a quiet determination. He was ready to learn, ready to contribute, ready to become a part of the Cedar Ridge tapestry, not as a fleeting thread, but as a strong, enduring one.

"I want to build something that outlasts me," Evan said, the thought crystallizing with surprising clarity. "Not a legacy of wealth or power, but a legacy of positive impact. A place where people feel supported, where they have the resources to pursue their passions, where the community itself is stronger because of the work we've done. That feels... more significant than anything I've chased before." He realized that his ambition had always been a solitary pursuit. This new ambition, however, was inherently communal. It was about lifting others up, about fostering shared success.

He looked at Lena, his heart full. "Thank you," he said, the words simple but laden with the weight of his gratitude. "Thank you for not telling me what to do. For showing me that the choice was mine. And for being the kind of person who makes that choice feel not just possible, but desirable." He felt a profound sense of relief, the kind that comes after a long and arduous journey, knowing that the destination, though still unfolding, was now in sight.

He had come to Cedar Ridge seeking an escape, a temporary respite. He was leaving with something far more precious: a sense of purpose, a community to call his own, and a love that felt as deep and as real as the earth beneath his feet. The crossroads was behind him, and the path ahead, though uncertain, was illuminated by the steady glow of intentionality.

CHAPTER TEN

A New Beginning

The morning sun, dappled and soft, painted the windows of the Cedar Ridge Collective with a warm, inviting light. Evan stood amidst the organised chaos of the main workshop, the scent of sawdust and fresh coffee a familiar, comforting perfume. It had been a restless night, filled with the quiet hum of a decision made, a new path charted. He'd replayed the conversation with Lena a hundred times, the echo of her gentle affirmation a steady beat against the lingering anxieties that still tried to surface. But the overwhelming feeling was one of clarity, of a profound rightness that settled deep in his bones. Today was the day.

He'd meticulously planned the announcement, not with the slick precision of a corporate boardroom presentation, but with the grounded intention of a craftsman explaining his vision for a new project. He wanted the message to be clear, unambiguous, and to carry the weight of his sincerity. He'd spoken to Lena the night before, confirming his plan, her quiet enthusiasm a bolstering presence. "Just be yourself, Evan," she'd said, her hand finding his. "Your intention is clear. They'll understand."

His first stop was Sarah, the Collective's unofficial matriarch, her presence a calming anchor in the often-turbulent waters of community projects. He found her tending to a tray of seedlings, her brow furrowed in concentration. "Sarah," he began, his voice steady, "I wanted to tell you something in person."

She looked up, her eyes crinkling at the corners. "Evan. Morning. You look like a man with something to say."

"I do," he confirmed, taking a deep breath. "I've been doing a lot of thinking, and a lot of talking, with Lena mostly. And I've made a decision. I'm staying."

Sarah's hands stilled, the tiny seedling held between her thumb and forefinger. A slow, genuine smile spread across her face, reaching her eyes. "Staying?" she echoed, a hint of disbelief tinged with joy. "You mean... really staying? Not just for another few months until the next big project calls you away?"

"Really staying," Evan affirmed, meeting her gaze directly. "I'm committing to the Collective. I'm committing to Cedar Ridge. I want to give it my full attention, my full effort, for at least a year. Probably longer. I want to see the projects through, to help build something sustainable here. This isn't a temporary fix anymore; it's an investment." He chose his words carefully, aiming for precision without sounding overly formal. "I'm not looking for an exit strategy. I'm looking to build. To contribute meaningfully."

Sarah set down the seedling and wiped her hands on her apron. She stepped closer, her expression one of deep appreciation. "Evan, that's... that's wonderful news. Truly wonderful. We've all seen what you've brought to the Collective, your energy, your ideas. But knowing you're committing, that you're willing to put down roots, it changes everything. It means stability. It means continuity. It means we can plan, really plan, for the future." She placed a warm hand on his arm. "This is more than just good news for the Collective; it's good news for Cedar Ridge."

He felt a flush of warmth at her words, the genuine emotion behind them a stark contrast to the often transactional acknowledgements he'd received in his previous life. "I want to help build that future," Evan said. "I want to see the greenhouse project completed, the new apprenticeship program flourish, and explore ways to expand our reach. I'm not looking to dictate, but to collaborate. To learn from all of you, and to contribute what I can."

Word, as it always did in Cedar Ridge, spread with remarkable speed. By the time Evan had finished his second cup of coffee, he was receiving nods of approval and quiet congratulations from passersby at the general store. Old Man Hemlock, usually a man of few words, gave him a gruff thumbs-up as he loaded a bag of flour into his truck. Mrs. Gable, her smile as warm as her famous apple pie, cornered him by the post office to express her delight, assuring him that "a good, steady hand is just what this place needs."

The relief was palpable. It wasn't the dramatic elation of a lottery win, but a deep, steady hum of contentment that resonated through the small community. Evan had arrived with a certain restless energy, a man accustomed to fast-paced decisions and immediate results. His presence had been a whirlwind, invigorating but also a little unsettling, hinting at a departure that always felt imminent. Now, his decision to stay, to commit, was like a grounding force, a signal that the momentum they had built together was not going to dissipate.

Later that afternoon, he found himself at the town square, ostensibly to check on the progress of the new park benches they were fabricating at the Collective. Lena was there, her laughter bright as she spoke with a group of children chasing a runaway ball. She looked up as he approached, her eyes alight with a shared understanding.

"So," she said, a playful glint in her eyes as she walked towards him, the children's boisterous energy trailing behind her. "The news seems to have travelled faster than a speeding bullet."

Evan chuckled, the sound easy and relaxed. "It seems so. Sarah was very... enthusiastic."

"She's thrilled," Lena confirmed, falling into step beside him. "We all are. You have no idea what a relief it is, Evan. To know you're here. To know that the plans we've been making, the ideas we've been nurturing, have a dedicated architect, not just a temporary consultant." She paused, her expression softening. "It means more than you know, to have you truly part of this."

"It means more to me than you know," Evan replied, the sincerity in his voice evident. "I was careful about how I phrased it. I didn't want to give the impression of an indefinite commitment, which wouldn't be honest, but I wanted to make it clear that this isn't a short-term arrangement. A year, maybe longer. Enough time to see things through, to truly embed myself, to build something tangible and lasting." He met her gaze. "I wanted to reassure everyone, including you, that I'm not going to vanish overnight. I'm here to invest."

Lena's smile widened, a genuine, radiant thing that reached her eyes. "That's the perfect balance, Evan. It's a significant commitment, one that shows your seriousness and your respect for what we're building. But it's also a timeframe that allows for honest evaluation. It's not a trap, and it's not a fleeting promise. It's a solid, measurable step towards integration." She linked her arm through his, a comfortable, familiar gesture. "And I have no doubt that once you're truly here, fully immersed, you'll find reasons to stay far beyond that initial year."

He felt a quiet confidence settle over him. This measured approach, this deliberate period of commitment, was precisely what had felt right during his long night of reflection. It wasn't about burning bridges behind him, nor was it about an endless, undefined commitment that could lead to burnout or future regret. It was about creating a space for genuine growth, for meaningful contribution, and for the possibility of a future that was built, not inherited or merely occupied.

"I think that's the hope," Evan admitted, his voice a low murmur. "I want to see what happens when I commit to a place, not just to a project. To understand the rhythms of a community, the needs that evolve over time, the subtle shifts that happen when people work together with a shared purpose. A year feels like enough time to move beyond the initial enthusiasm, to face the inevitable challenges, and to truly test the strength of the foundations we're laying."

As they walked through the bustling square, the sounds of cheerful chatter and the distant clang of hammers from the Collective workshop forming a familiar soundtrack, Evan felt a profound sense of belonging. It was a feeling that had been nascent for weeks, a quiet undercurrent beneath the surface of his actions. Now, with his decision publicly affirmed, it blossomed, a vibrant bloom in the fertile soil of Cedar Ridge. He was no longer just the city entrepreneur dabbling in rural revitalization. He was Evan, the man who was choosing to stay, to build, to be a part of this place.

The announcement wasn't a singular event, but the opening of a floodgate. Over the next few days, the confirmation of Evan's decision rippled through the community, solidifying into a quiet, underlying sense of optimism. Conversations at the diner now included mentions of Evan's involvement in future initiatives, not as a hypothetical, but as a certainty. The town council, usually a forum for addressing pressing issues and immediate needs, began to incorporate discussions about longer-term developments, knowing they had a skilled and dedicated individual ready to contribute.

Lena noticed the subtle shift in the town's atmosphere. "It's like a collective exhale," she commented one evening, as they sat on her porch, watching fireflies dance in the deepening twilight. "People feel more settled. More secure. They see your commitment not just as a personal choice, but as an investment in all of us."

Evan leaned back in his chair, the rough wood familiar beneath his hands. "It's about shared momentum," he agreed. "When one person commits, it encourages others. It validates the effort. I felt that when I spoke to Sarah, and I've felt it in so many conversations since then. It's not just about me staying; it's about what my staying enables for everyone else." He thought of the potential projects he now felt confident in pursuing – the expansion of the community garden, the development of a local artisan's co-op, the renovation of the old mill into a multi-purpose community space. These weren't just ideas anymore; they were tangible possibilities, fuelled by a commitment that had finally taken root.

He knew the period of adjustment would continue, that truly becoming part of Cedar Ridge was a journey, not a destination. There would be days when the ingrained habits of his former life would tug at him, days when the quiet predictability of small-town living might feel stifling compared to the constant urgency of the city. But those were minor eddies in the larger current of his newfound purpose. He had chosen this path, not out of obligation or a lack of options, but out of a deep-seated desire to build a life that felt meaningful and rooted. And with Lena by his side, and the quiet support of a community that had welcomed him with open arms, he felt ready for whatever lay ahead. The announcement was made, the news had spread, and a new beginning was truly, irrevocably underway.

Lena watched Evan as he navigated the small crowd gathered in the town square, his earlier conversation with Sarah and the subsequent ripple of confirmations still fresh in the air. A soft, almost imperceptible smile played on her lips. She hadn't realized, until this very moment, how much she had been holding her breath, how deeply she had anticipated this shift. His decision wasn't just a practical one for the Cedar Ridge Collective; it was a personal anchor, a silent testament to the quiet hope she had begun to harbor for their shared future.

She had always been fiercely independent, a trait forged in the crucible of self-reliance. Moving to Cedar Ridge had been a deliberate choice, a conscious step away from the expectations and pressures of her former life, a yearning for a slower pace and a more genuine connection. She had poured her energy into the Collective, finding purpose and satisfaction in building something tangible, something that served the community. But there had always been a solitary quality to her endeavors, a sense that while she was deeply invested in the town, she was still an observer, an outsider looking in.

Evan's arrival had disrupted that equilibrium. His drive, his innovative thinking, his sheer presence had injected a new dynamism into the Collective. And in the quiet moments, in the shared late nights planning projects, in the easy camaraderie that had developed between them, Lena had found herself drawn to him. She'd admired his intellect, his genuine desire to contribute, and, increasingly, the quiet kindness that underscored his ambitious nature. But she'd also maintained a careful distance, a practiced reserve, unwilling to let her hopes become too entangled with the possibility of his departure. His city life, his previous commitments, had loomed large, a constant reminder that his presence in Cedar Ridge might be transient.

So, when he had spoken to her the night before, outlining his intention to commit, to stay, a wave of relief had washed over her, so profound it had taken her breath away. It was a relief that transcended the practical implications for the Collective. It was the relief of seeing a possibility solidify, of a nascent hope finding its footing. His words had been measured, honest, and filled with a sincerity that resonated deeply. He wasn't making a grand, sweeping declaration, but a considered, practical commitment – a year, perhaps longer, enough time to truly invest and see the fruits of their labor. It was exactly the kind of grounded approach that appealed to her, a promise delivered not with fanfare, but with quiet conviction.

Now, watching him interact with people, his posture relaxed, his smile easy, she saw that conviction reflected in his demeanor. The subtle tension she had sometimes sensed in him, the slight edge of a man on a deadline or a man always looking for the next opportunity, seemed to have softened. He moved with a newfound groundedness, a sense of belonging that was palpable. It was as if a question that had been hanging in the air for months had finally been answered, and the response was the gentle hum of reassurance.

She walked towards him, the gentle murmur of conversations around them a comforting backdrop. The children who had been playing nearby, their laughter a bright counterpoint to the afternoon sun, now scattered as the town square began to buzz with a more adult energy. Lena reached him just as he turned, his eyes finding hers. There was a shared understanding in that glance, a silent acknowledgement of the significance of the day.

"It seems the word is out," Lena said, her voice light, a playful lilt to it.

Evan's smile widened, a genuine, unforced expression that reached his eyes. "It certainly appears that way," he replied, his gaze sweeping over the townspeople who were offering him nods of approval and quiet congratulations. "Sarah has a way of... disseminating information with impressive efficiency."

Lena laughed, a soft, melodic sound. "She's just happy, Evan. We all are. It's... it's truly wonderful news." She paused, her gaze holding his. "For so long, it felt like we were building something, but always with the understanding that the architect might pack up his blueprints and leave. Now..." she trailed off, the unspoken thought hanging between them.

"Now there's a commitment to the foundation," Evan finished for her, his voice steady. "To seeing the house built, not just drawn." He met her eyes, a quiet intensity in his own. "I wanted you to know, Lena, that my decision isn't just about the Collective. It's... it's about more than that."

The simple words, delivered with such earnestness, sent a warm ripple through Lena. She had consciously guarded her heart, shielding it from the potential sting of disappointment. She had told herself that her happiness shouldn't be contingent on Evan's presence, that her own sense of belonging in Cedar Ridge was solid enough. But to hear him acknowledge that his decision held a deeper significance, that he saw their shared future as intertwined with his commitment to the town, felt like a gentle unfolding of possibility.

"I understand," she said softly, the words carrying more weight than she intended. "And it means a great deal, Evan. Knowing that you see the potential here, not just as a project, but as a place to invest your time, your energy... your future." She linked her arm through his, a gesture of casual intimacy that felt both natural and significant. "It's not just about the greenhouse or the workshops anymore, is it?"

"No," he agreed, his thumb brushing lightly against her arm. "It's about building a life. And Cedar Ridge... it feels like the right place for that. Especially with you here."

The admission hung in the air, a sweet melody against the usual hum of small-town life. Lena felt a blush creep up her neck, a warmth spreading through her chest. She had found a sense of peace in Cedar Ridge, a quiet contentment that had been lacking in her previous life. But with Evan's presence, with this newfound hope for a shared future, that peace was deepening, blossoming into something richer, more vibrant. The unspoken tension that had often underscored their interactions, a subtle dance of attraction and reserve, seemed to dissipate, replaced by an easy anticipation, a shared excitement for what lay ahead.

"We have so much to do," Lena murmured, her gaze sweeping across the familiar storefronts, the quaint houses, the sturdy oaks lining the streets. "So many plans, so many dreams that now feel... tangible."

"And we'll do it together," Evan said, his voice low and resonant. "One project at a time. One day at a time. I'm not looking to rush anything, Lena. I want to learn. I want to grow with this community, and with you."

The sincerity in his voice was a balm to her soul. She had always been practical, grounded in reality. But there was a part of her, a part she had long suppressed, that yearned for a touch of romance, for a love story that unfolded organically, woven into the fabric of everyday life. Evan's presence, his quiet commitment, was offering her that possibility, a chance to believe in a future that was both grounded and magical.

As they walked through the square, acknowledging the greetings and smiles from their neighbors, Lena felt a profound sense of relief. It wasn't a dramatic catharsis, but a deep, steady calm. The weight of uncertainty had lifted, replaced by the quiet joy of shared purpose and the burgeoning hope of a deeper connection. She looked at Evan, his profile strong and thoughtful against the backdrop of the familiar town, and felt a profound sense of gratitude. Cedar Ridge had given her a home, a community, a purpose. And now, it seemed, it was offering her the chance for a shared future, a partnership built on mutual respect, shared dreams, and the quiet promise of love.

The following days were filled with a subtle yet significant shift in Lena's perspective. The anxieties that had occasionally pricked at her, the lingering doubts about her place in Cedar Ridge, seemed to recede, replaced by a quiet confidence. Evan's decision had, in essence, validated her own commitment to the town. His willingness to invest his formidable talents and energy into its future mirrored her own deep-seated belief in its potential. She found herself looking at him with new eyes, not just as a colleague or a friend, but as a partner, someone who shared her vision and her dedication.

Their conversations took on a new depth, flowing effortlessly from discussions about the Collective's projects to more personal exchanges. The unspoken tension that had sometimes flickered between them, a gentle undercurrent of attraction she had tried to ignore, now seemed to transform into a comfortable warmth, a mutual understanding. Lena found herself sharing more freely, opening up about her past, her dreams, her vulnerabilities, with a trust she hadn't extended to anyone in a long time. And Evan, in turn, was an attentive listener, his presence a steady, reassuring force.

One afternoon, as they were sorting through inventory at the Collective, a shipment of new tools and materials had arrived. The boxes were stacked high, the air thick with the scent of wood and metal. Lena found herself handing Evan a heavy box of specialized screws, their fingers brushing. The contact, brief as it was, sent a jolt through her, a reminder of the simmering attraction that was now, finally, allowed to surface.

"Thanks," Evan said, his voice a low rumble. He held her gaze for a moment longer than necessary, a subtle question in his eyes.

Lena felt her cheeks warm, but instead of looking away, she met his gaze, a small smile playing on her lips. "Anytime," she replied, her voice soft. "We make a good team, don't we?"

"The best," Evan confirmed, his smile mirroring hers. He didn't pull away, and neither did she. In that moment, surrounded by the organized chaos of their shared work, the simple act of handing over a box of screws felt charged with unspoken possibility. It was a silent acknowledgment of their burgeoning connection, a testament to the hope that had taken root in the fertile ground of Cedar Ridge.

Later that week, they found themselves at the town's annual summer fair. The air buzzed with the cheerful cacophony of laughter, music, and excited shouts. Children chased each other with brightly colored balloons, and the scent of popcorn and grilled food wafted through the air. Lena, who had always enjoyed the fair for its sense of community, found herself looking forward to it even more this year, knowing Evan would be there.

They navigated the bustling crowds, their hands occasionally brushing, their conversations interspersed with shared smiles and knowing glances. Evan had a way of making even the most mundane activity feel special, and Lena found herself utterly captivated by his presence. He pointed out the intricate woodworking of a local artisan's stall, his eyes alight with appreciation for the craftsmanship. He bought her a scoop of homemade ice cream from Mrs. Gable's stand, his smile warm as he watched her savor the sweet treat.

As the sun began to dip below the horizon, painting the sky in hues of orange and pink, they found themselves standing by the small bandstand, listening to the gentle strains of a local folk band. The crowd had thinned, leaving a sense of quiet intimacy. Lena leaned her head against Evan's arm, a sense of profound contentment washing over her.

"This is nice," she murmured, her voice barely audible above the music.

"It is," Evan agreed, his arm tightening slightly around her. "It's... everything I hoped it would be. Being here. Being with you."

Lena closed her eyes, savoring the moment. The relief she had felt at his decision had deepened into a quiet joy, a sense of rightness that settled deep within her. The uncertainty of their future, once a source of quiet anxiety, now felt like an exciting promise, a blank canvas waiting to be filled with shared experiences. She had always believed in the power of community, in the strength of human connection. And now, with Evan by her side, she felt that belief solidify, transforming into a tangible, hopeful reality. The unspoken tension had dissolved, replaced by the gentle hum of a shared future, a melody that resonated with the promise of love and belonging. Cedar Ridge, she realized, was not just a place she lived; it was a place where she was finally, truly, home.

The shift was subtle, almost imperceptible at first, like the gentle turning of a tide. It began with smiles, warmer and more sustained than the polite acknowledgements Lena had grown accustomed to seeing directed at Evan. Then came the nods, not just of recognition, but of genuine respect, accompanied by the occasional, hearty clap on the shoulder from a farmer whose tractor he'd helped troubleshoot, or a grateful squeeze of the arm from Mrs. Gable after he'd offered a hand with her perpetually overstuffed grocery bags. The initial quiet observation, the careful sizing-up of the newcomer, had gradually dissolved, replaced by an unambiguous embrace.

Evan found himself a frequent fixture at the Thursday night potlucks at the community hall, an event he'd previously attended out of a sense of obligation, a duty to Lena and the Collective. Now, he looked forward to them. The conversations weren't solely about the logistics of the upcoming town festival or the latest harvest yields; they veered into lighter, more personal territories. Old Man Hemlock, usually a man of few words, would corner him to discuss the merits of different apple cider recipes, his eyes twinkling with an unexpected passion. Sarah, whose efficiency in information dissemination was legendary, now took particular delight in orchestrating impromptu introductions, ensuring Evan was looped into conversations about everything from the book club's latest selection to the surprisingly fierce rivalries in the local bocce ball league.

Lena watched this transformation with a quiet joy that settled deep within her. She'd seen the way Evan, with his keen intellect and driven nature, had initially approached Cedar Ridge like a complex problem to be solved, a project with defined parameters and measurable outcomes. She'd recognized his innate desire to contribute, to make a tangible difference, but she'd also sensed his underlying struggle to truly *belong*. He'd been a builder, an architect of solutions, but not yet a resident, a root. Now, she saw the roots taking hold, nourished by the soil of genuine connection.

One Saturday, as Evan was helping Mr. Henderson repair a section of fencing along the edge of his property, the scent of freshly cut wood mingling with the earthy aroma of damp soil, Mr. Henderson's granddaughter, Lily, a bright-eyed girl of about seven, approached them. She'd been playing with a collection of brightly colored wooden blocks Lena had donated to the community center's childcare program. She held out a somewhat lopsided wooden birdhouse, its paint still slightly tacky.

"Mr. Evan," she piped up, her voice clear and eager, "I made this for you. So you have somewhere to keep your... your important city things."

Evan, who had been meticulously tightening a bolt, straightened up, a surprised smile softening his features. He knelt down, his movements careful not to appear intimidating to the child. "Well, Lily, that's incredibly kind of you," he said, accepting the birdhouse with genuine appreciation. He turned it over in his hands, admiring the uneven lines and the cheerful, if slightly smudged, coat of robin's egg blue. "It's perfect. Thank you."

Lily beamed, her small face alight with pride. She then turned to Lena, who had been observing from a short distance, a gentle smile on her lips. "Miss Lena, Mr. Evan's going to stay here, right? He's going to help us build the new playground?"

The directness of the question, the innocent assumption of his permanence, struck a chord with Evan. He glanced at Lena, and in her eyes, he saw a reflection of his own burgeoning sense of belonging. He knew that Lily's question, though childish, encapsulated the sentiment of the town. They weren't just accepting his help; they were accepting *him*.

"That's the plan, Lily-bug," Evan said, his voice warm. He ruffled her hair gently. "We're going to build the best playground Cedar Ridge has ever seen."

Lily clapped her hands with delight and scampered off, her mission accomplished. Evan watched her go, then turned back to the fence, his movements now imbued with a deeper sense of purpose. He was no longer just a skilled hand lending assistance; he was a future neighbor, a participant in the shared future of this small town.

The tangible benefits of this acceptance began to manifest in ways that went beyond mere social pleasantries. Invitations, once reserved for long-established residents, now found their way to Evan's doorstep. He was asked to join the organizing committee for the annual Cedar Ridge Harvest Festival, a role he accepted with enthusiasm. He found himself brainstorming ideas with Sarah and the other committee members, his input not just solicited but genuinely valued. He learned about the intricate dance of planning, the delicate balance of tradition and innovation that defined the festival, and he found a surprising satisfaction in contributing to something that held such deep meaning for the community.

He was also invited to a small, informal gathering at the O'Malley's farm, a gathering that was less about agricultural concerns and more about celebrating the recent success of their son's university application. It was an intimate affair, held on their porch overlooking rolling fields bathed in the golden light of late afternoon. Evan, initially feeling like an interloper, found himself drawn into conversations about family, about aspirations, about the quiet pride of seeing a child succeed. He shared a story about his own younger sibling's academic journey, a story he hadn't thought about in years, and he felt a connection, a shared human experience that transcended the boundaries of his previous urban existence.

Lena noticed how Evan's perspective had shifted. He was no longer solely focused on the grand projects, the large-scale initiatives. He began to appreciate the smaller gestures, the seemingly insignificant moments that formed the bedrock of community life. He started attending the weekly farmer's market, not just to procure supplies for the Collective, but to chat with the vendors, to learn about their families, to become a familiar face amongst the stalls. He'd strike up conversations with Mrs. Gable about her prize-winning jams, offer a word of encouragement to young Tom who was selling his homemade bird feeders for the first time, and even engage in playful banter with the town's resident jokester, Pete, over the best way to select a ripe tomato.

One evening, after a particularly productive work session at the Collective, Lena found Evan lingering, not by the blueprints or the supply lists, but by the window, gazing out at the quiet street. The streetlights cast a warm, inviting glow, and the distant sound of laughter drifted from a nearby house.

"It's different, isn't it?" he said, his voice softer than usual.

Lena joined him, leaning against the doorframe. "What is?"

"This," he gestured vaguely towards the scene outside. "The feeling. It used to feel... transient, even when I was working here. Like I was visiting, or just passing through. Now..." He trailed off, searching for the right words. "Now it feels like I'm part of the rhythm. Like I belong to the sound of that laughter, to the glow of those lights."

He turned to her, his eyes holding a newfound depth, a quiet sincerity that always made her heart flutter. "You talked about this, didn't you? About the tangible benefits of belonging. I'm starting to understand what you meant." He paused, a small smile playing on his lips. "It's not just about the projects we're building, Lena. It's about the people. It's about feeling... woven in."

Lena's smile widened, a genuine, unrestrained expression of happiness. "That's Cedar Ridge, Evan. It's a place that invites you to be woven in, if you're willing to let it." She reached out, her hand resting lightly on his arm. The gesture, so natural now, still held a spark of something new, something electric. "And you, Evan, you've proven yourself to be more than willing."

He covered her hand with his, his touch warm and steady. "I'm glad I did," he said, his gaze unwavering. "I'm so glad I did." In that quiet moment, surrounded by the remnants of their shared work, they both felt the profound shift – a transition from observer to participant, from outsider to an integral thread in the rich tapestry of Cedar Ridge. Evan was no longer just working *in* the town; he was working *with* it, living *in* it, and most importantly, he was becoming a part of it.

The carefully constructed walls he had carried with him from his previous life had begun to crumble, replaced by the open, welcoming embrace of a community that had finally, truly, claimed him as one of their own. He was no longer just Evan Hayes, the driven city architect; he was Evan, the man who helped fix fences, who appreciated homemade birdhouses, who looked forward to potlucks, and who was, undeniably, becoming a part of the very fabric of Cedar Ridge.

The hum of the generator, once a symbol of progress and a testament to their collective efforts in bringing electricity to the more remote homesteads, now felt different to Evan. It was no longer just about the successful completion of a task, the ticking off of another box on a project plan. Now, as he worked alongside Silas, a seasoned farmer whose hands bore the indelible marks of a life lived under the open sky, Evan felt a subtle yet significant shift within himself.

He wasn't just troubleshooting a faulty connection; he was ensuring Silas could keep his milk cold, that Mrs. Gable could bake her award-winning pies without worrying about the oven's fluctuating temperature, that young Lily could see her drawings clearly on the page in the dim evening light. The impact, he realized, wasn't measured solely in kilowatts delivered or systems optimized, but in the quiet thrum of everyday life made a little easier, a little brighter.

Lena observed this evolution with a quiet satisfaction. Evan's innate drive, his sharp analytical mind, had always been evident. He'd arrived in Cedar Ridge with a clear vision, a blueprint for efficiency and improvement that was, in many ways, a reflection of his own highly structured urban existence. He'd approached the Collective's needs with the same meticulousness he'd once applied to designing skyscrapers. But the seeds of change had been sown, and they were now taking root. He was beginning to understand that true progress wasn't solely about the speed of implementation or the elegance of a solution, but about the sustainability of its impact, the way it resonated within the heart of the community.

Their work sessions at the Collective had taken on a new dimension. While the core objective remained the same – to strengthen the town's infrastructure and resources – the methodology had softened, the focus broadened. Evan was no longer just dictating the most efficient course of action. He was engaging Lena and the small team of dedicated volunteers – the backbone of the Collective's operations – in a more collaborative dialogue. He'd ask questions that went beyond the purely technical. "What's the long-term maintenance plan for this system?" he'd inquire, but then he'd follow it up with, "And how can we ensure the person responsible feels empowered and supported to carry it out?" He was, for the first time, thinking about the *people* who would be living with and working with the changes they implemented, not just the changes themselves.

One afternoon, they were reviewing the plans for the new community garden's irrigation system. Previously, Evan would have meticulously calculated water flow rates, optimal pressure, and the most cost-effective pipe materials. This time, however, he'd spread the blueprints across a worn, wooden table that bore the faint scent of pine and countless years of shared meals. He'd invited Mrs. Gable, whose green thumb was legendary throughout Cedar Ridge, and young Mark, a recent high school graduate who'd expressed an interest in sustainable farming, to join the discussion.

"The initial plan is to use a drip irrigation system," Evan began, tracing a line on the diagram with his finger. "It's highly efficient, minimizes water waste, and delivers moisture directly to the roots."

Mrs. Gable, her eyes crinkling at the corners, peered at the intricate lines. "That sounds sensible, Evan. But will it be easy for anyone to manage? My arthritis flares up something fierce in the damp, and I don't want to be a burden when it comes to fiddling with valves and such."

Evan paused, his brow furrowing slightly. He hadn't factored in the physical limitations of some of the garden's most enthusiastic participants. "That's a valid point, Mrs. Gable," he conceded, pulling a fresh sheet of paper towards him. "Perhaps we can design a system with fewer manual adjustments. Maybe a central control panel, easily accessible, with timed settings? Or even a series of simpler, interconnected zones that can be managed with larger, more ergonomic handles."

Mark, who had been quietly observing, chimed in, "And what about rainwater harvesting? If we could integrate a system to collect runoff from the community hall roof, we could supplement the irrigation and reduce our reliance on the town's water supply even further. It would be more sustainable in the long run, and probably cheaper too."

Evan looked at Mark, then at Mrs. Gable, a genuine smile spreading across his face. These weren't just suggestions; they were contributions born from lived experience and a forward-thinking perspective that aligned perfectly with his evolving ideals. He hadn't simply presented a solution; he had created a space for collaboration, for co-creation. He felt a warmth bloom in his chest, a satisfaction far richer than the sterile triumph of a perfectly executed technical plan. This was about building something *together*, something that would serve the community not just efficiently, but empathetically and sustainably.

The shift in his approach extended beyond the formal projects of the Collective. He found himself more attuned to the subtle needs and rhythms of Cedar Ridge. He'd volunteer his time to help with tasks that, while not part of any grand plan, were crucial to the town's social fabric. He spent an entire Saturday helping Old Man Hemlock clear overgrown brush from around his prize-winning apple trees, not because it was a coded project, but because Hemlock had mentioned, in passing, that he was finding it harder to manage these days. Evan hadn't seen it as an obligation; he'd seen it as an opportunity to connect, to contribute in a way that eased a neighbor's burden.

He also started to view his own contributions through a different lens. The efficiencies he had once chased with relentless ambition now served a new master: lasting value. He wasn't just focused on the immediate fix; he was investing in the future. When they were upgrading the town's internet infrastructure, he didn't just push for the fastest, most cutting-edge technology available. He worked with Lena to understand the long-term growth projections for Cedar Ridge, to anticipate future needs, and to implement a system that could be scaled and adapted rather than requiring constant, costly overhauls. It was a slower, more deliberate process, but it felt infinitely more rewarding.

"It's like building a house," Lena mused one evening as they reviewed financial projections for the Collective. Evan had advocated for a slightly higher upfront investment in more robust, sustainable building materials for the planned expansion of the community center. "You can slap up a structure quickly with cheap materials, and it might stand for a while. But it won't weather storms, it won't be energy-efficient, and eventually, you'll be patching and repairing constantly. Or, you can take your time, invest in quality foundations and materials, and build something that will last for generations, something that becomes a true home."

Evan nodded, a thoughtful expression on his face. "That's exactly it. I used to be so focused on the 'completion' date, on the immediate 'wow' factor of a finished project. Now, I'm more interested in the 'endurance' factor. How will this serve Cedar Ridge in ten years? Twenty years? And more importantly, how will it empower the people here to continue serving themselves and each other?"

This redefined purpose wasn't just a professional shift; it was deeply personal. He realized his own sense of fulfillment was no longer tied to climbing a corporate ladder or achieving abstract professional accolades. It was rooted in the tangible improvements he helped facilitate, in the collective pride that bloomed when a community project, undertaken with shared effort and vision, came to fruition. He saw it in the way the children's faces lit up when the new playground equipment, designed with input from parents and children alike, was finally installed. He felt it in the buzz of the farmers' market, now more vibrant and organized thanks to the Collective's efforts to improve vendor accessibility and promotion.

He was no longer simply an architect of structures, but an architect of community resilience, a builder of lasting bonds. The frantic energy of his previous life, the constant striving for more, had been replaced by a quieter, more profound sense of purpose. He still possessed his sharp intellect and his drive for efficiency, but these qualities were now channeled into a desire for sustainable impact and genuine community well-being.

He was working *with* Lena and the Collective staff, not just to implement changes, but to foster a sense of ownership and pride among the townspeople. His focus had irrevocably shifted from quick fixes to building lasting value, a professional objective that was proving to be far more profound and infinitely more satisfying than he had ever imagined.

He was no longer just building in Cedar Ridge; he was building *for* Cedar Ridge, with Cedar Ridge, and in doing so, he was building a new future for himself.

The quiet hum of the generator, once a symbol of progress and a testament to their collective efforts in bringing electricity to the more remote homesteads, now felt different to Evan. It was no longer just about the successful completion of a task, the ticking off of another box on a project plan. Now, as he worked alongside Silas, a seasoned farmer whose hands bore the indelible marks of a life lived under the open sky, Evan felt a subtle yet significant shift within himself. He wasn't just troubleshooting a faulty connection; he was ensuring Silas could keep his milk cold, that Mrs. Gable could bake her award-winning pies without worrying about the oven's fluctuating temperature, that young Lily could see her drawings clearly on the page in the dim evening light. The impact, he realized, wasn't measured solely in kilowatts delivered or systems optimized, but in the quiet thrum of everyday life made a little easier, a little brighter.

Lena observed this evolution with a quiet satisfaction. Evan's innate drive, his sharp analytical mind, had always been evident. He'd arrived in Cedar Ridge with a clear vision, a blueprint for efficiency and improvement that was, in many ways, a reflection of his own highly structured urban existence. He'd approached the Collective's needs with the same meticulousness he'd once applied to designing skyscrapers. But the seeds of change had been sown, and they were now taking root. He was beginning to understand that true progress wasn't solely about the speed of implementation or the elegance of a solution, but about the sustainability of its impact, the way it resonated within the heart of the community.

Their work sessions at the Collective had taken on a new dimension. While the core objective remained the same – to strengthen the town's infrastructure and resources – the methodology had softened, the focus broadened. Evan was no longer just dictating the most efficient course of action. He was engaging Lena and the small team of dedicated volunteers – the backbone of the Collective's operations – in a more collaborative dialogue. He'd ask questions that went beyond the purely technical. "What's the long-term maintenance plan for this system?" he'd inquire, but then he'd follow it up with, "And how can we ensure the person responsible feels empowered and supported to carry it out?" He was, for the first time, thinking about the *people* who would be living with and working with the changes they implemented, not just the changes themselves.

One afternoon, they were reviewing the plans for the new community garden's irrigation system. Previously, Evan would have meticulously calculated water flow rates, optimal pressure, and the most cost-effective pipe materials. This time, however, he'd spread the blueprints across a worn, wooden table that bore the faint scent of pine and countless years of shared meals. He'd invited Mrs. Gable, whose green thumb was legendary throughout Cedar Ridge, and young Mark, a recent high school graduate who'd expressed an interest in sustainable farming, to join the discussion.

"The initial plan is to use a drip irrigation system," Evan began, tracing a line on the diagram with his finger. "It's highly efficient, minimizes water waste, and delivers moisture directly to the roots."

Mrs. Gable, her eyes crinkling at the corners, peered at the intricate lines. "That sounds sensible, Evan. But will it be easy for anyone to manage? My arthritis flares up something fierce in the damp, and I don't want to be a burden when it comes to fiddling with valves and such."

Evan paused, his brow furrowing slightly. He hadn't factored in the physical limitations of some of the garden's most enthusiastic participants. "That's a valid point, Mrs. Gable," he conceded, pulling a fresh sheet of paper towards him. "Perhaps we can design a system with fewer manual adjustments. Maybe a central control panel, easily accessible, with timed settings? Or even a series of simpler, interconnected zones that can be managed with larger, more ergonomic handles."

Mark, who had been quietly observing, chimed in, "And what about rainwater harvesting? If we could integrate a system to collect runoff from the community hall roof, we could supplement the irrigation and reduce our reliance on the town's water supply even further. It would be more sustainable in the long run, and probably cheaper too."

Evan looked at Mark, then at Mrs. Gable, a genuine smile spreading across his face. These weren't just suggestions; they were contributions born from lived experience and a forward-thinking perspective that aligned perfectly with his evolving ideals. He hadn't simply presented a solution; he had created a space for collaboration, for co-creation. He felt a warmth bloom in his chest, a satisfaction far richer than the sterile triumph of a perfectly executed technical plan. This was about building something *together*, something that would serve the community not just efficiently, but empathetically and sustainably.

The shift in his approach extended beyond the formal projects of the Collective. He found himself more attuned to the subtle needs and rhythms of Cedar Ridge. He'd volunteer his time to help with tasks that, while not part of any grand plan, were crucial to the town's social fabric. He spent an entire Saturday helping Old Man Hemlock clear overgrown brush from around his prize-winning apple trees, not because it was a coded project, but because Hemlock had mentioned, in passing, that he was finding it harder to manage these days. Evan hadn't seen it as an obligation; he'd seen it as an opportunity to connect, to contribute in a way that eased a neighbor's burden.

He also started to view his own contributions through a different lens. The efficiencies he had once chased with relentless ambition now served a new master: lasting value. He wasn't just focused on the immediate fix; he was investing in the future. When they were upgrading the town's internet infrastructure, he didn't just push for the fastest, most cutting-edge technology available. He worked with Lena to understand the long-term growth projections for Cedar Ridge, to anticipate future needs, and to implement a system that could be scaled and adapted rather than requiring constant, costly overhauls. It was a slower, more deliberate process, but it felt infinitely more rewarding.

"It's like building a house," Lena mused one evening as they reviewed financial projections for the Collective. Evan had advocated for a slightly higher upfront investment in more robust, sustainable building materials for the planned expansion of the community center. "You can slap up a structure quickly with cheap materials, and it might stand for a while. But it won't weather storms, it won't be energy-efficient, and eventually, you'll be patching and repairing constantly. Or, you can take your time, invest in quality foundations and materials, and build something that will last for generations, something that becomes a true home."

Evan nodded, a thoughtful expression on his face. "That's exactly it. I used to be so focused on the 'completion' date, on the immediate 'wow' factor of a finished project. Now, I'm more interested in the 'endurance' factor. How will this serve Cedar Ridge in ten years? Twenty years? And more importantly, how will it empower the people here to continue serving themselves and each other?"

This redefined purpose wasn't just a professional shift; it was deeply personal. He realized his own sense of fulfillment was no longer tied to climbing a corporate ladder or achieving abstract professional accolades. It was rooted in the tangible improvements he helped facilitate, in the collective pride that bloomed when a community project, undertaken with shared effort and vision, came to fruition. He saw it in the way the children's faces lit up when the new playground equipment, designed with input from parents and children alike, was finally installed. He felt it in the buzz of the farmers' market, now more vibrant and organized thanks to the Collective's efforts to improve vendor accessibility and promotion.

He was no longer simply an architect of structures, but an architect of community resilience, a builder of lasting bonds. The frantic energy of his previous life, the constant striving for more, had been replaced by a quieter, more profound sense of purpose. He still possessed his sharp intellect and his drive for efficiency, but these qualities were now channeled into a desire for sustainable impact and genuine community well-being. He was working *with* Lena and the Collective staff, not just to implement changes, but to foster a sense of ownership and pride among the townspeople.

His focus had irrevocably shifted from quick fixes to building lasting value, a professional objective that was proving to be far more profound and infinitely more satisfying than he had ever imagined. He was no longer just building in Cedar Ridge; he was building *for* Cedar Ridge, with Cedar Ridge, and in doing so, he was building a new future for himself.

The air in Lena's small cottage, usually filled with the comforting scents of drying herbs and brewing tea, seemed to hold a new kind of energy. It was the quiet hum of shared understanding, the gentle resonance of two lives aligning. Evan had made his decision, a conscious, deliberate choice that had settled into his bones like the deep roots of the ancient oak outside Lena's window. He wasn't just passing through Cedar Ridge anymore; he was planting himself here, alongside her.

They sat across from each other at her kitchen table, the remnants of a simple supper scattered between them. A half-finished loaf of bread, a bowl of salad glistening with olive oil, and two mugs of chamomile tea, long since cooled. The silence wasn't awkward, but comfortable, a testament to the deepening intimacy that had bloomed between them over the past few weeks. It was a silence punctuated by the soft ticking of a grandfather clock in the corner and the occasional sigh of the wind outside.

"So," Lena began, her voice a gentle murmur, her gaze steady and expectant. "You're really staying."

Evan met her eyes, a warmth spreading through him that had nothing to do with the fading sunlight filtering through the lace curtains. "I am," he confirmed, the words feeling both simple and monumental. "I've decided I want to stay. I want to... I want to be a part of this. Of *your* part of this."

He reached across the table, his fingers brushing hers. A spark, familiar and comforting, passed between them. It was more than just attraction now; it was a shared trajectory, a mutual recognition of purpose. He was no longer the outsider looking in, the consultant brought in for a specific task. He was becoming woven into the fabric of Cedar Ridge, and more importantly, into the fabric of Lena's life.

"That's... that's wonderful, Evan," Lena replied, her voice catching slightly. She intertwined her fingers with his, her thumb tracing the lines on his palm. "I confess, I wasn't entirely sure after... after everything. But seeing how you've embraced the work, how you've changed how you approach things... it's made me believe. It's made me hopeful."

Evan squeezed her hand. "It's because of you, Lena. You opened my eyes. You showed me that efficiency isn't just about speed or cost-effectiveness. It's about building something that lasts, something that nourishes. And that's not just true for the Collective, or for Cedar Ridge. It's true for... for us, too."

He paused, choosing his words carefully. This was uncharted territory, a landscape he hadn't mapped out with blueprints and calculations, but with intuition and a growing sense of deep-seated emotion. "I don't have a five-year plan for us, Lena. I don't have a five-year plan for Cedar Ridge, not in the way I used to. But I want to build something here, with you. I want to see what we can create together, not just for the town, but for ourselves. I want to be here to see what happens next."

Lena's smile widened, a genuine, radiant expression that lit up her face. "And what *will* happen next, Evan?" she asked, a playful lilt to her voice. "We've got so much on the go with the Collective. The community center expansion, the new microbrewery grant application, figuring out that old cannery building..."

"And that's just the Collective," Evan interjected, his eyes sparkling. "What about us? What about a garden that isn't just for vegetables, but for flowers too? What about exploring those hiking trails we haven't had time for? What about... learning to bake your pies, Lena? Really learn, not just watch." He chuckled, remembering his disastrous attempt at making a pie crust the week before.

"Oh, we'll get to the pie crusts," Lena promised, her gaze softening. "But first, there are more pressing matters. We need to talk about that old cannery. Silas mentioned they're looking for someone with your kind of expertise to assess its structural integrity. It's been sitting there for years, a big, empty shell. Imagine what it could become if we could revitalize it."

Evan leaned forward, his interest piqued. This was the kind of challenge that ignited his professional spirit, but now, it was infused with a personal motivation. "The cannery? I've driven past it. It's a substantial building. What are they envisioning for it?"

"That's the beauty of it, Evan," Lena said, her hand tightening on his. "Nothing concrete. It's a blank canvas. Some want to turn it into artist studios, others think it could be a much-needed storage facility for local businesses. Silas is even talking about a small-scale food processing hub, to help the farmers and producers in the region. But it needs someone to look at it, to see its potential, to figure out what's feasible and how to make it happen. Someone who can balance the practicalities with the dreams."

He recognized the implicit invitation. Lena wasn't just talking about the cannery; she was talking about their shared future, about the kind of collaborative vision that had become the hallmark of their interactions. "Someone like me," Evan stated, a slow smile spreading across his face. "And someone like you, who understands the heart of this town, who knows what it needs, what it dreams of."

"Exactly," Lena affirmed. "We'd be a good team, Evan. A really good team." The words hung in the air, a quiet declaration of intent. It wasn't a grand pronouncement, but a simple, honest acknowledgment of the path they were now choosing to walk together.

"So," Evan began, the excitement bubbling within him. "Let's start with the cannery. Tomorrow morning, first thing. We'll go take a look. See what's possible." He knew that "we" meant him and Lena, and perhaps a few others from the Collective who might be interested. It was the Cedar Ridge way.

Lena nodded, her eyes shining. "Tomorrow morning. And after that... maybe we can finally tackle that pie crust."

He laughed, a genuine, uninhibited sound. "Deal. But you have to promise to guide my hand. I suspect your definition of 'feasible' for a pie crust might be a little more forgiving than mine."

"I can do that," she said, her voice warm. "My approach to pie crusts, and to most things, is about patience and a little bit of love. Qualities I'm starting to see a lot more of in you, Evan."

He felt a profound sense of peace settle over him. The future, once a series of calculated steps and projected outcomes, now felt like an open field, full of possibility. It was a future he was choosing to build, not in isolation, but with Lena by his side, their hands working together, their hearts beating in a shared rhythm. He had come to Cedar Ridge to build, but he hadn't realized he was also building a life, a connection, a sense of belonging. And it was just beginning. The first steps, tentative yet firm, were being taken together.

The ensuing days were a whirlwind of activity, yet imbued with a new sense of deliberate pace. The assessment of the old cannery became their first major joint venture, a project that showcased their complementary strengths. Evan, with his architectural eye, meticulously examined the building's foundations, its structural integrity, and the potential for renovation. He sketched out floor plans, considered load-bearing walls, and calculated the costs associated with bringing the weathered structure back to life. Lena, meanwhile, engaged with the townspeople, gathering input, gauging interest, and weaving a narrative around the cannery's potential future. She spoke with Silas about a possible cold storage facility for his produce, with Mrs. Gable about a potential space for a community kitchen, and with a group of young artists who were eager for affordable studio space.

One afternoon, as they stood on the dusty floor of the cannery, shafts of sunlight slanting through the grimy windows, Evan found himself explaining the complexities of HVAC systems to a small group that included Silas and a few other community members. He wasn't just presenting technical data; he was translating it, making it accessible, and, crucially, explaining *why* it mattered – how an efficient system would reduce long-term costs and improve the working environment for everyone. He saw the understanding dawn in their eyes, the spark of possibility ignited.

"So, if we did it this way," Evan explained, pointing to a section of his meticulously drawn diagrams, "we could integrate a geothermal system. It's a higher upfront cost, yes, but the energy savings over, say, twenty years, would be significant. And it aligns with the town's growing commitment to sustainability. Imagine this place, buzzing with activity, powered by the earth itself."

Silas, his weathered face thoughtful, rubbed his chin. "Geothermal, huh? Never thought I'd see the day. But you make a good case, Evan. Keeping our overhead down is crucial if we want this to actually help us farmers, not just be another drain on our resources."

Lena, standing beside Evan, added, "And it would be a selling point too. A 'green' cannery, revitalized and environmentally conscious. It tells a story about Cedar Ridge, about our forward-thinking approach."

Evan felt a surge of satisfaction, not just from the technical challenge, but from the collaborative spirit. He was no longer just the expert imposing a solution; he was part of a conversation, a facilitator of shared vision. He found himself looking to Lena for her insights, for her intuitive understanding of the town's needs and aspirations. Her presence beside him felt natural, grounding.

In the evenings, their conversations would shift from the grand plans for Cedar Ridge to the quieter intimacies of their own lives. They discovered shared loves – old movies, quiet mornings with coffee, the taste of wild blueberries picked straight from the bush. They shared vulnerabilities too. Evan spoke about the pressure he used to feel, the constant need to prove himself, the emptiness that often accompanied professional success. Lena confided her own anxieties about the future, the weight of responsibility she felt for the Collective and the town.

One evening, as they sat on Lena's porch, watching the fireflies begin their nightly dance, Evan confessed, "I used to think success was about building empires. Now... now I think it's about building something that will last, something that makes a difference, piece by piece. And I think I'm finally learning how to build a life, too. Not just a career."

Lena leaned her head on his shoulder. "It's a different kind of architecture, isn't it? One that's built on trust, on shared dreams, on showing up for each other. And I'm so glad you're choosing to build it here, with me."

Their shared journey wasn't without its uncertainties. The path ahead for Cedar Ridge was still being forged, and their personal journey together was only just beginning. But there was a quiet confidence that settled between them, a mutual understanding that whatever challenges arose, they would face them together. They had moved past the initial stages of exploration and into a phase of deliberate commitment. The first steps had been taken, not just into a new project, but into a shared future. The foundation was being laid, not with concrete and steel, but with shared intentions and a deep, abiding hope. The future was unwritten, but for the first time, Evan felt he was writing it with the right co-author.

CHAPTER ELEVEN

Roots and Horizons

Evan found himself increasingly drawn into the fabric of Cedar Ridge, a departure from his initial, project-driven interactions. The meticulous planning and problem-solving that had defined his early days in town were now spilling over into the quieter, less tangible aspects of community life. It wasn't just about fixing the town's infrastructure; it was about understanding the people who lived within it, the subtle currents of connection that made Cedar Ridge more than just a collection of houses and businesses. He began to seek out opportunities to contribute, not as an outsider offering expertise, but as a neighbor lending a hand.

One crisp autumn Saturday, he found himself at the annual Cedar Ridge Fall Festival, an event he'd previously only observed from a distance. This year, however, he'd volunteered to help Silas man the farmers' market booth. It was a far cry from negotiating engineering contracts, but as he arranged crates of Silas's prize-winning apples and helped customers weigh their produce, he felt a different kind of satisfaction. He listened to Mrs.

Henderson lament the early frost threatening her late-season tomatoes, and he offered a sympathetic ear.

He chatted with young Tommy Miller about his enthusiasm for learning to drive, a milestone Evan remembered with a mix of excitement and trepidation. These conversations, seemingly mundane, were weaving him into the town's narrative. He was no longer just Evan, the consultant from the city. He was Evan, who helped Silas with the apples, who had a decent sense of humor, and who, apparently, knew a surprising amount about soil composition.

Lena observed this shift with a knowing smile. She saw him not just at Collective meetings or project sites, but at the local diner, engaged in conversation with regulars, his brow furrowed in genuine interest. She saw him, on another occasion, helping old Mr. Abernathy clear a fallen branch from his driveway, a task far outside the scope of any official Collective mandate. It was a small act of kindness, yet it spoke volumes about Evan's evolving perspective. He was no longer merely an architect of systems, but a builder of relationships. He was learning that the strongest foundations weren't always made of concrete, but of the shared experiences and mutual support that characterized a true community.

His involvement extended to other town initiatives. When the idea of revitalizing the old community theater came up – a project deemed too ambitious and resource-intensive by many – Evan didn't dismiss it outright. Instead, he attended the initial brainstorming sessions, not to offer a quick fix, but to listen. He heard the passion in the voices of the theater's supporters, the deep-seated desire to preserve a piece of Cedar Ridge's history. He asked probing questions, not to highlight potential problems, but to understand the underlying needs and aspirations. "What kind of programming are you envisioning?" he'd inquire, or "What are the biggest logistical hurdles you anticipate?" He brought his analytical skills to bear, not to shut down dreams, but to help shape them into achievable realities. He saw that his expertise could be a tool for empowerment, not just for project completion.

He also began to appreciate the interconnectedness of Cedar Ridge. He saw how the success of the farmers' market, bolstered by the Collective's efforts to improve infrastructure and marketing, had a ripple effect, bringing more people into town, boosting business for the general store and the bakery. He noticed how the revitalized town square, with its new benches and improved lighting, had become a gathering place, fostering spontaneous interactions and a stronger sense of shared identity. His initial focus on individual projects had broadened to encompass a holistic understanding of the town's ecosystem. He understood that true progress wasn't a series of isolated successes, but a carefully orchestrated symphony of interconnected efforts.

One evening, as he and Lena walked home from a late Collective meeting, the conversation turned to the challenges facing the town. Evan found himself speaking with a newfound intimacy about his observations. "It's fascinating, Lena," he mused, the streetlights casting long shadows around them. "I used to think of Cedar Ridge as a collection of individual problems to be solved. But now, I see it as a living organism. When one part thrives, it benefits the whole. The success of the new internet infrastructure, for instance, isn't just about faster downloads; it's about enabling Mrs. Gable to connect with her grandchildren online, about giving the local artisans a wider reach for their crafts, about making information more accessible to everyone. It's all intertwined."

Lena smiled, her hand finding his. "That's exactly it, Evan. You're starting to see the heart of Cedar Ridge. It's not about grand gestures, but about the countless small acts of connection and support that happen every day. It's about recognizing that we all have a role to play, no matter how small it might seem."

He felt a profound sense of belonging, a feeling that had eluded him for so long in his fast-paced urban existence. He realized that his desire to contribute had evolved beyond a professional obligation. It was now a genuine yearning to be a part of something meaningful, something that would endure beyond the completion of any single project. He wasn't just investing in Cedar Ridge's infrastructure; he was investing in its future, and by extension, his own.

His perspective on his own role had also shifted. He no longer felt the constant pressure to prove his worth through measurable achievements alone. The quiet satisfaction of helping Mr. Abernathy with his tree, or the simple joy of seeing children play on the new swings at the park – these moments now held as much significance as any successfully completed engineering plan. He understood that his presence, his willingness to engage, was itself a contribution. He was learning that belonging wasn't something that was earned through accolades, but something that was cultivated through genuine connection and shared experience.

This burgeoning sense of community wasn't just about formal volunteering or participation in town events. It was also about the everyday interactions that formed the bedrock of Cedar Ridge. He found himself stopping to chat with shop owners during his errands, learning about their families and their businesses. He started attending the occasional town council meeting, not to offer solutions, but to gain a deeper understanding of the challenges and opportunities facing the community as a whole. He realized that being a part of a community meant more than just showing up for scheduled events; it meant being present, being aware, and being willing to engage on a personal level.

The transformation was palpable. The man who had arrived in Cedar Ridge with a clear, albeit impersonal, agenda was now deeply invested in the town's well-being. He saw the town not as a problem to be solved, but as a community to be nurtured. He had shed the skin of the detached observer and was emerging as an active participant, a builder of connections, and, in his own quiet way, a true resident. His horizons had broadened, not just in terms of his professional scope, but in the depth of his human connection.

Cedar Ridge was no longer just a place he was working; it was a place he was becoming a part of, a place where he was finding a sense of home. He had come to build infrastructure, but he was staying to build something far more enduring: community.

The seeds of his integration were evident in the subtle ways he now navigated his days. His morning coffee at the diner wasn't just a caffeine fix; it was a chance to catch up on local news, to hear about upcoming events, and to offer a friendly greeting to whoever happened to be at the counter. He'd find himself offering unsolicited, but welcome, advice to young entrepreneurs looking to start businesses, drawing on his own experiences in a way that was both practical and encouraging. He was no longer the lone wolf of efficiency, but a collaborative spirit, eager to share his insights and learn from others.

One particularly memorable afternoon, the annual Cedar Ridge fundraising auction for the local animal shelter was held in the town hall. Evan, initially hesitant, had been persuaded by Lena to attend. He ended up volunteering to help set up chairs and organize donated items, finding a quiet satisfaction in the tangible tasks. As the evening progressed, he found himself bidding on a knitted quilt made by Mrs. Gable, not out of obligation, but because he genuinely admired the craftsmanship and the cause. He felt a warmth spread through him as the auctioneer announced his winning bid, a shared sense of accomplishment with everyone else contributing to a cause that was clearly important to the town. He saw the grateful smiles of the shelter volunteers, the enthusiastic applause from the attendees, and realized that contributing to a shared goal, even in a small way, fostered a powerful sense of collective pride.

His willingness to step outside his comfort zone extended to embracing the less glamorous aspects of community life. When the town decided to organize a clean-up day for the riverbanks, an initiative that promised muddy boots and early mornings, Evan was among the first to sign up. He spent hours wading through shallow water, clearing debris, and hauling rubbish, working alongside Silas, the mayor, and a handful of teenagers. The shared effort, the camaraderie born from a common purpose, created a bond that transcended their individual roles in town. He learned that true community wasn't just about grand projects or significant investments; it was about the everyday willingness to roll up one's sleeves and contribute, no matter how small the task.

Lena, watching him from her vantage point, saw a man transformed. The sharp edges of his urban drive had softened, replaced by a genuine warmth and an authentic desire to connect. He wasn't just performing community service; he was living it. He had moved beyond the transactional nature of his initial engagement and had embraced the relational essence of Cedar Ridge. He had learned that belonging wasn't a destination to be reached, but a journey of continuous engagement, a commitment to showing up, day after day, for the people and the place he was increasingly calling home.

His initial assignment had become a calling, his work in Cedar Ridge no longer just a chapter, but the beginning of a new narrative, one he was actively writing, word by word, deed by deed, with the entire town as his co-author. The horizon he had once looked towards with professional ambition now encompassed a far richer, more deeply personal landscape, one he was eager to explore and cultivate. He had finally found his roots, and in doing so, had discovered a horizon that was boundless in its possibilities.

The quiet hum of Cedar Ridge, once the predictable soundtrack to Lena's life, had begun to resonate with a new melody. It was a subtle shift, almost imperceptible at first, like the first hint of dawn on a familiar horizon.

Evan's presence, his earnest immersion in the town's rhythm, had acted as a catalyst, not just for his own integration, but for hers as well. She found herself looking at the familiar streets, the weathered storefronts, the very faces she'd known for years, through a slightly different lens. It was as if Evan's fresh perspective had been an invisible dye, bleeding into the existing fabric of her world, revealing hues she hadn't noticed before.

Her days had always possessed a certain comforting order. Mornings began with the ritual of the Sunrise Bakery's coffee, the gentle clinking of ceramic mugs, and the murmur of conversations that flowed as naturally as the creek behind the general store. Her work at the library, a sanctuary of quiet contemplation and curated knowledge, was a source of deep satisfaction. She knew the Dewey Decimal system like the back of her hand, understood the unspoken needs of her regular patrons, and cherished the hushed reverence of the reading room. This was her established world, a well-loved tapestry woven with threads of routine, community, and quiet passion.

But Evan's burgeoning connection to Cedar Ridge had inadvertently begun to tug at those threads, not in a way that threatened to unravel them, but in a way that suggested new patterns could be woven in. He'd ask her about the history of the old clock tower, not with a consultant's detached curiosity, but with a genuine interest that mirrored her own love for the town's past. He'd listen intently as she recounted tales of its construction, the stories of the families who had gathered beneath it, the way it had marked the passage of time for generations. He didn't just hear the facts; he absorbed the sentiment, the embedded history that gave the tower its soul. And in his listening, Lena found herself rediscovering the stories she'd held dear, seeing them anew through his attentive gaze.

One particular Tuesday, a day that would have otherwise unfolded with its usual gentle predictability, Evan appeared at the library with a proposition. "Lena," he'd said, his voice carrying a familiar blend of enthusiasm and thoughtful consideration, "Silas was telling me about the 'Little Free

Library' project you've been wanting to get off the ground. He's got some leftover lumber from that shed renovation, and I was thinking... if you have the time, and if it's something you're still keen on, we could tackle it this weekend."

Lena's heart had given a small, hopeful leap. The Little Free Library had been a persistent idea in her mind, a seed she'd planted with enthusiasm but hadn't yet found the fertile ground to nurture. It was a small thing, a charming addition to the town's already picturesque landscape, a way to share books and foster a love of reading in a more accessible, informal way. But the practicalities – the design, the construction, the sourcing of materials – had always seemed like hurdles too daunting to overcome on her own.

"Oh, Evan, that would be wonderful!" she'd exclaimed, a genuine smile spreading across her face. "I've been sketching ideas, but..."

"But you're the curator of Cedar Ridge's literary soul, not its carpenter," he'd finished with a grin. "Leave the hammering and sanding to me. We'll make it beautiful, and functional, and you can fill it with all the stories."

And so, the following Saturday, the familiar quiet of Lena's world was punctuated by the rhythmic thud of a hammer and the whir of a power saw. Evan, surprisingly adept with tools, had transformed Silas's salvaged lumber into charming, miniature libraries, each with a hinged roof and a welcoming shelf. Lena, armed with her paintbrushes, meticulously decorated them, adding touches of whimsy and local flavor – tiny painted versions of the town hall, the general store, the creek. As they worked side-by-side, amidst the scent of sawdust and fresh paint, Lena found herself engaging in a different kind of conversation than she was accustomed to. It wasn't about plot points or character development; it was about the practicalities of weatherproofing, the best height for small hands to reach, the ideal placement for maximum visibility.

This shared endeavor was more than just a community project; it was an exchange. Evan was helping her bring a long-held vision to life, and in doing so, he was introducing her to a new dimension of her own capabilities. He was demonstrating, through his own actions, that "expanding horizons" didn't necessarily mean venturing far from home. It could mean looking at the familiar with new eyes, seeing the potential for growth and creativity within the existing framework of one's life. He encouraged her to experiment with her designs, to think beyond the traditional, to infuse her personal touch into every detail. "Don't just build a box for books, Lena," he'd advised, wiping sawdust from his brow. "Build a little gateway. A place where imagination can take root."

His influence also nudged her out of her comfort zone in other, more subtle ways. She found herself attending town council meetings with him, not out of obligation, but out of a newfound curiosity about the broader machinations of Cedar Ridge. While she had always been aware of the town's governance, she had never felt a personal stake in its proceedings. Evan, however, approached these meetings with a quiet engagement, his thoughtful questions often sparking productive discussions. He'd then debrief with Lena afterward, not just recounting the decisions made, but sharing his insights into the underlying dynamics, the interplay of personalities, the collective will of the community.

"It's fascinating, Lena," he'd commented one evening, after a particularly lively debate about the proposed expansion of the community park. "You see how different concerns converge, how compromise is the bedrock of progress. It's not always about the most efficient solution, but about the most inclusive one."

Lena found herself nodding along, a quiet understanding dawning within her. She realized that Evan's perspective, honed by his professional experience in navigating complex systems, offered her a way to appreciate the practical artistry of community building. He wasn't just fixing infrastructure; he was helping to shape the town's future, and in his commitment to that endeavor, he was inspiring her to see her own role within that larger narrative.

Her routines, while still cherished, began to feel less like fixed boundaries and more like flexible pathways. The Sunrise Bakery coffee now often included a brief, animated conversation with Evan about his latest project or a shared observation about the town. Her library visits weren't solely about cataloging or recommending; they often involved discussing the Little Free Libraries, her excitement about their placement and the initial uptake from residents. She even found herself volunteering for the community garden's harvest festival, an event she usually observed with polite detachment, but this year, she helped organize the children's craft table, her creative energy flowing into a new outlet.

It was during these moments of shared experience, of working together towards common goals, that Lena felt the most profound sense of expansion. Evan's steady presence, his quiet encouragement, had given her the permission she hadn't realized she'd needed to explore these new facets of her life. He never pushed, never demanded, but simply offered his support and his perspective, an invitation to step beyond the familiar. He saw her inherent strengths – her keen observation, her deep empathy, her love for storytelling – and helped her channel them into new avenues.

For instance, when the town was considering ways to document its oral history, a project Lena had always felt passionate about but had been hesitant to initiate, Evan was the one who suggested she lead it. "Lena," he'd said, his gaze steady and encouraging, "you're the keeper of Cedar Ridge's stories. Who better to gather and preserve them? You have a gift for listening, for drawing people out. This is your horizon, waiting to be explored."

His words resonated deeply. He saw her not just as a librarian, but as a historian, a storyteller, a vital link to the town's past and future. He understood that her desire to connect, to foster a sense of belonging, extended beyond the pages of books. He encouraged her to think about how she could leverage her skills, her knowledge, and her passion to contribute to the town in a more active, outward-facing way.

This newfound confidence, this willingness to embrace new possibilities, wasn't a sudden transformation, but a gradual blooming, nurtured by Evan's consistent belief in her. She found herself approaching conversations with a bolder spirit, offering her insights more readily, and seeking out opportunities for collaboration. The world within Cedar Ridge, which she had always loved, now seemed to possess an even greater depth, an untapped potential that she was eager to explore. It was a beautiful paradox: in helping Evan find his roots, she had discovered a fertile ground for her own horizons to expand.

Their relationship was becoming a testament to the idea that true growth often happens when we are seen and encouraged by someone who believes in the best of us, someone who helps us to see the boundless possibilities within the world we already call home. She was learning that the familiar could be a launching pad, not a cage, and that the most exciting adventures could unfold right where she was, with the right companion by her side.

The hum of Cedar Ridge, once a familiar and comforting murmur for Lena, had recently begun to thrum with a vibrant new energy. It wasn't a jarring discord, but a harmonious addition, like a second melody weaving through a well-loved tune. Evan's presence, his genuine immersion in the town's fabric, had been the unexpected conductor of this subtle symphony. He had approached Cedar Ridge not as an outsider looking in, but as someone eager to understand and contribute, and in doing so, he had inadvertently encouraged Lena to see her own world with fresh eyes. The weathered storefronts, the familiar faces, the very rhythm of the days – all seemed to shimmer with a newly discovered potential, like a cherished painting revealed in brighter light.

Her days had always possessed a comforting order, a testament to her deep appreciation for routine and her quiet passion for her work. Mornings began with the comforting warmth of coffee from the Sunrise Bakery, the gentle chime of the bell above the door, and the low hum of conversations that flowed as easily as the creek behind Silas's general store. Her sanctuary was the Cedar Ridge Library, a place of quiet contemplation, where the scent of aged paper and the silent companionship of stories provided a profound sense of satisfaction. She knew the Dewey Decimal system intimately, understood the unspoken desires of her regular patrons, and reveled in the hushed reverence of the reading room. This was her world, a beloved tapestry woven with the threads of routine, community, and a deep-seated love for the written word.

Yet, Evan's burgeoning connection to Cedar Ridge had begun to gently tug at those threads, not in a way that threatened to unravel the established pattern, but in a way that suggested new, exciting designs could be woven in. He'd inquire about the history of the old clock tower, not with a detached curiosity, but with an earnest interest that mirrored her own deep affection for the town's past. He would listen intently as she recounted tales of its construction, the stories of the families who had gathered beneath its shadow, the way it had meticulously marked the passage of time for generations. He didn't just hear the facts; he absorbed the sentiment, the embedded history that gave the tower its soul. And in his attentiveness, Lena found herself rediscovering the stories she held dear, seeing them anew through his appreciative gaze.

One crisp Tuesday, a day that would have otherwise unfolded with its usual gentle predictability, Evan appeared at the library, a proposition lighting up his face. "Lena," he'd begun, his voice carrying a familiar blend of enthusiasm and thoughtful consideration, "Silas mentioned the 'Little Free Library' project you've been wanting to bring to life. He's got some leftover lumber from that shed renovation, and I was thinking... if you have the time, and if it's something you're still passionate about, we could tackle it this weekend."

Lena's heart had given a small, hopeful leap. The Little Free Library had been a persistent idea in her mind, a seed she'd planted with enthusiasm but hadn't yet found the fertile ground to nurture. It was a small, charming addition to the town's already picturesque landscape, a way to share books and foster a love of reading in a more accessible, informal manner. But the practicalities – the design, the construction, the sourcing of materials – had always seemed like insurmountable hurdles to overcome on her own.

"Oh, Evan, that would be wonderful!" she'd exclaimed, a genuine smile spreading across her face. "I've been sketching ideas, but..."

"But you're the curator of Cedar Ridge's literary soul, not its carpenter," he'd finished with a warm grin. "Leave the hammering and sanding to me. We'll make them beautiful, and functional, and you can fill them with all the stories."

And so, the following Saturday, the familiar quiet of Lena's world was punctuated by the rhythmic thud of a hammer and the whir of a power saw. Evan, surprisingly adept with tools, transformed Silas's salvaged lumber into charming, miniature libraries, each with a hinged roof and a welcoming shelf. Lena, armed with her paintbrushes, meticulously decorated them, adding touches of whimsy and local flavor – tiny painted versions of the town hall, the general store, the winding creek. As they worked side-by-side, amidst the scent of sawdust and fresh paint, Lena found herself engaging in a different kind of conversation than she was accustomed to. It wasn't about plot points or character development; it was about the practicalities of weatherproofing, the best height for small hands to reach, the ideal placement for maximum visibility. This shared endeavor was more than just a community project; it was a profound exchange.

Evan was helping her bring a long-held vision to life, and in doing so, he was introducing her to a new dimension of her own capabilities. He was demonstrating, through his actions, that "expanding horizons" didn't necessarily mean venturing far from home. It could mean looking at the familiar with fresh eyes, seeing the potential for growth and creativity within the existing framework of one's life. He encouraged her to experiment with her designs, to think beyond the traditional, to infuse her personal touch into every detail. "Don't just build a box for books, Lena," he'd advised, wiping sawdust from his brow. "Build a little gateway. A place where imagination can take root."

His influence also nudged her out of her comfort zone in other, more subtle ways. She found herself attending town council meetings with him, not out of obligation, but out of a newfound curiosity about the broader machinations of Cedar Ridge. While she had always been aware of the town's governance, she had never felt a personal stake in its proceedings. Evan, however, approached these meetings with a quiet engagement, his thoughtful questions often sparking productive discussions. He'd then debrief with Lena afterward, not just recounting the decisions made, but sharing his insights into the underlying dynamics, the interplay of personalities, the collective will of the community.

"It's fascinating, Lena," he'd commented one evening, after a particularly lively debate about the proposed expansion of the community park. "You see how different concerns converge, how compromise is the bedrock of progress. It's not always about the most efficient solution, but about the most inclusive one." Lena found herself nodding along, a quiet understanding dawning within her. She realized that Evan's perspective, honed by his professional experience in navigating complex systems, offered her a way to appreciate the practical artistry of community building. He wasn't just fixing infrastructure; he was helping to shape the town's future, and in his commitment to that endeavor, he was inspiring her to see her own role within that larger narrative.

Her routines, while still cherished, began to feel less like fixed boundaries and more like flexible pathways. The Sunrise Bakery coffee now often included a brief, animated conversation with Evan about his latest project or a shared observation about the town. Her library visits weren't solely about cataloging or recommending; they often involved discussing the Little Free Libraries, her excitement about their placement and the initial uptake from residents.

She even found herself volunteering for the community garden's harvest festival, an event she usually observed with polite detachment, but this year, she helped organize the children's craft table, her creative energy flowing into a new outlet. It was during these moments of shared experience, of working together towards common goals, that Lena felt the most profound sense of expansion. Evan's steady presence, his quiet encouragement, had given her the permission she hadn't realized she'd needed to explore these new facets of her life. He never pushed, never demanded, but simply offered his support and his perspective, an invitation to step beyond the familiar. He saw her inherent strengths – her keen observation, her deep empathy, her love for storytelling – and helped her channel them into new avenues.

For instance, when the town was considering ways to document its oral history, a project Lena had always felt passionate about but had been hesitant to initiate, Evan was the one who suggested she lead it. "Lena," he'd said, his gaze steady and encouraging, "you're the keeper of Cedar Ridge's stories. Who better to gather and preserve them? You have a gift for listening, for drawing people out. This is your horizon, waiting to be explored."

His words resonated deeply. He saw her not just as a librarian, but as a historian, a storyteller, a vital link to the town's past and future. He understood that her desire to connect, to foster a sense of belonging, extended beyond the pages of books. He encouraged her to think about how she could leverage her skills, her knowledge, and her passion to contribute to the town in a more active, outward-facing way. This newfound confidence, this willingness to embrace new possibilities, wasn't a sudden transformation, but a gradual blooming, nurtured by Evan's consistent belief in her. She found herself approaching conversations with a bolder spirit, offering her insights more readily, and seeking out opportunities for collaboration.

The world within Cedar Ridge, which she had always loved, now seemed to possess an even greater depth, an untapped potential that she was eager to explore. It was a beautiful paradox: in helping Evan find his roots, she had discovered a fertile ground for her own horizons to expand. Their relationship was becoming a testament to the idea that true growth often happens when we are seen and encouraged by someone who believes in the best of us, someone who helps us to see the boundless possibilities within the world we already call home. She was learning that the familiar could be a launching pad, not a cage, and that the most exciting adventures could unfold right where she was, with the right companion by her side.

Now, with the success of the Little Free Libraries a tangible testament to their collaborative spirit, Evan and Lena found themselves looking towards the future of the Cedar Ridge Collective. The Collective, once a nascent idea struggling for traction, had become a cornerstone of the town, a place of shared resources and mutual support. Evan, with his pragmatic approach and his knack for organizational development, and Lena, with her deep understanding of the community's needs and her unwavering passion for its well-being, were a formidable pair. Their combined vision was not just about maintaining the Collective's current momentum, but about propelling it forward, ensuring its vitality for years to come.

"The Collective is more than just a building, Lena," Evan mused, tracing the rim of his coffee mug one morning at the Sunrise Bakery, the morning sun painting streaks of gold across the worn wooden tables. "It's a hub, a nexus. And I think we're just scratching the surface of what it can be."

Lena nodded, her eyes alight with a familiar spark. "I agree. It's become a place where people feel connected, where they can find what they need, whether it's a skill-sharing workshop, a quiet space to work, or simply a friendly face. But you're right, we can do more. We *should* do more." The thought of expansion, of increased impact, sent a thrill of anticipation through her. She had always championed the Collective, seeing its potential for fostering a stronger sense of community, and now, with Evan's energy and vision alongside hers, that potential felt limitless.

Their conversations, which had once revolved around the immediate needs of the library or the logistics of a small project, now took on a more ambitious scope. They spoke of expanding the Collective's services, of weaving an even richer tapestry of offerings that would cater to a wider range of community needs. Evan, drawing on his experience in community development, began to outline possibilities for formalizing some of the Collective's informal programs. "We could establish dedicated mentorship programs," he suggested, his brow furrowed in concentration. "Pairing experienced artisans with aspiring craftspeople, for instance. Or perhaps a 'Tech Connect' initiative, where younger folks help older residents navigate the digital world."

Lena's mind raced, her librarian's instinct for organization and her deep knowledge of Cedar Ridge's residents kicking in. "And what about the artists and makers who use the Collective's space?" she countered, leaning forward. "We have so many talented individuals. We could create a curated online marketplace, showcasing their work and allowing them to reach a wider audience beyond Cedar Ridge. Imagine, a 'Cedar Ridge Made' portal, where people can buy unique, handcrafted goods directly from our community."

Evan's eyes widened with appreciation. "That's brilliant, Lena. It's about creating sustainable livelihoods for our creative community, leveraging the Collective as the platform. And it ties into another idea I've been mulling over: fostering stronger partnerships with local businesses. Not just for sponsorships, but for collaborative ventures."

He elaborated, sketching out a vision where the Collective could act as a conduit, connecting local businesses with the skills and resources available within the community. "Think about it," he said, his voice gaining momentum. "A local restaurant could partner with the Collective to source fresh produce from the community garden for their seasonal specials. Or the hardware store could offer discounts to Collective members for DIY projects, perhaps even co-host workshops on home improvement."

Lena found herself completely captivated. This was precisely the kind of forward-thinking approach that the Collective needed. It wasn't just about providing services; it was about creating an ecosystem, a network of mutual support that strengthened the entire town. "And the educational programs!" she added, her voice filled with renewed enthusiasm. "We could develop workshops that directly address the town's needs. 'Financial Literacy for Small Business Owners,' 'Sustainable Living Practices,' 'Introduction to Grant Writing for Non-Profits.' These are skills that can empower individuals and elevate the entire community."

Evan smiled, a genuine, warm expression that always seemed to put Lena at ease. "Exactly. We can tap into the expertise that already exists within Cedar Ridge, and also bring in external specialists for targeted programs. The Collective can become a center for lifelong learning, a place where anyone, at any age, can acquire new skills and knowledge." He paused, then added, "And for the younger generation, we can develop more structured after-school programs, tutoring, creative arts, STEM activities. Something that provides a safe and stimulating environment for them, while also fostering a sense of belonging and purpose."

The conversation flowed effortlessly, each idea building upon the last, a testament to their shared passion and complementary strengths. Evan's strategic thinking and his ability to see the bigger picture were balanced by Lena's deep understanding of the community's nuances and her heartfelt commitment to its people. They envisioned a Collective that was not only a functional space but a vibrant, dynamic entity, constantly evolving to meet the changing needs of Cedar Ridge. They talked about creating a 'Skills Bank,' a database of local expertise that could be accessed by individuals and businesses alike, fostering a culture of knowledge sharing and mutual reliance. Lena imagined an 'Intergenerational Storytelling Project,' where elders and youth could come together, sharing their experiences and preserving the rich oral history of Cedar Ridge, with the Collective serving as the central archive.

Evan was particularly keen on the idea of expanding the Collective's reach beyond its physical walls. "We need to think about how to make the Collective accessible to everyone, even those who might not be able to physically come here regularly," he stated, his gaze distant, as if visualizing the town spread out before him. "Perhaps a mobile outreach program, bringing some of our services – like digital literacy training or craft workshops – to different neighborhoods. Or a robust online platform that offers virtual access to resources and programming."

Lena, ever the champion of inclusivity, wholeheartedly embraced this concept. "Yes! We could even create a 'Community Resource Navigator' role, someone who can help connect residents with the services they need, both within the Collective and in the wider community. It would be a vital point of contact for anyone seeking assistance or opportunities."

They discussed the practicalities, the need for securing funding, of building a strong volunteer base, of cultivating even deeper relationships with the town council and local organizations. Evan spoke of developing a clear strategic plan, of setting measurable goals, and of implementing a robust evaluation process to ensure the Collective remained responsive and effective. Lena, meanwhile, was already mentally drafting proposals for grants, thinking about how to best communicate the Collective's evolving vision to potential donors and supporters.

"It's about building on the foundation we've already created," Evan emphasized, his voice calm and assured. "The trust that has been established, the relationships that have been nurtured – these are invaluable. We're not starting from scratch; we're evolving, growing, becoming even more of an integral part of Cedar Ridge's identity."

Lena felt a surge of pride and excitement. She had always believed in the power of community, in the profound impact that a shared space and shared purpose could have. Now, with Evan's partnership, that belief was being translated into a tangible, ambitious plan for the future. The Cedar Ridge Collective, under their shared vision, was poised to become an even brighter beacon, a testament to the enduring strength and resilience of a small town that dared to dream big. The horizons they were setting for the Collective were not just about expanding services, but about expanding the very definition of what it meant to belong, to contribute, and to thrive, together, in the heart of Cedar Ridge. Their shared vision wasn't just for the Collective itself, but for the collective spirit of the entire town, a spirit they were actively nurturing and empowering, one shared idea, one collaborative project, one hopeful future at a time.

Evan's realization about Cedar Ridge wasn't just about finding a place to settle; it was about discovering a dynamic ecosystem where stillness and movement coexisted. He had arrived with a desire for grounding, for an escape from the relentless churn of his previous life, and he'd found it in the quiet charm of the town. Yet, as he immersed himself, he began to see that stability wasn't synonymous with stagnation. It was more akin to the deep, unseen roots of an ancient oak, providing an unshakeable anchor while allowing the branches to reach for the sky, unfurling new leaves with each passing season.

He saw how the rhythm of Cedar Ridge, the predictable cycles of planting and harvest, of town festivals and quiet Sunday mornings, weren't restrictive chains but a steady heartbeat, a reliable pulse that supported innovation and personal evolution. The 'Little Free Libraries' were a perfect manifestation of this. They were a physical, tangible addition to the town's landscape, a new service, yet they were built upon existing resources – Silas's lumber, Lena's vision, their shared effort. They weren't a radical departure, but a natural extension, a testament to the idea that growth could sprout from established ground. This realization was a profound shift for him. He had carried a subtle fear that to truly grow, he needed to be in perpetual motion, constantly seeking new challenges in new places.

Cedar Ridge, through its quiet resilience and the active engagement of its residents, was teaching him a different, more sustainable kind of progress. He began to see his work with the Cedar Ridge Collective not as an end in itself, but as a platform for ongoing development, both for the town and for himself. Each successful workshop, each new partnership, each resident who found a connection or a resource through the Collective, was a testament to this balanced growth. It was the quiet satisfaction of seeing something sturdy and reliable flourish, not by its own frantic effort, but by the deliberate and thoughtful cultivation of its inherent potential.

Lena, too, was experiencing a parallel awakening. For years, her identity had been inextricably linked to Cedar Ridge, to the hushed aisles of the library and the comforting predictability of her routines. She had equated deep roots with a profound sense of belonging, a feeling that she was woven into the very fabric of the town. And while that was undeniably true, Evan's presence had begun to unravel a subtle thread of complacency. It wasn't that she had felt trapped, but rather that the horizons within her reach had felt finite, defined by the familiar contours of her life. Evan, with his fresh perspective and his genuine appreciation for Cedar Ridge, acted as a catalyst, prompting her to look at her home with new eyes.

He saw the potential in the town's history, the untapped talent of its residents, the inherent strength of its community spirit, and in his seeing, she began to see it too. The oral history project, which he had so eloquently encouraged her to lead, was a prime example. It wasn't just about preserving the past; it was about actively engaging with it, about creating new narratives by reinterpreting and sharing existing ones. She found herself spending hours at the Historical Society, poring over faded photographs and dusty ledgers, not as a curator of artifacts, but as an active participant in weaving the town's ongoing story. She discovered a thrill in connecting disparate pieces of information, in uncovering the hidden threads that linked generations, in understanding how the past informed the present and could shape the future. This process of discovery, of actively shaping and disseminating knowledge, was a form of growth that felt both deeply personal and intrinsically tied to her home. She realized that commitment to a place didn't necessitate an end to personal exploration.

Instead, the very groundedness of Cedar Ridge provided a fertile soil for her own horizons to expand. She could be deeply rooted in her community and simultaneously reach for new intellectual and creative heights. The library, once her sole domain, was now a springboard, a place where she could share her newfound knowledge and inspire others. She began organizing small talks, inviting residents to share their own family histories, creating a living archive that was constantly being updated and enriched. Her passion for stories, once confined to the pages of books, was now spilling out into the heart of the community, creating new connections and fostering a deeper appreciation for the collective narrative. This evolution wasn't a rejection of her past, but an expansion of it, a testament to the idea that growth could indeed flourish in the most familiar of soils.

The synergy between Evan and Lena was becoming a quiet force within Cedar Ridge, a testament to their individual evolutions and their shared commitment. They found themselves naturally gravitating towards projects that not only benefited the town but also challenged them to stretch beyond their previous limitations. The 'Cedar Ridge Collective' was evolving under their collaborative stewardship, becoming more than just a community center; it was transforming into a dynamic hub for innovation and personal development.

Evan's initial vision of a stable anchor point for the community had blossomed into something far more vibrant, a place where residents could not only find support but also actively pursue their own growth. He had discovered that by providing a stable foundation, he had inadvertently created the ideal environment for others to explore their own horizons. For instance, the mentorship programs he had envisioned were taking root, pairing seasoned artisans with eager apprentices. He'd witnessed firsthand the transformative power of this exchange, seeing a young woman who had always sketched in her notebooks blossom into a confident pottery artist under the tutelage of Mrs. Gable, a woman whose hands had shaped clay for over fifty years.

Evan would often pause by the Collective's workshop, observing the quiet intensity of their collaboration, the shared laughter that punctuated moments of painstaking detail. It was a tangible manifestation of his evolving understanding of growth: that it wasn't always about individual leaps, but often about the steady, supportive cultivation of collective talent. He saw how Mrs. Gable, in teaching, was also rediscovering her own passion, finding new joy in the act of imparting her accumulated knowledge. This reciprocal growth was a revelation, demonstrating that giving back could be as profoundly enriching as personal achievement.

Lena, equally inspired, was channeling her growing confidence into expanding the Collective's outreach. She had always been passionate about ensuring that Cedar Ridge's stories were not confined to the library walls, and now, with Evan's strategic vision, she saw a path to making that a reality. The 'Cedar Ridge Made' online marketplace was becoming a tangible success, a testament to the town's creative spirit and Lena's knack for organization. She had spent countless hours meticulously photographing local crafts, writing compelling descriptions, and building user-friendly interfaces, transforming a nascent idea into a thriving digital storefront.

She saw how this initiative was not only providing economic opportunities for local artisans but also fostering a deeper sense of pride and belonging within the community. Residents who might have felt isolated in their creative pursuits now found themselves connected to a wider network, their talents recognized and valued. Lena found a particular joy in seeing how this project encouraged personal growth in those involved. A shy baker, who had only ever sold her pies at the local farmers' market, was now receiving orders from across the state, her confidence blossoming with each positive review.

Similarly, a retired woodworker, whose skills had previously gone largely unnoticed, was now selling his intricate birdhouses to a national audience, his passion for his craft reignited. Evan often spoke of this phenomenon with a quiet sense of awe. "It's remarkable, Lena," he'd remarked one evening, watching her deftly manage inquiries from both a local artist and a potential buyer from out of town. "You're not just creating a marketplace; you're creating opportunities for people to redefine themselves, to discover capabilities they never knew they possessed. You're helping them to grow beyond their perceived limitations."

This idea of redefining oneself, of discovering hidden potential, resonated deeply with both of them. Evan found that his own need for stability had not diminished, but it had evolved. He no longer saw it as an endpoint, but as a launching pad. The security he felt in Cedar Ridge allowed him the mental space and emotional freedom to tackle more ambitious projects. He was learning to embrace the inherent tension between settling down and continuing to evolve, recognizing that the two were not mutually exclusive. His work with the town council, for example, had shifted from merely observing to actively contributing.

He had taken on a role in developing a long-term economic strategy for Cedar Ridge, a project that required him to draw upon his past experiences while also forging new approaches tailored to the town's unique character. He discovered that his ability to foster collaboration, honed by his work with the Collective, was invaluable in navigating the complexities of municipal planning. He wasn't just building programs; he was helping to build consensus, to foster a shared vision for the town's future. This, he realized, was a profound form of personal growth, a demonstration that stability could be a catalyst for leadership and meaningful contribution.

Lena, in turn, was actively cultivating her own horizons within the familiar landscape of Cedar Ridge. She had always loved the quiet introspection that her work provided, but Evan's encouragement had inspired her to seek out more outward-facing opportunities. She had recently taken on the role of coordinator for the town's annual historical society fundraiser, a task that initially filled her with a familiar sense of trepidation. However, as she delved into the planning, she found herself surprisingly invigorated by the challenge. She collaborated with local businesses, organized engaging events, and even delivered a heartfelt presentation on the importance of preserving Cedar Ridge's heritage.

The positive feedback and the palpable sense of community engagement that the event generated were immensely rewarding. She realized that her deep love for Cedar Ridge, once a quiet, internal passion, could be a powerful force for collective action and positive change. She discovered that by embracing new responsibilities and stepping outside her comfort zone, she was not diminishing her connection to Cedar Ridge, but deepening it. The town was not just a place where she belonged; it was a place where she could actively contribute, where her growth was intertwined with the community's well-being. She learned that putting down roots didn't mean being confined by them, but rather using them as a source of strength to reach for something more.

Their journey together was becoming a quiet testament to the profound truth that personal growth and a sense of belonging are not opposing forces, but rather complementary elements that nourish each other. Evan had found in Cedar Ridge the stability he craved, but he had also discovered that this stability provided the fertile ground for his own continuous development. He was learning that true contentment wasn't about escaping the past, but about building a future on a solid foundation, and that this future could be as dynamic and evolving as he was. Lena, meanwhile, was realizing that her deep connection to Cedar Ridge was not a limitation, but a source of boundless possibility.

By embracing new challenges and extending her reach, she was discovering new facets of herself and strengthening her bond with the community she loved. The horizons she had once perceived as distant and perhaps unattainable were now unfolding around her, nurtured by the familiar soil of her home and illuminated by the shared light of their evolving lives. They were proving, in their own quiet way, that the most profound growth often happens not in seeking distant lands, but in cultivating the rich soil of the place you call home, and in doing so, discovering that the most expansive horizons can indeed be found right where you are, especially when you have someone by your side who helps you see them.

The gentle hum of Cedar Ridge settled over Evan and Lena like a familiar melody, a counterpoint to the quiet conversation that flowed between them on their usual evening stroll. The sun, a molten orb, dipped below the western hills, painting the sky in hues of apricot and rose, a daily spectacle they had come to cherish. It was in these quiet moments, bathed in the fading light, that the unspoken found its voice. Evan had made his choice, a definitive turning of the page from a life of constant motion to one grounded in the rich soil of this small town. The decision, once a source of internal debate, now felt as natural as the turning of the seasons. He was here, not just as a resident, but as a participant, an architect of his own future within the steady embrace of Cedar Ridge. Yet, as he walked beside Lena, the weight of that choice, the sheer expanse of what lay ahead, settled upon him. It wasn't a burden, but a realization of the vast, uncharted territory that stretched beyond the comfortable familiarity they had cultivated.

Lena, her hand finding his, seemed to sense his thoughts. Her presence was a constant, soothing anchor, a reminder that his journey was now shared. "It's funny, isn't it?" she mused, her voice soft, almost lost in the rustle of leaves overhead. "How you can feel so certain about staying, and yet, the future feels like a book with all its pages still blank." A gentle squeeze of his hand was his unspoken agreement. They had spoken often of the roots they were laying, the tangible and intangible connections that bound them to Cedar Ridge. But the horizon, the vast, limitless expanse that beckoned them forward, remained a landscape yet to be fully explored. It was a prospect that, for many, might have bred anxiety. The unknown, the inevitable challenges that life invariably presented, could easily cast a shadow over even the most hopeful hearts. But as they walked, a different feeling bloomed between them – a quiet, resilient hope, an almost defiant optimism.

"I don't think I'm afraid of the blank pages, though," Evan said, his gaze sweeping across the darkening fields that bordered the town. "Not anymore. It's...invigorating, in a strange way. Like standing at the edge of a vast ocean, knowing you're about to set sail, but with a sturdy ship and a trusted crew." He glanced at Lena, his eyes reflecting the fading light. "And my crew is the best I could ask for." The sentiment was met with a warm smile, a silent acknowledgment of the shared understanding that had grown between them. They had built something here, brick by painstaking brick, idea by thoughtful idea. The Cedar Ridge Collective, the library programs, the burgeoning online marketplace – these were not just projects; they were testaments to their shared vision, and more importantly, to their ability to work together, to face the inevitable complexities with a united front.

Lena nodded, her gaze following his. "It's the intention behind it, I think. We're not just letting things happen to us. We're choosing this. We're choosing to build, to grow, to face whatever comes next, together." She paused, a thoughtful frown creasing her brow. "There will be days, won't there? When things don't go according to plan. When a proposal gets rejected, or a project hits a snag, or when life just throws something completely unexpected our way." The truth of her words hung in the air, a necessary acknowledgment of reality. Cedar Ridge, for all its charm and stability, was still a place subject to the ebb and flow of the wider world. Economic shifts, personal crises, the inherent unpredictability of human endeavors – these were all potential storms on their horizon.

"Absolutely," Evan confirmed, his tone steady. "And I think that's where the hope comes in. It's not a naive hope, the kind that expects everything to be perfect. It's a hope born of experience, of knowing we can weather those storms. We've already navigated some tricky waters, haven't we? Remember when the funding for the after-school program was in jeopardy? Or the initial resistance to the 'Cedar Ridge Made' marketplace? We found our way through those." He remembered the late nights spent poring over budgets, the impassioned community meetings, the moments of doubt that had threatened to derail their progress. But in each instance, they had found a way. They had rallied the community, creatively reallocated resources, or simply refused to give up. Each challenge overcome had added another layer to the foundation of their shared resilience.

"Exactly," Lena echoed, her voice gaining a quiet strength. "It's about the commitment. We're committed to this town, to each other, and to the idea that we can create something meaningful. That commitment is our compass when the path gets unclear. It reminds us why we started, and it propels us forward." She thought about the countless conversations she'd had with residents, the stories they had shared, the burgeoning sense of pride she witnessed. The oral history project, which had begun as a personal passion, had blossomed into a community-wide endeavor, connecting generations and forging new understandings. It was a tangible reminder that their efforts, however small they might sometimes seem, had a ripple effect, fostering a deeper sense of belonging and shared purpose.

Evan considered her words, the intricate tapestry of their lives in Cedar Ridge weaving itself into a cohesive whole. "And it's about intention, too," he added. "It's about making conscious choices. It's not just about 'staying.' It's about *how* we stay. How we contribute, how we engage, how we continue to learn and evolve, even within a stable environment. For me, that means continuing to work with the town council, not just as an observer, but as an active participant in shaping its future. It means finding new ways to leverage my experience, to help bridge the gap between what was and what can be." He had discovered a surprising satisfaction in the slower, more deliberate pace of municipal planning, a stark contrast to the fast-paced world he had left behind. It required patience, a deep understanding of the community's needs, and a willingness to build consensus, skills he had honed through his work with the Collective, but which found a new and more impactful application here.

Lena's mind drifted to the library, her sanctuary, her anchor. Yet, even within its quiet walls, she was discovering new horizons. "And for me, it's about continuing to push the boundaries of what the library can be," she said. "It's not just about books anymore, is it? It's about being a hub for connection, for learning, for sharing. I've been thinking about expanding our digital literacy workshops, perhaps even partnering with Silas on some basic woodworking tutorials for the online platform. And the historical society's fundraiser – that felt like a true test of my willingness to step outside my comfort zone. Organizing it, speaking at it... it was daunting, but incredibly rewarding. It showed me that my passion for Cedar Ridge's stories could be a catalyst for bringing people together, for fostering a sense of shared history and collective action." She had always been content with the quiet predictability of her life, but Evan's presence had subtly nudged her towards embracing new challenges, towards recognizing that her capacity for growth was far greater than she had previously imagined.

The unspoken agreement between them solidified with each shared glance, each synchronistic thought. They were not facing the future with a naive certainty that all would be smooth sailing. Instead, they were facing it with a deliberate embrace of the unknown, armed with a shared sense of purpose and a deep, abiding hope. Their commitment was not merely to Cedar Ridge, but to the life they were actively constructing within it, a life defined by intention, mutual support, and a willingness to adapt and evolve.

"We'll make mistakes," Evan acknowledged, his voice a low rumble. "We'll have disagreements. There will be days when we question everything." He turned to face her, his expression earnest. "But we'll face them. We'll talk them through. We'll learn from them. That's part of the building process, isn't it? You can't build anything truly lasting without encountering some resistance, without having to shore up the foundations." He thought of the architectural principles he had learned, the need for strong underlying structures to support even the most elegant of designs. Their relationship, their life in Cedar Ridge, was no different. It required constant attention, careful tending, and a willingness to address any cracks that might appear before they widened.

Lena leaned her head against his shoulder, the familiar scent of him a comforting presence. "And we'll celebrate the victories, big and small," she added softly. "Every successful workshop, every new artisan who finds their footing on 'Cedar Ridge Made,' every child who discovers a new favorite author at the library – those are the moments that fuel us. They remind us why this intentionality, this commitment, is so worthwhile." She envisioned the future, not as a predetermined path, but as a garden they were cultivating together. Some seeds would sprout easily, while others would require more care, more patience, more understanding. But the overall vision, the lush, vibrant landscape they hoped to create, was a powerful motivator.

"It's about creating a life that feels authentic, I suppose," Evan mused. "A life where our actions are aligned with our values. Where we're not just passively existing, but actively participating in the unfolding of our own story, and the story of this town." He felt a profound sense of peace settle over him, a calm certainty that transcended the usual anxieties about the future. He had found his ground, and from that ground, he was ready to reach. The uncertainty that once felt like a looming threat now felt like an open invitation, a testament to the boundless possibilities that lay before them.

The soft glow of streetlights began to flicker on, casting a warm, inviting light onto the quiet streets of Cedar Ridge. The air was cool and crisp, carrying the faint scent of pine and woodsmoke. They continued their walk, their steps in sync, a quiet rhythm that mirrored the steady beat of the town they now called home. They didn't have all the answers, and they certainly didn't have a crystal ball. But as they walked hand-in-hand, bathed in the gentle light of their shared future, they carried with them something far more valuable: a profound sense of hope, a steadfast commitment, and the quiet confidence that, whatever lay ahead, they would face it together, with open hearts and unwavering intention. The horizon stretched before them, not as a place of apprehension, but as a canvas waiting for the vibrant colors of their shared life to be painted upon it. They were not just settling down; they were settling *in*, and from that deep, intentional rootedness, they were ready to embrace the limitless expanse of what was to come.

CHAPTER TWELVE

The Road Ahead

The trust that now permeated Evan and Lena's relationship was not a fragile bloom, easily crushed by the slightest pressure. It was a robust, ancient oak, its roots deeply entwined with the very soil of Cedar Ridge, its branches reaching confidently towards the sky. This wasn't a trust that had materialized overnight, born from a single grand gesture or a shared, effortless moment. Instead, it was a meticulously constructed edifice, each stone laid with care, cemented by the mortar of shared vulnerability and hard-won understanding.

They had weathered storms, both external and internal, that had threatened to shake the very foundations of their connection. The early days, filled with the thrilling, yet sometimes disorienting, dance between Evan's innate restlessness and Lena's quiet yearning for stability, had been a crucible. He'd grappled with the fear of being tethered, of his spirit being confined by the very anchors he craved. Lena, in turn, had faced her own anxieties, the quiet whisper that perhaps her steady path was too predictable, too unexciting for a man who had lived a life painted in broader strokes.

But they hadn't faltered. Instead, they had leaned into those uncomfortable conversations, those moments of uncertainty where the easy path would have been to retreat. Evan remembered the sheer relief that had washed over him when Lena, instead of pushing him towards a decision about his future, had simply offered her quiet presence, her unwavering belief that he would find his way. It was in those silences, pregnant with unspoken support, that he felt truly seen, truly understood.

He had confessed his fears of losing himself in commitment, of the freedom he had so long equated with his identity being extinguished. Lena hadn't dismissed his anxieties; she had validated them, acknowledging the complexity of his internal landscape. "It's not about losing yourself, Evan," she had said, her voice a gentle balm, "it's about discovering new facets of yourself you never knew existed. It's about integrating your past with your present, not erasing it." Her wisdom, rooted in her own journey of self-discovery within the familiar embrace of Cedar Ridge, had been a revelation.

Similarly, Lena had found in Evan a catalyst for her own growth. He had a way of seeing possibilities where she saw limitations, of challenging her assumptions with a gentle curiosity that never felt confrontational. When she'd confessed her fear that her love for Cedar Ridge, her quiet contentment, might be perceived as a lack of ambition, Evan had countered with an earnestness that had disarmed her.

"Lena," he'd said, his eyes holding hers with an intensity that had made her heart skip a beat, "your connection to this town, your passion for its stories, its people – that's not a limitation, it's your superpower. It's what makes you, *you*. And it's what makes Cedar Ridge so special. Don't ever mistake rootedness for stagnation." He had a profound respect for the quiet strength she possessed, for the depth of her understanding of the community, a respect that had fueled her own confidence.

Their trust was also built on a shared understanding of their individual needs and a conscious effort to honor them. Evan, for instance, still needed his moments of solitude, his time to recalibrate and process. Lena had learned to recognize the subtle shifts in his demeanor that signaled this need, offering him space without making him feel as though he was pushing her away. She understood that his need for reflection wasn't a rejection of her, but a vital part of his well-being, a necessary recalibration for the man who was now so deeply invested in their shared future. He, in turn, had learned to appreciate Lena's need for connection, her quiet desire for shared experiences and affirmations. He made it a point to carve out time for their walks, for their impromptu coffee dates at the Cozy Mug, for simply being present with her, even when his mind might have been buzzing with project ideas.

This mutual respect extended to their shared endeavors. The Cedar Ridge Collective, the burgeoning online marketplace, the revitalized library programs – these were not merely projects they had embarked upon, but tangible manifestations of their collaborative spirit. They had learned to navigate the inevitable disagreements that arose when two passionate individuals worked together. There were times when Evan's more pragmatic, big-picture approach clashed with Lena's meticulous attention to detail, or when her desire for community consensus felt too slow for his action-oriented nature. But in those moments, they had learned to pause, to listen, to find the common ground. They had developed a language of compromise, a shared understanding that the success of their joint ventures was more important than individual "wins."

Evan recalled a particularly challenging board meeting for the Collective. A major funding proposal had been unexpectedly rejected, and the air in the room had been thick with disappointment and a simmering tension. Evan, feeling the familiar urge to strategize and push for immediate solutions, had seen Lena's quiet demeanor, her focus on the emotional impact of the news on the team. Instead of launching into a tactical barrage, he had found himself sitting beside her, offering a supportive hand. Later, he had learned that Lena's calm had been a deliberate choice, a way to ensure that the team felt heard and supported before diving into problem-solving. It was a subtle but profound lesson for him: that strength wasn't always about forceful action; sometimes, it was about gentle resilience.

Lena, too, had learned from Evan's willingness to embrace calculated risks. She had initially been hesitant about expanding the "Cedar Ridge Made" marketplace to include a wider range of artisanal goods, fearing it might dilute the core focus on local craft. Evan, however, had seen the potential for economic growth, for attracting a broader customer base and providing more opportunities for local entrepreneurs. He had patiently presented market research, outlined mitigation strategies for quality control, and ultimately, convinced her to take the leap. The subsequent success of the expanded marketplace had been a testament to his foresight, but more importantly, to their ability to trust each other's judgment, even when their perspectives differed.

Their trust was also fortified by their shared vision for Cedar Ridge. They weren't just building lives *in* the town; they were actively participating in its evolution. They shared a deep-seated belief in the power of community, in the potential for a small town to be a vibrant hub of innovation, connection, and opportunity. Evan's involvement with the town council, a role he had initially approached with a degree of professional detachment, had evolved into a genuine passion for shaping the town's future. He found immense satisfaction in the slow, deliberate process of governance, in seeing how thoughtful planning and community engagement could create tangible improvements. He had learned to navigate the intricacies of local politics, to build relationships with long-time residents, and to champion initiatives that would benefit the town for generations to come.

Lena, through her work at the library and her involvement with the historical society, had become a steward of Cedar Ridge's past and a visionary for its future. She saw the library not just as a repository of books, but as a dynamic community center, a place for learning, for connection, for shared experiences. Her expansion of digital literacy programs, her exploration of partnerships for skill-sharing workshops, and her dedication to preserving the town's oral histories were all testament to her commitment to fostering a richer, more connected community. She saw the threads of the past woven into the fabric of the present, and she was determined to ensure those threads remained strong, while also weaving in new patterns of growth and innovation.

This shared commitment to Cedar Ridge, this mutual investment in its well-being, had become a powerful binding agent for their relationship. It transcended the everyday ebb and flow of a romantic partnership; it was a shared mission, a common purpose that gave their lives a deeper meaning. They spoke about the future not in terms of individual aspirations, but in terms of collective growth. "Imagine," Evan had said to Lena just the other evening, watching the fireflies begin their nightly dance in the meadow behind their house, "imagine the library buzzing with activity during the day, with workshops and classes, and then in the evening, the town square filled with families enjoying the outdoor movie series we've been planning. Imagine the 'Cedar Ridge Made' marketplace becoming a destination for shoppers from neighboring towns. That's the future we're building, isn't it?"

Lena had smiled, a soft, contented smile. "It is. And it's a future built on a foundation of trust, Evan. Trust in ourselves, trust in each other, and trust in the potential of this town." She had reached for his hand, their fingers interlacing naturally, a gesture that spoke volumes about their unspoken understanding. The days of doubt, of questioning whether they could truly make this work, felt like a distant memory. They had navigated the complex currents of commitment and freedom, of individual journeys and shared paths, and they had emerged stronger, more resolute, and more deeply connected than ever before.

Their love was no longer a heady, intoxicating potion; it was a steady, nourishing stream, flowing with purpose and unwavering devotion. It was a testament to the fact that true connection wasn't about finding someone who completed you, but about finding someone with whom you could build, grow, and create something beautiful and lasting, together. Their trust, so carefully cultivated, was the fertile ground upon which the next chapter of their lives in Cedar Ridge would undoubtedly flourish.

The Cedar Ridge Collective, once a fledgling concept born from shared ideals and a mutual desire to breathe new life into their beloved town, had blossomed into something far more substantial. It was no longer merely a project; it was a living, breathing entity, a testament to the potent synergy that Evan and Lena had cultivated. Their combined strengths, so different yet so complementary, had provided the sturdy framework upon which its continued success was built.

Evan's pragmatic acumen, his ability to dissect complex business models and identify strategic growth opportunities, had been instrumental in navigating the often-turbulent waters of commerce. He possessed an innate understanding of market trends, a keen eye for operational efficiency, and a remarkable talent for fostering productive relationships with external stakeholders, from suppliers to potential investors. This wasn't the detached, purely analytical approach of his corporate past, however. Instead, it was tempered by a newfound appreciation for the human element, for the value of each individual contribution to the Collective's mission. He saw beyond profit margins; he saw the dreams of the artisans, the aspirations of the entrepreneurs, and the quiet determination of every person involved.

Lena, on the other hand, was the heart of the Collective, the embodiment of its deep roots within Cedar Ridge. Her innate understanding of the community's rhythm, its unwritten social contracts, and its deeply held values was invaluable. She navigated the intricate web of local relationships with a grace that was both reassuring and effective. Her warmth and genuine care for the people of Cedar Ridge were palpable, creating an environment of trust and open communication.

She was the one who remembered birthdays, who understood the unspoken needs of their vendors, and who could translate Evan's often-technical explanations into terms that resonated with everyone. Her tireless efforts in organizing workshops, facilitating mentorship opportunities, and championing the stories behind the products had fostered a sense of belonging and shared purpose that was the lifeblood of the Collective. She ensured that as the Collective grew, its commitment to its foundational principles – supporting local talent, fostering entrepreneurship, and strengthening community bonds – remained unwavering.

Their leadership, therefore, was a masterful blend of foresight and groundedness. Evan would meticulously map out expansion strategies, identifying new markets and potential collaborations. He would present data-driven projections, outlining the economic benefits and operational requirements. Lena, in turn, would then engage with the community, gauging the readiness for such expansions, ensuring that the proposed changes aligned with the town's character and the artisans' capabilities.

She would facilitate discussions, address concerns, and build consensus, transforming Evan's strategic blueprints into shared aspirations. This iterative process, marked by open dialogue and mutual respect, ensured that the Collective's growth was not only sustainable but also deeply ingrained in the fabric of Cedar Ridge.

The tangible results of their collaborative leadership were evident throughout the town. A palpable sense of optimism had begun to permeate Cedar Ridge. The Collective, with its curated selection of handcrafted goods, its vibrant online presence, and its increasingly popular community events, had become a beacon of entrepreneurial spirit. Local artisans, who had once struggled to find a consistent market for their creations, now saw their work reaching a wider audience, providing them with a stable income and the validation of their craft.

Small businesses that had partnered with the Collective, whether for logistical support or increased visibility, reported significant upticks in their own customer bases. Even the physical landscape of the town seemed to reflect this renewed energy. Storefronts that had stood vacant for years were being revitalized, often housing pop-up shops or studios affiliated with the Collective. The town square, once a quiet gathering place, now frequently buzzed with the energy of weekend markets, craft fairs, and outdoor concerts organized by the Collective.

Evan's involvement extended beyond the direct operations of the Collective. His role on the town council, initially driven by a desire to contribute to the community's development, had become more proactive. He found himself championing initiatives that directly supported the Collective's mission, such as advocating for improved broadband infrastructure to enhance the online marketplace's reach, or proposing zoning changes that would encourage the development of artisan studios and workshops.

He brought to council meetings a unique perspective, one that bridged the gap between economic development and community well-being, a perspective honed by his daily engagement with the challenges and triumphs of Cedar Ridge's entrepreneurs. His ability to articulate the economic multiplier effect of supporting local businesses, backed by the success of the Collective, had earned him respect and influence.

Lena's influence, while perhaps less overt in the halls of local government, was deeply embedded in the town's social ecosystem. Through her leadership at the library, she had fostered a culture of learning and skill development that directly benefited the Collective's members. Workshops on digital marketing, product photography, and financial literacy, offered free of charge through the library and often led by Collective members or external experts brought in through Evan's network, became incredibly popular. She had also spearheaded a "Cedar Ridge Stories" initiative, a project to document and share the personal histories of the town's artisans and small business owners.

These narratives, shared through the library's archives, the Collective's blog, and local media, not only celebrated individual achievements but also reinforced the collective identity and pride of Cedar Ridge. Her understanding of human connection meant that the Collective was more than just a business; it was a community hub, a place where people felt seen, supported, and valued.

The inherent viability of the Cedar Ridge Collective wasn't just about economic success; it was about its resilience, its capacity to adapt and endure. Evan and Lena had intentionally built a structure that was not solely dependent on their individual efforts. They had cultivated a team of dedicated individuals, empowering them with responsibility and fostering a sense of ownership.

Sarah, who managed the day-to-day operations of the physical storefront, had evolved into a trusted leader, capable of making quick decisions and handling customer service issues with efficiency and warmth. Mark, who oversaw the online platform, had become an expert in e-commerce, constantly innovating and improving the user experience. The artisans themselves were increasingly involved in governance, forming committees to discuss product standards, marketing strategies, and community outreach. This distributed leadership model ensured that even if Evan or Lena were temporarily unavailable, the Collective would continue to function smoothly, its momentum undiminished.

Their commitment was not just to the present success of the Collective, but to its long-term sustainability. They recognized that a thriving small town required more than just economic activity; it needed a robust social fabric, a sense of shared identity, and a continuous cycle of innovation. The Collective was designed to be a catalyst for all of these.

By providing a platform for local talent, it encouraged creativity and entrepreneurship. By fostering community events and workshops, it strengthened social bonds. By preserving and celebrating the town's unique heritage through the stories of its people, it built a strong sense of place. Evan and Lena understood that true revitalization was a multifaceted endeavor, and the Collective, under their thoughtful guidance, was serving as a powerful engine for that transformation.

There were, of course, still challenges. The economic landscape remained dynamic, with fluctuating consumer demands and the ever-present competition from larger online retailers. Supply chain disruptions, a persistent concern in the modern economy, could still impact the availability of raw materials for some artisans. Moreover, the inherent complexities of managing a growing organization, balancing the needs of diverse stakeholders, and making difficult decisions were constant considerations.

However, Evan and Lena approached these challenges not with dread, but with a seasoned resilience. They had learned to anticipate potential pitfalls, to adapt their strategies, and to draw strength from their shared purpose and the unwavering support of their community.

Evan often found himself reflecting on the early days, the tentative conversations, the initial uncertainties. He remembered the sheer audacity of their vision, the leap of faith they had taken. Now, looking at the bustling Collective storefront, seeing families browsing the aisles, or watching an artisan proudly explain their craft to an interested customer, he felt a profound sense of accomplishment. It wasn't just his accomplishment, or Lena's; it was Cedar Ridge's. The Collective had become a tangible symbol of what was possible when a community believed in itself and worked together.

Lena, too, would often pause during her busy days, a quiet smile gracing her lips. She would watch the interactions, the shared laughter, the easy camaraderie among the vendors and customers. She saw the way the Collective had fostered not just commerce, but genuine connection. It had provided a space for people to share their passions, to find support, and to feel a part of something bigger than themselves. This, more than any financial metric, was the true measure of its success. The continued vitality of the Cedar Ridge Collective was not an accident; it was the direct result of intentional commitment, unwavering belief, and the powerful synergy of two individuals who had poured their hearts and souls into creating a brighter future for their town. It was a testament to the enduring power of community, and a promise of what was yet to come. The road ahead, while always presenting its own set of twists and turns, felt steadier, brighter, and more full of promise, thanks to the foundation they had so carefully built, brick by brick, dream by dream.

Evan's sense of belonging in Cedar Ridge had bloomed, not as a sudden, dramatic flowering, but as a slow, steady unfurling, much like the wild roses that climbed the fences along the edge of town. He used to feel like a visitor, a temporary occupant in a life that was fundamentally elsewhere. His past was a series of transient addresses, a career path that prioritized mobility over permanence. Each move, each new city, had been an exercise in adaptation, in learning the local customs, in building temporary networks that would inevitably dissipate. He was good at it, at shedding his skin and adopting a new one, but it was a skill born of necessity, not desire. It had left him with a certain detachment, a feeling that he was always observing, never fully immersed.

Cedar Ridge, however, had subtly, irrevocably changed that. It wasn't just the success of the Collective, though that certainly played a part. It was the way Lena had woven him into the fabric of the town, not by force, but by invitation. It was the easy nod from Mr. Henderson at the hardware store, the genuine query from Mrs. Gable about his latest project at the council meetings, the way the younger artisans would seek his advice, not just on business, but on navigating the complexities of their own lives.

These weren't just professional interactions; they were moments of connection, small affirmations that he was seen, that he was *here*. He no longer felt the need to constantly assess his exit strategy, to keep one foot out the door. His feet were firmly planted, and the ground beneath them felt solid, fertile.

He remembered a conversation he'd had with Lena early on, shortly after they'd officially launched the Collective. He'd been outlining the projected growth, the potential expansion into new markets, the financial forecasts. Lena had listened intently, her brow furrowed in concentration, and then, with a gentle hand on his arm, she'd said, "Evan, this is all vital, and I value it more than I can say. But don't forget to look up.

Don't forget the people who are the heart of all this. Their stories, their dreams – that's the bedrock. The numbers are important, but the connection is everything." At the time, he'd nodded, appreciating her sentiment, but perhaps not fully grasping its profound truth. Now, he understood. The "connection" wasn't just a nice-to-have; it was the very engine of sustainable success, and more importantly, it was the source of his own newfound sense of belonging.

His transient past had, ironically, equipped him with a unique perspective. He could see the subtle shifts in Cedar Ridge, the ways in which the Collective was not just revitalizing commerce, but rejuvenating the town's spirit. He saw it in the increased foot traffic on Main Street, in the renewed pride in local craftsmanship, in the way people now spoke about Cedar Ridge with an optimism he hadn't heard in years.

He had been the outsider looking in, and now he was part of the inside, not as a gatekeeper, but as a contributor, an architect of this shared future. This was a freedom he hadn't anticipated – the freedom to choose where to invest his life, his energy, his passion. It was the freedom of commitment, of putting down roots, and finding that those roots not only held him steady but also nourished his growth.

The challenges he'd faced in his corporate life – the cutthroat competition, the relentless pursuit of profit above all else, the superficiality of many relationships – had left him with a deep-seated yearning for something more meaningful. He'd achieved a certain level of success, but it had always felt hollow, devoid of the genuine human connection that now defined his life in Cedar Ridge. He'd been building empires, but in doing so, he'd neglected to build a home. The Collective, and Lena, had given him that home, a place where his skills were not just utilized, but appreciated; where his intellect was valued, but his humanity was embraced.

He found himself thinking about his childhood, the constant moving, the feeling of never quite fitting in. There had been moments of fleeting camaraderie, but they were always overshadowed by the knowledge that another departure was on the horizon. He'd learned to be self-reliant, to find comfort in his own company, but that self-reliance had often tipped into isolation. Cedar Ridge had challenged that ingrained pattern. Here, he wasn't just self-reliant; he was interdependent. He relied on Lena, on Sarah, on Mark, on the artisans, and they, in turn, relied on him. It was a delicate, beautiful balance, a tapestry woven from shared effort and mutual trust.

The council meetings, which he'd once approached with a detached sense of civic duty, now felt like important forums for shaping the town's destiny, *his* town's destiny. He wasn't just presenting data; he was advocating for the dreams of his neighbors, for the future of the community he had come to call home. He still brought his analytical mind, his strategic foresight, but it was now infused with a deep-seated loyalty, a genuine desire to see Cedar Ridge thrive. He was no longer just a participant; he was an invested stakeholder, his own well-being intrinsically linked to the town's prosperity.

Lena often spoke about the importance of 'place,' of how our surroundings shape us as much as our experiences. Evan had always thought of 'place' as a backdrop, a stage upon which his life unfolded. But Cedar Ridge had shown him that it could be more. It could be the soil from which he drew strength, the ecosystem that supported his growth, the community that defined him. He wasn't just *in* Cedar Ridge; he was *of* Cedar Ridge. His transient past, once a source of pride in its adventurousness, now felt like a prelude, a necessary journey that had led him to this place of permanence, of belonging.

He'd spent years accumulating wealth and professional accolades, but he'd never felt truly rich. Now, he felt an abundance he couldn't quantify in dollars and cents. It was the richness of deep connection, of shared purpose, of knowing that he was contributing to something larger than himself, something that would endure. He realized that true freedom wasn't about the ability to go anywhere, but about the deep satisfaction of choosing to be somewhere, and then committing to making that place better. His life had been a series of open doors, leading to more open doors. Cedar Ridge had presented him with a sturdy, welcoming one, and he had walked through it, closing it firmly behind him, ready to build.

The feeling of being an outsider had been a constant hum beneath the surface of his life. It was a subtle dissonance, a feeling that he was always slightly out of sync with his surroundings. He'd learned to mask it, to project an image of competence and control, but internally, the feeling persisted. Here, in Cedar Ridge, that hum had faded. It had been replaced by a sense of resonance, of being in harmony with the people and the place. He could exhale, truly exhale, for the first time in years. He was no longer just Evan the businessman, Evan the strategist. He was Evan, a member of Cedar Ridge, a partner in its journey, a man who had finally found his place.

He saw it in the quiet moments too. Walking through the town square on a Saturday morning, the air alive with the chatter of the market, the scent of freshly baked bread mingling with the earthy aroma of local produce. He'd see familiar faces, exchange smiles, and feel a warmth spread through him that had nothing to do with the sun. He wasn't just observing the scene; he was a part of it, a thread in the vibrant weave of community life. This was the essence of belonging – not an entitlement, but a lived experience, earned through participation, through shared vulnerability, through genuine care. His past had been a journey of looking for a place to land; his present was the joyous discovery that he had found it, and that it was far more beautiful, and far more fulfilling, than he could have ever imagined.

Lena's gaze swept across the bustling market square, a contented sigh escaping her lips. The familiar sights and sounds – the vibrant colors of handcrafted textiles, the melodic calls of vendors, the easy laughter of neighbors – were a symphony that had always resonated deep within her soul. Cedar Ridge was more than just a place; it was the beating heart of her existence, the fertile ground where her roots had taken hold and flourished. She'd spent years nurturing this connection, tending to the community with the same care she'd give her most treasured garden, and the harvest was a profound sense of belonging that warmed her from the inside out.

Evan's arrival had been an unexpected bloom in her well-established garden. She'd initially viewed him through the lens of the Collective, a valuable asset whose business acumen could propel their shared vision forward. But as the seasons turned, and his presence became a more integral part of her daily life, her perspective had shifted, blossoming into something far richer and more complex. He brought with him a world beyond Cedar Ridge, a vast landscape of experience and ambition that, surprisingly, didn't diminish her own sense of place, but rather expanded it.

She watched him now, engaged in a lively discussion with Mrs. Gable about the provenance of some locally sourced wool for her knitting projects. His brow was furrowed in concentration, his hands gesturing expressively, a stark contrast to the reserved, almost corporate demeanor she'd first encountered. This Evan, the one who effortlessly navigated the intricacies of town council proposals and artisanal debates, was a revelation. He was learning the language of Cedar Ridge, not just its business jargon, but its heart language, the subtle nuances of community that were as vital as any balance sheet. And she found an exquisite joy in witnessing this transformation, in being a quiet observer, and sometimes, a gentle guide.

Her own understanding of continuity had always been tied to the cycles of the land, the predictable rhythm of planting and harvesting, of seasons giving way to one another. She believed in the enduring strength of tradition, in the importance of passing down skills and values from one generation to the next. Cedar Ridge embodied this deeply held principle, a living testament to the power of shared history and collective memory. Yet, Evan's arrival had introduced a new dimension to this concept, a sense of continuity that extended beyond the familiar boundaries of their small town. He represented a bridge to the wider world, a connection to possibilities she hadn't actively sought but now welcomed with an open heart.

Their shared future, once a nebulous concept discussed in hushed tones over cups of tea, was now solidifying into something tangible. The Collective was thriving, a testament to their combined efforts and shared vision. But it was more than just the success of the business that filled her with a quiet elation. It was the realization that she was building this future not just for Cedar Ridge, but *with* Evan. His presence had breathed a new kind of life into her days, infusing them with a vibrancy that was both exhilarating and comforting. He challenged her assumptions, broadened her horizons, and in doing so, deepened her appreciation for the life she had so carefully cultivated.

She recalled their early conversations about their respective paths. Evan had spoken of fleeting projects and the constant drive for outward success, a life lived in a series of transient landscapes. She had spoken of the deep-seated need for belonging, for a place to anchor her dreams. Now, their paths had converged, not by chance, but by a deliberate intertwining of their desires. He was finding his permanence in Cedar Ridge, and in him, she was discovering a new facet of love's capacity to enrich, to transform, to make the familiar feel exhilaratingly new.

The thought brought a warmth to her cheeks, a gentle flush that mirrored the blush of the late afternoon sun painting the sky. Love, she had always believed, was about deep roots, about shared history, about the quiet comfort of knowing someone intimately. And while that remained true, Evan was showing her that love could also be an adventure, a journey into the unknown, a willingness to embrace the unexpected with open arms. He was a constant reminder that even within the most cherished comforts, there was always room for growth, for discovery, for a love that continually reinvented itself.

She watched him now as he detached himself from Mrs. Gable, a warm smile gracing his lips as he headed in her direction. His gait was confident, his steps purposeful, a man who had finally found his footing. He no longer carried the air of an outsider, the subtle tension of someone perpetually on the verge of departure. Instead, he exuded a quiet assurance, a sense of being rooted, of belonging. This was a transformation she had facilitated, a testament to the power of community and the nurturing embrace of a place that felt like home.

Lena's own sense of self had evolved in tandem with the changes around her. The quiet satisfaction she once drew solely from the rhythm of Cedar Ridge was now amplified by the shared joy of her burgeoning relationship with Evan. Her world, which had once felt beautifully contained within the familiar embrace of the town, now felt boundless, filled with the promise of shared experiences and a love that was both deeply grounded and excitingly expansive. She had always valued continuity, the steady, reliable flow of life in Cedar Ridge, and Evan had shown her that this continuity could be enriched by new beginnings, by a willingness to embrace the unexpected with an open heart and a spirit of adventure.

She found herself reflecting on the concept of home. For years, home had been synonymous with Cedar Ridge, a physical location imbued with generations of history and shared memories. Now, home had begun to acquire a new meaning, encompassing not just the place, but also the person. Evan's presence had redefined her understanding of what it meant to be truly settled, to have found not just a dwelling, but a haven. His own journey of finding belonging in Cedar Ridge mirrored her own deepening connection to him, a reciprocal dance of finding and being found.

Their shared vision for the Collective was more than just a business plan; it was a testament to their shared values, their belief in the power of community, and their commitment to building something lasting. Lena had always been a steward of Cedar Ridge's traditions, a guardian of its heritage. But with Evan, she was also becoming a co-architect of its future, a future that embraced both the enduring strength of its past and the exciting potential of its evolving landscape. This blend of the familiar and the new was a delicate balance, one that she navigated with a newfound grace, her heart open to the myriad possibilities that lay before them.

She remembered their discussions about the future, the tentative explorations of what lay beyond the immediate horizon. Evan, with his strategic mind, would map out potential growth trajectories, new markets, innovative approaches. Lena, with her intuitive understanding of human connection, would always gently steer the conversation back to the heart of it all – the people, their dreams, their well-being. It was this synergy, this unique blend of foresight and empathy, that made their partnership so potent. He brought the structure; she brought the soul. And together, they were creating something truly remarkable.

The joy she found in her life was no longer solely an internal experience, a quiet contentment that bloomed in solitude. It was a shared joy, a vibrant energy that pulsed between her and Evan, a testament to the power of love to magnify happiness, to make even the most ordinary moments feel extraordinary. She was learning that love wasn't about possession, but about profound connection, about a willingness to embrace another's world, to expand one's own horizons in their presence.

She watched as Evan waved to someone across the square, a genuine smile lighting up his face. It was a smile of recognition, of camaraderie, of belonging. He was no longer the outsider looking in, the man who had once felt adrift in a sea of transient connections. He was here, firmly planted, his roots growing deeper with each passing day. And as she watched him, Lena felt a profound sense of gratitude, a quiet awe at the way life had unfolded, bringing them together in this small town, in this vibrant community, in this shared future. The road ahead was uncertain, as all roads must be, but with Evan by her side, she felt ready to embrace every twist and turn, her heart full of a love that was both timeless and ever-evolving.

The soft glow of the setting sun cast long shadows across Lena's small porch, painting the worn wooden planks in hues of apricot and rose. Evan sat beside her, his arm a comforting weight around her shoulders, the silence between them a tapestry woven with shared understanding and quiet anticipation. They weren't clutching at guarantees, nor were they dissecting every potential pitfall that might lie ahead. Instead, they were simply present, two souls charting a course through the unwritten chapters of their lives, their compass set towards a future defined by intention.

"It's funny," Lena began, her voice a low murmur, "I used to think a future had to be meticulously planned, like a perfectly drawn blueprint. Every room accounted for, every detail accounted for before a single brick was laid." She leaned her head against his shoulder, the scent of pine and something uniquely Evan – a blend of clean linen and quiet strength – filling her senses. "But life, it turns out, is much more like a garden. You prepare the soil, you plant the seeds with care, but you can't control the rain, or the sunshine, or the unexpected bloom that might surprise you."

Evan squeezed her gently. "And you've become an extraordinary gardener, Lena. You've cultivated a life here that's not just beautiful, but resilient. You've shown me that the strength isn't in rigidly controlling every element, but in nurturing growth, in adapting to what comes." He paused, his gaze sweeping across the familiar vista of Cedar Ridge, the distant lights beginning to twinkle like fallen stars. "I used to chase after predictable outcomes, chasing the illusion of certainty. It was exhausting, and ultimately, unfulfilling. Coming here, and being with you, it's taught me the profound liberation of embracing the unknown, of choosing to build something with someone, rather than just accumulating achievements."

Their journey to this quiet moment had been far from a straight line. It had been a meandering path, filled with moments of doubt, of tentative steps forward, and the occasional stumble. Evan's initial arrival, born from a business proposition, had been a catalyst, a disruption that had, in time, become an anchor. Lena, deeply rooted in the rhythm of Cedar Ridge, had found her world unexpectedly expanded, not diminished, by his presence. They had learned to speak each other's languages, Evan deciphering the subtle nuances of community life, Lena learning to appreciate the wider world he represented, and the ambition that had once defined him.

"Remember when we first talked about the Collective's expansion?" Lena mused, tracing a pattern on the armrest of the rocking chair. "You had spreadsheets for everything, projections stretching out for years, market analyses that could make anyone's head spin. And I... I was thinking about how much space Mrs. Gable would need for her pottery wheel, and whether the new apprentices would have enough natural light to practice their woodworking." A soft chuckle escaped her. "We were speaking different languages, weren't we?"

Evan's laugh rumbled in his chest. "We were, but we were both speaking them with the same goal in mind: to build something sustainable, something that mattered. You had a way of grounding my grand designs in the tangible reality of people's lives, in the heart of this town. You reminded me that numbers on a page are meaningless if they don't translate into well-being, into opportunity for the community we're trying to serve." He turned to her, his eyes reflecting the twilight. "And I, I suppose, nudged you to look beyond the immediate horizon, to see the potential for growth that extended beyond Cedar Ridge's familiar borders. It was a good balance, wasn't it? A necessary tension."

"A necessary tension," Lena echoed, the words feeling like a warm embrace. "That's exactly what it was. And it's that tension, that balance, that I think will carry us forward. We're not aiming for perfection, Evan. We're not expecting a life devoid of challenges or disagreements. We're choosing to face them together, with the intention of understanding, of compromise, and of unwavering respect for each other." Her heart swelled with a quiet certainty that had nothing to do with predictability and everything to do with commitment. "We're not looking for a finished product; we're choosing the ongoing process of building."

The concept of 'home' had evolved for Lena. For years, it had been intrinsically tied to Cedar Ridge, to the weathered buildings, the familiar faces, the unchanging rhythm of the seasons. Now, home had a dual meaning. It was still this town, this community, the place where her roots ran deepest. But it was also Evan. He had become an integral part of her definition of home, a space of comfort and belonging that extended beyond physical boundaries. His own journey of finding his place in Cedar Ridge, of shedding his past transient lifestyle, had mirrored her own deepening connection to him. They had found each other, and in doing so, had found a new sense of home within the shared space of their lives.

"I remember reading those old novels," Lena continued, her gaze distant, "where the ending was always this grand, definitive moment. The hero and heroine rode off into the sunset, and that was it. The happily ever after, neatly tied up." She smiled, a little wistfully. "It's a lovely fantasy, but it's not real, is it? Real life is the quiet moments after the sun has set, the everyday choices, the small acts of kindness and perseverance that make a life, a partnership, truly meaningful." She turned back to Evan, her expression earnest. "And I wouldn't trade these quiet moments, this everyday building, for any fairy tale."

Evan brushed a stray strand of hair from her cheek, his touch gentle. "Nor I. I used to think fulfillment came from external validation, from reaching the next rung on some imaginary ladder. I was so focused on the destination, I rarely appreciated the journey. But you, Lena, you showed me the richness of the journey itself. The beauty of the process, the value of the connections forged along the way. The Collective, our life here, it's not just about success in terms of growth or profit. It's about the shared purpose, the collaborative spirit, the quiet satisfaction of knowing we're building something good, something that contributes."

He spoke of their shared vision for the future, not as a rigid plan, but as a guiding star. The expansion of the Collective, the integration of new sustainable practices, the continued support of local artisans – these were not just business objectives, but expressions of their core values. They believed in the enduring strength of community, in the power of human connection, and in the responsibility to nurture the world around them. Lena, the steward of Cedar Ridge's heritage, was now also a co-architect of its evolving future, a future that honored its past while embracing new possibilities.

"It's about intention," Evan reiterated, the word resonating with the quiet conviction that had become his hallmark. "It's about choosing, every day, to invest in this life, in this community, in each other. It's not about waiting for happiness to find us, but about actively creating it, brick by brick, seed by seed. It's about saying yes to the adventure, even when we can't see the end of the road." He met her gaze, a profound depth of emotion in his eyes. "And knowing that you're by my side, choosing this path with me, makes all the difference in the world. It's not a guarantee of smooth sailing, but it is a guarantee of shared passage, of facing whatever comes with a united front."

Lena's hand found his, their fingers intertwining. The simplicity of the gesture spoke volumes. It was a silent acknowledgment of their journey, of the challenges they had overcome, and of the unwavering promise they made to each other. They had both arrived at Cedar Ridge with their own histories, their own expectations, their own definitions of success. But in the fertile soil of this small town, their paths had converged, weaving a new narrative, one of shared dreams and a future built not on certainty, but on the steadfast foundation of intention, mutual respect, and a love that had blossomed in the most unexpected and beautiful of ways.

"We've learned that the most profound joys aren't found in grand pronouncements or dramatic resolutions," Lena reflected, her voice soft but firm. "They are woven into the fabric of our daily lives. They are in the shared laughter over a burnt dinner, the quiet comfort of a hand held during a difficult conversation, the collaborative effort to solve a problem, big or small. These are the moments that solidify our connection, that build the resilience of our partnership." She looked at him, her heart full. "And this is the future I choose. Not a perfect, predictable one, but a real one, a rich one, a life lived with purpose, alongside you."

Evan turned to her fully, his expression one of profound contentment. "And I choose it too, Lena. I choose this life with you, in Cedar Ridge, with all its beautiful imperfections and its endless potential. We won't have all the answers, we won't be able to foresee every storm, but we will face it all together. With intention, with hope, and with a love that's grown stronger with every step we've taken, and every step we will take."

He brought her hand to his lips, a tender kiss sealing their unspoken vows. The road ahead was unwritten, but they would navigate it, side-by-side, their hearts aligned, their spirits joined in the quiet, powerful pursuit of a life intentionally built, and deeply loved. The sun dipped below the horizon, painting the sky in a final, breathtaking display of color, a fitting prelude to the vibrant tapestry of their shared future, a future they would weave together, thread by intentional thread.

Reference

The Cedar Ridge Collective: A Community Initiative

This initiative, central to the narrative, was envisioned as a multi-faceted organization dedicated to revitalizing the town of Cedar Ridge. Its core pillars include:

Artisan Support Program: Providing resources, workshops, and a platform for local craftspeople to showcase and sell their work.

Sustainable Agriculture Project: Encouraging and supporting local, eco-friendly farming practices, including community gardens and farmers' markets.

Community Hub Development: Transforming underutilized spaces into vibrant centers for gatherings, learning, and shared experiences.

The narrative explores the challenges and triumphs of expanding this collective, integrating new ideas while honoring the town's existing spirit.

Cedar Ridge: A fictional small town, characterized by its close-knit community, rich history, and picturesque natural surroundings. It serves as a backdrop for stories of personal growth and finding one's place.

The Collective: A community-driven organization in Cedar Ridge aimed at fostering economic, cultural, and social growth. It embodies the spirit of collaboration and shared purpose.

The Old Mill: A historic building in Cedar Ridge, repurposed and central to the narrative's exploration of community revitalization and the blending of past and future.

The Harvest Festival: An annual event in Cedar Ridge, symbolizing community unity, local bounty, and the celebration of shared traditions.

www.ingramcontent.com/pod-product-compliance
Lightning Source LLC
Chambersburg PA
CBHW030131310726
48970CB00005B/1388